Witches of Questionable Intent

JENN McKINLAY

ACE
NEW YORK

ACE
Published by Berkley
An imprint of Penguin Random House LLC
1745 Broadway, New York, NY 10019
penguinrandomhouse.com

Book design by Kristin del Rosario
Interior art: Title page frame © denisik11/Shutterstock;
books © Nikolaenko Ekaterina/Shutterstock

Library of Congress Cataloging-in-Publication Data

Names: McKinlay, Jenn author
Title: Witches of questionable intent / Jenn McKinlay.
Description: First edition. | New York : Ace, 2026. | Series: Books of dubious origin ; 2
Identifiers: LCCN 2026015815 (print) | LCCN 2026015816 (ebook) |
ISBN 9780593819777 trade paperback | ISBN 9780593819784 ebook
Subjects: LCGFT: Witch fiction | Romance fiction | Novels
Classification: LCC PS3612.A948 W586 2026 (print) | LCC PS3612.A948 (ebook)
LC record available at https://lccn.loc.gov/2026015815
LC ebook record available at https://lccn.loc.gov/2026015816

First Edition: November 2026

Printed in the United States of America
1st Printing

The authorized representative in the EU for product safety and compliance is Penguin Random House Ireland, Morrison Chambers, 32 Nassau Street, Dublin D02 YH68, Ireland, https://eu-contact.penguin.ie.

PRAISE FOR

Witches of Dubious Origin

"A delightful treasure! With a wonderful cast of characters, a fabulous spellbook, and a library you'll want to live in, *Witches of Dubious Origin* is one of those books that you fall more and more in love with until suddenly it's two in the morning, and you've lost track of the world. Such a fun and fantastic read!"

—Sarah Beth Durst, *New York Times* bestselling author of *The Spellshop*

"This book is perfect for everyone who loves libraries and magic as well as comfort, adventure, and romance. These characters—including the books, they're characters, too—are tremendously entertaining, and I'm looking forward to many more shenanigans with Zoe, Jasper, Miles, Tariq, and Olive!"

—Kevin Hearne, *New York Times* bestselling author of the Iron Druid Chronicles

"With an irresistible found family, tons of magic, and a dash of romance, this book is a rollicking, delightful adventure from start to finish."

—Jen DeLuca, *USA Today* bestselling author of *Haunted Ever After*

"McKinlay has conjured a world so rich in bookish charm and magical oddities, readers will never want to leave. I loved it! Now, seriously, how do I get a job in the Books of Dubious Origin department?"

—Auralee Wallace, national bestselling author of *In the Company of Witches*

"The perfect story for readers who've always dreamed of stepping into a world where books take on a life of their own and enchantment is waiting with every turn of the page. Brimming over with magic, mystery, and just the right dash of romance, *Witches of Dubious Origin* is a must-read!"

—Stacy Sivinski, national bestselling author of *The Crescent Moon Tearoom*

"[A] smart, fast-paced novel. . . . This is the kind of escapist reading that keeps a reader reading." —*The Colorado Sun*

"Jenn McKinlay writes a spellbinding (no pun intended) novel that takes the reader on a highly imaginative adventure with fascinating characters and creative challenges for a group of folks with differing magical abilities. A thrilling read to be sure."

—Fresh Fiction

"Deftly matching an ingeniously inventive plot with an engagingly quirky cast of characters, including an adorable bookish feline, and adding a hint of flirtatious romance as well as her signature snappy wit, McKinlay casts a spell readers will find impossible to resist." —*Booklist* (starred review)

"McKinlay's magically delicious contemporary cozy fantasy . . . will appeal to fans of the TV show *The Librarians*, as well as anyone who loves stories that combine witchcraft, mystery, and romance with compelling quests and fascinating adventures."

—*Library Journal* (starred review)

TITLES BY JENN McKINLAY

Paris Is Always a Good Idea
Wait For It
Summer Reading
Love at First Book
The Summer Share

BOOKS OF DUBIOUS ORIGIN

Witches of Dubious Origin
Witches of Questionable Intent

HAPPILY EVER AFTER ROMANCES

The Good Ones
The Christmas Keeper

BLUFF POINT ROMANCES

About a Dog
Barking Up the Wrong Tree
Every Dog Has His Day

CUPCAKE BAKERY MYSTERIES

Sprinkle with Murder
Buttercream Bump Off
Death by the Dozen
Red Velvet Revenge
Going, Going, Ganache
Sugar and Iced
Dark Chocolate Demise
Vanilla Beaned
Caramel Crush
Wedding Cake Crumble
Dying for Devil's Food
Pumpkin Spice Peril
For Batter or Worse
Strawberried Alive
Sugar Plum Poisoned
Fondant Fumble

LIBRARY LOVER'S MYSTERIES

Books Can Be Deceiving
Due or Die
Book, Line, and Sinker
Read It and Weep
On Borrowed Time
A Likely Story
Better Late Than Never
Death in the Stacks
Hitting the Books
Word to the Wise
One for the Books
Killer Research
The Plot and the Pendulum
Fatal First Edition
A Merry Little Murder Plot
Booking for Trouble

HAT SHOP MYSTERIES

Cloche and Dagger
Death of a Mad Hatter
At the Drop of a Hat
Copy Cap Murder
Assault and Beret
Buried to the Brim
Fatal Fascinator

For my mother, Susan Norris McKinlay, for teaching me life's most valuable lesson: Books are magic.

Love you forever, Mom.

Witches of Questionable Intent

1

"Ziakas, you're not focusing." Olive Prendergast looked peeved. A few months ago, this would have intimidated me—fine, it still intimidated me—but I no longer wanted to hide under the nearest table.

Olive was an extremely powerful witch, her origin story a mystery as she wasn't one to share anything personal. She was tall and thin with long black hair, a face that was handsome rather than pretty, and her dark eyes were framed by arching black brows, one of which had a scar slicing through it. She always wore all black and today's outfit was a wool pantsuit over a cashmere sweater. It made her pale face seem eerie in the soft light of the main room of the Books of Dubious Origin, a collection at the Museum of Literature which was housed in a mansion on Museum Mile in New York City.

I had recently taken a job in the BODO, as we called it, after I came here looking for help when I inherited my family's grimoire. I was still new to the world of witches, mages, and magic, but I was learning.

"Sorry, I'll try again." I put my hand on the small black

leather book on the table beside me. The cover was so dark it seemed to absorb light and it was locked with a silver metal band engraved with runes I couldn't decipher that latched into a hexagonal lock with a small depression in its center.

"Your grimoire can't help you now," Olive chided me. "We're calling up the magic inside of you, not casting a spell."

A feeling of irritation came from the book, and I had to squelch my smile. The Donadieu grimoire had been passed down through the maternal side of my family until it came to me, the last of the line, after the passing of—or more accurately the murder of—my mother. I hadn't wanted it or anything to do with magic when it arrived, but as I'd attempted to decipher it, I'd discovered the grimoire was not just a book but rather a sentient being that communicated its emotions quite clearly to me.

I was still engaged in trying to crack the code in which the Donadieu grimoire was written. After my initial reluctance in joining the BODO team, it hadn't taken me long to realize that this library was exactly where I belonged and not just because it gave me access to thousands of volumes to help me decipher the magical family tome.

"Again, Ziakas," Olive ordered. My first name was Zoe, but Olive only used surnames, not just for me but for all the junior staff. I sighed and straightened my back.

We were standing in the main reading room, which was made up of three stories of open shelving of every conceivable type of book since humankind had begun scratching knowledge into rocks. What made our collection different was that every item was dubious, meaning the books, papyri, tablets, or scrolls had magical properties of some sort and many we had yet to decode, like my own grimoire, while others were full of dark magic that needed to be carefully monitored.

"Was that going to be today or Thursday, Ziakas?" Olive crossed her arms over her chest.

"Today," I said, sounding a little huffy. Olive was unimpressed.

I closed my eyes and held my hands out at chest height while I concentrated on what Olive had been teaching me about calling up my magic from my core. I had been practicing for months, and while it was becoming easier to access the magical power within me, I was still struggling to control it.

I focused on the warmth I could feel in my center. The color associated with my magic was red, so I concentrated on that color and the warmth started to unfurl inside of me. Today's lesson was about calling forth weather. Olive seemed to think every beginning witch should be able to call a thunderstorm, snowstorm, or sunshine on command. I had yet to manage any of that.

The magic rush came swiftly, like a blush filling my face when I was embarrassed. This was not good. I needed to contain it. I could feel my anxiety spike, causing my heart rate to increase.

"Breathe," Olive instructed. "Remember your goal is to use the atmosphere surrounding you to craft a tiny little rain cloud over that metal trash can at your feet. Do not let it get away from you."

Her words did not reassure me. I tried to breathe and keep the rain shower small, but the force I was pulling from both inside and outside of me was big, and keeping it tiny took a lot of energy. My shoulder-length hair was whipped back from my face as a swirl of wind hit and the smell of rain filled the room. The storm was brewing. I just had to let a little bit of it out.

Between my open hands, I could feel the temperature drop. This was a good sign. I opened my eyes and watched as heavy gray clouds formed between my palms. The ping of raindrops sounded and my eyes went wide when I saw that it was raining right into the trash can per Olive's orders.

I glanced up at her with a grin. I'd been trying to accomplish this for weeks and now *it was happening*! Olive, being Olive, looked bored. I was determined not to take it personally and focused on making it rain harder. The rain grew in volume until it was hard to hear over the pinging in the metal can.

"All right." Olive nodded. "You can end it now."

"End it." I nodded. I would have preferred to let it rain a bit longer and glory in my small triumph but Olive looked impatient. I loosened my hold on the rain, thinking it would diminish. It did not. Instead, the thick cloud between my hands doubled in size and the rain started coming down in sheets.

"Ziakas, you don't lessen your hold on magic to manipulate it, you tighten it." Olive curled her fingers into a fist as if to demonstrate.

Flustered, I tried to lock back in on the storm, which was now tossing my hair about my face while the rain pelted down bigger than the trash can, creating a puddle on the parquet floor. I focused on the cloud, trying to draw my magic back inside of me, while releasing the atmosphere surrounding us. It felt like a taffy pull and I was confused as to which part to pull and which to push.

Olive's scarred eyebrow rose a tick and I felt a drop of sweat run down the side of my face.

After finally achieving a storm, I was going to blow it by not being able to end it. Frustration surged through me and a low ominous rumble of thunder emitted from my little storm.

"Ziakas." Olive's voice held a note of warning.

"I know," I snapped. We were in a three-story room full of rare one-of-a-kind manuscripts; letting a rainstorm loose in here would be catastrophic.

"Ewey!" Tariq Silver cried his native Nigerian exclamation for happiness as he dashed into the main room from his office. His cheerful face was animated as he cried, "Guess what?" Then his feet hit the puddle and he skidded across the floor with his arms windmilling as he fought to keep his balance.

"We're about to be flooded?" Olive said. She snapped her fingers and an umbrella appeared over her head, opening right as my storm cloud rose above her.

Miles, the head of Special Collections, peered out of his office. "What's this?"

"Ziakas managed a storm, but she's having trouble controlling it," Olive said.

"Oh, yes, that is the flip side to conjuring." Miles cupped his chin with one hand while he considered my cloud, which rumbled with another ominous thunder roll. His glasses had slid down his nose, his white hair was unkempt as usual, and he was wearing slippers with his corduroys, a plaid flannel shirt, and his favorite beige cardigan. Miles rocked the absent-minded professor vibe wholeheartedly. Born and raised in New York, he had been friends with my grandmother when she first arrived in the States from France. It was one of the many reasons I had a soft spot in my heart for him.

"Listen, I have news!" Tariq patted his chest with one hand. He was wearing a pristine white lab coat over his dress shirt and pants. How he crafted his many potions and never spilled anything on his coat baffled me. Then again, maybe he had a cleaning spell for that.

"The only news we need right now is how to get Ziakas's storm under control," Olive said. "Focus, Ziakas."

"I'm trying," I said through gritted teeth. The magic was thrumming like a dragon poking its head out of its lair. I tried to contain it but it was extremely stubborn.

"But he's back!" Tariq protested.

"Who?" Miles and Olive asked at the same time.

"Ja—" Tariq started to answer but was interrupted by a familiar voice that blew my focus up as effectively as a stick of dynamite.

"Good morning, esteemed colleagues." Jasper Griffin strode through the iron door—yes, literally through the closed door—that was warded to keep the BODO collection safe. My head snapped in his direction and I felt my insides sigh. He was just as handsome as I'd remembered and his deep British accent had the same effect it always had on me, scattering my wits like falling leaves in an autumn breeze.

It had been two months since I'd seen him, as he was the containment specialist for the department, securing items that were problematic out in the world at large. He'd been teaching me energy manipulation before he left, and we'd shared several romantic dates right before he was sent on a very hush-hush assignment. The only person who knew where he'd gone or what he was doing was Miles.

"Jasper!" I cried in surprise. I was hit with equal parts delight at seeing him again and annoyance that I hadn't heard one word from him while he was gone. My overload of emotion poured right into my rainstorm, and a bolt of lightning shot out of it, headed straight for him. "Oh no! Look out!"

Jasper dodged the bolt by spinning to the side and it sliced into the floor, leaving a three-foot-long scorch mark and the smell of burning wood. Panicked, I lost control of the storm and watched as it roiled above us with a deafening crack of thunder. At any second I expected we'd all be pelted with hail or, worse, electrocuted by lightning.

Instead, there was a popping noise. When I lowered my arms and looked down, Miles was holding a midsized decanter into which the storm was pouring itself. When the last bit of cloud was sucked into the glass bottle, Miles stoppered it with a cork.

"Nice work for your first storm, Zoe." Miles handed me the bottle. "Most witches can't conjure lightning for years . . . if ever."

The burst of pride I felt was tempered by mortification. The lightning had come from a loss of control at seeing Jasper, and I'd almost blasted the guy who, in my defense, had ghosted me for two months. Still, it was utterly mortifying. I couldn't even look at him.

I held the glass bottle in my hands, watching the gray clouds swirl by as flashes of lightning randomly lit up the interior. I set it gently down beside the grimoire. The proverbial lightning in a bottle, who'd have thought that was possible?

"Jasper, it's good to see you." Miles stepped forward and clasped Jasper's hand while patting him on the shoulder. "I take it your trip was successful."

"Very." Jasper nodded. He gestured to the black leather backpack he had slung over one shoulder. "I brought the item right here."

My eyes darted to the backpack. What was it that had sent him away for two months? I was dying of curiosity despite being annoyed at his disappearance.

"Let's have some tea and take a proper look at it, yes?" Miles asked.

"Brilliant," Jasper said.

It was then that I noticed the dark shadows under his eyes, the pallor of his skin, and his overall haggard appearance. I'd been so surprised to see him, I hadn't looked past his handsome face to see the bone-weary exhaustion.

When he glanced at me with a tentative gaze, I smiled in encouragement and he returned it with obvious relief. The spark of awareness that had existed between us from the very first time I saw him flared to life. As the others crossed the room to Miles's office, I turned to Jasper and said, "Sorry about the lightning."

"Don't be. That was bloody impressive." His dark hair fell over his forehead as he leaned close to me and said, "I've missed you, Zoe."

I felt a warmth bloom inside of me that had nothing to do with magic, but I wasn't ready to let him off the hook just yet.

"I could tell from all the phone calls and text messages I received."

"Ah, you're cross." He nodded as if this was what he'd expected.

"Not cross," I corrected. "I mean, just because we went on a few dates before you completely vanished, why would I be cross?"

"Disappointed then," he said.

"Not that either." I glanced at him. "I think *confused* would be the best description."

"I'm sorry," he said. "I hated leaving so quickly, and I really hated that I couldn't reach out to you while I was gone."

"Why couldn't you?" I asked.

"The assignment," he said. "I couldn't risk putting you in danger if I blew my cover. I hope you understand. I really did miss you quite desperately."

I'd have to be made of stone not to forgive him. "I missed you, too."

He grinned and I felt it all the way to my core. "At the risk of being presumptuous because it's horribly last-minute, can I ask if you have a date for the Booklover's Gala tomorrow night?"

"You can ask." I pressed my lips together to keep from smiling.

He huffed a small laugh, giving me a side-eye with his pale blue eyes. "Right. *Do* you have a date for the gala?"

I watched as Tariq followed the others into Miles's office. Jasper and I hadn't kept our previous dates a secret exactly, but they weren't common knowledge either.

"I do not." My heart was fluttering so hard in my chest it was difficult to breathe.

"Brilliant." Jasper caught my hand in his. "Ms. Ziakas, would you do me the great honor of allowing me to escort you to the Booklover's Gala?"

His gaze was intent on mine and I was hit with the crazy urge to launch myself at him and bear-hug him within an inch of his life. I didn't. My pride demanded that I play it cool at least for the moment.

"I will allow that, Mr. Griffin." I tried to sound blasé, but I knew he could see the frantic pulse in my throat.

"Excellent." Jasper raised my hand to his lips, a gesture that should not have been as charming as it was, and kissed the backs of my fingers. My brain glitched. Not one coherent thought was forthcoming.

I was charmed even more when Jasper laced my fingers with his and pulled me toward Miles's office. As we stepped inside, Jasper released my hand after giving it a quick squeeze and slid the backpack off his shoulder.

Miles's office was in its usual state of chaos. Magical tomes and implements littered every surface and were stacked on the floor as well. I understood Miles well enough by now to appreciate that he knew what was in every single pile, but that didn't soothe my librarian rage for order.

Miles was seated in an armchair while Tariq and Olive shared one of the couches, leaving the other one for Jasper and me. A tall silver teapot was pouring tea into individual cups without anyone holding it. It had taken me a while to get used to inanimate objects performing functions on their own in the BODO, but Miles's magical teapot from the Victorian era was one that still fascinated me.

Jasper and I sat and he cleared off a space on the coffee

table and set his backpack on it. He took a moment to pull on a pair of cotton gloves before he unzipped it and pulled it open. Gently, he removed a volume from it and said, "Witches and mages, I give you the one-thousand-year-old *Liber Umbrarum*, otherwise known as the *Book of Shadows*."

2

I wasn't sure what I expected, but the tome Jasper set on the table looked *new*? Its cover was glossy, the leather a deep burgundy polished to a high sheen with brass studs set in each corner of the front and back cover, most likely to protect the leather when it was set on a table. There was no title, just the embossed letters *L* and *E* molded into the leather with a wreath of flowers circling them on the front cover.

Miles pursed his lips while he studied the book. "Interesting."

Olive crossed her arms over her chest and leaned back into the couch. "Is it really all that they say it is?"

Jasper shrugged. "I haven't had a chance to examine it. My team and I managed to secure it and I thought it best to get it here straightaway."

"And your team is fine?" Miles asked.

"Carrington suffered some minor injuries during our . . . departure, but the London healer said she'd be sorted soon enough." Jasper sipped his tea but his hands weren't exactly steady, and I knew whatever had happened had rattled him.

I mean *injuries*? Of course he was rattled. I knew Jasper's work as the containment specialist came with some risk but hearing him state it so plainly made me anxious. What if it had been him? Would we have known if he was in trouble? I didn't like this. Not at all.

"May I?" Tariq gestured to the book.

"Absolutely." Jasper pushed it toward him.

Tariq pulled on gloves before he lifted the book up, turning it over in his hands while he examined it. "Hand-stitched leather over what I believe are oak boards, judging by the heft. I'm not sure what the wreath around the letters signifies."

"Death," I said.

They all turned to look at me. "The wreath is belladonna, also called deadly nightshade. You can tell by the pointed leaves and the large round berries. It's a well-known poison, so my assumption is that it means death."

"Quite right, Zoe." Miles nodded, looking pleased, and I felt like a star pupil.

Jasper bumped me ever so slightly with his elbow, which I took as an *atta girl* nudge, which made me smile.

"What's the book's provenance?" I asked.

"That's the interesting thing, no one can quite agree on *how* it came to be." Miles was practically aglow with delight at the mystery surrounding this new acquisition. "Rumors have circulated about it for a thousand years, but there was never a sighting until just a few months ago. We weren't even sure the rumors were real."

"Why is it called the *Book of Shadows*?"

"Some witches say it was written not by a witch or a mage but by the shadows of demons," Olive said. She looked uncomfortable at the mere thought of such a thing.

"Others insist it was the lifelong project of an eccentric witch-scholar who dwelled in darkness, preferring to live in the shadows, crafting these spells only on nights of the new moon," Tariq added.

I glanced at their faces to see if they were trying to haze me, the newest staff member, with wild tales, but when I glanced at Miles, he nodded, indicating their theories were well known. He watched as Tariq opened the volume and examined the interior pages.

"Vellum." Tariq held a page up close to his face and studied it. "Interesting. Did you note the ink, Jasper?"

"Carbon ink." Jasper nodded. "Unusual for a European manuscript that is said to be one thousand years old."

"Carbon ink, made of soot mixed with gum or glue, is more common in the Middle East or Asia a millennia ago," I said.

"Precisely," Miles agreed. "Judging by the mixed media, I'd say this book got around."

"Maybe the demon shadows moved it around." Tariq glanced at Olive and let out a chilling macabre laugh.

"Stop that!" She sent him a glare that would have had me diving behind the couch. Tariq just laughed.

"Where did you acquire it?" I asked Jasper.

Jasper and Miles exchanged a look. I noticed that both Olive and Tariq had leaned forward, indicating they wanted to know, too.

"For now, that information needs to remain classified," Miles said.

Olive pursed her lips in annoyance. "At least tell us what sort of being was in possession of such a book."

Jasper frowned. He glanced at Miles, who nodded.

"The worst sort," Jasper said.

"Human billionaire." Olive's voice was full of contempt.

"Just so." Jasper sipped his tea.

We were all quiet, contemplating how badly this could have gone if the billionaire managed to gain access to the book by employing someone with magical abilities.

"What do you plan to do with it now?" I asked Miles.

"Authenticate it," he said. "Once I catalog it, we'll secure it in the vault, where its powers can't be misused."

"What sort of power does it have?" I asked.

"No one is certain, but it's believed that the *Liber Umbrarum* has a spell to alter reality as we know it." Miles's voice was grave and it was clear he was concerned that the book could actually do just that.

Alter reality *for everyone*? Well, that was terrifying.

"When they said we were to dress as a fictional character for the Booklover's Gala, I didn't anticipate you choosing Hester Prynne." Jasper looked me up and down with an intrigued gaze.

"What? You mean you don't have fantasies about having your way with a Puritan gal?" I sent him my sexiest wink.

Jasper's pale blue eyes widened and he ran his hand through his thick dark hair. His ridiculously attractive British accent became noticeably deeper when he said, "Well, when you put it like that . . ."

I crossed the decorative parquet floor to him. I was the picture of Puritan chic. I had my bonnet, my wide white collar over my gray sack-like dress, and the large scarlet *A*—the characteristic Nathaniel Hawthorne's Hester Prynne was best known for—stitched on the front of my gown's bodice. The museum's costume department had outdone themselves. But Jasper hadn't seen the best part.

I reached up and pulled the bonnet off my head and tossed it aside. I started to twirl, holding my hands over my head, creating a deep red ball of light between my palms. I dropped my hands and the light shattered above me, draping me in an explosion of sparkles. As I finished spinning, my Puritan dress was no more. I stood instead in a low-cut, body-hugging scarlet dazzler of a gown.

Jasper's jaw dropped. He put his hand over his heart and said, "What was that? Zoe Ziakas, you are stunning, and I might be having a heart attack."

I laughed. His reaction was everything I'd hoped it would be. I leapt into his arms and kissed him with all the longing I'd felt while he was gone during the past few months. He clutched me close and returned the kiss with one hand in my hair and the other on my lower back, pulling me in tight. When we paused to breathe, his gaze smoldered. I shivered in response.

"Zoe, you showed him your latest magic!" Tariq stepped out of his office and we jumped apart, attempting to look casual. His Nigerian accent was a gentle rebuke when he added, "You were supposed to wait."

I fanned my face, trying to calm myself. Jasper was right beside me and when the back of his hand brushed against mine, I could have sworn actual sparks flashed between us.

"I'm sorry, but it took me forever to master that spell. It

was too epic not to share." I turned to face Tariq. "I plan to twirl it out several times tonight."

"That's fair," Tariq conceded.

I reversed the spell by twirling in the opposite direction, holding my hands over my head to pull the red back into the ball, and shrinking it between my palms until it was extinguished. Once I was returned to my previous dowdy dress, I put my bonnet back on and noted that Tariq's clothing matched Jasper's. They both wore full-sleeved white shirts and brown trousers tucked into high black boots.

"And you two are . . . ?" I asked.

Miles came dashing out of his office with a stack of garments over his arm. He, too, was dressed exactly as Jasper and Tariq. I searched my mind for what literary characters would require three very different men to be dressed alike. I couldn't hazard a guess.

Miles tossed a sleeveless blue velvet tunic at Tariq and another at Jasper. I watched as Miles dropped a matching one over his own head. There was a fancy embroidered silver cross on each of them, and I realized it was more of a tabard than a tunic. Miles then reached into a bag and tossed a tricorn hat with a huge silver feather hanging off the back at Tariq and then Jasper before slapping one on top of his own head.

"Now do you see?" Tariq asked as the three of them stood together.

I frowned. There were three of them, dressed exactly alike in garb from the Middle Ages. I didn't have a clue, which was really annoying. I shrugged.

"Swords!" Miles said. "We need our swords."

He hurried back to his office and returned with three prop swords. He handed them out and the three of them held the swords in the air with the points meeting over their heads.

"Now guess," Miles said. His eyes were shining with delight. He reminded me of a kid getting dressed up as their favorite character for Halloween.

I grinned. "The three musketeers, of course."

"I told you people would get it," Tariq said.

Jasper rolled his eyes. "But not without the swords."

"So, who is who?" I asked. "Porthos? Athos? Aramis?"

Miles, Jasper, and Tariq lowered their swords and studied one another. Obviously, they hadn't gotten as far as character selection.

"Porthos, I'm definitely Porthos," Miles said.

"I thought I was Porthos," Tariq argued.

"No, you're Athos and Jasper is Aramis," Miles said.

"Why is he Aramis?" Tariq sputtered.

"He's Aramis because he's the youngest," Olive called from above.

We craned our necks to see her. The BODO housed three stories of open-floor bookcases set back behind fancy wrought iron railings and accessible by two spiral staircases leading to the upper levels. Olive was all the way up on the third floor and as I leaned back, I took in the gorgeous domed ceiling above, which was painted to resemble the sky, bright blue with fluffy white clouds, giving me the sense of being outside even though we were three stories belowground. It truly was the most beautiful library I'd ever seen.

As we watched, Olive opened an umbrella and floated up over the railing. I gasped, which was ridiculous because Olive was a witch and clearly wasn't going to fall to her death, but I still wasn't entirely used to these things.

I felt my jaw slacken. I squinted at her, taking in her outfit from her black straw boater hat festooned with daisies and cherries to her long fitted navy coat with white piping on the lapels, her matching ankle-length navy skirt, and lace-up, narrow-heeled black boots. The open umbrella acting as her parachute clinched it.

"Are you . . . Mary Poppins?" I asked.

"Nice to hear you've read the classics, Ziakas, or should I call you Hester?" Olive landed beside us and closed her umbrella, the handle of which was a parrot, naturally.

"But I . . . of all the characters in literature, you chose a British *nanny*?" I couldn't let it go. My brain simply could not reconcile Olive as Mary Poppins.

"Clearly." Olive held her arms out and twirled. "Mary Poppins is a no-nonsense, intelligent, self-actualized, magical woman. Of course I chose her."

I thought about how stern Mary Poppins could be when one of her charges stepped a toe out of line. "You're right. It's perfect."

"I think you mean 'practically perfect in every way,'" Olive corrected me. She turned to the musketeers. "Are we ready? Let's get this over with. You know how much I loathe these things."

"Yes, I do." Claire Carpenter, the director of the Museum of Literature, entered the BODO with her husband, Sam, by her side. She wore a long red gown that accentuated her height and curves paired with a flowing blond wig that reached to her lower back. Sam looked dashing, costumed in a blousy black shirt, tight black pants, and high black boots, with an eye mask covering the upper half of his face. Obviously, they were Westley and Buttercup from *The Princess Bride.*

With them was Agatha Lively, my bonus mom, who was also my mentor and friend. Agatha had been my mother's childhood best friend and had become my guardian when I was fourteen and my mother could no longer take care of me. I was forever grateful to have Agatha in my life. I took in her costume. Her curly gray hair was pinned in a knot on the top of her head. Her clothes were a mishmash of bright colors. I knew immediately whom she was dressed as.

"Mrs. Whatsit?" I inquired, giving her a quick hug.

Agatha grinned. "I went with the actress Alfre Woodard's costume from the film version of *A Wrinkle in Time.* But I added a little something." She spun around and a pair of bright-colored wings sprouted out of her shoulders and flapped. "One has to be prepared to transform, after all."

"Naturally." I gestured to my dowdy dress.

Agatha leaned in and whispered, "Did you show Jasper?"

"Of course."

"And?" she pressed. Agatha was one of the few who knew of my feelings for Jasper.

"He said something about a heart attack," I murmured.

"Who had a heart attack?" Claire asked. Her sharp gaze took in the two of us and I went for a diversion.

"Just an expression. You and Sam look amazing. A couple costume triumph." I turned to Jasper. "Next year, we should . . ." My words trailed off. Jasper and I had only met four months ago and two of those months he'd spent chasing down the

Book of Shadows. I didn't want to sound as if I was overly invested in our situationship, which was so new we hadn't even put a label on it.

Agatha, no doubt sensing my panic, asked Claire a question about the expected attendance for the gala, and Jasper and I were forgotten as everyone in the room began to chime in. *Phew.*

Jasper sidled up next to me. His pale blue eyes met mine and there was a knowing twinkle in them. His voice was barely audible when he asked, "What were you thinking? Daisy Buchanan and Jay Gatsby? Or would we want to steer away from tragic pairings and go for a happier one like Mr. Darcy and Miss Bennet?"

My heart did a tiny somersault of joy because he was right there with me. Before I could answer him, Claire said, "I stopped by to congratulate you, Jasper, on successfully retrieving the *Liber Umbrarum* for the collection. Our benefactors are very pleased."

Jasper gave her a half bow. "Thank you. I won't say it was easy, but it was definitely worth it. The *Book of Shadows* is now locked up safe and sound in the high-security vault to which only Miles has access."

"Is the book that valuable?" Sam asked.

Claire exchanged a look with Miles. He nodded, making his silver feather bob, then turned to Sam and said, "Beyond measure."

Sam leaned back and eyed the three stories of shelving with interest. I didn't know how much Claire had told her husband about the Books of Dubious Origin collection or about the staff who worked here. While Claire was not a witch, she was committed to the mission of the museum, founded by Mabel Stewart, who had been an extremely powerful witch.

Mabel had been married to the love of her life, Thomas Stewart, who had not been a mage but rather a steel industrialist, who doted on his wife and built the Stewart mansion specifically for her. Upon Thomas's death, Mabel turned the Stewart mansion into the Museum of Literature to protect and preserve literature from all over the world and to keep those books and manuscripts that wielded powers yet to be understood in the Books of Dubious Origin collection until they could be deemed harmless or not. The books without magic went into the main library upstairs while the books like the *Liber Umbrarum* stayed here, where they could be contained.

"Tonight is the biggest fundraiser of the year for the Museum of Literature." Claire tucked her hand into her husband's elbow, drawing his attention back to her. She glanced at each of us in turn. "I will expect all of you to be on your best behavior."

"Meaning no . . . shenanigans?" Tariq asked with a quick glance at Sam.

"Exactly," Claire confirmed. "I will expect the utmost professionalism from each of you."

"You have my word, Princess Buttercup, as a member of the King's Guard." Miles doffed his hat and held it to his chest while he executed a low bow. "I will keep order in the ranks."

Claire laughed and exchanged a smile with her husband. "I know you will, Sir Miles. Now arise and, everyone, go and have fun. That includes you, Mary Poppins."

Olive sighed. "It would be a lot more fun if I floated in over the crowd via my umbrella."

"I would pay to see that," Sam said. "Is there a wire or something you'd be using?"

"It doesn't matter, the insurance liability would cripple us," Claire answered. She gave Olive a meaningful look before she turned and led her husband from the room.

Olive tucked her umbrella under her arm and fell into step behind them. "How long do we have to stay at this thing?"

Claire glanced over her shoulder and said, "Until the bitter end."

I didn't have to see Olive's face to know she was frowning.

Jasper crooked his elbow and said, "May I escort you, Miss Prynne?"

"Merci beaucoup, Monsieur Aramis. I just need one moment." I hurried out of the main room and into my office.

Yes, I had an office. It was a small room nestled between Olive's and Jasper's, but it was all mine. After years of sharing office space in a small public library in Connecticut, this felt like luxury to me. My large ornately carved walnut desk sat in the middle of the room surrounded by four walls of bookcases. I had started to fill the shelves with my references and resources, slowly staking my claim on the space book by book.

On the center of my desk was a marble bookrest where I kept my family's grimoire. The small black book and I had taken on a dark witch together several months ago, and even though I was still working on deciphering it, we had come to a tentative understanding. I rarely let the powerful little book out of my sight, and I had learned to respect it enough to keep it in the loop when I did leave the collection and not take it with me.

"I'm going to the gala upstairs," I said as I patted its matte black cover. "I won't be long."

The book's metal band was fastened into the hexagonal latch on its front cover. The book was spelled to open only when a drop of blood was spilled onto the center of the latch from the Donadieu witch who possessed it. Presently, that was me. I waited, trying to sense what the grimoire was communicating to me. If it didn't want to be left, I would take it with me. Weirdly, I felt nothing. No, wait. There was something. It felt like a . . . snore?

Well, that answered that. I exited my office, closing the door behind me. I crossed the room and took Jasper's arm as we hurried to catch up to the others.

To get to the Books of Dubious Origin department, there were two magicked doors, a series of tunnels, and a very steep spiral staircase. Even though I had been employed in the BODO for several months, I was still unused to the number of stairs I was required to climb every day and by the time we reached the top, I was winded. Self-respect demanded that I not show it, but it was an effort.

The entrance from our staircase into the museum was a nondescript heavy iron door at the end of a large gallery. As we stepped through the door, we were greeted by Claire's assistant, Sebastian Hanover. I had never seen him in anything other than meticulously pressed designer dress shirts and trousers, but tonight he was costumed as Sherlock Holmes, his wool deerstalker cap and overly large pipe making it obvious.

"Good evening, Princess Buttercup and Dread Pirate

Roberts," he greeted Claire and Sam. "Oh, Mary Poppins, how . . . unexpected."

"Wine, where is the nearest wine?" Olive asked.

"There are several pop-up bars in the museum, the main lobby, and the library." Sebastian indicated with a sweep of his arm.

"Thank you," Olive said. "If anyone needs me, I'll be drinking."

"I want in on that," Miles said. His sword banged against his leg as he offered Olive his arm. Together they made their way across the room.

"Claire, Sam, the mayor is dressed as Willy Wonka and he's asking to see you two," Sebastian said. "Shall I escort you to him?"

"Yes, please." Claire studied the guests in the room and smiled. "I'm delighted that it's a crush but I doubt I could find him in this crowd even in a top hat."

They departed with a wave, and I stepped into the former ballroom turned museum turned ballroom again and gasped. Thousands of twinkling lights illuminated the space while massive freestanding books were staged about the room, making it a booklover's dream. I glanced at the enormous book beside us. It was at least six feet tall and its faux leather cover was open, exposing its rough-edged pages. On one page was an ink drawing of a castle and on the opposite one it read, "Once upon a time . . ." in a decorative loopy script.

"That's fantastic." I turned to find Jasper watching me. The warmth in his smile made my heart flutter.

"That's just the fairy-tale book," Tariq said, oblivious to the moment happening between Jasper and me. "Look there.

That's the mystery book, then there's the sciences and history, and look! There are little reading nooks with life-sized literary characters."

The museum items that were usually housed behind freestanding glass display cases remained, but the rest of the room was done up with more enormous books and large cutouts of literary characters with groupings of armchairs and small faux fireplaces scattered about the room as if the party planner's idea of a Booklover's Gala was to design dozens of little reading cubbies. As a lifelong book nerd, I had to say they nailed it.

"Zoe, did you want to—" Jasper began, but Tariq interrupted.

"Come on." Tariq grabbed my hand and began to pull me across the room. "I must introduce you to my favorite curator Sarah and her partner Liam, the museum's registrar. Wait until you hear about their adventures in Greece. Sarah swears she was visited by Aphrodite."

"What?" I couldn't even imagine. "Is she a witch?"

"No, but she may have some witchlike tendencies because her story is that wild." Tariq chatted as he pulled me through the crowd. I turned and grabbed Jasper's hand, making certain I didn't lose him, as I really wanted to know what he'd been about to ask me.

We moved through the room, passing every literary character imaginable and some so obscure even I had no idea who they were, and I considered myself very well read. We found the curator Tariq was seeking and her partner. They were dressed, unsurprisingly given what Tariq had told me, as Aphrodite and Hephaestus.

Tariq badgered Sarah into telling me all about their hunt for an artifact in Greece. It was an epic tale. Sarah was an animated storyteller and her partner Liam had a charming Irish accent that punctuated the exciting parts with his droll observations.

"Do you hear that, mhuirnín?" Liam's voice softened with the Irish endearment. "They're playing our song."

"We don't have a song." Sarah frowned in confusion.

"We do now," he corrected her. "How else am I going to get my Aphrodite to myself for a minute?" With an unrepentant nod at us, he swept her toward the makeshift dance floor in the far corner of the room. The five-piece band was playing a slow jazz number and more couples crowded onto the floor.

"Clever," Jasper observed. "Zoe, I—"

"There you are!" Miles joined us. "The three musketeers have to stick together."

"Says the one who abandoned us for the bar," Tariq scoffed. "It's my turn now. Zoe, let's dance." He stuck out his elbow and I glanced at Jasper, who looked about to protest. Before he could, Tariq hauled me to the floor.

"This is the perfect moment to showcase your dress," Tariq said.

"I don't know." I hesitated. "Claire was very clear that we're to behave ourselves."

"People will believe it's part of the costume." Tariq waved off my concerns.

I *had* worked on the spell for a really long time. I glanced over my shoulder to see my handsome musketeer, watching us with an expression of consternation. When I glanced back at Tariq, I narrowed my eyes and asked, "Wait. Did you invite me to dance on purpose to thwart Jasper?"

"I have no idea what you could be talking about," Tariq protested. Then he spun me out onto the floor and said, "Let her rip!"

As if sensing we were about to take over the dance floor, the crowd parted. Potentially, this was due to Tariq's flamboyant dance style but I liked to think they could feel something magical rising within me.

I tossed my bonnet to Tariq and started to twirl. I raised my hands and formed my ball of red light, and when it was the size of a bowling ball, I released it and the magic rained down on me in a waterfall of sparks, revealing my sparkling red gown.

There were several cheers and quite a lot of applause. Claire met my gaze across the floor and raised her eyebrows. I grinned and she shook her head and then lifted her glass of champagne in a silent toast to me.

"That was amazing!" a woman dressed as a Scarlett O'Hara gushed.

"Truly, spectacular," her partner, Rhett Butler, agreed.

"Thank you." I felt my face get hot. I wasn't used to being the center of attention and truthfully, I wasn't comfortable under so many watchful eyes. If I hadn't worked so hard on perfecting the spell, I never would have busted it out like that. Lesson learned.

"If you get to go from dowdy to dazzling, I feel that at the very least I should be allowed to fly above the crowd with my umbrella," Olive said when we finished our dance and joined them.

"You can't." Miles gestured up at the ceiling with his rocks glass that appeared to have two fingers of whiskey in it. "You'll get caught in the strings of lights and garlands."

"How inconvenient." Olive sipped her overly large glass of wine. It was a very generous pour.

"Excuse me." Jasper pushed his way into our group. "Zoe, a word?"

"Shall we let him take her?" Miles asked. A small smile was visible behind his beard.

"I suppose we've had our fun," Tariq agreed.

"You mean . . . ?" Jasper frowned.

"We just wanted to make sure you appreciate our Zoe since you left her for two months while you chased down the *Liber Umbrarum*," Miles said.

So, apparently, our colleagues had noticed the mutual admiration between Jasper and me before he left.

"Which was an assignment you sent me on," Jasper protested.

Miles shrugged.

I turned to Jasper. "I had nothing to do with this."

"I don't doubt it. Some 'one for all and all for one' you lot turned out to be." Jasper sent Miles and Tariq a mock glare, which made them laugh. Then he took my arm and escorted me away, which was fine with me.

Partygoers continued to praise my costume change, making me even more self-conscious. When we reached the perimeter, Jasper opened the large French doors that led to the veranda. It was February in New York City so I knew it would be cold, but the sudden gust of wind was a slap in the face. I stepped out onto the stone floor and watched my shadow move. Wait. It moved, but I hadn't.

Before I could even register what I thought I'd seen, Jasper pulled me fully outside and into his arms. I opened my mouth to tell him about the shadow, but he kissed me and I completely forgot what I was going to say. I knocked his hat onto the snow-covered ground when I looped my arms about his neck. Neither of us cared.

The feel of his mouth against mine blotted out any other thought or feeling. He'd been gone for months, leaving just after winter solstice, when we'd met only a few weeks prior. I knew his job was to be the department's fixer and that he could fly off at any time for another emergency. If I had any sense of self-preservation, I wouldn't get involved with him, but I'd always been a sucker for a British accent.

When I'd first been told about his role in the department, I thought his extraordinary good looks and delicious accent were what made him so successful, but now that I knew him better, I knew it was because he was a very gifted mage—a male witch. I had learned much from him before he left and I was eager to get back to training with him, but more than that, I just wanted to kiss him until the missing him I'd been suffering from eased.

We separated reluctantly with the need to breathe. The winter air was cold and it burned my lungs when I inhaled. A chilly wind swept across the veranda and I shivered.

"Sorry, love," Jasper apologized. "I was so desperate to get you alone, I completely disregarded how cold it is."

"No worries." I turned to stand in front of him with my back pressed against his front. Jasper's hands went instinctively to my hips, almost distracting me from my purpose, but the icy wind brought my attention back to the cold.

I held my hands out the way Olive had been teaching me and focused on the warmth of my magic in my core. Slowly, as if I were crafting an enormous soap bubble, the ball of energy made from my hands grew until we were fully surrounded by a clear shield that I filled with warmth. It was impervious to the wind and freezing temperatures and we could walk around in it.

"Zoe!" Jasper spun me around and I stumbled into his arms. "This is incredible. Your magic is truly becoming a part of you."

It was the perfect thing to say. I twined my arms around his neck and kissed him, memorizing the feel of his lips against mine as I buried my fingers in his dark hair and pulled him closer, surrendering to the desire humming between us.

"Um, love, I think we're about to give ourselves away," Jasper whispered as his mouth slid down the side of my neck. I blinked and then my eyes went wide.

"Oh!" The bubble I'd created was now swirling with ribbons of black and red. The first time Jasper had kissed me, I'd discovered my magical color was red—which was why I had chosen Hester Prynne and her scarlet *A*—and his color was black. A witch's signature color showed up in a variety of ways. But for me, it roared to life whenever Jasper touched me . . . thus the colorful swirls.

I started to fan my face with my hands, trying to cool it down. If anyone saw this bubble of color, we would have some explaining to do. Claire had been very clear that we were to behave ourselves. Jasper reached up and gently brushed back the hair hanging over my eye with the backs of his fingers. The bubble immediately went bright red, and I let out a small nervous laugh. Potentially, this bubble had not been my best idea.

"Maybe we should walk," I said.

"Of course." A small smile played on his lips as he laced his fingers with mine.

We crossed the veranda and went down the steps to the barren garden beds that surrounded the lawn. The walkway had been cleared of snow and as we strolled, I felt the awareness sparking between us ease. The desire lingered, but as he told me about his trip to London to retrieve the *Liber Umbrarum*, I was caught up in the details and able to get a handle on my rioting emotions.

Jasper and his three field operatives had staked out the London home of a billionaire for weeks before they could verify that he had the *Book of Shadows* and that he was planning to sell it to the highest bidder.

"Why wouldn't he hire a magical person to help him use the book to gain greater riches?" I asked.

"The sorts of witches and mages that could wield the power in the *Book of Shadows* would never ever be a lackey to a billionaire, and Alfie knew it," Jasper explained.

"Alfie? Seriously?" I asked.

"His full name is Alfred Smudge," Jasper said. "But everyone calls him Crooked Alfie. How he got his hands on the book, I couldn't ascertain, but I'm certain it wasn't by legitimate means."

"And he sold the book to you?" I asked.

"Not exactly. We got intel that the demon whose offer Alfie accepted planned to renege on their deal, murder Alfie, and steal the book." Jasper turned to me with a look of chagrin. "We saved Alfie's life and took the *Liber Umbrarum* as payment."

"Oh." I frowned. "I assume the demon wasn't happy about that."

"Under-world-statement," he quipped.

"Is that how one of your operatives got hurt?" I asked. "Taking on the thwarted demon?"

"Carrington? Yes, but she's fine," Jasper said. "She's got some selkie in her that makes her hard to kill."

He said it so matter-of-factly that I felt my anxiety spike. Demons. An operative who was part selkie. Sometimes I was so boggled by how my life had changed in the course of a few months, it was hard to wrap my brain around it all.

When we finished our stroll around the large rectangular lawn, the bubble's surface was clear again.

"Why did Miles send you to retrieve the book?" I asked. "I thought you were the containment specialist, only called in when things go wrong."

Jasper stopped walking and turned to face me. His expression was very serious in the lamplight and with the austere three-story stone mansion behind him, it felt very gothic novel to me. I had a hard time focusing on him when my reader sensibilities were busy soaking up the atmosphere.

"About that, love, there's something I've been meaning to tell—"

"Jasper!" I clutched his arm and pointed at the museum. "Look!"

He spun around and we watched an ominous dark shadow

in the shape of a large hand move over the outside of the building. The fingers were spread wide as if the shadow hand was grabbing hold of the 154,000-square-foot building. The hair on my arms and the back of my neck prickled and I didn't need to be told to know this was something very bad.

"What is it?" I gasped.

"Demon," Jasper said.

3

D-demon?" I stammered. The bubble of heat I'd created around us popped and the night's cold air rushed in, causing me to shiver. "As in, an evil spirit?"

"They're not *all* evil." Jasper sounded slightly defensive. At my surprised expression, he gestured to the museum. "But this one probably is. It's too much of a coincidence that it's here when we've just recovered the *Book of Shadows* and there's a gala happening."

I glanced at the stone building as it was engulfed by shade as thick as night. "Miles said that the *Book of Shadows* had a spell that could alter reality. How would that interest a demon?"

"With such a spell, a demon—or anyone really—could alter how everyone experiences life," Jasper said. "The demon would control how people perceive him, probably as a god or chosen leader. Any attempted rebellions would be remembered as disasters no matter the outcome. Resistance would feel futile even when it wasn't. The world would believe it's already conquered, and armies would surrender without even fighting. Humanity would never escape the demon's hold."

I felt my jaw drop as a feeling of horror swelled inside of me. This was a terrifying prospect. "We have to get back in there."

"Agreed." Jasper squeezed my fingers. "But carefully."

I nodded. We crept toward the door, stepping into the shadow. If I'd thought I was cold before, it was nothing like the frigid darkness that enveloped us. My bones felt as if they were encased in ice.

Jasper pulled open one of the French doors. The five-piece band that had been playing jazz had changed their style of music to a cacophonous discordant screeching that didn't resemble music at all.

It appeared that every guest in attendance was dancing. I saw Olive—*Olive!*—go by with Miles. They were spinning and twirling, crashing into other dancers and not slowing down or stopping.

"Olive! Miles!" I shouted but their vacant expressions didn't change, and as the music got faster and louder, they kept pace with it.

The saxophone player hit a sharp shrill note and I clapped my hands over my ears, but even as I tried to shut out the noise, my right foot started tapping as if there were anything even rhythmic about the frenzied squeaks and bleats the musicians were making. Before I could stop it, my left foot started to tap, too. My legs seemed to have a mind of their own and they moved toward the dance floor that was a sea of bodies all moving and flailing and gyrating. They were so close together, dancers were punched and shoved and stepped on, but no one seemed to care. I didn't want to dance. I didn't want to be a part of this mosh pit from hell.

"Jasper!" I cried. I glanced over my shoulder at him and his legs had started bouncing, too. He grabbed my hand and pulled me back to him before I was swallowed by the crowd.

Pressed up against him, we started to move, but it was awkward and disjointed. It felt as if we were puppets on strings and not a couple who wanted to dance together.

"What is happening?" I whispered. My inability to control my own body was starting to freak me out.

"A spell of some sort," he said. "Hang on tight. We've got to run."

Taking me with him, Jasper forced his way across the ballroom. One guest dressed as Peter Pan blocked our path by doing an impossibly fancy jig with high kicks, triple shuffles, and hop toe steps. He was red-faced and sweaty and even though he staggered doing a Donnybrook step he kept going. Jasper finally shoved him aside and we reached the door that led down to our basement department.

I felt as if my very skeleton was being pulled back into the ballroom and commanded to dance. As soon as the heavy iron door shut behind us, I sagged against it. Jasper hugged me close and then abruptly let me go to cup my face and examine my eyes. "Are you all right? Do you feel in control again?"

"Yeah, I'm good." I nodded and pulled away. Pointing to the ballroom, I said, "That's not normal."

"No, it isn't." He took my hand in his and we hurried down the three-story spiral staircase. "Let's see what we can determine from the safety of the BODO."

We hurried down and around until we reached the landing. Decorative lasers protected the iron door. Jasper held my hand even though I no longer needed help getting through the magically protected door. A few steps forward and I felt as if I was being absorbed and then spat out by the door. We ran down the white-tiled hallway, very subway chic, until we reached the second set of doors. Again, we had to magic our way through them, which Miles had taught me to do months ago.

Despite being here every weekday, I still tensed up when I passed through the doors. I had an irrational fear that one day I would get stuck in the door and live there forevermore. I didn't share this fear with anyone because I didn't want them to think I wasn't up to the task, and so the anxiety remained.

Once we entered the BODO, Jasper took my hand and we dashed across the main room to Miles's office. In the far corner was an oval mirror with an ornate gilded frame. It very much reminded me of the wicked stepmother's mirror in the Brothers Grimm fairy tale "Snow White."

Jasper made right for it. I thought it was an odd time to choose to fix his hair but what did I know. I watched as he gently tapped on the glass with the knuckle of his index finger three times, once on the top, then the middle, and lastly the bottom.

"Narcissus, reveal the gala." Jasper spoke to his own reflection. He reached back and grabbed my hand, pulling me into the frame with him. We were reflected together for a mere moment when the entire mirror went black.

"What?" I whispered.

"Just watch," Jasper whispered, his mouth beside my ear.

Slowly the opaque glass began to clear. It was a bird's-eye view of the gala. We leaned forward to watch the frenzy of arms and legs. Mercifully the mirror didn't provide sound. I could see our friends and colleagues trapped in this dance. Now Tariq twirled Olive and they careened off the dancers around them. I saw Agatha dancing by herself in the corner. I squinted. I could swear she was trying to fight off whatever had taken possession of her body. I scanned the room but there was no sign of Miles. I hoped he was all right. A person could get trampled in that crowd if they had the misfortune to fall.

"What is happening?" I asked. "What spell are they under? And how were we able to escape it?"

"I suspect someone has bewitched the band, which has in turn bespelled the guests, compelling them to dance." Jasper leaned close, studying the gala with narrowed eyes while his mouth formed a deep frown. "Because we were outside when the spell was cast, we escaped its direct hit, allowing us to get away."

"It's not a prank gone awry, is it?" I knew it wasn't but I wanted desperately to be wrong.

"No, this is the work of someone with an agenda." Jasper stepped back from the mirror. "Thank you, Narcissus."

The mirror returned to normal. I had so many questions, I thought they'd all explode out of me, but I knew it had to wait.

"We have to stop the music," I said. "You saw everyone. They're hypnotized. I'm afraid someone is going to die or at the very least be seriously injured."

"Agreed." Jasper's voice was grim. "Do you know sign language?"

"American." I answered by making a fist and mimicking the way a person nods their head with it, which was the sign for yes.

"Me, too. Excellent." Jasper clapped his hands. "I'm going to block our hearing so that we can't be caught under the spell of the band's music."

"Music?" I shook my head. "It sounds like the band is actively trying to torture everyone."

"If I'm guessing right, a spell was put on the musicians and as they played it swept up everyone in the room, and the longer it goes on the worse it gets. We were fortunate to be outside when it began," he said. "We have to unplug the band's equipment and speakers. Hopefully, the lack of music will break the spell."

"All right. Let's do it." I was impatient to get back upstairs and find Agatha and the others.

Jasper raised his hands to my ears. He cupped them with the palms of his hands and as he counted down from ten, my hearing faded until I could only see his lips moving with no sound. He did the same to himself and then signed for me to follow him. We headed back upstairs to the gala. I only hoped we weren't too late. The Peter Pan fellow had looked like he was on the brink of collapse.

When the door slammed shut behind us and we were back in the gala with the large books, reading nooks, and literary character cutouts, the gala attendees swirled around us, still dancing in their maniacal fashion, but there was no sound this time, making the sight even more macabre.

Jasper plunged into the thick of it, making a beeline for the stage with the musicians. He'd grabbed my hand as soon as we entered the room and was pulling me along behind him, his grip tight, as if afraid he'd lose me.

A dancer collided into us, breaking his hold and sending

me spinning. Jasper looked back as I caught my balance. Dancers clogged the space between us and I waved him on, signing that I'd catch up. He nodded and plowed back into the throng.

I started to follow when the dancer who'd collided with me popped up in front of me. She was swaying back and forth but not in the out-of-control way that the others were. She was dressed in a pale blue velvet gown adorned with deep blue gems. If they were real sapphires, the dress would be priceless. They couldn't be, could they?

Of its own volition my hand reached out to grasp one of her long angel sleeves to examine the gems more closely. The woman, who stood a head taller than me, slapped my hand away. I glanced up and noted that her eyes were the same dark blue as the gems. Her pale hair was scraped back into a tight bun at the nape of her neck, and a diadem of white gold with the same blue gems set in the pattern of a snowflake circled her head. She was dressed as the Snow Queen from the fairy tale by Hans Christian Andersen. It was an impressive costume. I shook my head. I didn't have time for this.

"Excuse me." I went to move around her, but she grabbed my arm. Even through the fabric of my sleeve, her fingers felt like ice that was so cold it burned. When I glanced up, she was staring at me with an intensity that put me immediately on guard. I felt a shiver move through me as I realized she didn't have the vacant gaze of everyone around us.

"Is it you? Did you do this?" I gestured to the chaos around us.

She released my arm and lifted her hand and, as I watched, icicles formed on the tips of her fingers. It didn't take an advanced degree in *uh-oh* to know that I was in deep shit. Instinctively, I cupped my hands, forming the same heated bubble

I had put around Jasper and me when we were outside. I had barely gotten it around me when the Snow Queen launched her first icicle, aiming straight for my head. My entire body clenched but the icicle melted as soon as it hit my shield. Well, how about that?

The Snow Queen looked furious. Her nostrils flared and her dark blue lips were moving, either in a spell or chewing me out, I couldn't tell thanks to Jasper's soundproofing. I needed to help him, but I couldn't just let her go if she was responsible for all of this. I thought about the energy manipulation Jasper had been teaching me before he went on his mission. I had practiced while he was gone and gotten pretty good at controlling objects using their own energy.

Raising my hands inside my bubble, I focused on the long angel sleeves of the Snow Queen's outfit. They practically reached the floor and should give me enough to work with. While she was busy shouting and calling forth more ice, I manipulated her sleeves to wrap around a nearby pillar, pulling her along with them.

As her dress moved under my command, she turned a furious gaze toward me and launched what felt like a full-scale blizzard at me. It all melted as soon as it hit the bubble. Not gonna lie, I was feeling very Glinda the Good Witch at the moment. I wrapped the ends of her sleeves around the pillar and tied them tight. I was confident that the Snow Queen wasn't going anywhere.

She tried to pull herself free, but she was plastered against the pillar and unable to work any magic with her hands bound so tightly. As my bubble was jostled by more dancers, I let it pop and bolted for the stage to help Jasper.

The band was set up on a temporary dais in the far corner of the room. The musicians had the same dazed expressions as the dancers and they jumped around the stage as they played as if they couldn't help but move. The closer I got the more merciful my lack of hearing felt. I scanned the stage, looking for Jasper, and spotted him behind the drummer.

I hurried around to the back of the stage. No one seemed to notice us or care that we were there. I crouched down low and crept along the wall until I was beside Jasper. He looked perturbed and gestured from the stage to the main power supply, which was clearly switched off.

He signed to me that he had shut the power down but nothing happened. The band kept playing and the dancers kept dancing. We exchanged a frown.

Jasper gestured to the many power cords running from the equipment on the stage to the power supply. Together, we started unplugging them. Surely, the band would have to stop now. They didn't. They kept playing. The dancers kept dancing. It was creepy and weird and I was so over it.

I gestured to Jasper that we needed to hear what was happening. He nodded in agreement but then signed that we should do it from outside. I agreed.

This time I grabbed his hand and led him back through the same French door we'd first exited through less than an hour before. We passed people who were slumped on their feet but still dancing. One woman in a wicked pair of high-heeled sandals had blood running from where the straps dug into her ankles. She slipped on the blood but kept dancing.

We had almost reached the doors when Tariq appeared in front of us. His tricorn hat was askew and his feather was beginning to droop. His face was slack as if he was sleepwalking. He was swinging his sword as if he'd slash at anything that stopped him from his grisly dance. I wanted to grab him and shake him.

Jasper must have sensed my intentions, because he turned me away from Tariq and dragged me out into the cold night air.

Once outside, I slammed the door behind us. Jasper lifted his hands to cup my ears and *pop,* just like that, I was able to hear again. He then did the same to his own ears.

"Why didn't it work?" I asked. "I don't understand."

"I don't know." Jasper ran his hands through his hair. "It should have. If the spell was on the musicians and it's their music trapping the others, then unplugging them should have stopped it. Except it didn't. Listen."

We were both silent and the musicians muffled by the closed door were clearly audible. The noise they were making had become even more screechy and discordant as their exhaustion kicked in. Somehow their instruments were as loud as ever. They shouldn't have been, with the speakers of the PA system and their own amps, monitors, and microphones unplugged, but nevertheless their hideous music thrummed through the building as if it would shake loose the mortar from between every stone.

"If we can't unplug them, we have to drown the noise out with something else," I said. "Is there an alarm system in the museum that we could activate that would be louder than the music? Should we call in a fire and get the firetrucks blaring their sirens here?"

Jasper looked at me and then cupped my face and kissed my forehead. "Brilliant!"

"Huh?"

"You're right, Zoe. We need to make a noise louder than the musicians." He snapped his fingers. "But it has to come from a power source equal to whatever spell is happening in there."

"How do we know what its equal is?" I asked.

"There's only one sound in the magical realm that can bring creatures, both magical and mortal, to their knees," Jasper said.

"And that would be?" I prompted.

"A banshee," he said. "And I know just the one."

4

A banshee." I had no idea why I repeated him. It wasn't as if he hadn't been clear. It was just that out of all the things he might have suggested, I hadn't expected him to say *banshee*.

"Yes." He was patting the pockets of his costume as if looking for something.

"Is there a banshee hotline of which I'm unaware?" I asked.

The corner of his mouth twitched. "Funny."

I watched as he retrieved a small black pouch from his pocket. I'd seen this mage emergency kit before. I couldn't wait to see what he pulled out of his magic bag this time. Olive was in charge of curating the items in the kit. As yet, she hadn't seen fit to give me a bag of my own as, according to her, my magical skill set wasn't up to par.

"Stand back, love," Jasper instructed.

I moved to stand against the wall. The wailing music was louder there but I shut it out and focused on the circle Jasper was drawing on the stone floor with a blunt piece of charcoal. Within the closed circle, he sketched a sigil that was a spiral of tears. Satisfied, he put the charcoal away and pulled what looked like a short piece of bleached wood out of the bag. I watched in fascination as he licked his lips before he put the end of the small pipe to his mouth. When he blew through the opening, it played a mournful sound like a keening wail and I felt it echo in my chest and fill me with such a deep sadness that tears sprang to my eyes.

Jasper began to slowly walk around the circle in a clockwise direction as he played. The exterior wall sconces shone on the small instrument. I watched his fingers move up and down, covering the holes and changing the sound of the mourning cry. It took me a moment to recognize that the tiny flute wasn't made of wood. Rather, it was carved from bone.

The realization cut off my sorrow. Again, I was filled with so many questions. Where does one acquire a flute made of bone? Whose bone was used in the creation of such a thing? Human? Animal? Supernatural being? I was betting on that one. And, finally, would I be issued a bone flute when Olive finally deemed me worthy of having an emergency spell bag? I wasn't sure how I felt about that.

As Jasper made his third lap around the circle, the ring he'd drawn with the charcoal started to glow with a pulsing white light. Jasper kept playing but he met my gaze across the circle and I could see he was relieved that it had worked.

The melody he played became increasingly louder, and the stone pavers within the circle began to ripple as if they were no more substantial than water. The mournful lament coming from the circle grew in volume until Jasper lowered his instrument. He moved to stand beside me and we watched together as a petite silver-haired woman wearing a diadem of bright white bones—oh goody, more bones—on top of her head and a long dark gray cloak rose up out of the circle. Her arms were raised, her back arched, and her face tipped up to the sky as she continued to keen until she was standing fully realized on the sigil Jasper had drawn.

"Lira Luna, I've called you here to pay the debt you owe me," Jasper said.

"Well, that's a fine how ya, isn't it, Jasper Griffin?" The woman dropped her arms and glared at him. Her voice wasn't British like Jasper's, rather it was softer and with more of a lilt. I guessed she was Irish.

She was as pale as the bone flute Jasper had played. Her features were sharp with prominent cheekbones, a beak of a nose, and a pointy jaw. Her teeth were crooked, her lips thin, and her eyes as black as the coal Jasper had used to draw his summoning circle. I felt my heart race at the sight of her and had to remind myself that banshees were spirits who warned of impending death and were not known for doing harm, as far as I knew.

"I don't hear from you for ages, and then when I'm enjoying a quiet evening minding my own business in my fairy mound, you call me"—Lira paused to glance around the veranda and up at the museum building—"to wherever this place is."

"New York City," I said. Both Jasper and Lira turned to look at me and I pressed my lips together.

"New York City?" Lira stared at Jasper. "Are you mad?"

"Sorry to disturb you, Lira." Jasper held his hands out in a placating gesture. "But it's a dire situation and you're the only one who can help."

Lira tossed her hair over her shoulder, clearly pleased with the praise, then she leaned back on her heels and studied Jasper with a calculating gaze. "What is it you require of me, Jasper Griffin?"

"It seems the musicians in the gala"—he paused and gestured to the door—"have been bewitched and we need to release them and the guests by creating a noise louder than theirs."

"Noise?" Lira crossed her arms over her chest. It was clear she didn't appreciate that word choice.

"Not noise," Jasper amended immediately. "I meant to say *sound*, we need a sound, a melody, if you will, that's louder than theirs."

"A melody?" Lira tapped her chin with one bony finger as if considering.

I glanced at the door. The glass was fogged on the inside, from the heat of hundreds of bodies trapped in an exuberant dance, making visibility into the ballroom limited. Even so, I caught sight of Agatha as Mrs. Whatsit as she danced by. She was drenched in sweat, her face ashen, her pretty wings drooping. Panic thrummed inside of me. Agatha was the only family I had and I was not about to lose her.

"It really is an emergency," I said. "People are going to die."

Lira's head snapped in my direction. Her black eyes latched onto my face with a sudden intensity that put me instantly on high alert. Her pale lips pulled back in a sneer. "What do you care if anyone dies?"

"I care because they're my family and friends and no one should die like this." I gestured wildly at the ballroom.

Lira gave me a side-eye. "I know what you are."

"Scared? Desperate? On the verge of a nervous breakdown?" I offered.

She shook her head and the bones of her diadem glowed in the glare of the outside lights. "I warn people about death. I try to save them, but not you. You let them die and then you disturb their rest by bringing them back. Oh yes, I know exactly what you are, death caller."

She said it with so much disdain and contempt, as if I were a grave robber digging up bodies and stripping them of their valuables. It was clear she didn't like me, which stung. Ridiculously, I felt the need to defend myself.

"For the record, I have not raised any dead," I said. "I thought I did once, but it turned out that I didn't, so you can just stop judging me now."

"Oh, I'm judging." Lira looked me up and down and I had to force myself not to squirm.

Instead, I looked at Jasper and said, "A little help here?"

"Lira, Zoe is not one of the bad necromancers. She wouldn't be here working at the BODO if she was." His voice was calm and reasonable and I was surprised to see Lira nod. "She was instrumental in helping us get rid of a dark witch."

Lira turned from me to Jasper and back. "Well, fair play to you, death caller."

"Death caller?" I asked, thoroughly annoyed. "Really?"

"We have bigger issues, love," Jasper reminded me.

"Fine." I shrugged aside my feelings. "Are you going to help us or not?"

"For a price," Lira said.

"No." Jasper held out his hands in a *stop* gesture. "You owe me a favor and this is what I'm calling in."

"Ah, but you're desperate," Lira cackled. "Which means I

have the power, and I want more than to just wipe the slate clean between us."

The music pounded from inside and the sound of the dancers flailing about in their exhaustion was impossible to miss. Lira had us and she knew it.

"What do you want?" Jasper asked.

"Her." Lira pointed to me.

"Me?" I squeaked at the same time Jasper said, "Absolutely not."

"Why do you want me?" I asked.

"That's my business, isn't it?" Lira asked.

"She hasn't raised anyone as yet." Jasper's tone was gentle. "She can't bring back your wean, Lira."

Lira's head and shoulders drooped, and I felt my heart plummet. I knew that *wean* was what the Irish called a child. The stark pain on Lira's pale face was no longer that of a banshee but rather a heartbroken mother mourning her baby.

"Maybe, when I learn to raise the d—" I began, but Jasper cut me off.

"No."

Lira's head snapped up and she glared at him. The fury in her black eyes was frightening to behold. She started to sway with a serpentine grace.

"I want her!" Lira tried to grab my arm but Jasper was quicker and pulled me out of reach.

"Lira, don't do this." Jasper tucked me behind him.

"But I need her." Lira's voice became a keening whine.

"You're only here because I'm claiming the favor you owe me." Jasper's voice was stern. "You know the rules of a magic-made bargain. You can't change the terms without suffering. You will lose your ability to warn of death and become a harbinger of it instead."

"Noooooo." She wailed and the high-pitched sound pierced my eardrums. I clapped my hands over them, watching as Lira began to spin in her charcoal circle. Her silver hair flew about her face and she opened her mouth, revealing jagged teeth, as her wailing grew in intensity.

Jasper grabbed my arm and signaled that we needed to open the doors to the ballroom. We ran for them and jerked them open. I couldn't hear the musicians playing over Lira, but I could see them sweating over their instruments while the guests bobbed in front of them. I felt as if I was watching a horror movie.

Jasper and I stood on each side of the opening, studying the crowd, hoping for a behavior shift, an awakening, anything while Lira keened loud enough to make my ears bleed. Nothing happened. I glanced back at Lira Luna. She had dropped to her knees, her hands crossed over her chest as she rocked back and forth. She was giving it her all.

Agatha danced by the door and on instinct I reached in and yanked her outside. She stumbled into my arms and I hugged her tight. "Agatha, can you hear me?" I yelled.

She pulled back and as her gaze met mine, I could see her eyes focusing on my face. She drew in a deep breath and glanced around the veranda. She pushed her gray curls out of her face and then clapped her hands over her ears. She jutted her chin at Lira and said, "A banshee, really?"

I laughed in relief and gave her another quick squeeze. I

glanced at Jasper and gestured that we needed to pull the musicians outside where Lira could drown out their playing and clear their minds, stopping the music and saving the guests. He nodded, leaving me to haul guests out of the ballroom while he went for the band.

I leaned close to Agatha and yelled what I needed her to do, hoping she could hear me. She nodded and hurried down the steps into the center of the lawn. Jasper pushed the guitar player out and then the bass player, both still strumming their instruments. As soon as they heard Lira's wailing, they stopped playing and clapped their hands over their ears.

By the time we had emptied half of the ballroom, Agatha had used her kitchen witch magic to make it snow just as I'd requested. The overheated guests wandered the grounds, marveling at the beauty of the big fluffy flakes while cooling off from their exertion.

"Who is making that infernal racket?" Olive staggered out of the ballroom, clapping her hands over her ears and glaring at Lira. "Luna, I might have known."

Having heard Olive, Lira stopped keening. She dropped her hands from in front of her and slowly rose to her feet. "Olive Prendergast, how does it feel to be saved by me?"

"Saved?" Olive's eyebrows shot up. She opened her mouth to argue, when Miles and Tariq came skidding out of the ballroom behind her.

"Lira! Delightful to see you as always!" Miles cried. He was sweaty and disheveled much like Tariq, but he strode forward and bowed to the banshee as if she were royalty. "Jasper tells me you've saved the night."

Lira lifted her chin and managed to look down at Miles even though he stood a head taller than her. "I've told Jasper what I want in return."

I felt my stomach drop.

"No, there was no bargain made." Jasper's voice was firm as he half dragged, half carried the saxophonist, who still clutched his instrument. "You owed me, Lira, and I called it in. Your debt is paid."

"We'll see, Jasper Griffin, we'll see." She turned to me, her dark eyes boring into mine with a feverish intensity that made my skin crawl. "Until we meet again, death caller. And make no mistake, we will meet again."

Before I could utter anything more than a quiet sound of distress, she melted into the stone pavers at her feet. As quickly as she'd appeared, Lira Luna was gone.

"Don't take her seriously," Olive chided me. "Banshees are always *so* dramatic." She rolled her eyes and I wished it made me feel better, but when I glanced at the circle where Lira had stood, I saw a pair of dark eyes watching me and one winked before they faded from sight completely. I shivered.

"Would someone tell me what happened in there?" Tariq removed his hat and wiped the sweat from his forehead with his sleeve. "One minute I was talking to Sarah and Liam about the collection and then next thing I knew Jasper tackled me and dragged me out here."

Miles, Tariq, and Olive turned and stared at Jasper and me in question. Clearly, none of them had any recollection of the last hour. How to explain? I waved my hands at Jasper, indicating he should tell them.

"From what Zoe and I witnessed both outside the museum and down in the BODO, I believe a demon put a spell on the band and the guests," Jasper said. "I suspect it was to cause a distraction, and the only reason I can think of is because of the *Book of Shadows*. We need to check the vault to be certain it's safe."

"Well, that explains why my legs are cramping." Miles straightened up and pushed his glasses up on his nose. "Tariq, can you calm the crowd? They won't remember what happened either and they'll likely suffer some agitation because of it."

Tariq considered the people out on the lawn and the veranda. "I can use one of my aromatic potions to help soothe their psyches, if that's what you mean."

"I do. Excellent," Miles said. "Everyone else, let's go check the vault." He turned on his heel, causing his tabard to swish around his hips as he led us back inside.

"Wait!" I cried. "There was a woman. She tried to stop me when Jasper and I were going to stop the music."

"Was she a demon?" Jasper asked.

"I don't know." I shrugged. "I've never met a demon."

Jasper glanced away and Olive raised her eyebrows. Olive glanced from Jasper to me and back. "Are you sure you've never met a demon, Ziakas?"

"Pretty sure," I said. My voice held a note of sarcasm that I would normally never deploy on Olive, but it had been a very stressful evening.

"If you say so," Olive said. There was something about her tone that I knew in my soul did not bode well for me.

5

If we could focus on the current crisis." Miles frowned. "Zoe, what did this woman look like?"

"Blue," I said. Miles, Jasper, and Olive stared at me in surprise. "I mean, she was costumed in shades of blue. I'm not a blingy gal generally, but I think she had actual sapphires adhered to her gown. It was spectacular. I think she was dressed as the Snow Queen from Hans Christian Andersen. She even shot some lethal icicles at me."

"What happened to her?" Olive asked.

I glanced around the ballroom looking for the pillar where I'd left her. "I used the angel sleeves of her costume to tie her up." I spotted the pillar and gestured to it. "She was right there."

They all turned to examine the empty space. "We'll talk more about that later," Miles said. "Right now, we must check on the *Liber Umbrarum*."

He led us through the ballroom, weaving his way among the stragglers who were headed for the exit now that the spell was broken with the end of the music. I listened to the guests we passed, curious to know what they'd thought of the past forty minutes.

"I've never had so much fun," a woman dressed as Holly Golightly gushed to the man beside her, who was clearly costumed as Truman Capote. They were both red-faced and sweaty but smiling. The woman frowned and asked, "We were dancing, weren't we?"

"We must have been. I'm so out of breath I think I must have blacked out." Capote laughed. "I'm so impressed with us."

They joined the rest of the gala guests outside and I wondered if the spell that had taken over the gala had caused everyone to experience it in a positive way, unaware that they'd actually been held captive and tortured by magic. If not, I had no doubt that Tariq would make it so with one of his concoctions.

I followed the others down the spiral staircase, through the first warded iron door at the beginning of the long hallway, until we reached the entrance to our department. I brought up the rear, and as I stepped through the heavily secured second door into the BODO, a hedge witch's spellbook came careening across the room right at my face. I ducked, covering my head with my arms. "What the hell?"

"Zoe, down here!" Jasper grabbed my hand and pulled me to the floor.

I dropped to all fours and crawled beneath a table with him. Miles and Olive were under the table next to ours. Miles's glasses were askew and a deep line of concern formed between his brows. Olive sat with her arms crossed over her chest, looking extremely peeved.

"What's happening?" I cried as a book flew past the table.

I glanced out at the library, which was in chaos. Books were flitting between the shelves frantically shelving themselves in the wrong places. The reference books that we kept in the main room for easy access were all turned around so the pages faced out, almost as if they were trying to hide. The Greek papyri had rolled themselves up so tight they were as thin as reeds.

"The collection is upset," Miles said. "Likely because someone got through the wards."

"It wasn't like this when we were down here, checking the magical mirror in your office," I said.

Miles glanced at Jasper. "What did you see in the mirror?"

"I asked Narcissus to show us the ballroom," Jasper said. "And while I watched, I saw a shadow moving among the crowd. It was not attached to a being but moving independently."

"Definitely a demon." Miles nodded.

I thought about the moment Jasper and I had left the ballroom. I'd seen my shadow move on its own. At least, I'd thought it was my shadow. Maybe it wasn't. Maybe the demon had piggybacked onto me or perhaps it was the same shadow that we'd seen crawl over the building and I just happened to cross paths with it. I shivered.

What did a demon even look like? As far as I knew, I'd never seen one. I started to panic sweat.

"Regardless of what caused this, we need to get this collection under control before these volumes destroy themselves," Olive said.

"I've got it." Miles peeked his head out from under the table and a furry gray book launched itself at him with a yowl. Miles opened his arms as Freya, a book of Old Norse mythology, which was also a cat, burrowed into his arms. The book's exterior was the soft fur of a gray tabby, and the front cover of the book revealed the cat's face, when she wanted it to, while the upper corners were her ears, but again, only when she wanted to be seen. Freya and I had gotten off to a rocky start when I accidentally levitated her, but she'd been slowly warming up to me. I'd even been able to stroke her spine and cause her tail to appear. I didn't think her tail was going to appear anytime soon after this.

Miles rose to stand beside the table, ducking when a thick tome of Druid tree spells careened toward him. He clutched Freya closer.

"You're all right!" Miles straightened up and made his voice carry throughout the three-story room with an impressive amount of authority. "Settle down. You're all right."

The response wasn't immediate. Slowly, as if recognizing the head of the department was there and order was being restored, the books stopped flitting between the shelves. Some fell right from midair to the floor with loud thumps and bangs.

"This is going to be a pain in the ass to clean up," Olive huffed as she slid out from under the table.

A horrible thought hit me. My grimoire! I'd left it in the office. I bolted out from under the table, smacking my head. "Ouch!" I clapped my hand to my scalp and kept going.

"Zoe, what's wrong?" Jasper called after me, but I was in too much of a hurry to answer.

I slammed open my office door, expecting to see the havoc

that was outside in here but my shelves were intact, my books in place, and my grimoire sat on its marble stand exactly where I'd left it. I sagged against my desk with relief. I put my hand on the book just to be sure that it was in fact real and unharmed.

"Oh, of course." Jasper followed me into my office. He gently put his hand on my upper back. "All right, Zoe?"

"Yeah." I picked up the book and clutched it close. It was the only tie I had to my grandmother and my mother. Its value was beyond measure. "I'm going to need a vault of my own."

Jasper nodded. "We'll make it happen."

I slipped the grimoire into the bottom drawer of my desk, the one with the lock. "This is just until we examine the vault. I'll be right back."

A groggy acknowledgment was all I got from the book. Nice to know the raid on the BODO hadn't disturbed its sleep.

As we left my office, I leaned close to Jasper and asked, "Did we do this when we were down here before? Did someone . . . a demon . . . follow us in here?"

Jasper blanched as if he, too, was afraid we were responsible.

"Unlikely," Miles answered. "The BODO is one of the most secure collections in the entire world but that doesn't mean it's foolproof. Nothing is."

"I don't think a fool caused all of this." Olive waved her hands at the mess that was now the library.

"This can wait," Miles said. "We need to check the vault." Gently he placed Freya on a shelf with a few soothing words before striding out of the main room and into his office.

As soon as we entered, I knew something was very wrong.

"Narcissus!" Miles cried and ran across the room to where

the mirror had been less than an hour ago. Now it was just a frame hanging crookedly on the wall with shattered pieces of mirror on the ground below it.

I gasped and put my hands over my mouth. This was bad. I knew without being told this was very, very bad.

"Bloody hell!" Jasper cursed while Olive stared at the pieces consideringly.

"We can deal with this after." Olive put her hand on Miles's shoulder, which was interesting because Olive was not one for comforting others. "The vault."

Miles sighed and approached the bookcase behind his desk. He pulled out several books and rearranged them. As soon as he put the last one in place, a mechanism clicked and the bookcase slid back several feet before moving sideways into the wall and disappearing from view.

I glanced into the opening, expecting to see a deep dark tunnel lit by torches and guarded by a troll. Instead, it was a light and airy arch-shaped passageway, illuminated with art deco sunburst wall sconces, a black-and-white geometric marble floor, and elaborately carved statues sitting on pedestals, stationed every ten feet as if guarding the area.

I paused beside one to study its face. It was carved of white marble and resembled a tiger with wings. Before I could track its movement, the tiger opened its jaws impossibly wide and I saw an enormous gaping darkness inside of it.

"Now, now, Leonides, Zoe is with me." Miles slid between me and the statue. "We've talked about this. We don't eat the guests."

Leonides snapped its jaws shut and turned its head away from Miles.

"It's best not to linger in front of the guards," Miles said to me. "They get bored and forget their manners."

"They're alive?" I was pleased my voice didn't come out as shaky as I felt.

"As much as the books upstairs are," Olive said, clearing up my confusion not at all.

Miles continued forward and Jasper moved to my side, which I appreciated.

The arched hallway ended at a massive stone gargoyle with its wings spread and its unblinking gaze leveled on us. Miles didn't hesitate but stepped up to the gargoyle and placed his hands on the clawed feet right in front of him. Remembering the tiger, I went rigid, but Jasper put his hand on my back in a soothing gesture.

We watched silently as a white aura began to form around Miles. It started to pulse, growing brighter and brighter until I was forced to glance away. I turned to face Jasper, who was shielding his eyes with his hand.

"What's happening?"

"The vault can only be opened by Miles using his magical aura signature," Jasper said. "In other words, the vault is keyed to Miles."

I nodded. That made sense. No, it really didn't, but I wasn't going to quibble. I knew Miles's magical color was white, which was likely why his aura was so blindingly bright. Unable to resist watching, I peeked through my fingers.

The bright light coming from Miles flared and like a lightning strike it was absorbed into the gargoyle through its waterspout of a mouth until the entire gargoyle was glowing. With the sound of stone grinding upon stone, the wings, which had been folded down, lifted, revealing a doorway beneath its clawed feet.

"Thank you, Graven." Miles patted the gargoyle's feet and led the way inside.

I let out a weak laugh and followed Olive with Jasper at my back as if he knew I was afraid to be last in case Graven also felt peckish.

The vault was another surprise. It was not a dank, musty cave with piles of treasured books, magical artifacts, or gold. No, it looked exactly like the safe-deposit boxes in a bank vault, with one distinct difference. Instead of locks that required keys or passcodes, these drawers all had a single eye where normally a handle would be. And at the moment, all the eyes were watching us. In other words, nightmare fuel.

6

Steady, love," Jasper whispered in my ear. "They can't harm you."

"My psyche begs to differ," I muttered. The eyes swiveled in my direction and then blinked as one. I felt my knees go slack.

Miles moved across the room and gently placed his hand over one of the drawers, closing its eye. All the eyes faded into the flat metal front of their drawers except the one Miles had touched, which popped open when he removed his hand.

A rush of air exited my lungs. Maybe it was my own discomfort at being the center of attention, but having so many eyes on me was creepy as hell and I could see how it would act as a deterrent for wannabe criminals.

"Open." The eye closed and the drawer slowly opened as he'd commanded. Miles glanced inside and went still. "It's not here."

"What?" Jasper strode forward. "That's impossible. You're the only one who can access the vault."

"Apparently not." Olive rotated in a circle, examining the drawers and the vault itself. "Is there any way the demon who caused the ruckus upstairs could have spirited Miles away and used him to open the vault without him knowing?"

"But we saw you and Miles dancing, didn't we?" I glanced at Jasper. "Unless whoever grabbed Miles did it while we were summoning Lira."

"Do you remember anything of your time upstairs, either of you?" Jasper asked.

Both Miles and Olive shook their heads.

"We have to check all of the drawers," Jasper said. "Just in case it was misplaced."

I scanned the room. There were hundreds of drawers. How were we going to open every—

Miles spread his arms wide, casting his aura out in waves. The drawers started popping open. Well then.

"Everyone choose a wall," Olive said. "Close each drawer that you check so we don't repeat ourselves. Remember you're looking for the *Liber Umbrarum*."

I nodded. I had only seen the book once when Jasper had arrived from London with it yesterday. But I remembered the cover was thick burgundy leather with a glossy sheen, studded with brass, and embossed with a wreath of nightshade.

I took the wall at the far end of the room and started on the top drawer. Most of the drawers were empty, making quick work of my search. I did get distracted halfway through when a drawer revealed a small vial nestled in a velvet lined box. Intrigued, I picked up the vial and held it up to the light. It was filled with ashes.

"The ashes of the first phoenix," Miles said. "It's believed to bring anyone back from death, but it can only be used once."

I carefully put it back in its box and gently closed the drawer. There were more curiosities and I tried not to get sidetracked by a pearl the size of my fist, a wedding veil that shimmered, a battered silver cup that vibrated in its drawer as if asking to be picked up.

"Don't touch that one," Olive instructed. "It's a poison maker. Anything poured into it, even water, will turn into pure poison."

I slammed the drawer shut. There were several books but none were the *Book of Shadows*. The final drawer I checked contained a seemingly unassuming dagger.

"So, that's where you went," I said. I ran my finger along the blade. The Dagger of Death. We had become acquainted months ago when I'd been battling for my life. I leaned in close and whispered, "In case I never said it, thank you."

The blade gleamed and I couldn't tell if it was a trick of the light or something more. Either way, I closed the drawer and turned to face my colleagues. "No luck in any of these."

"Here either," Jasper said.

"Same." Olive sighed.

Miles closed the last drawer on his side of the vault and faced us. Worry made the lines on his face deeper and his expression was one of grave concern. "Olive and I will redo the wards down here. Jasper and Zoe, I need you to find Claire. We must have a meeting as soon as we're done."

"On our way," Jasper said. I nodded and followed him out the door, or more accurately, out the gargoyle's wings.

We sped past the creepy statues and along the art deco

hallway until we stepped through the bookcase and back into Miles's office. Jasper took out his cell phone.

"Claire, we have a situation in the BODO and Miles would like you to come down as soon as possible," Jasper said. Even in the most dire circumstance, Jasper's British flair for understatement remained. He listened for a beat and said, "See you soon."

"Well?" I asked.

"The party is back in full swing. She's finishing up with the mayor and will be down after that," he said. "I'm sure she's doing as much damage control as she can."

"How did a demon get in here?" I gestured to the shards of Narcissus on the floor. "And why would they only take the *Book of Shadows*? Not for nothing, but it seems to me if I had access to phoenix ashes, I'd be taking those, too."

"Potentially, if they discovered how to break into the vault, they likely assumed they could come back anytime they wanted." Jasper knelt beside the shards, picking up pieces and studying their shapes.

"What about the new wards?" I crouched beside him. "They won't be able to breach them, will they?"

"The old wards didn't stop them." Jasper fit two pieces together and I wondered if his plan was to glue the mirror back together.

"But how could someone replicate Miles's aura enough to fool Graven?" I found two pieces that fit together and added them to his.

"No idea, but it's definitely a cause for concern." There it was again. Jasper's remarkable unflappability.

The door to Miles's office opened and Claire and Tariq strode into the room. They both looked a bit worse for wear. Claire's red gown was wilted and her long blond wig frizzy. Tariq's feather drooped on his hat and he had sweat stains under his armpits.

"What's happened?" Claire asked, taking in the mirror on the floor. "Is everyone all right?"

"Narcissus!" Tariq dropped to his knees beside us and started helping with the shards as if we were all working on a large jigsaw puzzle.

"We're all fine," Miles said as he and Olive stepped through the bookcase. "But the *Book of Shadows* is gone."

"Gone!" Claire gasped and put her hand over her mouth.

"I'm afraid so," Miles said. "We have no idea how they were able to get into the BODO or break into the vault or even how they escaped."

"I actually have a theory," Jasper said, glancing up from the pieces of mirror.

"When you and Jasper used the looking glass to observe the gala, did you see me?" Miles asked.

Jasper and I exchanged a look. He turned to Miles and said, "No. I remember because before we left the gala, you were dancing with Olive, but when we observed through Narcissus, Olive was dancing with Tariq."

"We danced?" Olive asked Tariq.

"I have no idea." He shrugged.

"Well, there's a blessing," Olive muttered.

"If I wasn't there, that means the demon used me." Miles sounded horrified. "Me. I'm the one who led him into the BODO and the vault. I'm the reason the *Book of Shadows* was stolen."

"No." Claire shook her head. "*If* it was you, then you were kidnapped and your powers were used to gain access." Miles began to protest but Claire cut him off. "I will not debate this with you."

Miles opened his mouth and then closed it. Still, his eyes had a haunted look as if he wasn't sure what had been done to his person and he felt violated. I couldn't imagine how awful that must feel, especially when he had no memory of the ordeal.

"It's imperative that we discover who did this and where the book is," Claire continued. "We were entrusted by the Global Council of Magisters to keep the *Book of Shadows* secure. I will call the American councilperson first thing in the morning and apprise her of the situation."

I knew it was bad when Miles, Olive, Tariq, and Jasper all flinched.

I glanced at the shards at my feet, wondering how we were supposed to catch a demon. I glanced at the piece of mirror in my hand. A bit of shadow moved across its surface and then spilled out of my hand and onto the floor, where it slid toward the door.

I jumped to my feet and pointed. "Shadow! Moving! On its own!"

As if it sensed that it had been spotted, the little bit of darkness doubled its speed and it shot across the floor and into the main room of the BODO.

"Catch it!" Miles cried. "It might be our only clue to whoever did this!"

We tumbled after it into the brightly lit main room of the BODO. I saw the shadow slip under a table and I dove for it.

It slipped right beneath my fingers and through Tariq's legs. He drew his prop sword and sped after it.

"Try not to harm it," Olive said. "We need as much of it intact as possible."

"Got it!" Jasper grabbed a bit of shadow near his shoe, but it was his own, so he let it go.

The little bit of shadow circled the room, dodging and weaving while it looked for an exit. One by one, we dove, fell, and clutched at the little bit only to come up empty-handed time and again.

"Where is it going?" Tariq asked. His Nigerian accent was thicker with his ire. "Does it really think it can get through the warded doors?"

"Maybe it can," Olive said. "Did we ever test for shadows crossing?"

"We did," Miles said. "It can't leave this room. We should just wait until it tires itself out."

He gave a side-eye to a pile of books on his left. I frowned. Miles was up to something. I glanced at Jasper and he seemed to draw the same conclusion.

"That could take all night," Jasper said.

"We've got nothing but time." Miles started to whistle and gestured for us to move away from the table where the little bit of shadow was trying to blend into a table leg. As soon as we gave it some space, the little dark spot shot out from under the table toward the main door. A tremendous yowl sounded and Freya, the book-cat, launched herself from the top of the bookshelf where she'd been and landed on the little shadow, catching it between her furry gray covers.

"Excellent work, Freya." Miles scooped her up and even from ten feet away, I could hear the book purring.

Tariq ducked into his lab and came out with a glass test tube. He held the tube against Freya's pages and a little bit of dark was squeezed right into it, and he stoppered it with a cork. He held it up to the light and the dark spot curled itself into a little ball, like poking a caterpillar with a stick. I almost felt sorry for it.

"How?" I asked.

Olive glanced at me and for once there was no disdain in her voice when she said, "The demon must have used Narcissus to escape. The mirror is enchanted to show you any person or place you ask to see, but it can also be used as a portal to that same place."

"Did they break the mirror so that no one could follow them?" I asked.

"Most likely," Jasper said. "We can repair it, but the information of who used it and where they went is gone."

"We do know that it was a demon." Miles handed the tube to Jasper. "There's only one way for us to identify them. I'm sorry, Jasper, but you know what you have to do."

I glanced at Jasper's face and noticed that his jaw was set and his eyes flat as if he was steeling himself for something. He took the test tube and nodded. "I'll go tomorrow morning."

"Go where?" I didn't like the bad vibe I was getting. I glanced at Claire and Miles and noted the concern in their eyes. Tariq looked worried while Olive showed no emotion, as usual.

"And, Griffin, you'll bring Ziakas with you," Olive said.

"No." Jasper refused.

"Yes." Miles backed Olive.

Jasper looked as if he'd argue, but Olive said, "Ziakas is the most suited to keep you on task, Griffin, and you're going to need that."

They stared at each other and silent understanding passed between them. Jasper glanced away first. His fingers tightened around the test tube and he nodded. "Excuse me, I have to go make some arrangements. Zoe, I'll meet you here tomorrow morning at eight."

He strode out of Miles's office, leaving me staring after him. I glanced at the others and in unison they all made shooing gestures with their hands. I didn't hesitate and chased after Jasper.

"Jasper, wait!" I cried. He was almost at the door but he turned when I called his name. His face was tight, the muscles in his jaw clenching. I put my hand on his arm. "Tell me what's happening. Where are we going tomorrow? I need to be prepared."

Jasper glanced from my fingers clutching his forearm up to my face. His gaze softened and he said, "I'm sorry. You're right. That was incredibly rude of me. I'm just processing, and not very well, apparently."

"Where are we going tomorrow?" I repeated the question. His stony expression was beginning to alarm me. Jasper was silent for a beat and then he sighed.

"We're going to meet my father." His gaze met and held mine. "He's a demon and he'll be able to identify to whom this bit of shadow belongs."

Jasper's father was a demon. I blinked. That meant . . .

"I'll see you tomorrow, love." Jasper slipped through the door.

Jasper. Was. A. Demon.

7

I wasn't sure how long I stood there, trying to grasp that my would-be boyfriend was a demon . . . part demon . . . half demon? Was there a technical term for such a thing? Mage-demon? Demonmage? My librarian brain raced through the possibilities.

The pungent scent of rosemary interrupted my panic spiral and I turned to see Tariq with his ever-handy aromatic diffuser standing beside me. I felt my shoulders drop and I smiled at him, although it was strained.

"Thanks, I needed that."

"I figured," Tariq replied.

"Why me?" I asked. "Why did Olive say I should go with Jasper?"

"Because Jasper and his father get a bit chippy, and while Jasper would feel free to let his temper loose if he was alone or if one of us was with him, he won't do that if you're with him," Tariq explained.

"Because I'm a baby witch with no real power?" I asked, trying not to pout.

"No, because he cares for you and he won't do anything that might put you at risk, including antagonizing his father," Tariq said.

"Oh." I nodded. "That makes sense."

"Go home, Ziakas," Olive ordered. "We'll take care of things here. You need to prepare for tomorrow."

"Prepare?" I asked.

Miles nodded. "Agatha is expecting you upstairs."

"We have a car and driver waiting to take you both home," Claire said.

"But—" I gestured to the mess.

"We can take care of this," Miles assured me. "Go."

Too befuddled to argue, I dashed back to my office to grab my grimoire and then made my way through the doors and up the stairs to the museum above. I pushed the door open to find Agatha just as Miles had said. She looked much recovered with her usual sparkle in her eyes and her Mrs. Whatsit costume set to rights.

She took one look at my face and frowned. "What's wrong?"

"Something's happened. I can't explain here." I gestured to the partygoers all around us. "But the upshot is that I'm going with Jasper to see his father tomorrow morning."

"Ah." Agatha's eyes went perfectly round behind her glasses. "That explains why Miles mentioned you would need my help."

"Should I be worried?" I asked as a young woman dressed as Juliet jostled by us, dragging her Romeo behind her.

"No, but we have a lot of work to do." She grabbed my hand in a firm grip and moved through the crowd with the efficiency of a snowplow. "The car is waiting. We can talk on the way."

A big black Suburban was parked at the curb and once he determined that we were his designated passengers Agatha Lively and Zoe Ziakas, the driver rushed to open the door for us. There was a privacy glass between us and the driver, but Agatha put a finger to her lips indicating that I shouldn't speak until she had put a soundproof spell all around us.

Once the clear shimmering wall divided us from the driver, she turned in her seat to face me.

"What happened?"

I told her about the chaos in the BODO, the mirror, the vault, the missing item, and the bit of shadow Freya had captured. I ended with Jasper telling me that his father was a demon. "Does that make him a half demon? It does, doesn't it?"

"Technically, he's a cambion—half-demon, half-mortal, because mages and witches are mortal," Agatha said.

"You knew this?" I asked. "And you didn't think to mention it to me?"

"I assumed Jasper would tell you when the time was right," she said. "It's not like you're an official couple or anything. Are you?" One gray eyebrow quirked up and I shook my head.

"He's been away for months." I shrugged. "I was so happy to see him and I think he felt the same, but then tonight went horribly sideways and now I don't even know if we're dating."

"And with this new information you're not sure you want to?" Agatha probed.

"It's not that," I protested. "I have no knowledge of what

being a half demon entails and I don't think I can make any sort of decision until I do."

"That's fair." Agatha patted my knee. "But for now, your bigger problem is that you have to meet his father, Lord Griffin."

"I'm sorry, did you say 'Lord' Griffin?" An uneasy feeling began to flutter in my stomach.

"Yes, Lord Eliath Griffin, a British aristocrat of the highest order," Agatha said. "Your first meeting is critical. If you want him to respect you, you have to set the tone immediately."

"And that tone would be?"

"That you are a badass witch who is not to be messed with," Agatha said.

"Ha ha! You're hilarious." I patted the grimoire in my pocket. "I can't even decipher the spells in my own grimoire and I'm supposed to present like I know what I'm doing?"

"I'm serious, Zoe. You need to channel your inner Olive Prendergast and have the attitude as well as dress the part, otherwise Lord Griffin will eat you for lunch," Agatha said.

I stared at her. "That's metaphorically speaking, right?"

Agatha just stared at me. Okay then.

As soon as the driver dropped us off at Agatha's house in Wessex, Connecticut, the village where we both lived, she dragged me upstairs to her bedroom. "We have to outfit you in a way that establishes your worth from the moment Lord Griffin meets you."

"How about my awesome librarian skills?" I asked. "I feel like that's my strongest trait."

"While admittedly fabulous, that is not what speaks to

Lord Griffin." Agatha pushed me to sit on the edge of her bed. "We're going to need some haute couture for you, my dear."

"Hot what?" I gaped at her.

"Very funny." Agatha stepped into her massive walk-in closet and started throwing clothing out. "Oscar de la Renta, maybe; Louboutin, definitely; Stella McCartney, perhaps; oh, there you are, Prada."

I watched as blouses, pants, dresses, and shoes landed on the bed beside me. Agatha was a head shorter than me and definitely more curvy. I didn't know how she thought I could wear any of these bespoke items.

I picked up a dress that was all pouf and sparkle. The girlie part of me loved it, but it did not seem like something a person wore to meet a member of the peerage. Also, it was nowhere near my size.

"I love you for doing this, Agatha, I do."

"I hear a *but*." A blue Chanel blazer came out of the closet like it was shot by a cannon.

"But there's no way any of these clothes are going to fit me." I desperately did not want to hurt her feelings, but seriously, I would wear my own serviceable librarian attire of a wool skirt and a sweater.

"Am I not a kitchen witch?" Agatha plunked her hands on her hips.

"You are." I nodded.

"Do I not make the most amazing lemon chiffon cakes?"

"You do."

"Is my house not always fastidiously clean?"

"It is." I decided that I wouldn't mention the clutter. Agatha had a hard time throwing anything away. That being said, you could eat off her floors—you know, if you could find them.

"Then why would you question my ability to tailor these clothes to fit you to perfection?"

"Clearly an oversight," I said.

"That's right." She wagged a finger at me. "Now start looking for something to wear and do not doubt me."

"My mistake. Won't happen again." I picked up the blazer. The fabric was like butter and the stitching meticulous. Was it possible to fall in love with clothing? I thought I might have an affair with this jacket.

"This is it!" Agatha popped out of her closet cradling a burgundy dress. She held it up, and I noted it was long-sleeved, with a high neckline, a tiered midi skirt, and a narrow matching belt with a delicate gold buckle in the shape of a lotus flower.

"It's stunning." I loved it even more than the blazer.

"And with a pair of black patent leather low-heeled boots, you'll look the part of a badass witch," Agatha said. "Come on. I have work to do."

By the time Agatha was done using her stitch witchery to reconfigure the dress to fit me, I was exhausted from standing in my underwear with my arms out while the dress unstitched itself and then restitched itself to my size. Once the burgundy dress was finished and paired with the knee-high boots Agatha suggested, which had also been magically reconfigured, I had to admit I looked like I could hold my own with a lord or a president or a king. I just hoped I looked like I could go toe-to-toe with a demon.

As Agatha fussed with the skirt, getting it to hang just right,

I stared at my reflection and saw my mother staring back at me. No, not really, but I looked so much like her that sometimes I felt like she was on the other side of the looking glass.

"I wish Mom could see this," I said.

Agatha straightened up and rested her chin on my shoulder as we gazed at our reflection. "You look so much like her, sometimes I have to look twice to be certain it's you."

"I miss her," I admitted. "I miss how she was when I was a child, always smiling and laughing and filling our days with her particular type of magic."

"She loved you with her whole heart," Agatha said.

"Enough to leave me," I acknowledged. It had taken me years to understand that my mom had been on the run with me, her only child, from a very bad dark witch and that the greatest sacrifice she'd ever made was to leave me under Agatha's protection.

"Yeah." Agatha's voice was gruff as she smoothed my hair. "She broke her own heart to keep you safe. And now look at you."

"Badass witch," I muttered and we exchanged watery smiles.

When Agatha went to bed, I popped into her library and searched for any information I could find about demons. Unfortunately, Agatha's library, like the rest of her house, was not organized in a way that made sense to me, which was maddening given that she'd been the library director of our village of Wessex for most of her life.

The books I found were not encouraging and several were

quite contradictory. Scoggins's *Codex Daemonica*, a thin volume that was almost one hundred years old, listed a variety of attributes for demons that I took issue with. I knew for a fact that demons didn't have visible horns. I would have noticed when I shoved my fingers into Jasper's hair and kissed him. Right? Unless as a half demon, he didn't have them. Another volume by Lucy Paletti, entitled *Chronicle of the Banished*, was equally light on facts, based more on Lucy's experience as a demon bride, which also seemed suspicious. Disappointed, I went to sleep in my room, which Agatha had left unchanged since my teen years when I'd spent school holidays with her.

I nestled into my bed, pulling the fluffy lavender-scented comforter over me. While waiting for sleep to come, I reviewed the events of the evening in my mind but kept circling back to the fact that Jasper was part demon.

My grimoire sat on my nightstand and it brought me comfort. Inheriting the family tome made me feel closer to my mother and grandmother and less like an imposter in this world. Would Lord Griffin be able to see past the bougie dress and boots and spot my insecurity? Probably. Did it matter? No.

The most important thing was to identify the demon who'd broken into the BODO and stolen the *Book of Shadows*. Bonus points if Lord Griffin could help identify the woman who'd been dressed as the Snow Queen. Those ice shards she'd fired at me hadn't been for grins. I'd gotten the feeling she hoped to take me out. Permanently.

I passed the night in a fitful sleep. My dreams were invaded by bits of shadow. They were scattered on my bedroom floor. Not here at Agatha's but in my own modest house across town. In my dream, I kept trying to catch the little bits and put them in my pocket, but I couldn't get a grip on them as they slid from the floor up my body to cover my nose and mouth, suffocating me.

Gasping for air, I bolted upright. I opened my eyes and put my hand on my throat. My heart was racing and I wondered if the dream was a result of my overactive imagination, the horrifying events at the gala, or if it was a warning from an otherworldly creature like the demon who had stolen the *Book of Shadows*.

I threw aside the covers and hurried downstairs, where I was greeted by the calming sight of Agatha in the kitchen, making breakfast. She pushed an omelet at me with a side of toast and a hot cup of coffee. "Eat up. You're going to need it."

"That's reassuring." I toasted her with my coffee mug.

"Lord Griffin is not someone to take lightly," Agatha said. "I suspect that's why Jasper didn't tell you that he was his father."

"Hmm," I mumbled in agreement through a mouthful of egg. The omelet was fluffy and delicious but also very spicy. I coughed and my eyes filled with tears. "What's in these eggs?"

"Cayenne pepper. It protects you from evil spirits." Agatha slathered her homemade raspberry jam onto a piece of toast and handed it to me.

"How? By killing me?" I bit into the toast, hoping for relief.

"You can thank me later." Agatha sent me a pointed look over the rim of her coffee cup.

I swallowed the toast, relieved that the burn had faded. It

was going to have to be a *one bite of eggs, one bite of toast* breakfast. "Is Lord Griffin evil?" I tried to keep my voice measured so that she didn't parse out the subtext, but this was Agatha, who had known me all my life and raised me for the latter part of it.

"I don't believe that Jasper is like his father," she answered my unasked question. "Jasper's mother is a very powerful Swedish witch and when he wasn't at Eton, she raised him in Brighton and kept his contact with his father to a minimum."

"That must have been hard on him." I thought about losing my own father at a young age and realized Jasper and I had more in common than I'd realized.

Agatha reached across the table and patted my hand. "Your driver will be here in half an hour, you'd better get ready."

I shoveled in the last bite of egg and let it burn its way to my belly. *Take that, Lord Griffin.* I was ready to face him or so I tried to convince myself.

Jasper was waiting for me in front of the museum when I arrived at eight o'clock sharp. He looked ridiculously handsome in a black wool overcoat over a dark suit with a white dress shirt and black tie. I scooped up my own coat and stepped out of the car when Jasper opened the door for me.

His eyes went wide as he took me in from the tight chignon at the nape of my neck to the pointy toes of my boots. "Zoe, you look—"

"Like a badass witch?" I asked. "Because that's what Agatha was going for."

"You do." He laughed. Then he leaned close and kissed my cheek. His voice was low when he added, "But I would argue that you're a beautiful badass witch."

I grinned. "Excellent, because that's what *I* was going for."

He took my long beige cashmere coat and held it open for me. I slid my arms in and fastened the large buttons on the front.

"My father's place is just across Central Park. I thought we could walk if that's all right?"

"Of course." I was hoping he would give me a quick briefing on how to approach his father, but instead he was quiet, lacing his fingers through mine and walking slowly as if trying to draw out the time.

I was burning with so many questions it almost felt like a fever. Instead, I focused on the bare limbs of the trees overhead, the bite of the wind against my cheeks, and the dark gray of the sky overhead. Central Park was quieter than usual and I appreciated the stillness as it gave me a moment to catch my breath before meeting the father of the man I was dating, who also just happened to be part demon.

"You haven't asked about my father," Jasper said as we climbed one of the winding paths that cut across the park.

"I figured you'd tell me whatever you wanted me to know." This felt like a nice neutral non-probing response.

"For the record, I was about to tell you about him last night at the gala," he said.

I glanced at his profile and remembered he'd said he had something he wanted to tell me. "You can tell me now."

"My father was unaware of my existence until I was ten," Jasper said.

I said nothing, allowing him to tell me whatever he wanted to in his own way.

"My mother left him when she discovered she was pregnant. She couldn't go home to Sweden because she knew he would look for her there, so she raised me in Brighton with frequent secret trips to Landskrona to visit the aunts."

"Your parents were married?"

"For a brief time, less than a year, in fact." He squeezed my fingers. "My mother says it was still too long."

I nodded, not knowing what to say.

"When he discovered my existence, he fought for custody," Jasper said. "That didn't go well. The compromise was that I was shipped off to Eton."

"Oh." Again, I nodded. It occurred to me that being sent to private school was yet another thing we had in common.

Jasper released my hand and put his arm about my shoulders as if he needed more contact. I slipped my arm around his waist, happy to oblige and not just because I was cold. I understood the devastation of suddenly being sent away, but at least I'd had Agatha to look out for me.

"Yeah, it was difficult," Jasper admitted. "What is a ten-year-old boy supposed to do with the knowledge that he is half-demon, half-mage?"

"Nothing good, I expect."

A wisp of a smile flitted across his face. "Many an afternoon was spent in the headmaster's office. I went on to Cambridge to study mythology just to piss them both off. When I took the job at the museum, my father opened a branch of his company here in New York. He said it was to be close to me, but I think it was to avoid certain legal situations in Europe."

"His company?" I asked.

"My father deals in art and antiquities."

"Like Christie's or Sotheby's?" I slipped on a bit of ice, but before my foot even shot out from under me, Jasper caught me and steadied me. Why hadn't I noticed that his reflexes were unnaturally fast before?

"Similar, but my father's objets d'art are of the magical persuasion," Jasper said. "A word of caution, when we're in his house, be sure not to touch anything."

"Anything?" This felt like a tall order.

"Just stay beside me," Jasper said.

I nodded. We exited the park onto Central Park West and while I didn't want to badger Jasper about his life, I couldn't hold in my questions anymore.

"Jasper, what attributes do you share with your mother and your father?" The words came out in a rush. It was the most roundabout way I could think of to ask what was on my mind. "If you don't mind my asking."

"I don't mind." He kept his arm around me, so I took him at his word. I glanced up at his face and I could see the tension in his jaw and the fine lines around his eyes. We paused at the crosswalk to wait for the walk sign to change.

"My mother is a witch, a powerful one much like the women in your family. I get my magical ability from her."

Jasper was an impressive mage. He'd been teaching me how to manipulate energy before he was sent to retrieve the *Liber Umbrarum.* I glanced at the two people nearby, worried that they could hear us, but the woman had large headphones on and the man was talking to someone as evidenced by the wireless earbuds he wore.

"From my father, I inherited a decided attraction to chaos." He glanced at me from beneath his lashes, and his light blue eyes hit me with a blast of charm that left me weak in the knees.

"Are you calling me 'chaos'?" I pointed to myself.

"My life has been infinitely more interesting with you in it." His lips curved up in a small smile that should not have been as attractive as it was given that I wasn't sure if he was complimenting me or not. I glanced away, refusing to be sucked in by his magnetism, which was plentiful. Was that part of being a demon, too?

"What else?" I burrowed into his warmth as we waited on the curb.

"Being only half-demon and refusing to be tutored by my father or his minions in demonship, my demonic abilities are limited. I can sense strong emotions, like desire or fear. I have an immunity to curses or mind control, that one comes in handy working in the BODO and likely helped me get us out of the gala last night before we were bewitched. I also have enhanced strength and stamina, and—" He turned away as if checking to see when the light would change and his words were lost in the sound of the traffic.

"Sorry, I didn't catch that." I tried to meet his eyes but he remained turned away.

"Iagemursloly." His words were mushed together and I grabbed his arm to get him to face me. Before he'd fully turned toward me, his words hit me like a blast of ice water.

"You age more slowly?" I asked. "Exactly how much more slowly?" I leaned in and stared at his face. It was a beautiful face. "How old are you?"

"Not as old as Olive," he said.

My jaw went slack and I staggered back.

"Light changed!" Jasper caught my hand in his and pulled me across the street.

"How old is Olive?" I asked as we stepped onto the curb.

"No idea." He kept my hand in his and continued walking.

"Then how do you know—" I stopped walking and dug my heels into the sidewalk. The only way Jasper was going to get me to move was to drag me. "You told me that Miles recruited you from Cambridge."

"He did." Jasper leaned back and stared at the tall building beside us.

"How did you meet Miles?" I asked. Miles had once told me that he was an adjunct professor at Cambridge, but that was thirty years ago.

"You really are very clever," Jasper said.

"Complimenting my intellect will not derail this conversation," I said. "How old are you, Jasper?"

"Promise you won't freak out," he said.

"No."

"That's fair." He nodded. His gaze met mine when he said, "I'm fifty."

I put my hand on my forehead as everything went gray and I started to see spots. I felt like I might pass out. "Fifty."

"It's not that old." He sounded a little offended. "I'm only fourteen years older than you."

"Yes, but you look like you're in your thirties like me," I protested. "So, how does it work? When you're eighty, you'll look forty?"

"It's not an exact thing, I just age slower than a human but not as slowly as a full demon," Jasper said. "Besides, I could get injured or disfigured in my work and then all bets are off."

"That's not as comforting as you'd think," I said.

"I would have thought you'd be more concerned about my ability to sense strong emotions." He took my hands in his, keeping me in place as we faced each other. "I didn't mean to keep my being a half demon from you. If I hadn't been sent out into the field right after our second date, I would have told you, but—"

"But?" I asked.

"But if you want to change your mind about—"

"About?" I had never seen Jasper struggle for words. It was endearing to see him so flustered.

"About this?" He gestured between us. "I know we're just . . . actually, I have no idea. What are we doing, love?"

Demon or no, the second this man called me "love" my treacherous heart fluttered in response as if it was tuned specifically to his frequency.

"I . . . we're . . . the thing is . . ." I stammered. I didn't know what we were and I wasn't sure I wanted to declare it just now having learned he was a demon, rather a half demon, and an older man, too.

"I'll understand if you've changed your mind—"

"Ahem. Excuse me, Jasper, but your father is waiting." A very British voice interrupted whatever Jasper had been about to say.

Jasper sighed and said, "Let's finish this discussion later."

I nodded, feeling oddly relieved to get a reprieve. I glanced at the man who had spoken. He had a round head, with a bulbous nose that appeared to have been broken a time or two. His body was equally round, but I suspected it was more muscle than flab. Judging by the size of his hands, he looked like he could rip a man's head off his body if he was feeling duly motivated.

"Nice to see you, Corey." Jasper let go of my hands and stepped forward to give the man a hug. My entire body grew tense, but Corey hugged Jasper in return, slapping him on the back as he did so.

"It's been too long, mate." Corey looked him over and seemed satisfied. Then he turned to me. He smiled and the glint from several gold teeth temporarily blinded me. "Nice to meet you, Ms. Ziakas."

"Call me Zoe," I said.

His grin broadened. "Corey."

"A pleasure." I inclined my head.

Jasper took my hand in his as Corey led the way into the towering building in front of us. I'd been so busy grappling with the age difference between Jasper and me that I hadn't realized we'd arrived. Large highly polished steel letters spelling out **GRIFFIN'S** were perched above the oversized black glass doors. Above the name were several flags; the United Kingdom's Union Jack, the United States' Stars and Stripes, as well as several European flags, clearly establishing it as a place of international business.

The lobby was austere, with two very large paintings that were roped off by stanchions, and a fountain that ran down the length of the wall in the corner. I glanced at it, realized something wasn't right, and glanced back. It was a fountain, but it wasn't water that trickled down the wall. It was liquid gold.

"Is that . . . ?" I pointed and Jasper nodded.

"Liquid gold," he confirmed.

"But gold has a melting point of 1,947 degrees Fahrenheit," I said.

Jasper blinked at me as if surprised that I knew such a random fact.

"The fountain is made of a furnace and a crucible," Jasper said. "It's rumored to have belonged to King Midas."

"The ruler of Phrygia in seventh century BCE known for his golden touch?" There was absolutely no way I could keep the shock and awe out of my voice.

"That's the one." Jasper led me away and leaned in and whispered, "Mouth closed." I snapped my jaw shut with a loud clack. If an artifact of King Midas was in the lobby, I couldn't imagine what the rest of Griffin's contained.

A beautiful woman in a formfitting bright blue dress sat behind an austere black glass desk at the far end of the lobby. At a guess, she was about thirty, with a killer figure and her honey-blond hair styled in a severe bob. She glanced at us over the top of her cat-eye glasses as we walked by. She stared at Jasper as if she'd like to stab him. Ex-girlfriend? I found I didn't like that thought at all, so I banished it.

"Mr. Griffin." Her voice was tight when she greeted us.

"Ms. Bengt, please tell my father we're on our way." He didn't introduce us, which was fine with me. The tension in the lobby was thick enough to cast a shadow.

There it was. That was the question I'd been wanting to ask Jasper since last night but hadn't gathered the courage to do so.

Jasper led me to an elevator at the far side of the lobby.

The doors were fancy copper inlaid with turquoise in geometric patterns. Jasper pressed the button and the doors slid open. We stepped inside and I ignored the toile wallpaper that decorated the interior, which was a feat because even at a glance I could see the repeating images were all of the underworld, including Cerberus, the three-headed dog, Charon on his ferryboat, and a young woman I believed to be Persephone, holding a pomegranate with a look of satisfaction on her face.

"Can you do it?" I asked Jasper as he pressed the button for the top floor.

"That's a broad inquiry," he said. "Can you narrow it down a smidge?"

"Can you command your shadow to do things?"

"Oh." His expression became impassive and I worried that I'd hurt his feelings.

"I'm sorry," I said. "That was rude. It's none of my business."

"Of course it is." Jasper reached out as if he'd take my hand, but then he didn't. "No matter what happens between us on a personal level, you are my colleague and you should feel free to ask me anything."

"Thank you." With great intention, I reached across the space between us and took his hand in mine. Then I grinned and asked, "So, can you?"

His lips twitched and he said, "I don't want to disappoint you."

"Not possible," I said. "Remember, I've seen you inhabit birds."

"It is impressive, isn't it?" The teasing glint was back in his eye.

"So impressive." I fanned my face with my free hand and he laughed.

"I suppose had I been raised among other demons, I might be able to wield shadows, but to answer your question, no, I never learned that particular skill and I honestly don't know if I'm demon enough to pull it off."

"Well, you're more than enough demon for me," I teased. I could feel the tension in him start to release, and I wondered if this was another reason Olive had insisted he bring me with him.

Jasper's smile widened and he pulled me close. I did know him well enough to know when he was about to kiss me. I leaned in. We were mere inches apart and he was lowering his head when the doors whooshed open and the most terrifying being I had ever seen was standing there, glaring at us.

"Hi, Dad," Jasper said with a sigh.

8

"Don't faint. Don't faint. Don't faint," I whispered to myself as I gripped Jasper's hand and allowed him to pull me out of the elevator to face the *man*? in front of us.

Lord Griffin was easily six foot four. Presently, he was shirtless and his skin was a deep crimson color and his upper body bulged with muscles. There were horns poking out of his thick dark hair, which had patches of silver at his temples. The pupils of his yellow eyes were elongated and he had a meticulously trimmed beard that came to a sharp point. He was wearing some sort of silky gold-and-black-striped lounge pants and he was barefoot. This was Jasper's father. Holy shit!

"Nice," Jasper drawled. He gestured at his father's half-naked body. "Is this for my benefit or Zoe's?"

Lord Griffin smiled and I fully expected him to have pointy teeth. He did not and I was a little disappointed. Then he turned to face me and I wished I knew enough magic to make myself invisible.

"Zoe?" His voice was so deep it sounded like thunder and

when his gaze raked over me, I was surprised I didn't blister from the heat of his scorn. "You're a witch."

He said it with the same disdain I'd use to refer to a person who kicked puppies.

I felt my grimoire, which I'd tucked into my coat pocket, hum. I didn't think it liked him any more than I did, but I also got the distinct feeling that it was trying to remind me of who I was. I was a witch *and* the last of the line of Donadieu witches who specialized in necromancy, and while I had yet to bring anyone back from the dead, I'd certainly managed to send a dark witch there. My grimoire anchored me in my power.

I tipped my chin up and met his stare. "And you're a demon. How thrilling." My tone reeked of sarcasm and when Jasper coughed into his fist to hide his laugh, I knew I'd nailed it.

Lord Griffin's eyebrows rose. He tipped his head to the side and said, "Interesting."

Then he turned on his heel and strode out of the foyer and into the penthouse apartment. I gulped in some air as Jasper escorted me inside. We crossed the threshold to find Lord Griffin, looking nothing like the creature who had greeted us.

He was fully clothed in a black bespoke suit and designer shoes, there were no horns on his head, his skin was no longer red, and the pupils of his brown eyes were round. He retained the neatly trimmed beard and looked every bit a member of the British aristocracy.

"Tea?" He gestured to a rolling cart beside the couch and two armchairs that were arranged around a large marble fireplace.

"No, thank you," Jasper said. "We really don't have the time."

"There's always time for tea." Lord Griffin gestured to the chairs.

I glanced at Jasper, who sighed. He led me to the couch, keeping me close to his side, and we sat down.

"Would you care to pour, Zoe?" Lord Griffin asked me.

I hesitated. If I deferred to Jasper, I looked weak. I was not having that. Yet, if I went blithely along with Lord Griffin's request, I looked malleable and not very bright, especially since Jasper had warned me not to touch anything. What if the teapot was enchanted? It could have a venomous bite for all I knew.

There was no help for it. I was going to have to play hardball. It wasn't the tone I'd wanted to set with the father of my potential boyfriend, but what was a witch to do? I reached into my coat pocket and took out the rune that Agatha had given me before I left Wessex that morning.

Carved into a square of polished hematite, the rune was a closed eye. Agatha had told me to set it between me and the demon to keep him from being able to use his demonic power on me. It blocked him from my mind, body, and spirit, which was just fine with me.

Lord Griffin reared back at the sight of it. "Is that necessary?"

"You tell me," I countered.

"That's my witch," Jasper muttered, and I could hear the pride in his voice, which bolstered my courage.

Lord Griffin said nothing and I poured the tea into the three delicate bone china cups on the decorative silver tray. Lord Griffin added milk and sugar to his while Jasper and I ignored ours. It was a shame to waste it, but I was following Jasper's lead. If he didn't drink the tea, neither would I.

"Things are going well at the BODO?" Lord Griffin sipped his tea.

"You know exactly how things are going." Jasper leaned back and studied his father.

"I do, don't I?" Lord Griffin grinned and his pupils elongated for just a moment before becoming circular again.

The demon was not very far below the surface. I glanced at the rune on the table and sent a silent thank-you to Agatha for it.

"You had some excitement." Lord Griffin set his cup down and flicked a piece of lint off his pant leg.

"If by that you mean a demon broke into the museum and stole the *Liber Umbrarum* from the vault, then, yes, we have."

"Isn't that the book you spent two months hunting down in London?"

"It is."

"A highly coveted item." Lord Griffin crossed his arms over his chest.

The tension between the two men was so intense it was almost painful, like being forced to listen to a high-pitched alarm that wouldn't stop ringing.

"It is." Jasper reached into his coat pocket and pulled out the test tube with the remnant of shadow in it. "I was hoping you could identify who our culprit is."

"Tsk tsk tsk. How very sloppy of them to leave a bit of their shadow behind." Lord Griffin went to take the vial but Jasper held it out of reach.

"I'm going to need some assurances before I let you examine it."

"I'm your father."

"As I said, I'm going to need some assurances," Jasper repeated.

Lord Griffin waved his hand at him. "Go on."

"If you can identify who this shadow belongs to, you do not try to broker a deal with them for the *Book of Shadows*," Jasper said.

Lord Griffin raised his brows. "I would never." It sounded like a lie.

"You do not warn the demon in question to garner favor with them."

"I think I'm offended." Lord Griffin frowned.

"You swear on my life as your son that you will do nothing with any information you gain from this meeting." Jasper leaned forward in his seat, holding his father's gaze.

Lord Griffin rolled his eyes, clearly annoyed, which I suspected was because he'd just been thwarted. I deconstructed Jasper's words just to be certain there was no loophole for Lord Griffin. It seemed like an airtight deal to me.

"Fine. I swear." Lord Griffin held out his hand for the vial. Jasper hesitated for the merest moment before he set the stoppered glass tube in his father's hand.

Lord Griffin held the tube up to the light. "Funny thing about a demon's shadow: It's like an extension of them. Little-known fact: If a fragment gets cut off from the rest, it could go rogue."

A shiver shot right down my spine.

"It will whisper to you, tempting you, taunting you, making you doubt your sanity if it's strong enough," Lord Griffin continued.

Jasper shifted beside me and I wondered if the shadow had whispered to him. He hadn't mentioned it, but maybe he hadn't known. I glanced at him and saw the muscles in his jaw clench repeatedly. That couldn't be good.

"Can you identify who this particular shadow belongs to or not?" Jasper asked.

His father watched the shadow move around the vial as if looking for a way out. It flattened itself against the glass, then curled up into a tiny ball. It shot up toward the cork as if it could pop it out but then rebounded back to the bottom of the tube, where it stayed as if it had knocked itself out.

Lord Griffin unstoppered the vial and poured the shadow into his palm. The shadow immediately tried to slither free, but Lord Griffin tightened his fingers about it. I wondered if he was going to squeeze the magic out of it. When it lay limp in his hand, Lord Griffin poured it back into the vial and stoppered it.

He handed the vial back to Jasper. "When you get back to the BODO, lock that up where no one can get near it."

"You recognize it?"

"Yes, it belongs to a demon named McWrath." Lord Griffin picked up his tea, studying the inside of his cup. When he glanced up his expression was grim. "He is not a demon to be toyed with."

"He should have thought of that before he stole my book," Jasper said.

His father shook his head. "You sound just like your mother—foolish and brave. How is she?"

"None of your concern," Jasper said.

"That's fair." Lord Griffin's lips curved up in a small smile that was tinged with regret.

"Why would this McWrath want the *Book of Shadows*?" I asked. "I mean, I know it's powerful, but what do you think he would use it for, specifically?"

"McWrath hates the Global Council of Magisters. He resents that they maintain order between all the factions of the magical world, making certain that no one abuses their power," Lord Griffin said. "I suspect he plans to use the power of the *Liber Umbrarum* to alter reality and bend the council to his will, allowing him to seize power, after which he'll destroy the council."

"Bloody hell," Jasper cursed.

"It will be if he gets his way," Lord Griffin agreed. For the first time, I noticed that he sounded genuinely concerned.

"How do you suppose he managed it?" I asked. This had been bothering me ever since we entered the vault. It had seemed so impenetrable. How had McWrath done it?

Lord Griffin took a deep breath and said, "You said this bit was found in the BODO?"

Jasper nodded.

"Then I'd make the educated guess that McWrath used whoever controls the security of the BODO—*Miles*?—to gain entrance. McWrath likely bespelled Miles to believe he was somewhere else doing something else and then, in his shadow form, McWrath used Miles's body to gain access to the highly secure area and access to where the book was kept. McWrath's only mistake was leaving a bit of his shadow behind."

"Nothing is foolproof," I said, remembering Miles's words.

"Indeed."

"Where do I find him?" Jasper stood, indicating that our time here was done.

"He's elusive." Lord Griffin stood as well. "I'll see what I can do to locate him."

"I'd appreciate that." Jasper turned and held his hand out to me, pulling me to my feet.

"McWrath is very powerful," Lord Griffin said. "If you go after him, you're going to need help."

"Are you volunteering?" Jasper asked.

"I'd be open to brokering a deal," Lord Griffin offered.

"Always a deal," Jasper said with a mirthless chuckle. "Thanks, but I'm not interested."

"The offer stands." Lord Griffin escorted us to the door. "Be careful . . . son."

Jasper nodded. We stepped into the foyer and Lord Griffin was about to shut the door, when I asked, "Does McWrath associate with any witches that you know of?"

Lord Griffin pursed his lips and gave me a reproving glance. "Witches and demons do not generally associate with one another."

Jasper tipped his chin up as if daring his father to say another word. I was amazed that Jasper didn't point out that his father had clearly done more than "associate" with his mother. I doubted I would have shown as much restraint.

"Really?" I asked. "That seems limiting."

Lord Griffin stared at me for a beat and then frowned.

"There is one witch that McWrath was rumored to have an understanding with. She's the high priestess of the High Bridge Coven."

"Odessa Van Doren?" Jasper asked.

His father nodded. "The coven meets in the Highbridge Water Tower in Washington Heights on the Manhattan side of the old High Bridge, which was part of the Croton Aqueduct."

"Because that's not creepy at all," I murmured.

Lord Griffin actually cracked a small smile. "Odessa is a very powerful witch, and she is not one to be crossed."

"Oh, we've met," I said. "And we've crossed." I was positive that the witch who had assisted McWrath at the gala was Odessa Van Doren. "I believe she has a Snow Queen kink."

Lord Griffin let out a surprised chuckle. "That would be Odessa. She likes to fire icicles at people who displease her."

"I've noticed." I nodded at him. "Thank you for that information."

"Happy to help." He sounded as if he meant it.

Jasper led me through the building and back outside into the light, or what passed for it on this chilly, overcast February morning. He hailed a cab and we sped back to the museum, which was fine with me as I was eager to hear what Miles thought of the information we'd gathered.

When we entered the BODO, the entire staff was seated at the largest study table in the main reading room as if they had been waiting for us.

Tariq jumped up from his chair as we approached. "How did it go? Could Lord Griffin identify the shadow?"

"He did." Jasper took the vial out of his coat and handed

it to Miles. "We need to keep this locked up. My father reminded me that a demon's shadow is an extension of their person and if a fragment were cut off from the rest, it could go rogue if not kept in isolation."

Miles nodded. "I've heard of snippets of demon shadows being used in spells by dark witches, usually to incite madness."

"That's a thing?" I took my grimoire out of my coat pocket and set it on the table. Judging by its stillness—I couldn't feel any emotion coming from it—I suspected it was listening to the conversation.

"Who does the shadow belong to?" Olive asked. Her eyebrow with the slit in it was raised in inquiry.

Jasper took a short breath and said, "A demon called McWrath."

"Oh, shit." Tariq let out a low whistle. "That's not good, in fact, it's bad, so very bad."

"It makes sense," Olive said to Miles. "Only a demon of his power could have used you to get into the BODO and remain undetected."

"We still need to discover exactly how." Miles frowned.

"He had help," I said. "Lord Griffin told us that McWrath associates with the witch Odessa Van Doren."

Olive hissed.

"And I believe she's the witch I tangled with during the gala, the one dressed as the Snow Queen," I said. "She actively tried to stop me from assisting Jasper and she was definitely not bespelled like the rest of the gala attendees."

Olive rose from her chair and started to pace. "Odessa is our way to reach McWrath."

"How so?" Miles asked.

"She's power hungry," Olive said. "She always has been and she has the loyalty of a weather vane, shifting in the direction of whoever can give her what she wants."

"With McWrath in possession of the *Book of Shadows*, that would be him," Tariq said. "I don't see how we can pull her allegiance away from that much potential power."

"Simple." Olive waved a dismissive hand. "We offer her something even more powerful that she doesn't have to grovel to a demon for."

"And that would be what?" I asked.

Olive spun to face me, her dark eyes locked on mine, and she said, "You."

9

"No!" Miles, Tariq, and Jasper shouted as one.

"Absolutely not," Jasper added as if that would be the end of it.

"While I appreciate your confidence in me . . ." I began, but Olive interrupted me.

"Oh, no, I have less than no confidence in you or your abilities, but what you do have is a grimoire of questionable intent and a decided lack of magical training, which makes you attractive to power seekers," Olive said. "I think you need to infiltrate the High Bridge Coven and convince Odessa to take you under her wing."

I felt my grimoire then. It took me a moment to read the emotion, but when I did, I had to resist the urge to roll my eyes. My little black book was feeling decidedly smug.

I reached out and tapped the cover with my forefinger. "Stop that."

Olive cocked her head to the side, a small smile on her lips. "It agrees with me, doesn't it?"

"You're certainly giving its ego a stroke," I said.

"I don't like the idea of using Zoe and her grimoire as bait," Tariq said. "No offense, Zoe, but I don't think you have enough control of your magic yet to take on a witch like Odessa."

I thought about how I'd managed to tie Odessa up by her dress sleeves, and then I remembered that she'd escaped. "No offense taken."

"I agree with Tariq. Too many things could go wrong." Jasper crossed his arms over his chest. "It's better if I confront Odessa."

"And warn her that we're onto her?" Olive asked. "She's a brilliant witch; she'll see through you before you land at her coven's doorstep. Zoe is an unknown, an ingenue reeking of innocence. If we start a rumor among the witches we know that Zoe is an untrained witch with a powerful grimoire and that she's new in town and looking to join a local coven, Odessa will hear about it immediately. You know how witches talk, gossip spreads faster than a snap spell for boiling water." Olive snapped her fingers for emphasis. "Looking for a coven is the perfect cover for Ziakas, and the temptation for Odessa to invite Ziakas into her coven to gain access to the Donadieu grimoire will be too much for Odessa to resist."

"I'm sorry, but isn't it my job to be the containment specialist?" Jasper asked. "This is exactly what you hired me for. Right, Miles?"

The room went completely quiet. I got the feeling all three stories of books surrounding us were listening. Miles pushed his glasses up on his nose and glanced from Olive to Jasper and then to me.

"How do you feel about this, Zoe?" Miles asked. "You've

faced down Odessa already. Do you think you can convince her that you want to join her coven?"

"Honestly? I have no idea." I shrugged. "I suppose I have nothing to lose by trying."

"Nothing to lose?" Jasper cried. "She could murder you or worse."

"There's something worse than murder?" I asked.

"She could turn you into a houseplant," Tariq offered. "One of those office plants that always looks a sickly shade of yellow."

"Or a doormat." Olive shuddered. "Having people wipe their feet on you for eternity."

"I know a mage who angered his wife and she turned him into a vacuum for a month," Miles said. "He still coughs up the occasional bit of carpet."

They were pranking me. They had to be. I glanced at each of their faces. "A witch can actually do those things?"

"One without a moral compass can," Jasper said. "How do you think Narcissus became a mirror?"

"Well then." I paused to think about the ramifications of pissing off the witch that I had *tied up by her sleeves*. It seemed likely that any meeting between us in the future was going to be fraught with danger—for me.

I mentally tried to get a lock on my grimoire to sense how it felt about this, but it was giving me nothing. The decision would be solely mine. I cleared my throat. "I don't see that we have any choice."

Jasper was not happy. He and Miles holed up in his office strategizing the best way to approach the coven, while I spent several long days being instructed by Olive so as not to embarrass myself when I appeared before the High Bridge Coven.

If I'd thought Olive was tough before, now she was positively relentless. When I arrived home at my cute little cottage in Wessex, Connecticut, every evening, I longed to pass out from sheer mental and physical exhaustion, but I was thwarted. While Olive put me through my paces magically, Agatha met me at home to instruct me on the history of the High Bridge Coven.

Agatha became my guardian when my mother sent me to Wessex Boarding School when I was fourteen. Life with my mother had been challenging as we moved constantly in the wake of the deaths of my father and grandmother. My mother kept us moving every season and while I knew she loved me, I was also aware she had changed after my father died. She was closed off to me and my tween years were incredibly lonely.

Despite the emotional distance between us, I had resisted being apart from my mom and her placing me in boarding school. For reasons I came to understand as an adult, it was necessary for her to leave me where she knew I'd be safe. Agatha, who was my mother's childhood best friend, took me under her wing and I spent my school holidays at her house and my free afternoons after classes visiting her in the Wessex Public Library, where she was the director. It didn't make up for the abandonment I felt at my mother leaving me, but it eased the pain a bit.

Small wonder I followed in her footsteps and became a librarian in Wessex. The shift to working at the BODO had been a significant life moment for me, but Agatha had encouraged me to take the opportunity. As a bonus mom, she was top-tier, and not just because she was a kitchen witch who loved to cook.

She was waiting for me when I stepped into my little cottage. The house smelled amazing and I paused to breathe in the scent of real food versus the packaged chicken potpies I tended to live on in winter.

"Is that . . . ?" I began, but Agatha, who was sitting in one of the armchairs by the fireplace, which had a crackling blaze going, interrupted and said, "Beef Wellington."

Exhausted as I was, I did a happy food hop. "Yay!" I kicked off my boots, hung up my coat, and unwound my scarf, dropping everything on the bench beside the front door.

"It'll be ready in fifteen minutes." Agatha gestured to the chair across from hers. "Take a seat and tell me about your day."

"It was a rinse and repeat of yesterday," I said. "Honestly, I think Olive is ready to put me in a sack and throw me in a river."

Agatha smiled. "Olive's not as brutal as she seems."

"We're talking about Olive Prendergast? The witch who can make even the unflappable Miles flinch?"

Agatha lifted the teapot that sat on a small table between us and poured me a cup, pushing the honey jar toward me. These items belonged to Agatha but she kept them here because my utilitarian cookware didn't possess the magic her kitchen witchery required.

"Is this tea tea or *tea* tea?" I asked, meaning was it imbued with her culinary magic.

Agatha pushed her reading glasses up on her head to hold

back her silver ringlets. She gave me a look that clearly indicated of course it was *tea* tea. "It's brewed to give you energy but not keep you awake. Ginger for warding off stagnation, apples for vitality, and cinnamon to spark your inner fire," she said. "And you can add some honey to sweeten your disposition."

This last step didn't sound optional. I added honey and stirred clockwise as my grandmother had taught me as a child to draw energy into myself. I cupped the mug with both hands and let the heat sink into me before I took a sip. I could feel a zap of energy hit as the liquid warmed my core.

"Thank you, Agatha." I reached across the space between our chairs and took her heavily beringed hand in mine. "I don't know what I'd do without you."

Agatha squeezed my fingers and then released me. "Starve, I suspect."

"True." I laughed and sipped more of her tea. It was delicious. It went against Agatha's kitchen witch code to make things that tasted terrible.

We sat in silence, sipping our tea and staring into the flames of the fire, which emitted a delightful heat against the February chill that seemed determined to infiltrate every crack and crevice of my petite cottage.

When I finished my tea, Agatha pushed out of her seat and said, "Come on, we can talk over dinner."

I set the table, while Agatha served the meal. Beef Wellington was a Lively family recipe, handed down through the generations of Lively witches, most of whom were kitchen witches like Agatha. Rumor had it that one of the first Lively witches had been an enslaved cook, working under the direction of Martha Washington. It would not surprise me in the least, as the Livelys had settled in Wessex when the town was founded two hundred years ago.

The pastry-wrapped slice of beef on my plate looked amazing and I barely retained enough manners to put my napkin in my lap before I tucked in. Agatha watched me with a contented smile as if nothing gave her greater joy than feeding people, whether with food or books, it didn't matter which.

"Where did I leave off on the history of the High Bridge Coven last night?" she asked.

"We got through the lives of the covens that existed along the Croton River, how they dealt with the construction of the aqueduct, and their impact on the cholera outbreaks of the mid-1800s as they placed charms and spells on the aqueduct to keep the water pure." I paused to take another bite and chew. "I think you were telling me about the coven's need to go to ground during the industrial age when we stopped."

"You mean when you fell asleep?" Agatha asked, glancing at me over the top of her glasses.

"Sorry about that." I'd woken up this morning tucked into my bed like a toddler. It had been nice.

"Don't be." Agatha's voice was kind. "I know how hard you're working to prepare."

"I wish I knew what to expect when trying to infiltrate a coven." I took a sip of water. "It's not like joining a sorority, is it?"

"Even if it was, you were never much of a joiner." Agatha speared a piece of summer squash in a butter dill sauce.

"Facts," I agreed.

"The industrial revolution forced the coven to go into hiding," Agatha said. "Mostly because the enlightened age used legal means to prosecute anyone claiming to be a witch for fraud, which could be financially devastating and include prison time.

"The aqueduct expanded during this period of growth, giving the coven plenty of places to meet, like ventilator shafts and forgotten stone chambers. Reports from Hudson Valley workers at the time tell of women offering 'protection charms' to laborers building bridges and rail lines—the payment being in coins or the occasional lock of hair."

"I wonder how a husband would explain a missing chunk of hair to his wife," I said.

"More easily than missing coin," Agatha replied.

"After the industrial age, what happened to the coven?" I asked.

"They remained," Agatha said. "When the aqueduct was decommissioned, they centered themselves in the Highbridge Water Tower, which was built on a bluff above the Harlem River and pumped the water that came to it from the Croton Aqueduct, which was carried by the High Bridge, the oldest bridge in the city, to bring fresh water to the higher sections of Manhattan. The coven still meets there, although, since the water tower has been refurbished and designated a landmark, it's all kept very hush-hush. Needless to say, no one joins the coven without the invitation of the high priestess."

"Odessa Van Doren." I put my fork down. The thought of meeting up with her again gave me stomach cramps. I had asked Olive why she couldn't be the one to meet Odessa and she said they "had history," which made her being invited to join the coven extremely unlikely.

"She's very powerful, Zoe." Agatha put her fork down, too. "You have to be extremely cautious should you get invited to the coven."

Her face was creased in concern and I knew there was nothing I could say to ease her anxiety as we both knew I was in way over my head. So, I went with the same thing I'd always said to her when I was an overconfident teen. "Don't worry. What could possibly go wrong?"

Agatha rolled her eyes and huffed out a small laugh. "You sound just like you did when you were sixteen." Then her face grew serious. "I made a promise to your mother that I would always watch over you. I'm going to craft some protection for you."

"Like the rune I used with Lord Griffin?" I asked. "You should have seen his face." I hoped Agatha would laugh but she didn't.

"You had Jasper beside you then." Agatha fretted her lower lip with her teeth. "You'll be on your own in the coven, Zoe. You must stay on high alert."

"I will." I reached over and squeezed her forearm. "I promise."

Instead of meeting with Olive the next morning, I entered the BODO to discover a staff meeting was about to take place. Jasper, Olive, Tariq, and Miles were seated at the largest table in the main room. There was a pot of coffee and a pile of pastries on a tray in the center.

"Someone's birthday?" I asked as I pulled my messenger bag over my head and set it on the table while I shrugged out of my coat.

"Sadly, no," Miles said. "Tariq is updating us on his plan for you to infiltrate the High Bridge Coven."

"Oh." I slid onto the seat next to Jasper. He poured me a cup of coffee and dished up a raspberry pastry, setting it in front of me. How did he know that was my favorite? I'd never told him. Lucky guess? Or was he just that observant?

"The coven recruits new members at the Midnight Market, so I believe we should go," Tariq said.

"That sounds . . . fun?" I bit into my pastry and Olive stared at me from across the table with her lip slightly curled as if finding me lacking, which was no different than any other day. I ignored her.

"It can be." Miles's voice was very measured. "It can also be very dangerous. There is a lot of magical bargaining happening and sometimes it gets dicey."

"We'll all be with you," Jasper said. "You don't need to worry."

"I'm not worried." I took another bite.

"You should be," Olive chastised me. "The most powerful witches in the city will be there, one of which is Odessa Van Doren. If she's holding a grudge from your last meeting, she'll turn you into a lampshade before any of us can stop her."

I dropped the remainder of my pastry onto my plate and took a bracing sip of coffee. I met Olive's gaze and said,

"Well, then she isn't that great of a witch, because I am the only one who can open the Donadieu grimoire, and she'd be an idiot to give up access to that much power."

Olive's curled lip unfurled into a small smile. "That's better. Know your worth, Ziakas. You'll need to once you're in with the coven."

A compliment? From Olive? I honestly wasn't sure how I felt about that . . . oh, wait. Yes, I did. I was distinctly unsettled.

10

Like all magical things, access to the Midnight Market was complicated. Apparently, there were portals all over the city and we had to get to one at precisely 12:12 a.m. and make an offering to the gatekeeper to be allowed entrance. I was not generally a night person, so it was already a challenge to be up this late.

"Which portal are we using?" Jasper asked Miles as we stepped out of the museum into the frigid night air. A large black SUV and a driver were waiting for us in front of the building.

"*The Boy and the Hammer,*" Miles said. "233 West Seventy-Ninth Street."

"Isn't that a street art piece by Banksy?" I asked.

"It is." Olive gestured for me to get in the back seat of the car. Tariq and Jasper joined me while Olive and Miles took the middle row. The driver closed the door after us.

"Is Banksy a mage?" I whispered to Jasper. I might as well have shouted as Olive with her super hearing glanced over the seat at me.

"Why do you think no one has caught him?"

That made sense. A notorious anti-authoritarian street artist who popped up in the nineties, the Bristol-born Banksy's identity was still up for debate after all these years. Remarkable.

"No one knows for certain," Miles said. "But we have our suspicions."

"So, street art is the portal to the Midnight Market?" I asked.

"It keeps traffic moving to have many points of entry," Tariq explained.

"What other artists are used?" I asked.

The driver got in and Miles gave us a warning look before he said, "Other murals and street art of interest are Keith Haring on the Houston Bowery Wall, Yuko Shimizu's *Yes!* mural in DUMBO in Brooklyn, the Audrey Hepburn mural on Mulberry Street, and—"

"The Welling Court Mural Project in Astoria is the most popular," Olive said. "With over one hundred fifty murals."

I nodded. I was glad we were going with the Banksy, which was relatively close to the museum. I wanted to ask how we used the mural to get to the Midnight Market, but Miles had made it clear that we weren't to speak in front of the driver, so I held my curiosity in, but it was a struggle.

I patted my coat pocket, making certain my grimoire was with me. I had been so resistant to its presence in my life when it first showed up, but now it was more important to me than my phone or my handbag. Its solid weight, the accumulated knowledge of generations of my ancestors, calmed me.

The driver let us out at the corner of Broadway and West

Seventy-Ninth. The wind whipped up the street, which, even for this time of night, was busy with people coming and going mostly in and out of the Irish pub nearby.

When the street was relatively quiet, Miles took a velvet pouch out of his pocket and handed each of us a coin. It was silver, bigger than a quarter but smaller than a half-dollar. There was a fox engraved on one side and the numeral three on the other.

I glanced at the coin and then at Jasper. He smiled and said, "You have questions."

"Sooo many questions," I said.

Miles glanced at his watch and said, "We have a few minutes before the portal will open. Tell me first, what do you think the sides of the coin represent?"

I studied the fox. There was something sly about his expression. Maybe I was imagining it, but I didn't think so. "He reminds me of a kitsune, a Japanese fox spirit, which acts as a messenger of the gods and also a guide or a trickster for travelers."

"Very good," Tariq said. "That's exactly right." He grinned at me. "What about the other side?"

I shook my head. "Three. Is that the value of the coin? The cost of the portal?"

"Think about the parts of a journey," Jasper suggested.

"The beginning . . ." Olive rolled her hand in an impatient gesture.

"The middle and the end," I said. "Clever."

"It's almost time," Miles said. "When it's 12:12, we will go through in single file. We have one minute. Plenty of time."

I felt my anxiety spike. One minute? What if I dropped my coin? What if I was rejected? What if the portal wouldn't open for me?

Jasper's hand settled on my lower back. "We'll walk you through it. Don't worry."

"We never leave a team member behind," Tariq said.

I nodded. I knew that. They'd proven it before.

"And we're off! Step lively!" Miles strode up to the mural. He held his coin out between his thumb and forefinger. There was a shimmer in the air and the coin disappeared. The boy in the mural slammed his hammer down and then he faded into the brick as a smoky archway appeared. Without hesitation, Miles stepped inside. "Hurry! The portal will close in exactly one minute."

Olive held up her coin and it, too, disappeared in a shimmer of air, then Tariq, and then it was my turn. I stepped forward and held up my coin. It was then that the portal keeper took shape in front of me. He wore a hooded cloak that covered his face. His skeletal fingers reached out from his long sleeves and he snatched the coin from my hand. It took everything I had not to yelp.

"Go ahead, the others are waiting," Jasper encouraged me.

I patted the grimoire in my pocket and stepped through the shadowed doorway into an explosion of light and color and exotic scents mixed with a cacophony of sound. It was such a punch in the face, I staggered. Jasper stepped up behind me and steadied me with his hands on my shoulders.

"All right, love?" he asked.

I was not. Towering long-limbed trees dripped with massive multicolored globes of light, casting the market in shades of purple and red and blue and green. Shouts and laughter filled the night as creatures hawked their goods to the customers wandering through the endless rows of booths.

"Where are we? Because we didn't walk into the building we were standing outside of, and I've walked most of Central Park and this isn't it," I said.

"We're in the Netherveil, an alternate plane that exists between light and shadow, seen and unseen. It's only accessible by the magic of the waning moon," Jasper explained.

"Wow." I felt the magic inside of me open like a flower unfurling in the sun, responding to all the magical stimuli surrounding me.

"Oh, that won't do," Miles said.

"What?" I asked.

"You're leaking," Olive said with a sigh.

"Huh?" I glanced down at my body and saw ribbons of red swirling around me.

"The first visit to the market causes some witches to lose control of their magic." Tariq shrugged. "It happens."

"Not to me." Olive's scarred eyebrow ticked up. "You can't walk around like that, you'll be a target for any witch or mage with nefarious purposes."

I sighed, feeling like an idiot. I didn't want to have to leave.

"Not to worry," Jasper said. "I prepared for this." He reached into his pocket and pulled out a small square of fabric. It was as black as the cover of my grimoire but studded with silver as if it had been hit with an exploding star.

I watched as he flicked the fabric and it unfolded into a long-hooded cloak. He dropped it over my shoulders and pulled the hood up over my hair, which now had vibrant red streaks.

"How did you know I would need this?" I asked.

"I'm in charge of containment, so I try to plan for any contingency," he said. "Also, this is the same cloak I wore on my first visit to the Midnight Market and for the same reason."

"Thank you." I pulled the fabric more tightly about myself. It was soft to the touch like velvet and yet weighed nothing.

"What's the plan?" Tariq asked.

"Let's operate as normal," Miles suggested. "If we stay in a huddled group, we'll draw attention to ourselves. Zoe can walk with each of us in turn, which would be expected of a witch visiting the market for the first time."

Jasper opened his mouth to protest, but Miles held up his hand. "You can keep an eye on her from a distance."

I wasn't sure how to respond to Miles's acknowledgment of Jasper's protective feelings, and I really loathed being the center of attention, so I turned to Olive and said, "Lead on."

Olive's eyebrows rose and a small smile tipped her lips. "Don't worry, Griffin, I'll make sure she doesn't get turned into a toadstool."

"That's not funny," Jasper said.

Olive laughed, a sound I had never heard before, and it was as musical as the noise coming from the market and I found myself smiling in response.

"Come on, Ziakas, I have some things to buy," Olive said.

"Keep an eye out for aetherleaf," Tariq said. Olive raised her hand in acknowledgment and started walking.

I sent Jasper what I hoped was a reassuring glance as I fell into step beside Olive. She was taller than me and her stride longer. I hurried my pace.

"How do you buy things here?" I asked. "Or do they take debit cards?"

Olive's lips twitched. "I'll show you." We stopped by a booth that appeared empty until a tomte popped up from behind his table, standing on a wooden box to raise him to eye level. He had the requisite white beard and pointy red hat.

"Olive Prendergast." His thick Swedish accent did not mask his tone. He was clearly unhappy to see her.

"Mossgrim." Olive crossed her arms over her chest as they stared each other down.

I glanced behind me to see if Jasper was nearby. Jasper being half-Swedish, I wondered what he'd make of the Swedish gnome. I didn't see him, so I turned back to the interaction, racking my brain to remember what sort of power the tomtar wielded.

"That sigil mark you gave me for my bloodroot resin was lacking." Mossgrim's beard puffed with his annoyance.

"Careful, gnome," Olive said. "You won't get any more from me if you insult what I've paid you before."

"Humph." Mossgrim turned away, unimpressed.

I felt my heart start to pound. I would never have the audacity to slight Olive. Ever. Also, what was bloodroot resin?

"Fine. If my sigil is of no value to you, I will find Skogmar and do business with him. I'm looking for phoenix ash to make a balm, and I doubt you have it anyway." Olive turned to leave.

"You doubt I have phoenix ash? Ha! And you're going to ask Skogmar?" Mossgrim spun around to face her. His eyes were round under his cap as if he couldn't believe the blasphemy of what he'd just heard. "I should let you. That would serve you right."

He jumped off his box and yanked open the door of the cupboard behind him. He shuffled through shelves of small glass jars until he found one that contained a bright red powder. He hopped back onto his box and slapped the jar down on the table between them. "Go ahead. See if Skogmar has this quality of phoenix ash."

Olive lifted the jar with one hand while manifesting a bright blue orb of light with the other, which she used to shine into the jar. She tipped her head to the side and said, "Three sigil marks and not one more."

"Pah!" Mossgrim scoffed. "Do you know what I had to do to obtain that ash?"

"Buy it from a passing peddler and package it as your own?" Olive asked.

Mossgrim glared. Olive glared back. Not being the sort of person who invites conflict, I felt myself start to sweat.

"Five sigil marks," Mossgrim declared.

"Three," Olive countered.

Mossgrim's lips disappeared into his beard. "Four. And that's my final offer."

"Deal," Olive agreed.

She reached into the pocket of her long black coat and pulled out four thick pieces of paper. She put them down on the counter and I noticed that they each had a decorative sigil on them that glowed blue as if the ink was made of light.

Mossgrim snatched them up and pocketed them in the

time it took me to blink. "Pleasure doing business with you, Olive Prendergast."

"I'd say the same, but it isn't." Olive inclined her head as she pocketed the small jar. "Until next we meet, Mossgrim."

He touched his cap and we turned and walked away. I waited until we were a few yards away before I started firing questions at her.

"What is a sigil mark? How do you get them? And the phoenix ash—are those actual ashes from a phoenix that went up in flames? How are they different than the ones in the vault of the BODO? And what is bloodroot resin?" I asked all my questions at once, not wanting to forget anything.

Olive raised her hand to indicate I should stop talking. "Easy there, Ziakas, you're going to hurt yourself."

"But I have so many—" I began, but she interrupted.

"Questions, yes, so I gathered." Olive strode along the booths, stopping to examine the goods for sale. A witch was selling hearthstones, which were smooth palm-sized stones that emitted a gentle heat and smelled faintly of cinnamon. Another vendor was hawking self-stirring teacups, which made me think of Agatha, and I contemplated picking it up for her birthday, but of course I had no sigil marks.

My desire to buy one must have shown on my face because Olive said, "Sigil marks are the only currency accepted here. You have to create a sigil that is unique to you and then infuse it with a bit of your magic. The stronger the witch, the more valuable the sigil."

"So, a lesser witch might have had to pay ten sigil marks for the phoenix ash?" I asked.

"Precisely." Olive nodded. "Also, phoenix ash comes from exactly where you'd expect. After the phoenix is consumed in flame and is then reborn, there is residual ash. It has potent magic and, as you can imagine, it does wonders for magical burns. The difference between this and the one in the vault is that those ashes are from the first phoenix. Those are the only ashes that can be used to bring back the dead."

"Right, yes, of course," I mumbled. Meanwhile I was still trying to wrap my brain around the fact that phoenixes, plural, existed.

"As for bloodroot resin," Olive continued, "it's sap that is used to bind oaths, making them as strong as iron."

"Cool," I said, when what I was thinking was, What sort of oath needed to be strengthened like that?

I glanced around the market feeling as out of place as I had at every new school I started when my mom had us moving every few months during my childhood. I hadn't known until just recently that we were outrunning a dark witch. I understood why my mother hadn't told me but at the same time wondered what it would have been like to grow up knowing about this world. Feeling like I was a part of it instead of always being the oddball who didn't seem to fit in.

"Zoe, there you are!" Tariq jogged over to us. "It's my turn to take Zoe around. I've managed to procure the aetherleaf I was looking for, and at a bargain." He patted his pocket. "Now I want to show Zoe my favorite vendor."

"She's all yours, but remember your real purpose, both of you," Olive chastised us before disappearing between two very tall witches, dressed as if they were on a Paris runway.

One had purple hair and the other green, and they both wore outfits that almost appeared to be upside down, as the tops were puffed-out balls of shiny pink fabric and the bottoms were leg-hugging tights in deep green. They looked like flowers and were laughing as they shared a paper bag of something that smelled like cinnamon rolls, but they couldn't have anything as ordinary as that here, could they?

"What are those two witches eating?" I tipped my head in their direction.

Tariq stared at the witches and then said, "Those are spiderweb cakes, they're made of spun sugar and sprinkled with cinnamon. They're said to attract luck or spiders."

"Oh, no thank you then," I said.

Tariq laughed. "Come on. I want to show you this. As a librarian, you'll love it."

He waved for me to follow him and we dove back into the wandering throng. We wound our way to the edge of the market and the last booth in the corner. I could see the sign over it read **MARVELLO'S MISCELLANEA**.

When we arrived, a man who looked every inch the scholar with his round glasses, curled mustache, and the pipe he held clenched in his teeth, glanced up at us. When he saw Tariq, he removed the pipe and broke into a broad grin. He was shorter than me and quite a bit wider, and he was wearing a lavish waistcoat over his dress shirt, giving him the air of belonging to a different century.

"Tariq, my old friend, how are you?"

"Excellent, Marv, and you?"

"Equally well, thanks." They shook hands and then Marv

turned to me, studying me through his glasses. "Zoanne Zi-akas, I'm Marvello, but everyone calls me Marv. What a pleasure to meet you."

I blinked. "How did you know my name when we haven't been introduced?"

"Sorry, sorry, that was quite rude of me," Marv said. "It's my spectacles. They're bewitched to spell out the names of people I meet because I am terrible with names."

"Oh, that is handy," I said.

"Isn't it?" Marv asked. "But I sometimes forget to wait until a formal introduction has happened."

There was something very genuine about Marv. I decided I liked him.

"Zoe is our newest librarian at the BODO," Tariq said. "I knew she would love your booth. All right if we browse?"

"That's why I'm here." Marv grinned. "Have fun and I'm happy to answer any questions."

"Excellent." Tariq took me by the elbow and dragged me into the booth while Marv went back to the recliner and small woodstove he had set up in the corner. He opened his book and promptly ignored us. He was definitely my kind of people . . . er . . . mage.

"Check this out," Tariq said. He opened a small box, and nestled inside was an ancient-looking monocle. He lifted it out by its engraved ivory handle and handed it to me.

"What does it do?" I asked as I held it up to my eye. I turned to a nearby bookshelf and grabbed a slender leather volume, flipping the cover open to see if it improved my vision. Instead, I was hit with an emotional punch in the chest that took my breath away. Heartbreak for a first love flooded my senses and tears sprang to my eyes as I felt the absolute devastation of loss wreck me.

"Oh dear, that's enough." Tariq pried the glass from my hand and the emotions immediately receded. I set the book down and turned to Tariq.

"What was that?" I asked.

He held up the monocle. "It's called an Archivist's Lens and it allows you to experience the emotion the author was feeling at the time they were writing."

I blew out a breath. "That's wild."

"Isn't it?" He grinned. "Don't you love it?"

"It certainly makes reading a next-level experience," I said.

I glanced around Marvello's trove of items. There were clocks, mirrors, sets of dishes, maps, lanterns, and books . . . so many books. It was easy to see why Tariq loved Marv's booth the most. Leaving the lens behind, I began to sort through the titles of books, looking for items of interest. I was reaching for a volume on a nearby shelf when a tiny flicker of flame shot out at my fingers, followed by a puff of smoke.

"Ouch!" The flame had grazed my finger but hadn't burned me. My exclamation was more from surprise and anticipated pain. "Marv, I don't want to alarm you, but I think there's a fire in your books!"

"Oh, no!" Marv and Tariq hurried over to the shelf.

"Right there!" I pointed. Sure enough, another little lick of flame appeared.

Marv laughed and said, "Oh, don't worry, that's a bookwyrm hatchling."

I glanced at Tariq in confusion and he explained, "A baby dragon."

11

I clapped my hand against the side of my head a few times as if I was trying to dislodge water. "I'm sorry, could you repeat that, because it sounded like you said *baby dragon*?"

"I did." Tariq gestured to where Marv was moving aside books and reaching into the shelf.

I felt my jaw drop when Marv pulled his hand out of the opening, and pinched between his thumb and forefinger by the scruff of its neck was a tiny black dragon, no bigger than a baseball.

"That's not . . . you're pranking me," I said.

"Hold out your hand," Marv said. "This little fellow is named Titus. He won't hurt you."

My hand trembled, but I held it palm up and Marv dropped the bookwyrm hatchling into it. The petite fellow stretched his neck, sniffing the air between us. He was stupid cute and I desperately wanted to pet him or squeeze him, but I didn't want to terrorize him as he was so tiny, so I didn't do anything.

He circled my palm, his tail twitching and his leathery

wings flapping, like a dog trying to settle into the best position for a nap. As soon as he relaxed, Titus folded up his wings and tucked in his tail. A puff of smoke came out of his nostrils and he closed his eyes. I would have thought I was hallucinating, but I could feel the pinpricks of his tiny talons on my palm, his steady heartbeat, and his slow inhale and exhale.

"But . . . I don't . . . isn't it dangerous to have a little guy who emits fire near your books?" I asked.

"Oh, he's not the only one," Marv said. "I have five bookwyrms. They eat mold and dust, and their fire is like witch fire, where it doesn't burn but does clean the books quite nicely."

"He is just the sweetest thing," I said. "Are the others here?" I glanced around the booth but didn't see any.

"Yes, they hide when strangers come around." Marv pointed at Titus. "He's the boldest of their clan."

"I had no idea that bookwyrms existed," I said. "We should have a clan at the BODO."

"We talked about it, but Claire wasn't comfortable with the idea, given that our collection is occasionally opened to the board members and explaining a bookwyrm would be . . ." He shrugged.

"Impossible?" I offered.

"Yeah, that," Tariq agreed.

"Still, he's just precious," I said. The pocket where I kept my grimoire suddenly got warm and I glanced down to see if it was aflame. It wasn't, but there was a decided green glow and the warming sensation continued. Was my grimoire jealous?

I was about to reassure it when Jasper and Miles arrived at

Marvello's booth. Forgetting about my grimoire, I cupped Titus and spun around.

"Jasper, look!" I cried. "A bookwyrm! I've never seen one before."

"Cute little poppets, aren't they?" Jasper smiled. He stroked Titus's head with one finger and the baby dragon let out another puff of smoke that curled in the air as if signaling his contentment.

"I'm sorry to dash in and out, Marv," Miles said as he shook Marv's hand. "We're introducing Zoe around and have a lot of ground to cover."

"Of course." Marv held out his free hand and I carefully slid the sleeping dragon into his palm. He tucked Titus into the pocket of his sweater and little puffs of smoke rose from the opening. "It was wonderful to meet you, Zoe. Be sure to come by next time."

"I will," I promised.

As Jasper took my elbow and led me away, I leaned close and whispered, "What's happening?"

"We saw some of the High Bridge Coven witches at another booth and Miles thought it might help your odds of being invited into their group if we placed you in their line of sight." He glanced at me and his eyes narrowed. He pushed aside the dark cloak he had given me and gestured to my coat. "Why is your pocket glowing green?"

"Huh?" I glanced down and sure enough, the green glow in my pocket was now a pulsing green light. "You know, I really adored the bookwyrm, but they're not nearly as wonderful as having your own grimoire as your companion."

One of Jasper's eyebrows ticked up, and I winked at him, indicating that he should play along.

"You think so?" he asked. "A book isn't a baby dragon, after all."

My grimoire pulsed bright green and I met Jasper's gaze and he gave me a small nod, indicating that he was tracking the mood of the book, too.

"No, it's infinitely better," I said. I wondered if I was laying it on too thick, but the glow was dimming, so I went with it. "I mean, you have to feed baby dragons and clean them and they likely demand your attention at all hours. Books are just perfect companions. There when you need them and waiting patiently when you don't." I paused and noted that my pocket was no longer glowing like a beacon and was now more just a little phosphorescent.

"I can't argue with that," Jasper said. "And you're so lucky to have such a special grimoire all your own."

"I am!" I enthused. "I just love the Donadieu grimoire."

The glow went out like someone snapping off a light, taking the warm sensation with it. I smiled up at Jasper and his lips twitched. What a moody little book I had.

"Over here!" Miles waved to us from several booths ahead. Tariq was beside him and they were in close conversation as we caught up.

"I don't think we should leave her alone," Tariq said.

"She won't be," Miles insisted. "We'll keep an eye on her but from a distance."

"Are you talking about me?" I asked.

"There's so much that could go wrong here," Tariq said.

"I just don't think gaining access to the coven is worth putting Zoe in jeopardy."

"I agree," Jasper began and then added, "with both of you. Zoe, what do you think?"

"I think if the only way the witches are going to approach me is when I'm alone, then that's what we have to do," I said. "And as Miles said, if you pick different spots to observe from, I won't really be alone."

"Fair point," Jasper said. "Although, the idea does make me uneasy."

"Olive has found the witches," Miles said. He pointed to one of the orbs of light above us in the market. It was a few rows over and its color had changed to a searing shade of orange.

"Olive's signal," Tariq explained.

"Let's walk over there," Miles said. "Zoe, you stay in the center of the path. I've got your six, while Tariq takes the left flank and Jasper the right. We'll be far enough away that no one will see us, but you'll know we're there. Okay?"

My nerves were a tangled mess of panic and pride. I didn't want to let anyone down, but my social battery was already at an all-time low. This was going to be tough. "Got it. The sooner I meet these witches the better."

"Proud of you," Jasper said.

I felt my face get warm and I was glad the hooded cloak hid it from sight. I was a grown woman. It was ridiculous to be so flustered by praise from this man.

The market was in full swing. There was music and laughter and good-natured shouts. A pair of mages were trying to outdo each other in spellcasting and a crowd gathered around to watch. The taller one conjured a large pie on the table in front of him. I slowed my walk to see what sort of pie it was. Apple? Cherry? Hunger made me desperate to know.

The mage grabbed the center of the top crust and pulled it back, revealing that the inside of the pastry was filled with live blackbirds. The crowd oohed and aahed and clapped. The second mage shook his head, unimpressed, and with a surge of magic that stopped me in my tracks, he turned the blackbirds into paper cranes and arranged them to hang in the air in the shape of a heart.

The crowd went wild and I, too, was caught by the spectacle as one of the cranes floated down in front of me. I held out my hand and it settled on my palm. The first mage demanded a rematch, but the second one waved him off and started walking straight toward me.

He was tall and lithe, and his features were delicate, giving him an almost feminine beauty. He was wearing a long black trench coat with black lace-up boots. His shoulder-length wavy blond hair was so pale it was almost white. But it was his eyes that held my attention. Their color was a brown so deep that his pupils blended into the irises, making them solid darkness. It was very unnerving.

I glanced around looking for Jasper, Tariq, or Miles, but they were staying in the shadows. With every step closer the mage took, I could feel my own magic stir as if in response. I tried to shut it down, but the paper crane resting on my palm fluttered its wings and I couldn't look away.

The mage stopped in front of me. He was even better looking up close, with chiseled cheekbones, full lips, and a square jaw. I forced my eyes back down to the crane.

"Impressive," I said.

"You're too kind." His lips ticked up on one side in a lopsided smile that was unexpectedly charming. "It's nothing compared to a witch who can raise the dead."

My gaze shot to his and I knew I must look surprised.

"Yes, I know who you are, Zoe Ziakas," he said. "In fact, I doubt there's a witch or mage here who doesn't."

I glanced around the crowd, most of whom were ignoring us, or were they? I was suddenly very self-conscious and really hoped one of my colleagues was about to save me—*any moment now.* I glanced up at the orange orb and because I knew it was a signal from Olive, I felt her impatience as clearly as if she were standing there tapping her foot.

"I don't know about that." I tried to hand him back the crane but he waved me off. "Keep it. It's an invitation."

"Is it?" I glanced at the paper bird, which abruptly folded itself flat. "To what exactly?"

"You'll see." His smile deepened. There was a slyness about him that I did not trust. I didn't care what the invitation was for, I was going to decline.

"Thank you, I guess? If you'll excuse me, Mr. . . ." I wanted his name so I could ask Miles about him later. Whereas Marvello had been delightful and Mossgrim entertainingly cross, this mage made me edgy.

"Rowan," he said. "My name is Rowan Thorne."

Of course it was. "Nice to meet you, Mr. Thorne, but I'm afraid I have to go and find my colleagues." The hair along my arm prickled as I pocketed the crane.

"I won't keep you then." He hesitated for the briefest moment, looking as if he wanted to say something more, before he stepped out of my path. "Until we meet again, Ms. Zi-akas." I felt a surprising warmth enfold me as he walked past. It was comforting and I felt my suspicion of him ease. I watched until he turned a corner and faded from sight, taking the warmth and my sense of calm with him.

12

I turned back to the market. The crowd had dispersed but I still didn't see Miles, Tariq, or Jasper. I glanced up at the orbs in the trees, looking for Olive's high-alert orange one, but it wasn't there. Somehow in the time I'd been talking to Rowan, it had changed color. Damn it!

Did that mean Olive was in trouble? Was that why there was no sign of the others? Had they rushed off to help Olive?

"Jasper! Miles! Tariq!" I hissed into the shadows. No one near me paid any attention and it was then that I noticed something felt off about the market. The energy was different. There was a hazy vibe as if everything were wrapped in cotton. Oh no, was this another enchantment like the night of the gala? Was that why the guys had abandoned me? Were they dealing with something bad?

A flash of annoyance surged. They should have told me. Yes, I was still learning the basics, but I could help. I started to jog.

I aimed for the orb I was certain I'd been walking toward even though it was no longer orange. I hurried past vendors and jostled my way through the crowd, which seemed to be moving in slow motion.

I had almost reached the row where I believed Olive's light had been. I took a sharp turn around a mage hawking magic carpets. At any other time, my curiosity would have demanded that I stop, but I had to find out what was happening with my colleagues.

I was running full-out when a puppy as black as midnight shot out of a merchant's booth, and I had to stop short to avoid colliding with him. I lost my balance and flailed. I was too late and too uncoordinated to save myself and landed on the ground with a jarring thump. Thankfully, I hadn't landed on the puppy or my grimoire and, judging by the relief I felt coming from my pocket, I wasn't the only one who thought so.

The puppy took this as a sign that I wanted to play and he jumped on me—he was strong for such a little fella—and licked my face. Slobber covered me from my chin to my eyebrow. *Gah.*

"Hound!" A woman burst out of the booth from where the puppy had run. She was short and stocky, wearing a navy tracksuit with a whistle on a cord about her neck. Her gray hair was scraped back from her face, making her overbite seem more prominent, and she had jowls that shook when she bellowed, "Get back here now!"

The puppy growled, clearly not interested in listening to the woman, who I assumed, by the whistle, was his trainer.

"There's always one, every litter, there's always one that should be put in a sack and tossed into the river," the woman snarled. I glanced behind her into the booth and saw three other puppies just like this one, sitting in a perfect line as if awaiting her next command. She shoved the sleeves of her jacket up to her elbows, revealing muscled forearms. "Come here, hound."

"What did he do?" I asked the woman as I pushed up to my feet.

She turned toward me and examined me from head to toe, her eyes narrowed, and then she nodded as if she'd come to a conclusion about me. I didn't suppose it was a flattering one. "He does not obey. If he remains untrainable, he will be put down."

I gasped. "But he's just a puppy." I looked at the wriggling black body, so full of life and joy, and thought I'd be sick. How could she casually suggest ending him like that?

"Come here, hound," the woman ordered through gritted teeth.

The puppy jumped in the air, barked forcefully, and took off at a run.

"Maybe if you'd stop yelling at him, he'd come on command," I said.

A slow smile that lacked any warmth spread across the woman's face. "It is done. He's yours now."

"Excuse me?" I cried. "How do you figure that?"

"You think you can handle him?" the woman asked and swept her arm in the direction the puppy had gone. "Be my guest. I suggest you fetch him before someone else captures him. Who knows what this lot would do to a poor little puppy."

I glared at her. How heartless could a person be? If I did manage to catch him, there was no way I was turning that sweet puppy over to the likes of her. No way. No how.

"Fine." I turned and ran after the puppy, convincing myself that this was more important than getting in with the High Bridge Coven and that my colleagues in the BODO would surely understand. I didn't dwell on how Olive was likely to respond. Best not to think about that right now.

"Dog!" I ran through the booths, looking for the puppy as well as my colleagues. I had covered two rows and was doubling back when the puppy darted across my path again. I stumbled and fell, landing on my knees with a hard thump. The puppy wiggled his way over to me as if he thought cuteness was going to get him out of trouble with me. Of course it did.

"My guy, what are you doing taking off all by yourself? I know that lady is mean, but you can't just book it. Is there another caretaker I can bring you to?" I asked him, wondering if there was any chance he could understand me. We were at a magical Midnight Market, after all.

The puppy barked three times. Was that an answer? It was an impressive bark. I scratched his ears. "It's okay, buddy, we'll find you a new fam." I cupped his slobbery jowls and studied his features. "You look like a Diego to me."

He tipped his head to the side, considering. "Don't worry. It's just temporary until we get you where you belong. Diego is much more dignified than Hound or Dog."

Diego licked me again. I wiped my face with my sleeve and pushed off the ground to standing. As soon as I was upright, I noted the quiet. The cacophony of the market was gone. The only sound now was Diego panting and a soft whisper of breeze passing through the trees. Trees.

I glanced up. The orbs were gone and so was the night. Daylight illuminated the world around me and it wasn't the world I had just been standing in a few moments ago. The market had vanished and so had every person and creature other than my puppy companion. I spun around, taking in my surroundings. I was standing in a field of wildflowers, and it was beautiful.

The breeze was soft, gently tugging at my cloak. I pushed back my hood to let the sunshine fall on my face. I could hear birds chirping and the lazy drone of the bees on the blooms surrounding me. The scent of the flowers wasn't overly strong and there was an enticing hint of vanilla to it. A surge of euphoria hit me low and deep and I felt myself smiling.

I glanced down at Diego, who was sitting beside me, wagging his tail as if he felt the same all-consuming joy I was feeling.

"It's amazing, isn't it?" I asked him.

Diego barked, whether in actual answer or just because he felt the need to respond, I had no idea. But I laughed in response and threw my arms out wide and started to twirl. I felt a joy I hadn't experienced since I was a child and my parents were alive and we were a happy family, full of love and laughter. Joyous tears streaked down my cheeks as I spun and spun until I was out of breath and staggering on my feet.

Diego hopped around me, leaping into the air and barking. It was as if he was trying to join me. I had no idea where we were, but the need to run was so strong I couldn't resist it. We darted through the field, startling birds and plowing through the black-eyed Susans, Queen Anne's lace, and purple lobelia with no direction in mind.

My breathing became labored and I glanced up and noticed a man standing on the far edge of the field. He was backlit but I could see his powerful build. He was waving his arm over his head, beckoning to me. Jasper? I was ridiculously happy to see him. I began to run faster with Diego doubling back to run at my side.

We were halfway across the field when a raven swooped down, cutting me off and startling me. I stumbled and crashed to the rough ground, grazing both of my palms. My hands stung and when I checked them, they were bleeding.

The raven let out a sharp cry and rose into the sky to circle overhead as if it was watching me. There was something significant about the raven, but my brain was fuddled and I couldn't remember. I sat there, feeling my mind slipping away. My heart started to race with panic when Diego pounced on me, licking my face until I put my hands up to block him. *Urgh.*

His method was gross but effective. I felt more centered. I patted his head. "Thanks, pal."

I went to stand and felt the weight of my grimoire in my pocket. My grimoire. Yes, that was what I needed. I sat back down.

Diego flopped down beside me as I pulled the book out of my pocket. The grimoire was sealed with a family blood oath, and the only way to open it was to use a drop of my own blood on the hexagonal lock on the front of the book. I let the bloodier of my two hands drip onto the lock. Instantly the lock released the metal band that held the book closed.

The Donadieu family grimoire could only be opened by a Donadieu. I was the last of the line so it was just for me. Of course, the grimoire was written in a code I had yet to crack, but as I'd learned before in dire circumstances, the grimoire could come to my aid if I needed it. Given that I was lost and my brain getting fuzzier by the minute, I couldn't think of a better time than now.

"Zoe!" a man's voice called. It sounded familiar. A vision of a man with dark hair and pale blue eyes filled my mind. J—Ja—I couldn't remember his name. My memories were fading. "Zoe!"

I recognized the voice as belonging to a person who was important to me. I trusted him. I dropped my grimoire on the ground and started to rise. I would go to him. He would help me. Diego nipped my fingers.

"Ouch!" I plopped back down and gave the puppy a reproving look. He didn't seem to care. He lay down on his belly and nudged my grimoire with his nose, pushing it toward me. I dragged the hefty puppy onto my lap. He weighed a ton and it felt like having a small horse on my lap, but I wanted his warmth and weight to keep me centered and in the moment.

"All right." I set the grimoire on the ground beside me, ignored the man who was still calling my name, and said, "Help me, please."

The grimoire immediately started flipping through its pages back and forth until it found what it wanted. It stopped and I studied the page. It was written in the same code as the others and I had no idea what it meant. I remembered being in a similar situation, and that time I'd put my hand on the page and the grimoire deciphered the code for me. I'd tried it again and again since that day and it hadn't worked. I hoped the situation was dire enough that the book chose to help me now.

I put my hand on the centuries-old paper and held my breath. After a bit the code started to shift, the shapes reforming themselves into words. I sounded them out, hoping my pronunciation was close enough. *Reverti domum. Reverti domum. Reverti domum.*

I said it three times, with one arm around Diego and the other hand on my grimoire. The ground started to shake. Earthquake? Diego whimpered and burrowed his nose under my arm. I clutched him close. The flowers began whipping back and forth as black clouds rolled across the blue sky, and the gentle breeze turned vicious, lashing at us.

I glanced up and saw the raven blown across the sky, careening through the air with no ability to fly away. I cried out, knowing this was bad but not certain of why. My throat grew tight and my heart raced and I knew with a sudden absolute clarity that we were in grave danger.

The shadowy figure from the edge of the field appeared just yards away, striding toward us with one hand outstretched as if he would grab us. The stinging wind forced me to squint and my eyes filled with tears, blurring everything. I couldn't get a good look at him but everything inside of me screamed, *Run!*

I grabbed my grimoire and clutched Diego close, muttering the phrase that I hoped would save us. *Reverti domum. Reverti domum. Reverti domum.*

And then the world exploded.

13

I was knocked onto my back as a ripple of light in a violent shade of red rolled out from under us, wiping out everything in its path as if it were a tsunami. As the wave of light faded from crimson to cerise to rose to pink, I noticed the orbs were again hanging overhead. I heard the sounds of the marketplace, chatter and laughter, and haggling over prices. I let go of Diego and rolled up to a seated position.

"What the hell was that?" I asked him. I pocketed my grimoire, grateful to have had it with me. It took me a moment to realize I was back in the booth where I'd seen the woman with the litter of puppies, except the booth was empty, she was gone, and so were the other dogs. Weird. Had she taken them and gone to look for Diego? Would she be back? Did I need to hide him? Because I was definitely not letting her have him back even if I had to borrow sigil marks from my coworkers to buy him.

"Zoe!" a man shouted. I felt my shoulders jerk up defensively, thinking it was the man from the field, but then Jasper appeared in the crowd. He was sprinting toward me and he looked frantic. My heart fluttered and I stood. The past few minutes had rattled me and I desperately wanted a hug, which was extraordinary as I wasn't a huggy sort of person.

I stepped forward and Diego moved with me. He pressed himself against my side, as if afraid I was going to leave him.

"Don't you worry, Diego." I patted his head, scratching him behind his ears. "I am not letting you go back to that nasty woman. I'll buy you myself if I have to."

Diego let out a bark and jumped up and licked my face, clearly approving the plan.

"We need to work on that." I wiped the drool off my face, although I wasn't clear whom I was talking to, myself or the dog.

"Zoe!" Jasper skidded to a halt just outside the booth. His eyes were huge and his mouth slightly agape. Miles, Tariq, and Olive appeared behind him, looking equally alarmed. Yes, even Olive.

"What's wrong?" I asked. "You all look weirded out. Did something happen? Because I just had the most bizarre experience—"

"Listen to me carefully, love." Jasper held his hands out in a calming gesture. "Don't panic. Just slowly step away from the hound."

"Why?" I asked. "Is the nasty woman he ran away from looking for him? Because she can't change her mind. I'm not letting her have him back."

Tariq and Miles exchanged questioning looks.

"What woman?" Olive asked.

"There was a woman in this booth," I said. "Really muscular, wore a whistle around her neck. I assume she's a dog trainer? She was very mean to Diego. I can't let him go back to her. She said something about putting him in a sack and throwing him in the river. That's not happening. Not on my watch."

"You mean the *Ash Mother*? You spoke to her?" Tariq asked. His voice was high and squeaky and he cleared his throat.

"I don't know who she was," I said. "I just know that she was awful." I patted Diego on the head. "I mean, he's just a puppy. Who would threaten a puppy?"

"A puppy?" Tariq repeated as if he couldn't comprehend. "Zoe, as your friend and colleague, I am imploring you to move away from that beast *right now*."

"Why? He's a sweetie." I kissed Diego on the snout to prove my point and turned back just in time to see Tariq's eyes roll back into his head as he did a slow slide to the ground.

"Tariq!" I cried.

Miles quickly conjured a fainting couch for Tariq to land on, which he did with a small bounce. I stepped out of the booth and asked, "Is he all right? Oh no, he's not afraid of dogs, is he? Diego is so sweet. Honestly, he's just a little excitable. He wouldn't hurt anyone."

"Zoe." Jasper grabbed me, lifting me off my feet as he clutched me close in a fierce hug.

I heard Diego growl from the booth as I patted Jasper's back, trying to reassure him. "I'm all right."

Jasper released a pent-up breath and set me gently on my feet. He cupped my face and studied my eyes. "Are you sure? It didn't hurt you?"

Diego's growl got deeper and I was worried he felt abandoned. I turned my head and said, "It's okay, buddy, these are my friends." He stopped growling and tipped his head to the side, considering the others. I turned back to Jasper. "Not only did he not hurt me, I think he saved me. He's very brave for being such a young puppy."

Jasper slowly turned us so that he was standing between Diego and me. "Love, that isn't a puppy, that's a full-grown hellhound, and the woman who was with him was the Ash Mother."

"The who?" I asked.

"She's the caretaker of hellhounds from the time they're born out of ash until they are old enough to serve their masters," Miles explained.

"Hellhound? Ash Mother? You can't be serious. I mean, look at him. He's adorable. I don't think hellhounds are this cute." I pushed Jasper aside and gestured to the booth. Instead of my rambunctious puppy, an enormous black-furred beast with crimson eyes stared at me. I felt my heart thud in my chest. What the hell? Had this monster swallowed my puppy?

"Diego?" I whispered.

The ginormous beast dropped to the ground and commando crawled toward me. His head was a big square block, his jaws massive, and his teeth were pointy and dripping saliva. His shoulders rippled with muscles and his paws had claws that looked like they could tear flesh like paper. I swayed on my feet and felt Jasper grab my arm to steady me. This was not my puppy, this was a hellhound who looked like he could bite my head off.

Panic began to thrum in my core, but then I saw his tail.

As the beast crawled toward me, his tail was wagging back and forth. Then he whimpered and I recognized that plaintive sound.

I shrugged off Jasper's hold and strode forward, crouching in front of the canine. "Diego?"

He whimpered and put his big, blocky head on my shoes. I tentatively reached out and rubbed his ears. His tail thumped the ground even harder. I glanced over my shoulder to see Jasper, Miles, and Olive, watching with varying degrees of alarm.

"I don't understand," I said. "Why did I see him as a puppy?"

"It could be that the Ash Mother had them appear in that form so as not to scare potential buyers," Olive said. She gestured to Diego and me. "An effective strategy, apparently."

"Buyers?" I asked. "I always thought hellhounds existed for the purpose of keeping condemned souls in hell."

"Some do," Miles said. "But most don't. Hellhounds serve in a variety of capacities, much like service dogs in the nonmagical world. Since Diego bonded to you, it appears he failed overseer of the gates of hell as a career choice, choosing to be a guardian hound instead."

"Guardian?" I repeated.

"Yes," Miles said. "Guardian hellhounds bond to one soul and their only purpose is to protect it and the body in which it resides."

I was a bit taken aback. I'd avoided pets all my life, not wanting the emotional attachment. But after what the puppy and I had been through, how could I reject him?

"I don't want to leave him here, but I'm not positive I'm the person he should be bonding to," I said.

"You don't have a choice," Olive said. Jasper's head

whipped in her direction and Olive shrugged. "He's a hellhound and he's chosen her. He will be by her side until one of them dies."

Okay, that was more of a commitment than I was looking for, but as I stroked the velvet ears of the beast drooling on my shoes, I knew there was no helping it.

"We'd better rouse Tariq and get out of here," I said. "I think any chance I had to be invited to join the High Bridge Coven is likely dusted and done."

Olive roused Tariq with one of his own diffused potions. He blinked awake and Jasper helped him to stand. He looked sheepish when he met my gaze. "Sorry, I don't usually scare so easily."

Diego pounced forward and licked Tariq's face before sitting back down. Tariq's entire body clenched and he wobbled as if he'd faint again. I grabbed him by one arm and Jasper caught his other before he went down. Olive handed him a washcloth that she'd conjured and he wiped his face with it.

"Sorry about that," I said. "Apparently, he's a guardian hellhound."

"Right. That makes sense." Tariq nodded. "I'm just not a dog person." He looked at Diego. "No offense."

Diego tipped his head to the side as if considering but he didn't seem offended.

"Listen." Tariq gestured for all of us to move in closer. When we were gathered loosely in a circle, Tariq threw up a clear barrier between us and the rest of the marketplace. "This is not the ideal place, but we need to speak in a quick cone of silence."

"Why?" Jasper asked. "Did you learn something?"

"Yes, when we all got separated, I used a dissembling spell on a couple of hedge witches. What they told me explains why Zoe saw a puppy instead of a hellhound," Tariq said.

"You all got separated?" I asked. I didn't mean to interrupt, but I'd wondered what had happened to everyone else while I'd been trapped in that field. "What happened?"

"I was walking through the stalls one moment and the next I was in London," Jasper said. "Hyde Park."

"The hedge witches were telling me about McWrath and the *Book of Shadows* and then I was suddenly in Nigeria," Tariq said. "With my grandmother."

"Teaching," Miles said. "I was lecturing a class of witches and mages on thaumaturgical mathematics."

"Using geometry, numerology, and equations to structure spells?" Olive asked. "Anything groundbreaking in your hallucination?"

"No," Miles said. "It was very low-rent as far as mind control went. What about you?"

We all glanced at Olive. She jutted out her chin and said, "Whatever spell was cast did not affect me. I was here waiting for all of you to show up because I saw Odessa Van Doren."

"Odessa was here?" I asked. Olive lifted her eyebrows as if she couldn't believe I was asking her to repeat herself.

"As I said," Olive confirmed.

This was all so disturbing. A mass hallucination had sent us all in different directions. I didn't know if it had been real or if I'd just been lying in that booth, dreaming I was in a field the entire time.

"Wait." I glanced at Jasper. "You were in London? Then you weren't in the field with me?"

"What field?" He frowned.

"Diego ran away from the Ash Monster—" I began, but Tariq interrupted.

"Ash Mother."

I glared at him and he pressed his lips together and said, "Sorry."

"One second I was chasing Diego through the market, and the next, we ended up in a field of wildflowers and I had this incredible feeling of euphoria." I paused and pressed my hand on my chest as if I could still feel it.

Jasper scrutinized my expression as if trying to make sense of what I was saying. "Why did you think I was in the field?"

"There was a man on the edge of the field and he was calling my name," I said. "I assumed he was you, so Diego and I started to run toward him."

"And." Olive gestured for me to keep going.

"I was halfway across the field when a raven swooped down in front of me, stopping me. I couldn't remember why the raven was important but I knew it was warning me away."

"You didn't remember my aviankinesis ability?" Jasper asked.

I shook my head. "No, in fact, in the time I was there, it was as if my memories were being drained. I went from knowing your name to not being able to recall it within a matter of minutes. When I fell, I bloodied my hands, so I used the blood from the scrapes to open my grimoire and ask it for help. It gave me the spell that got me out of there."

Jasper grabbed my hands and turned them over. They were completely healed with no sign of any scrapes.

"I swear they were bleeding," I said.

Tariq nodded. "I believe you. The hedge witches said there was a powerful demon here tonight with a legendary spellbook and that he was looking for a particular witch—Zoe. That was all I got out of them before I found myself in Nigeria with my yaya."

Miles's eyebrows shot up behind his glasses. "Did they name the demon?"

"McWrath," Olive and Jasper guessed together and Jasper added, "It has to be."

"I believe you're right." Tariq glanced outside the bubble as if he expected the demon to appear out of the shadows. "According to the hedge witches, the demon planned to use the *Book of Shadows* to manipulate reality for everyone here tonight, Olive and the hedge witches excepted, which could be why Zoe saw the hellhound as a puppy instead of its true self. He used the dog to lure her away."

"Bloody hell," Jasper cursed. "He was here and we had no idea, and he's using the book to get to Zoe. He could have snatched her and we never would have known."

"But he didn't." Miles gestured to the barrier around them and the market beyond. "I suspect Olive and the hedge witches and potentially some others were left out to bear witness to McWrath's abilities."

"I believe I'm immune to that particular spell." Olive's scarred eyebrow lifted as if daring us to argue. "That being said, your theory makes sense. If we all suffered from an episode of altered reality, who would be left to verify that everyone had gone a bit mad?"

"Did we?" Miles asked.

"Yes." Olive gestured to the market outside their bubble.

"It didn't last very long but it seemed as if most everyone was in a weird sort of daze."

"Now that we know what we're up against, we can protect Zoe," Miles said.

"Can we?" Jasper asked. "He altered reality for most of us. If he decides to do it to all of us, how can we possibly stop him?"

I reached out and took Jasper's hand in mine. I knew if the situation were reversed and he was being targeted by a demon, I would feel the same helplessness.

"We managed it tonight." I gave his fingers a squeeze before releasing him. "Someone was looking out for me. That raven very specifically knocked me down to keep me from running to the man across the field."

Miles glanced at Jasper. "Are you sure it wasn't you?"

"Maybe it was." He frowned. "Like Zoe, my memories got fuzzier the longer I was in the altered plane, but I do remember thinking that I needed to find Zoe. I was tracking her magic when I tried connecting to a raven outside the park, in a different plane."

"You can follow my magic?" I asked.

"I can follow magical trails," he said. "One of the handier gifts of demon kind. I do remember mentally connecting with a raven on another plane. I've never managed that before. I honestly don't remember what happened until I woke up back here."

"We need to leave. Things feel off here." Olive glanced at the market around us. "Let's get back to the BODO and discuss it there."

"Agreed." Miles nodded and Tariq removed the silencing cone from around us.

Miles and Olive led the way, walking side by side, leaving the three of us to follow. Diego had tolerated being excluded from the huddle we'd been in, but now he nudged his way in between Tariq and me.

Tariq sent him a nervous glance and moved forward to walk with Olive and Miles. I put my hand on Diego's shoulder, which came up to my ribs. I suspected if he stood on his hind legs, he would be taller than me. How I was going to walk through the streets of New York with him without freaking people out, I had no idea.

"Do we leave the same way we entered?" I asked Jasper. We were no longer holding hands, but our fingers brushed occasionally and it was a comfort.

"There's no token involved, but we will arrive where we started," he said.

"I'll have to walk back to the museum," I said. "I don't think I'll be able to get a driver to pick Diego up."

"I'll walk with you," Jasper said. "I don't trust that we've seen the last of McWrath."

As we wound our way through the booths to the exit, I listened to snippets of conversation. It seemed everyone had come to the realization that someone powerful had been at the market and had manipulated their sense of place and time.

I would have thought they'd be outraged but they weren't. Instead, they all seemed impressed and curious to know more about this powerful entity.

"Exiting the market is not nearly as interesting as entering," Miles said when we arrived at a shadowy doorway. "I'll go first and, Jasper, you take the rear. Zoe, keep your hand on Diego at all times so he can pass through with you."

I nodded and watched as Miles, Olive, and Tariq vanished. I put my hand on Diego's back and together we walked through. I felt the hound lower himself as we passed through the darkness and I wondered if he was afraid.

"It's okay," I encouraged him. "It only takes a few seconds." When we stepped out onto the sidewalk in front of the Banksy mural, I checked to see if he was okay and found myself looking at the adorable little puppy he'd first been.

I dropped to my knees, almost tripping Jasper, who stepped out onto the sidewalk behind me.

"What's this?" he asked.

"Interesting, very interesting," Miles said.

Diego was wiggling and wagging and I hugged him close. "Wait. Does this mean McWrath is nearby and using the *Book of Shadows* on us again?"

"No." Miles shook his head. "I believe it means this hound has the ability to alter his appearance. I think you kept seeing him as a puppy because he presented himself to you as such, while we saw him as a hellhound because he wanted us to see him that way, probably to protect you."

I crouched down and faced Diego. "Is this true?" He barked and waggled around me as if someone had wound up his back end.

"Well, this does make the situation more manageable," Jasper said as he crouched beside me. He held out his hand and Diego sniffed him, checking his vibe, I assumed. The wagging intensified and Diego licked Jasper's face.

"I think that's approval," I said. "I'm still trying to speak hellhound."

"A car is on its way," Miles said. "And they'll allow the hound. Try not to transform, Diego."

I patted the puppy on his head and stood, feeling ridiculously relieved that keeping him was not going to be as hard as I'd feared. The February air was cold and I stuck my hands in my pockets to warm them up. I felt a folded bit of paper brush against my fingers.

"It has been an eventful night, but it's unfortunate that Zoe didn't get an invitation to meet with the witches of the High Bridge Coven," Miles said.

I grasped the paper, wondering what it was, when an image of Rowan Thorne's face flitted through my mind. Oh, right, the paper crane. So much had happened I'd forgotten the encounter entirely.

"Actually, I might have met someone." I pulled the flattened crane from my pocket and opened my palm. The folded crane snapped back into its full origami form. Its wings started to gently flap but it didn't fly away. I glanced up at my colleagues and noted their varying looks of surprise. "Anyone heard of a mage by the name Rowan Thorne?"

"That bastard." Jasper glared at the paper crane. "I'll kill him for this."

14

"Where did you get that?" Olive asked.

"We were on our way to meet you after seeing your signal, and somehow I was separated from the others in the crowd and I watched two mages have a sort of magic-off, if that's a thing," I said.

"That's not a thing." Tariq shook his head.

"Knowing Thorne, it was staged for your benefit." Jasper glowered. Oh, there was a backstory there that I was dying to hear.

"Thorne was the one who made this paper crane fly into my hand," I said. "He approached me after their demonstration and told me it was an invitation."

Miles and Olive exchanged a look before Olive said, "Well, open it."

"Should I?" I asked. "I mean, what if there's some sort of spell attached to it or something?"

"We're all here," Miles said. "We'll protect you."

Diego leaned against my leg as if assuring me of his support as well.

"All right then." I gently plucked the crane from my palm with my free hand and carefully unfolded the bird. In the center of the paper was an invitation just as Thorne had said.

It read, *Zoe Ziakas, you are cordially invited to the next meeting of the High Bridge Coven on the night of the next new moon at the Manhattan High Bridge. This invitation will be extended only once.*

There was a mark stamped onto the paper. A circle with a line across it, with three wavy lines below the line and a crescent moon above. When I ran my thumb over it, it pricked my fingers as if the mark was made of nettles.

"Ouch!" I dropped the paper onto the ground. Jasper took my hand and examined my thumb. The pain was already gone and there was no mark on my skin. I squeezed his hand with mine and said, "I'm all right."

Miles, Tariq, and Olive all leaned over to study the paper on the ground. "Odessa," they said together. That figured. Odessa must have had Thorne deliver the invitation for her.

"What does one wear when invited to a coven?" I asked. I was desperately trying to keep the tone light and not let on how incredibly nervous I was.

"I would suggest a hellhound." Olive's tone was dry. Although, I noted she was looking at me with approval, a first, so that felt pretty good.

A breeze kicked up and the paper folded itself back into its origami crane form and floated into the air above our heads, where it immediately burst into a ball of icy blue witch flame.

"We have much to discuss . . . in the morning," Miles said. "For now, I suggest we all get some rest. We're going to need it."

An oversized SUV pulled up to the curb and the driver glanced at us through the window. Her gaze landed on Diego and she nodded, confirming that she'd expected the dog. Diego was put in the back and we assumed the same seats we'd had on the way here.

"When is the new moon?" I asked. I suspected this was something any self-respecting witch would know automatically, but I was still a rookie and I was too tripped out by the night to try to fake it.

"In three days," Jasper said. He sounded extremely unhappy about it.

We arrived back at the BODO a little after three in the morning. Miles suggested I spend the night at the museum since it was too late to catch a train back to Connecticut. I had an office all to myself in the department and it had a small couch in it. Diego and I could sleep there for the night. Honestly, after the night I'd had, it would be a comfort to be surrounded by books.

I climbed out of the car and opened the back for Diego. He hopped down and I waved at the others before shutting the door. The SUV pulled away to take the rest of them to their homes in the city, and I turned to find Jasper standing on the sidewalk with Diego sitting beside him.

"You didn't think I was going to abandon you now, did you?" Jasper asked.

"I'm so tired, I didn't really think about it." I staggered toward him, falling into his open arms. "Truly, I don't think I've ever been this exhausted in my entire life."

"The overload of magic in the market will knacker you on its mellowest night and tonight was a hell of a lot more than that." He held me for a few minutes, resting his cheek on the top of my head as we soaked in the calm of the quiet winter morning. "Come on. I'll tuck you in."

And that, right here, was why Jasper was the first man I was interested in dating in forever. It wasn't that I needed his help. I was more than capable of getting myself squared away without any assistance, but it was his awareness of me and what I was feeling as I tried to grasp this magical world I was now inhabiting that made me appreciate him so much.

"Thank you," I said. I patted my leg and Diego trotted along beside me, his nose to the ground as he took in the smells of his new home.

The museum was dead quiet. We crossed the beautiful first floor of dark paneled and ornately carved oak, through the main museum, to our secret staircase at the back. Once we passed through the door, Diego morphed from his playful puppy body back to his large shaggy hellhound form.

Jasper and I exchanged a glance and I asked, "He knows it's safe to be a hellhound here?"

"Or he's on alert because he senses danger." Jasper frowned. "Stay close."

Jasper kept one hand on my arm as he guided me, while Diego picked his way down the spiral steps, clearly having never been on such a tight and winding staircase before.

We magicked our way through the iron doors into the BODO. I was relieved that Diego was able to slip right through. I hadn't been sure how the wards would feel about a hellhound, but apparently he was given automatic clearance.

Jasper led me right to my office. In moments a fire was lit in the fireplace, making the room toasty warm. It was a magical fire, naturally, Being three floors belowground, we didn't have wood fireplaces or natural gas and relied on Miles's bespelled fireplaces to produce warmth and flames.

I set my grimoire in its proper place on the bookshelf behind my desk. As I considered how I would sleep on the couch—I didn't have a blanket or a pillow in here—and what I would use to fashion a dog bed for Diego, Jasper motioned for me to follow him back out of my office to a door I had never noticed before. Was it a linen closet? Now, that would be handy.

"Go on in," he said. "You'll find everything you need in there and I'll have your office ready for you when you're done."

"Is this new?" I asked. "I don't remember a door here before."

"It's always been here, although it's not always accessible," Jasper said. "Mabel Stewart put it here when she opened the BODO more than a century ago. A witch must be in real need for it to appear, and judging by how cold your hands are and how you keep shivering, I think it's appeared just for you."

"Am I that needy looking?" I straightened up, using the last of my energy to do so.

"You look like you're about to collapse." Jasper leaned forward and kissed the top of my head, then opened the door and pushed me inside, closing it behind me.

Warmth immediately enveloped me and I glanced into the room and saw, by the light of dozens of candles, an enormous claw-foot tub filled with steaming water and soap bubbles. Yes, please. Beside the tub was a small table with a pot of tea and a plate of small cakes. I closed my eyes and breathed in the soothing scent of lavender. If I was hallucinating this, I did not want to wake up.

I opened my eyes. Everything was still there. Without hesitation, I stripped out of my clothes and climbed into the tub, letting my troubles pop like the soap bubbles that floated in the air all around me.

I had no idea how long I soaked. It felt as if the water never cooled and when I checked my fingers, they didn't even prune. Huh. I sipped the tea and ate the cakes and felt as if I was being restored back to myself moment by moment, especially as I was certain I had dozed for a power nap or two.

I climbed out of the tub and dried off, pulling on the flannel pajamas and matching bathrobe that hung on a hook beside the tub. The robe was thick and fluffy and covered me all the way to my ankles. I slid my feet into the soft slippers and felt extremely coddled by the strange room.

There was a gentle knock on the door, and Jasper called, "Have I lost you forever, love?"

I laughed and wrapped my wet hair in a towel before crossing the small room to the door. I opened it and found Jasper leaning there. My heart warmed at the sight of him and when he opened his arms, I stepped into them. He was solid and real and when I rested my head on his chest, I could hear his heartbeat. It steadied me.

"How's Diego?" I asked.

"After foraging in the kitchen with me for some choice cuts of meat, he's out cold in front of the fire." Jasper put his hand on the small of my back and led me back to my office.

I expected my office to be exactly as I'd left it but with a blanket and pillow scrounged from somewhere. I was so wrong. My little couch was now a big, fluffy bed, which matched the dog bed that Diego was presently sprawled across, with his feet up in the air and his head hanging over the side while he snored like a champ.

I glanced at Jasper. "This is amazing." I bounded across the room and jumped on the bed. I bounced and then laughed. "I feel like a princess in a fairy tale."

"Well, princess, time to get some shut-eye," Jasper said as he pulled back the covers. "It's been a night and a half."

I dutifully kicked off my slippers and shrugged out of my robe, climbed onto the bed, and slid under the covers. A yawn slipped out and the weariness I'd felt earlier came back tenfold. Jasper arranged the covers around me and reached up to brush a lock of hair back from my forehead.

"When the reality-altering spell broke and I woke up in the market and couldn't find you tonight . . ." He paused and took a steadying breath. "I was scared, love. More scared than I can remember being in a very long time."

"I would have felt the same." I reached up to cup his cheek and then kissed him. It was supposed to be swift and sweet, but I couldn't help myself. I didn't mean for it to pack the passionate punch that it did, but Jasper Griffin was absolutely my type and I found him completely irresistible.

Before the kiss could get completely out of control, he pulled away. His breath was ragged and I took some satisfaction in that, even as he eased me away from him and pulled the covers up to my chin as if there were some magical binding spell included in the duvet that would keep me from seducing him. As if. I gave him my best come-hither look, which was ruined by a yawn.

"Nice try, love, but I'd be a complete cad if I took advantage when you are clearly exhausted." He sat beside me, leaning against the headboard. "How about I stay here until you fall asleep?"

It was probably for the best. We hadn't had much of a chance to talk about his being a half demon. I still had so many questions and I hadn't decided how I truly felt about him aging so much more slowly than me. It didn't bode well for a lengthy relationship because assuming we were in this for the long haul, I definitely didn't want to be seventy with a partner who was eighty-four but looked forty. The horror!

"Are you spending the night in the BODO, too?" I asked. "I don't want to keep you if you'd rather go to your apartment."

"I'm staying." He nodded. "My office is set up and waiting."

"Okay then." I snuggled into the bed. My eyes felt gritty and I was having a hard time keeping them open. "Tell me about Rowan Thorne," I said.

"That loathsome toad?" Jasper asked. "Why?"

"There's a history there," I said. "And I want to hear it."

"Is that the only reason?" he asked.

"Of course, why else?"

"I've heard most women find him attractive." Jasper's scathing tone let me know what he thought about that.

"I suppose I can see that."

"What?" Jasper cried. "You think he's good-looking?"

"*I* don't, no." I shook my head, then I met his gaze and said, "I'm not most women."

A slow smile curved his lips. "No, you're not."

"So, tell me about him," I said. "If I run into him at the coven meeting, I want to know how to handle him."

"Consider him to be the mage embodiment of horse manure and avoid him at all costs," Jasper said.

"I'm going to need to know why you dislike him—" My words were cut off with another yawn. Sleep was winning. Darn it.

"Rest, love, we can talk about this more tomorrow." Jasper kicked off his shoes and lay down beside me, pulling me into his arms. The beating of his heart beneath my ear soothed me, lulling me to sleep.

"I'm just resting my eyes, don't leave yet." It was a lie. I was fighting sleep for all I was worth because I didn't want to let go of this moment with him. I had missed him fiercely while he was gone and it was so nice to have him back, even though I had no idea what sort of relationship the future held for a new witch and a half-demon mage.

"Of course not." His voice was low and deep and he rested his cheek on my head. Despite the potential danger of McWrath coming after me again, in this moment with Jasper, Diego, my grimoire, and the magical BODO surrounding us, I felt perfectly safe.

I woke up to a snout just inches from my face. Hot breath puffed across my skin and it took me a moment to realize it was Diego. We were in my office. Oh, and an arm was slung around my waist and my back was nestled against someone's chest. I carefully turned my head and found Jasper dead asleep with his head on the pillow beside mine.

The man was a stunner when he was awake, but asleep the half-mage, half-demon looked enticingly vulnerable and

I had to resist the urge to run my finger over his features. Only my wish not to disturb his rest curbed the impulse.

A soft woof sounded and I turned to see Diego staring at me from beneath his bushy black eyebrows.

"Do you need to go out?" I whispered.

A soft woof was his answer, which I suspected was a yes in hellhound-speak.

"All right, give me a second," I said. I gently lifted Jasper's arm from about my waist and slid out from under it. He didn't stir as I eased off the bed and shrugged on my robe as I searched the floor for the slippers I had kicked off the night before. I put my finger over my lips, hoping the hellhound understood the universal sign for quiet, and crept toward the door, leading Diego with me.

I glanced back at the bed. Jasper was sprawled across his side of it, still dressed but without his shoes. Another blanket had appeared and covered him, keeping him warm as the fire was now just embers. I stepped back to the bed and gently tucked the blanket more securely about him.

I opened the door, and Diego and I stepped into the main room of the BODO, quietly shutting the door behind us. I expected the library to be empty. It was not.

"It's about time, Ziakas," Olive said. "I thought you were going to sleep the day away."

"Yah!" I yelped, taking in the sight of Olive, Miles, and Tariq all seated at the round table in the center of the room, where we generally had our meetings.

"Oh, I see you found Mabel Stewart's chamber," Miles said. He looked pleased.

"Huh." I wasn't following. All I could think was that Jasper was asleep in my office and how it would look if he came wandering out right now. It wasn't that we were keeping our interest in each other a secret, it was just that we were trying to keep it professional.

"Your robe." Tariq gestured to my clothing. "It's exclusive to that chamber."

I tightened the belt around me and said, "Yes, it was amazing." I glanced at the blank space of wall where the door had been last night. "Does it move around or does it always appear there?"

"It moves," Miles said. "And how did Diego do last night?"

"Slept like a champ," I said. "And now he needs to go out. Should I take him to the lawn or up to the rooftop garden?"

"The garden." They all spoke together.

"It might be best to keep him out of sight for the time being, and he should assume his puppy form outside of the BODO," Miles said. "Until we know whether the Ash Mother wants him back or not."

"She doesn't. She said he was mine and I'm going to hold her to that." I put my hand on Diego's head and he licked my wrist. I hated the idea of having him go back to that terrible woman.

"I'll put out some feelers just to make sure," Tariq said. "It was weird that she was at the market. That's not a place she would normally frequent—"

"Unless someone sent her there," Olive said. "If they did, we need to discover who sent her and why."

"I wish Diego could tell us," Tariq said. "That would certainly make things—"

"Zoe, did you find your clothes?" Jasper appeared in the

doorway to my office, looking adorably rumpled and disheveled. He paused as he took in the faces all staring at him. "Uh . . . good morning."

Miles, Olive, and Tariq looked at Jasper, then me, then Jasper, and then me again. I felt my face get hot even though there was absolutely no reason for it.

"That wasn't what it sounded like," I said.

Miles, Olive, and Tariq stared at us. Miles looked bemused, Olive impassive, which I weirdly appreciated in this instance, but Tariq snickered.

"Right," he said. And then, much to my embarrassment, Miles laugh-coughed into his hand and Olive turned her head and let out a huff of amusement. I glowered at Jasper. He was the containment specialist. Shouldn't he be stealthier than this?

"I'm taking Diego up to the garden," I said. When Jasper looked as if he'd join me, I held up my hand. "Oh, no, you stay here and explain yourself. I'll be right back."

Diego and I made for the stairs without looking back.

The garden on the top of the Museum of Literature was mostly dormant. The raised beds were barren for the winter. The wind whipped across the roof and I regretted not having on more than pajamas and a bathrobe. I cupped my hands, preparing to craft a bubble of heat.

"Zoe!" I turned to see Jasper striding across the rooftop toward me. He was wearing the same clothes he'd had on the night before and he was carrying my cloak. He draped it around my shoulders and I was immediately warmed.

"Thank you." Too embarrassed to look at him, I kept my gaze on Diego, who was in full wiggly puppy mode.

"Hey." He gently cupped my chin and turned my face to his. "Are you all right, love?"

"I'm fine." I met his pale blue eyes and felt my face grow warm. "Just a little mortified by what our coworkers surmised about the relationship between us."

"Why?" He dropped his hand and tipped his head to the side, much like a bird. "They're not wrong."

"Um . . ." I blinked at him. "I'm pretty sure they think something happened that didn't."

"Oh, that." He shook his head. "Don't worry. I set them straight."

"Did you?" I glanced back at Diego, who was nosing around the dead plants in Olive's poison garden.

"Of course." He put his hands on my shoulders and drew my attention back to him. "But they aren't wrong about how I feel about you."

My heart started to thud in my chest. We were having this conversation *now*? When I had a scorching case of bedhead? And I was monitoring a hellhound? Okay, fine. So be it.

"Tell me, Jasper Griffin, how do you feel about all of this?" I gestured to my entire person. I expected him to have a reality check and flinch at the sight of morning me. Instead, he grinned.

"I like you, Zoe Ziakas, I like you a lot." His gaze held mine and I knew he meant what he said. It made me dizzy, which was not something I'd ever felt before. Maybe I was just hungry. Jasper lifted his eyebrows and said, "This is usually the part where you tell me how you feel."

"There's something you should know," I said.

"Oh?" He looked wary.

"I don't do emotional entanglements," I said. His eyebrows lifted higher. "Not that I haven't dated or been involved, I have, but I can't say that I ever . . ."

"Ever what?"

"Maybe we should go see what the others are doing," I said. "They must be planning my visit to the coven. I should be in on that." I ducked under his hands on my shoulders and turned to go inside.

I only got a yard away when he caught my hand, stopping me. "You don't actually think I'm going to let you go without finishing that sentence, do you?"

"I . . ."

He pulled me toward him and he looked so solid and strong, and the memory of waking up in his arms and feeling as if I was exactly where I belonged worked against my sense of self-preservation, and before I had the wherewithal to resist him, I was gently tugged into his arms.

"So, tell me, love, how do you feel about me?" he asked.

"Fine." I huffed and my breath plumed on the air between us. "I like you, too."

He grinned. Then he leaned down and kissed me. His lips were cool against mine and I twined my arms around his neck and pulled him in close, allowing his heat to warm me from the inside out. It was a hotter fire than any magic I could conjure and I welcomed it. The longing for him, to be close to him, took over and I threaded my fingers into his hair, reveling in the way the soft dark locks twined about my fingers.

He slid his hands to my hips and pulled me in closer. The

wind whipped my cloak around us, as if encouraging this passionate moment between us. It would be so easy to get swept away by him and the desire that burned between us. But I still had questions that needed answers.

"Tell me about Rowan Thorne," I whispered against his lips.

15

Jasper tipped his head back and groaned. "Now? You want to talk about that backside barnacle now?"

I checked on Diego, who had moved to Tariq's garden bed, where he was digging up a root with his massive paw. I decided he was tilling the soil, and was confident Tariq wouldn't mind.

"Yes, now. I fell asleep last night with my questions unanswered." I stepped back from him and stared up into his handsome face. "I need to know what I'm dealing with."

"That's fair," Jasper agreed. "Thorne isn't to be trusted. If he gave you that note, it's because he's seeking either your power or a favor from someone who wants your power. Someone like Odessa."

"That makes sense given that it's her coven," I said. "Do you think he works for her?"

Jasper stared across the rooftop, studying the Manhattan skyline. "Her or somebody like her."

"Meaning?" I asked, watching his jaw clench.

He turned and met my gaze. "Thorne and I used to be friends."

Surprised, I went very still. I tried to picture Jasper and Thorne being pals and I just couldn't see it.

"Like me, he is half-mage and half-demon. It's a rare combination and we formed a friendship bond quickly because of it. He was different then." Jasper's tone was rueful. "He was . . . is . . . a brilliant mage. He was doing really advanced stuff even when I first met him thirty years ago."

Jasper started to pace, so I looped my arm through his and together we strolled the path between the garden beds. Diego abandoned his root and followed us.

"What happened?" I asked.

"He always wanted more," Jasper said. "More power. More influence. No matter what he achieved, it was never enough. He aligned himself with witches like Odessa and demons like McWrath without any reservations despite their reputations for dark magic. I couldn't be a part of that."

"You had a falling-out," I said.

"A big one."

We paused at the edge of the rooftop. It was a flat roof with a carved stone balustrade that ran all the way around it. From here, our view of the Jacqueline Kennedy Onassis Reservoir was unimpeded as the leaves had fallen from the trees and the morning sun danced on the water with a cheerfulness that wasn't present up here on the roof.

"I'm sorry," I said.

He shrugged. "It's my own fault that I didn't realize who he really was from the beginning. I always made excuses for him because he was put up for adoption as a baby and had no idea he was a mage or a demon. His entire life was a struggle to catch up to what the rest of us are born knowing." Jasper paused to look at me. "Even if we don't embrace it."

I knew he was remembering my reluctance to accept magic and witchcraft into my life when we first met. I smiled. "It just takes some of us longer. What precipitated the end of your friendship?"

"Someone I cared about was hurt by him so much that I cut ties with him. I only regret that it took me so long. What's that brilliant quote? 'When someone shows you who they are, believe them the first time.'"

"Maya Angelou." I nodded. "Very wise."

Jasper put his arm around me and pulled me close. I snuggled into our combined warmth, while Diego snuffled along the stone railing, as if hoping someone had dropped a cookie there.

"We tangled again just last year." Jasper blew out a breath and it plumed on the air like an engine letting off steam.

"What happened?" I asked.

"I was retrieving an enchanted book of poetry for the BODO when Thorne showed up and tried to steal the item from me," Jasper said. "I turned him in to the Global Council of Magisters for judgment. The prat likely talked his way out of any punishment. He even had the audacity to appear when we were retrieving the *Book of Shadows* from Crooked Alfie."

"He does have charm, I'll give him that," I said. Jasper glowered and I added, "I mean, I don't think he's charming, but I can see where others might."

"Promise me, when you go visit the coven, you will stay

on your guard. Do not trust any of them, especially Thorne." Jasper pulled me in tighter.

It was an easy promise to make as I didn't trust any of them, especially Thorne. "I pro—"

That was all I got out before Diego let out a sharp bark and jumped in the air, morphing from happy puppy to full hellhound in a blink. He knocked Jasper and me back a few steps and took our spot, standing on his muscled hind legs with his front paws braced on the balustrade.

"Diego, be careful!" I cried.

The hellhound turned his big blocky head in my direction and his red eyes focused on me as he let loose a howl that sounded like a war cry. The hair on the back of my neck stood on end in response and it was then that I saw a tendril of shadow slither over the stone railing and wrap itself around Diego's leg. The hellhound snapped his teeth at the shadow tentacle, but it was no use. The shadow slithered up the hound's body, twining around him in a tight grip. Diego let out a yelp, but I couldn't tell if it was pain or fear or both.

"Diego!" I jumped forward but Jasper grabbed me and shoved me behind him.

"No! Stay back!" he ordered.

I didn't have my grimoire on me—damn it—and my developing skills were definitely not up to fighting a demon's shadow. Not yet at any rate. I stood behind Jasper, wringing my hands and feeling useless. I made a promise to myself to never ever be without my grimoire again.

Jasper opened his hands and a ball of pure white light formed. It was blinding in its intensity and I had to shield my eyes and look away.

"Don't move, mate. You'll be all right," Jasper said. The shadow moved over his face and Diego whimpered, which broke my heart into a million itty-bitty pieces. Jasper tossed the ball right at Diego and it burst into thousands of tiny pin-pricks of light that attached themselves to the shadow, illuminating it right out of existence.

"Brilliant!" I cried.

"But unfortunately, also temporary." Jasper grabbed my hand and whistled at Diego. "Let's go!"

Diego shoved off the balustrade with a snarl and a show of very impressive teeth. Sure enough, another tendril of shadow appeared on the ground and Jasper yelled, "Run!"

We were flat-out sprinting for the door on the far side of the roof. Diego was sending up sprays of gravel with his enormous paws while Jasper shot white light out of his fingertips. I was certain we were going to make it. We were so close.

I was in the lead, reaching for the door handle of the enclosure that protected the stairs, when a thin coil of shadow the size of a vine dropped from the doorjamb and twined itself around my neck and my waist, yanking me up the side of the building and holding me locked in place with my back against the cold stone.

I struggled against the hold, and the shadow tightened in response. I gasped for breath, clawing at my throat as I tried to breathe, but I only found my own flesh. Everything went fuzzy and I started to see squiggles of light in my peripheral vision.

Diego was barking and Jasper shouting, but the sound was muffled as if they were far away. I could faintly see the bright white light Jasper had used to free Diego, but I knew it wouldn't work this time. Instead, we had to find a new way to fight this shadow. I stopped struggling. I didn't have enough air to stay conscious unless I remained completely still and breathed in little sips.

The shadow held me by my waist and throat but another tendril moved up my body and caressed my cheek. It gave me the ick and I would have recoiled, but I didn't dare move and lose the tiny bit of air I could manage to suck in.

Instead, I ignored the groping shadow and focused on my magic. Olive had been drilling me for weeks on manipulating the elements. I had gotten decent with water and earth, while air and fire were fussier. None of those elements could help me now, but it occurred to me that manipulating day and night shouldn't be that much more difficult. I dug into my core and felt the warmth unfurl. A brisk wind kicked up on the rooftop. Jasper and Diego jumped up, repeatedly trying to grab me, but the shadow held me just out of reach.

I closed my eyes and envisioned my grimoire in my office downstairs. I had discovered over the past few months that my little black book was able to read my emotions just as I could sense its. I didn't know if it could do so when it was out of my presence, but I had to try. I forced all of my energy into forging a connection with my grimoire. To my profound relief I felt alarm and then fury coming back at me. The book knew I was in trouble!

I'd assumed it would flip through its pages and find a spell to help me, but instead, I felt it muscle me aside in my own mind. If I wasn't about to pass out from lack of oxygen, I would have been alarmed. Instead, I let the book all the way in.

I closed my eyes and saw dark ink spilling over a piece of

paper, soaking into its fibers and turning it completely black. Without opening my eyes, I sensed night creeping across the rooftop. The wind grew stronger, the air had the smoky scent of magic, and the atmosphere grew even colder. When I felt the shadow tendrils around my neck and waist disappear as they were absorbed into the darkness, I opened my eyes. I registered the complete loss of my sense of sight just before I plummeted to the rooftop.

A strong pair of arms grabbed me, but my momentum was so great I took us both down to the gravel covering the rooftop. I landed with a thump on top of a hard body, who groaned.

"Jasper?"

"Beneath you." His voice sounded strained.

A puff of hot breath and a snout nuzzled my cheek as I pushed off Jasper. "Diego?"

His response was to lick me from my chin to my eyebrows. I was so relieved I didn't mind a bit.

"How?" Jasper asked. "How did you manage that?"

I couldn't see him, so I reached for him in the dark and ran my hand down his arm until I could lace our fingers together.

"Honestly, it wasn't me," I said. "And I don't know how long it will last. We have to go."

"Right," Jasper agreed. He stood and pulled me up with him. "We need to find the door. Let me see if I can craft some light."

He let go of me and a very faint orb of light formed between his two hands. It couldn't cut through the darkness beyond his fingers, rendering it useless.

A door slammed and the three of us started. I glanced toward the sound and there was the door to the roof, wide open and shining light into the darkness, as Olive, Miles, and Tariq stepped out.

"What is this?" Miles asked.

"No time." Jasper grabbed me by the hand and Diego by the scruff—impressive given how large the hellhound was—and dragged us toward the door. "There's a demon shadow up here! Get back inside."

As one, all three of our colleagues ducked back into the narrow staircase that led to the BODO. Jasper pushed Diego and me inside and then turned and warded the doorway, keeping any shadow from entering, before he shut and latched the door behind him.

Miles led the way back to the BODO and we all fell in line behind him. No one spoke until we reached the main room. As we took our seats at the table, Miles conjured a coffee urn and a basket of muffins.

He looked at me and said, "Eat. You look alarmingly pale."

I took a muffin and a cup of coffee, as did the others. No one spoke until our muffins were gone and we were on our second cup of coffee. I tossed a muffin in the air for Diego and he leapt up to catch it, transforming into his puppy self before his feet hit the ground. He still managed to swallow it in one bite.

"It tastes better if you chew it," I said. He wagged, unrepentant about his lack of manners.

"What happened up there?" Miles asked.

"A demon shadow slithered over the railing. Diego warned us away, but it wrapped around him. I managed to chase it back by blasting it with light, but when we reached the door, it captured Zoe, pulling her up against the side of the building and out of reach. She managed to escape by cleverly using darkness to absorb the shadow," Jasper said with a note of pride.

"How did you—" Tariq began, and then stopped.

"Turn the rooftop into night?" I asked. He nodded. Olive and Miles were both watching me, Miles looking impressed and Olive skeptical. When I glanced at Jasper, his expression was one of reassurance.

"It wasn't me, it was my grimoire," I said.

"Did you have it with you?" Olive asked.

"No, but I . . . I . . . called to it and it answered," I said. "I was about to black out, so I thought it might sense I was in trouble and help me. It did by turning the roof into night." I bit my lip, trying to figure out how to explain the next part. "Honestly, I let my grimoire into my mind and it cast the spell that saved us."

Miles and Olive exchanged a look that I couldn't interpret and at the moment I wasn't sure I wanted to.

"Did it feel invasive?" Jasper asked. His voice was very measured. "Or was it more like it was assisting you?"

"Definitely the second one," I said. "It was as if we had a mind meld going and it guided me on calling the night. Speaking of which, shouldn't we do something about that? The entire roof is encompassed in darkness."

"Without you up there to hold it in place, it will have faded by now," Miles said. "Very clever of you to use your grimoire like that."

"I'd like to take credit," I said. "But my grimoire answered the call and was the architect of that power play."

I felt a surge of pride come from my office and I knew my grimoire was pleased.

"But where did the shadow come from?" I asked. "Was it another snippet left over from the gala?"

"Highly unlikely," Miles said. "It would have revealed itself before now. No, I suspect it was a bit of shadow weaponized to come for you."

"Me?" I asked. "But why?"

They all stared at me expectantly, waiting for me to put it together.

"Oh, right." I nodded. "It's not me they want so much as my grimoire. Having the *Book of Shadows* and my grimoire would give them immense power. That's why I was invited to the coven, isn't it? They want my grimoire. Do they not know that it'll only open for a Donadieu?"

"I suspect they know but believe that if they can get you to join the coven, they'll be able to control you and have access to your grimoire," Miles said.

I rolled my eyes. "That's never going to happen."

"Of course not." Olive waved her hand dismissively. "Have you ever been invited to a coven or even a gathering of witches before?"

"Only if you count Agatha's kitchen witch cookie exchanges during the winter solstice," I said.

Olive blinked at me as if she couldn't comprehend such a thing. I made a mental note to have Agatha invite her next year.

"Go get dressed. We have work to do to get you ready and only three days to get it done," Olive said. "Be at my office in ten minutes."

With that she pushed back from the table and strode to her office across the room.

"Don't worry," Tariq said. "She really is mostly bark and no bite."

"Mostly?" I asked.

"I can hear you," Olive said before she stepped into her office and shut the door with a loud bang.

"I'd better go." I stood and Diego rose to follow me. Jasper, Miles, and Tariq sent me sympathetic glances, none of which made me less nervous about my time with Olive.

Once inside my office, Diego flopped onto his doggy bed, which remained by the now cold fireplace. No doubt he needed a little recovery time after that shadow had grabbed him.

I shut my office door behind us and glanced at the shelf where I kept my grimoire. It was on its stand exactly where I expected it to be, but after what Miles had told me about the possibility that the shadow had been sent after my grimoire, relief surged through me. That grimoire was my connection to my mother and grandmother. To lose it would kill me.

My clothes from the night before were cleaned and neatly folded and I hurriedly dressed, taking just a minute to tame my wild hair by fastening it into a ponytail at the nape of my neck. There was a gentle knock at the door and I called, "Come in."

Jasper entered the office, looking ridiculously handsome despite being rumpled. His light blue gaze lit on me and a small smile curved his lips. "I see you found your clothes."

Maybe it was the relief that we'd managed to escape the roof intact, but I found myself smiling in return. "I don't know if I thanked you for all of this." I gestured to my clean clothes and the bed. "Last night would have been infinitely less comfortable without Mabel's room and that big fluffy bed."

"Do you want to keep it?" he asked. "You might need a lie down when Olive gets done drilling coven etiquette into you."

I glanced at the bed. Truthfully, I could have slept another ten hours right then and there. Better not tempt it. "I wish I could but there's too much to do. You can send it back? Reconfigure it? Where did that bed come from anyway?"

"The bed is your couch," he said. "I just took some liberties with its physical properties. Just as Diego's bed was formed out of one of the couch pillows."

"Oh, just toying with the physical properties of actual objects." I waved my hand as if it were no big deal while my mind was trying to wrap around the mere idea of such a thing. "That's all."

"I'll teach you how when we have our next lesson if you'd like," he promised.

"Yes, please."

Jasper gave me one confirming nod and then turned back to the fluffy bed. He raised his arms and I almost stopped him. It really was a comfortable bed. But instead, I watched, eager to learn how.

Jasper held his hands out at the couch and said, "Wake and tighten, stitch and seam, no longer for slumber, withdraw the dream." The bed jolted as if shaking off its own sleep, and in a blink it was gone and my old, lumpy tweed couch with the faint smell of wet dog was returned to me.

"A spell?" I asked. "That couch became a bed from a simple spell?"

"Yes, and it was returned to its original form by another spell," he confirmed. "How did you think I did it?"

"I don't know," I said. "I thought maybe you'd sent the

couch into some pocket dimension and replaced it with a bed from the same."

He shook his head. "Sorry, no pockets."

"That disappoints." I tsked.

He grinned and pulled me into his arms. "Well, I can't have that." Then he leaned down and kissed me. It was swift and sweet as if he knew how easy it would be for us to get distracted. I appreciated that even as I was disappointed that I couldn't just hole up in my office and be with him and hide from my impending visit to the High Bridge Coven.

"You'd better go," he said. "Olive is not a patient person."

"Really?" I feigned surprise and he laughed.

I grabbed my grimoire, reluctant to go anywhere without it, and tucked it into a deep pants pocket. I paused in the doorway, taking him in for just a moment. We hadn't declared it yet, but I was feeling a very girlfriend-boyfriend situation happening and, most shocking of all, I wasn't opposed.

"See you later," I said, leaving the office before I changed my mind.

"You're late," Olive said when I entered her office.

"How can I be late when we didn't have a set time to meet?" I asked. "You said ten minutes and by my count nine minutes and forty-two seconds have passed since you said that."

"And that is etiquette lesson number one," Olive said. "Do not argue with the head witch."

Immediately my mind flashed to my mother and how she had taken on the high priestess of the local coven when I was a child. It hadn't gone well and ultimately cost my father his life. I had a lot of *feelings* about head witches and I wasn't sure I could keep a lid on them if tested.

"You can't be late and you must address the head witch as 'high priestess' unless instructed otherwise," Olive said.

I squinted at her. Olive was the most badass witch I'd met to date, to put it mildly, and I had a hard time picturing her addressing anyone in such a way. "Do you belong to a coven?"

"Hell no." Olive made a face like she'd stepped in something gross.

"Why not?" I asked.

Olive stared at me and I felt as if her dark eyes were examining the corners of my very soul. I fully expected her to snap at me to mind my own business. Instead, her voice became unusually soft. "It's complicated."

Amazed that she'd admitted that much, I respected the trust she'd just shown me and nodded. "Okay, what else?"

"Keep your magic contained," Olive said. "This is critical. They will test you and if your aura flares or you leak any magic whatsoever in an emotional response, you will be seen as weak and undisciplined."

"I thought you said that's what made me attractive to power seekers," I said.

"No, I said what made you attractive was that you have a grimoire of questionable intent and a decided lack of magical training, which is not the same thing as being unable to control your magic," Olive corrected me. "You will be perceived as dangerous if your magic leaks, and they might reject you."

I closed my eyes. I had been nervous before but now I was feeling a little queasy. Up to now, as evidenced by my out-of-control trash can storm, I could barely conjure what I intended to conjure. Controlling magical leakage, well, that was a tall order. I put my hand over the pocket that contained my grimoire and felt a calmness come over me.

"I think my grimoire can help contain my magic, so long as I keep it close," I said.

Olive studied me for a beat. "Good idea. Between your grimoire and Diego you should be able to manage, but let's go over the details of coven etiquette so that you don't inadvertently anger one of the witches."

"What would happen if I did?" I asked.

Olive's scarred eyebrow lifted. "Best outcome, you'll offer some of your own magic in atonement."

"And the worst?" I asked.

"Death."

I didn't like that answer. Not at all.

16

By the time Olive was done with me, my head was spinning. So many coven rules to remember. Don't interrupt a spell. Greet the circle before entering and purify with salt. Don't enter until invited. Never turn your back to the altar. Mind the direction you move in—clockwise (deasil) for blessings, counterclockwise (widdershins) for banishments—mix them up and it would insult the spirits. My head hurt and I knew I had two more days of these instructions before the new moon. It didn't feel like enough time to prepare.

I escaped to the upper floor of the collection. It was quiet there and I tucked myself into one of the alcoves. I'd been thinking about my family's grimoire quite a lot since it had saved me from McWrath at the Midnight Market. I'd only managed to use the grimoire a few times, and it had always been when I was in dire need.

The past few months had been spent with me trying to decipher the code that the grimoire was written in to no avail. Every time I'd managed to use it, I'd asked the grimoire for help. The book had flipped to the page I needed, and I'd put my hand on the coded spell and the strange cipher had transformed into something legible. Was that the secret then? Was that how the grimoire worked? It had to decode the spell for the witch. This did not seem practical at all.

I set the book on the floor and studied the black cover and the silver band that was secured by the hexagonal lock on the center. To prove my theory, I would have to open it, which required a drop of Donadieu blood. Fine.

I unfastened the dainty pearl brooch I had taken to wearing, after I acquired the grimoire, for just this purpose. The pin was a Lively family heirloom that Agatha had given me when I graduated with my master's degree in library science. With the business end, I pricked the tip of my finger and squeezed until a tiny bead of blood appeared, then I held it over the little dip in the middle of the hexagon. As soon as the blood touched it, the lock clicked and turned, releasing the bands. Now was the moment of truth. Except, what was I supposed to ask the book? Previously when I'd used the book, it had entailed life-and-death situations.

I closed my eyes and focused on the magic inside of me. I felt the warmth unfurl. Good. Maybe if I was in a magical state, the book would respond to that. I opened my eyes and jumped. Freya, the book-cat who resided in the BODO, was upright beside the grimoire. When Freya wanted to hide, her cat features disappeared into her gray cover, but at the moment her cat face was visible on the cover and her ears, in the corners, were twitching. I saw her tail brush my grimoire and I wondered if she was trying to determine whether the book was a friend or a foe.

"Hello, Freya," I greeted her.

Her eyes rolled in my direction and I could hear her purring. I didn't want to be rude, but I was busy at the moment. "Did you need something?"

Her tail twitched in that way cats did when they were up to something. Freya was a book of Norse folklore written in Old Norse. She was named Freya after the goddess because cats were Freya's sacred animal. I watched as Freya's tail swept over the cover of my grimoire repeatedly, and the next thing I knew the cover opened and the pages began to flip, back and forth, as if my grimoire was looking for something. Were the two books able to communicate?

"Is there something I should know about here?" I glanced between the two books, feeling frustrated. "I wish my mom or Mamie were here. How am I ever going to decipher you, grimoire?"

The pages flipped faster and Freya's tail fluffed with agitation or potentially excitement? I couldn't tell. When the book finally landed on a page toward the back, I watched as Freya drifted up into the air until she was hovering over the open pages. Usually, I could read the emotions of my grimoire, but at the moment it was completely closed off to me. Something wasn't right. I reached for Freya but before I could grab her, she was swept up into a small whirlwind and disappeared into the book.

"What the hell?" I cried. I leaned forward, studying the page, but the grimoire slammed shut and the metal bands latched back into the lock with a click. My grimoire had just swallowed another book. A book-cat to be precise. I put my hand on my forehead, feeling a bit sick.

How was I going to explain this to Miles when I knew

how fond he was of Freya? I slumped back onto the floor so that I was staring up at the shelves surrounding me. I was so screwed.

I don't know how long I lay there. A face appeared upside down, with a frown line in between his dark eyebrows as he stared down at me, his light blue eyes studying my face with obvious concern.

"Are you all right, love?"

"No," I mumbled. How was I supposed to go to a coven meeting with a witch who likely had a grudge against me when I accidentally just disappeared a cat? Not just a cat but a rare book-cat named for a god. Gah.

Jasper crouched and then sprawled beside me, mimicking my position by staring up at the ceiling. "What happened?"

"My grimoire ate Freya."

"What?!" Out of the corner of my eye, I saw his head snap in my direction. He quickly cleared his throat. "I mean, I'm sure there's a way to rectify the situation."

"Are you?" I asked. "Because I'm trying to picture telling Miles what happened, and I think I'd rather just lie here until I turn to dust."

Jasper let out a soft grunt, which weirdly made me feel better. I mean, if he could laugh, then he wasn't that freaked out about Freya disappearing, which meant he thought it was fixable.

"Tell me what happened," he said.

I pushed up to a seated position and wrapped my arms around my knees. With a sigh, I described the events leading up to Freya's disappearance and nudged my grimoire with my toe as if I could push the book into coughing Freya up.

"Interesting." Jasper picked up the grimoire and studied it. He held it out to me. "Have you tried to open it?"

"I was too nervous to try." I didn't take the book. "It slammed shut so fast it felt as if it was shutting me out."

Jasper nodded. "Potentially, or it had to close to keep whatever spell it was weaving for Freya contained so that it didn't take you, too."

"*Was* it weaving a spell for Freya?" I asked. "How do we know it didn't just eat her?"

A pang of hurt zinged my chest, and I gasped and glanced at the book in Jasper's hands. I took the book from him and glared at the cover. "Oh, now you want to share your feelings?" *Pfft.*

"I feel like I'm missing something." Jasper studied my face as if trying to read the subtext.

"I've mentioned before that the book makes its feelings well known to me." I paused and Jasper nodded. "Yes, well, when it was disappearing Freya, it shut me out completely."

"Oh." Jasper's mouth formed an O. I glanced away. There was no way that should be as attractive as it was. "Perhaps it can't emit feelings while performing magic."

I glanced at the book in my hands. "Is that true?"

The book went dark again. It was like trying to read the emotions of a brick. I glanced up at Jasper and sighed. I set the book down and returned to my pricked finger. I squeezed the tip until I had another bead of blood and dropped it into the face of the hexagonal lock.

Nothing happened. I wondered if I hadn't used enough blood, or maybe the book needed more recovery time after swallowing a book-cat. Jasper leaned forward, and when I glanced at him, he was frowning, equally perplexed. Just when I was about to give up and freak out, the lock turned and the bands unlatched.

Leaning over the book, I said, "Show the page that Freya went into."

Reluctance was the response, like asking a library borrower to pay their late fees, and the pages flipped one at a time, slow enough for me to scan each one. *What the hell?*

"I've never seen it do this before." Jasper voiced my own observation. "It's like the book is stalling."

"Exactly!" I cried. "But why?"

"We should go talk to Miles." He pushed up to his feet and held out his hand to help me up.

I slid my hand under my grimoire, holding it on my open palm, while taking Jasper's hand with my free one and using him to pull myself to my feet.

I wasn't eager to go see Miles, and as we navigated the spiral staircase to the first floor, I thought of a million reasons to duck, but the reality was, I had no idea what had happened and it made me faintly ill to think of Freya trapped somewhere like the Netherveil because of me and my grimoire.

Jasper led the way to Miles's office. He rapped on the door three times and we heard Miles call, "Enter."

Jasper pushed the door open and gestured for me to lead. Inside, the office appeared more chaotic than usual, with books scattered everywhere, some hovering in midair, and several beakers with what appeared to be shadows inside of them, sitting in a wooden holder on the worktable in the corner where Miles and Tariq were seated.

I lifted my eyebrows in surprise. A large whiteboard was

on a rolling stand beside them. It was covered in scribbles, none of which made any sense to me, and I couldn't determine whether bad handwriting was the culprit or if it was some sort of code.

Miles sat up straight at the sight of us. "Excellent. Just the people we needed to see."

Jasper and I exchanged a wary glance. One never knew with Miles whether being needed was a good thing or not. Still, if it gave me the opportunity to stall, I'd take it.

"What can we help with?" I asked. I set the grimoire on the coffee table in front of the couch, where it continued to flip through its pages.

"We're working on a counterspell to thwart McWrath," Miles explained. "Since you two got the closest to him, with you stepping into his altered plane in the Netherveil, Zoe, and you able to follow her there as a raven, Jasper, it's your wisdom we need to figure out how to counter his use or any magical being's use of the reality-altering spell in the *Book of Shadows*."

There were so many times that I'd felt I was out of my depth since joining the BODO, but this moment was beyond all of those. I had no insight to offer Miles about McWrath and I felt like a complete and total fraud, one who had inadvertently just disappeared his cat. Jasper must have suspected how I was feeling because he spoke up immediately.

"It was a wild night," he said. "I don't know that we have any insight to offer given that we were running for our lives."

Miles raised his hand and nodded as if he understood this. He turned to me and said, "It's the details I want. You said you were in a field, the sun was out, and there was a man in the distance."

I nodded. "Yeah, that's exactly what it looked like."

"Can you name the types of flowers, what time of day you thought it was, what exactly did the man look like as he approached, what did it smell like? Those sorts of things."

This I could do. "It might be easier if I write it down."

"Of course." Tariq handed me a pen and a blank pad of paper. Then he turned to Jasper, who nodded, and Tariq handed him one, too.

We sat quietly on the couch. I closed my eyes, willing every single detail of the encounter to come back to me. I scribbled until I filled two pages, and there wasn't anything else I could think of to share.

When we were finished, Jasper gave the notepads to Miles, who looked them over and muttered, "Excellent." He handed them to Tariq to read and looked back at us. "Oh, but what did you come to see me about?"

Moment of truth. I felt like I was in the principal's office awaiting punishment. I held up my grimoire and said, "My grimoire disappeared Freya."

Miles's eyes went wide behind his glasses, and Tariq glanced up from the notepads and said, "Did you just say—?"

"Yes." I described what had happened and instead of freaking out, like I would have, Miles cupped his chin in thought.

"Do you think Freya was called into the book?" Tariq asked.

"It's possible," Miles agreed.

"I'm sorry," I said. "How is that possible?"

"The last thing you said before Freya disappeared was that you wished your mother or grandmother was there to help you decipher the grimoire, right?" Tariq asked.

A stillness came over me when I answered. Had I done

this by wishing for help? How would Freya's disappearance help me? My voice was low when I said, "I did."

"It could be that Freya used your grimoire to travel to your mother or your grandmother, or potentially, it's the other way around and your grimoire sent Freya to them," Miles said. "To let them know you needed help?"

I slumped back against the couch like I'd been shot.

"It's just a theory," Tariq said. "But your grandmother did mention that your mother had been hiding in time. Your grimoire might know exactly where to find her."

I cradled my head with my hands. It was true. After my mother had left me at boarding school under Agatha's supervision, she would show up unexpectedly, usually with gifts that were antique, as if they'd come from another time. Agatha had hypothesized that my mother, who'd been on the run from a dark witch, had used a time-travel spell in the grimoire to hide, and during our one brief visit last autumn, Mamie had confirmed it. My magic hadn't been strong enough to hold Mamie in the present for more than a few minutes then, and it surely wasn't strong enough to call her back now.

Defeat weighed down my shoulders. One of the reasons I'd been so desperate to decipher the book was to be able to use that time-travel spell to see my mother again. And here Freya, a book-cat, had just popped into the grimoire potentially to go and see my mom. *What the hell?*

A large warm hand landed on the middle of my back, grounding me. Jasper's soothing voice said, "Look at the positives. Now you know that your grimoire is capable of such a thing and that you're that much closer to manifesting the outcome you want."

I swallowed the frustration. He was right. I'd seen the page. I knew I could find it again. I turned to him and gave him a weak smile, the best I could manage, and said, "You're right. I'm one step closer."

He squeezed my shoulder and gestured to the book. "Take a look."

The grimoire had stopped sifting through its pages. It sat open. I peered at the pages in front of me. I recognized the one on the right. This was definitely the page Freya had disappeared into.

"She was flicking the grimoire with her tail as if she was looking for this particular spell." I turned to Miles. "Can Freya do magic?"

He shrugged. "She is a book with a cat face, ears, and a tail. I'd always assumed she was created by a witch, but maybe she is a witch hiding in a book that's a cat."

"Whoa." Tariq's voice was full of awe.

We all sat with that theory for a moment. I glanced at Miles and Tariq and asked, "What is Freya's backstory? Where did she come from?"

Miles said, "She's always been here. As far as I know, she was one of the first books that Mabel put in the Books of Dubious Origin collection."

"Because she's a book and a cat?" I asked.

"You can't really have that sort of item up in the regular collection," Tariq said. "People wouldn't be able to handle that."

"But she comes and goes as she pleases," I said. "And we really don't know where she goes when she goes, do we?"

"We don't," Miles confirmed. "Because . . . cat."

Newly motivated to decipher my grimoire, I shoved my

finger into the book to mark my place and closed the volume, holding it with my thumb and remaining fingers. "If you don't need me for anything else, I'm going to my office."

Miles and Tariq exchanged a glance and then shook their heads. I didn't wait to see what Jasper said. I wanted to be alone with my grimoire and my thoughts. I strode from the room, my mind awhirl with all this brand-new information.

The next two days were miserable. Olive grilled me until I almost snapped at her. Thankfully, I had enough self-preservation to keep myself in check. But I simply didn't care about the coven or the meeting or McWrath. I was too consumed with my own desire to figure out where Freya had gone, how she'd done it, and whether she was traveling through time even now. So many questions and no answers. It was maddening. My grimoire was no help whatsoever.

Every night I turned my office couch into a bed. I didn't want to lose any time studying the grimoire to take the train to and from my house in Connecticut. I also refused to see anyone but Olive, only making time to study coven etiquette with her, and that was grudging at best.

The night of the new moon arrived. Agatha appeared at my office with an armful of clothes. Glancing up from my grimoire, I started in surprise.

"You don't come home, you don't call, tsk tsk," Agatha chided me. "Just what is so all-consuming that you have no time for your bonus mom?"

"I'm trying to decipher the spell Mom used to travel through time," I said.

Agatha dropped the clothes she was holding onto the floor. "Are you saying . . . ?"

"I think I might be able to find her," I said.

"Oh, honey." Agatha's eyes filled with tears. If there was anyone who had grieved the loss of my mother as much as I had, it was Agatha, who was Mom's childhood best friend.

I stood and crossed the room to give her a quick hug. She swiped at her tears with the backs of her hands and shook her head, making her silver ringlets dance. Her deep brown gaze held mine as she drew in a restorative breath. "That is very exciting news, but we have to get you prepared for tonight. I really don't like you walking into this coven meeting alone."

"I know." I nodded. "But the invitation was just for me. I have the grimoire that we suspect they want to increase their power, and they have a tie to McWrath, who has the *Book of Shadows*, which we are determined to reclaim. I have to go."

Agatha scooped up the clothes she'd dropped and shook them out. "I made you these. They're bespelled to give you some protection. Natural fibers are required by the coven, so the velvet is from silk dyed red, because that is the color of your magic, plus, red signifies strength and courage and protective energy."

I was not a person who dressed colorfully. I liked fading into the background by dressing in shades of black, beige, and, when I was feeling wild, gray. My Hester Prynne costume had suited me because it had been drab with just a splash of color in the letter *A*. The ability to turn that costume into a red sparkler had appealed mostly because I could go back to drab in an instant. This, however, was not a dress that would ever belong to a wallflower.

"Agatha—" I started, but she interrupted.

"You need to make an entrance," she said. "Just like Diego will be in full hellhound mode, so should you."

"Hellhound, huh?" I held up the garment. It was a mock-turtleneck, long-sleeved, formfitting maxi dress that was as soft as butter under my fingers, and it was dyed a red so deep it reminded me of the burgundy long-stemmed roses that were sold on every street corner on Valentine's Day.

"Get changed," Agatha ordered. "I have more to add to this outfit."

"Yes, ma'am." I slipped out of my clothes while Agatha fussed with the rest of the items she'd brought.

The dress fit like a dream, hugging my curves and dropping all the way to my ankles. Long enough for coverage and warmth but not so long I'd trip when I walked. Agatha handed me a pair of boots. They were pointy-toed but with a thick heel and an inside zipper.

"Spelled to keep your feet warm," she said.

"Just like when I was a kid," I said with a smile.

Next she handed me a necklace. It was made from liquid silver, called that because the tiny narrow silver cylinders were strung on thread, making the silver look like liquid. There was a witch's knot pendant hanging from the silver. This particular one was a circle of black obsidian with four tear-shaped stones of labradorite that met in the circle's center and fanned out like the petals of a flower.

"Black obsidian deflects ill will, reveals hidden truths, and neutralizes dark magic, while the labradorite protects the aura, conceals your magical signature, and strengthens intuition," Agatha explained. Her voice sounded choked up as she fastened it around my neck.

"Hey." I took her hands in mine and gave them a gentle squeeze. "I'll be all right. I promise."

"Keep your grimoire on you at all times," Agatha said, ignoring my assurances.

"Will do." I let go of her hands and stashed the grimoire in the pocket of my cloak. "I'll be under surveillance by Jasper during the meeting. I'll have Diego with me. And my grimoire. If I get into trouble, my grimoire will save me. It has before."

"The Donadieu witches knew what they were doing when they crafted that book of spells," Agatha agreed.

I draped the dark cloak Jasper had made for me the night of the market over my arm. I didn't feel ready to face a bunch of strange witches in some creepy remote location, but I didn't expect I ever would.

"Best get it over with," I said. Agatha nodded and we left the safety of my office for the main room, where Jasper, Tariq, Olive, and Miles were waiting.

Jasper took in the sight of me and I saw his eyes widen. His expression remained neutral as I crossed the room, my skirt swishing around my ankles. Diego trotted forward to sit beside me. He was in full hellhound mode, and with his dark coat and red eyes, we made quite the matched set. Also, he looked like he'd rip off the head of anyone who crossed him, and I found that ridiculously reassuring.

"Not bad, Ziakas," Olive said. She had her arms crossed over her chest, assessing me. "You're missing one thing."

I glanced down at my pendant, dress, boots, and the cloak on my arm with my grimoire tucked into the pocket. I was certain I had everything. "What?"

"This." Olive held out a small black velvet bag.

My mouth dropped open in surprise. "Is this—?"

"Your BODO emergency kit," she said. "Don't read too much into it. I don't think you're ready for most of it, but I can't in good conscience send you into a coven meeting with Odessa Van Doren without some magical backup."

"Thank you," I said. I was extremely touched.

She waved me off and I knew better than to say anything more.

"There is a bog gas globule in there," Tariq said. "I added that. If you need to make a quick getaway, use it but be prepared to run. You'll never get the methane smell out of your clothes if you don't."

Olive rolled her eyes and I almost laughed.

Miles stepped up and put his hands on my shoulders. "Your safety is our highest priority, Zoe. If anything feels off or if you believe you're in danger, leave immediately. We'll get to McWrath another way."

"Understood." I shrugged on the cloak and slipped my emergency kit into the pocket without my grimoire. I patted Diego on his big, blocky head, turned to Jasper, and said, "Let's go."

He gestured for me to lead, and with Diego by my side, I magicked us through the metal door without looking back.

17

That dress, love," Jasper said as we walked through the deserted museum. His voice sounded lower than usual, and a shiver ran down my spine in the most delicious way.

"What about it?" I asked. I was trying for coy, but I doubted that I pulled it off given that my voice came out a bit breathy.

"It's a heart attack in velvet." Then he grinned. "And what a way to go."

He looked so cheerful at the prospect that I laughed. "That might be the nicest compliment I've ever gotten on an outfit. Thank you."

"I meant every word." He paused by the door to allow Diego to transition into his puppy self before he opened the front door of the museum for me. Together, we stepped out onto the street to see our car waiting. The driver held open the back door for us, looking anywhere but at the happy drooling dog we were letting into his pristine car. If only he knew. Miles had hired a high-end car service for exactly this discretion.

Jasper was in a black overcoat over a black sweater and

jeans. I had no idea where he was going to be while I was in the coven meeting, but I knew he would use his aviankinesis to watch over me, just as he had at the Midnight Market. It was a comfort.

The ride to the High Bridge was quiet, aside from Diego's panting. I was trying to keep my nerves in check while inside I felt as if I were going to fly apart at any moment. Jasper reached across the seat and took my hand in his.

"At what point do you think you'll use that bog gas globule that Tariq gifted you with?" he asked.

That surprised a laugh out of me and I squeezed his fingers, feeling my nerves ratchet down. "I expect I'll use it on Odessa when she annoys me." It was a satisfying thought to imagine.

"You're going to be all right," Jasper said. "Diego and I will be with you every step of the way."

I nodded. It was reassuring to have a hellhound and a badass mage at my back.

Our driver stopped at the entrance to the park on University and West 170th. He asked no questions. I suspected in his line of work he saw stranger things than a couple and their dog going to a park in the middle of the night. We had decided to approach the tower from the pedestrian bridge on the far side of the river, hoping to draw the attention of whoever might be watching and allow Miles, Olive, and Tariq to station themselves in the neighborhood surrounding the tower.

Jasper got out and held the door for me. Diego leapt out before me and began sniffing the area as if he planned to root out any bad guys with his nose.

"Thanks, mate," Jasper said to the driver, who nodded.

He turned to me and offered his arm. My boots were warm and had thick heels with nice tread so I was able to manage the paved path without stumbling.

We waited until the driver departed before we slipped into the closed park. Diego took three steps into the area, which was enclosed by a brick wall with spiked wrought iron fencing surrounding it, and shed his puppy facade like discarding a jacket, and the muscled hellhound with the red eyes returned. I put my hand on his shoulder and he leaned in. I didn't get the feeling he was nervous so much as uneasy. That made two of us—I felt a flutter of anxiety coming from the grimoire in my pocket. Okay, three of us.

Despite Olive's grilling, I really had no idea what this meeting with the coven was going to entail. Every bit of information we were operating on was pure speculation. Was Odessa out for revenge for my tying her up at the gala? Or did she want my grimoire? Was she working with McWrath, who also wanted my grimoire, and would she just hand me over to him? The questions chased themselves around my mind.

"Don't overthink," Jasper whispered as we passed a squat square stone building with black metal doors. "Trust your instincts."

I nodded but he wasn't done.

"Especially in regard to any rogue mages who try to dazzle you with paper cranes," he said.

"Thorne," I said. "I understand I'm not to trust him."

"Not even to give you the correct time," Jasper ground out as we started down the steps that led to the High Bridge.

"Given your recent history with him trying to steal that enchanted book of poetry and appearing in London when you were acquiring the *Book of Shadows*, I can see why you feel that way." I nodded.

"I don't care about any enchanted book as much as I do you." Jasper stopped walking and turned to face me. The wind whipping up the Harlem River sent my cloak fluttering around us. I pulled it more tightly about me. "If Thorne puts you in harm's way—"

"I don't think this meeting is going to come to that," I said. "They're checking me out. I'm checking them out. If the rumors that Olive spread about me and my grimoire and how I'm now looking for a coven were believed, then as far as we can surmise, the coven wants me for my grimoire and my potential power while I want to use them to find McWrath and the *Book of Shadows*. There are a lot of cross-purposes happening tonight. Most likely we'll get an assessment of each other and retreat to our separate corners."

Jasper cupped my chin and his thumb stroked my cheek. "Witches and mages do not pull their punches ever. Show one sign of weakness and they'll close in for the kill."

My eyes went wide. "What happened to your reassurance that you and Diego are going to be with me every step of the way and I would be all right?"

"That was before we arrived." He pulled me in and hugged me while Diego leaned against my side. "I hate having to leave you unguarded even for a moment."

I rested my face on the soft wool of his coat. I could have just stayed there, cocooned safely in his warmth. I pushed away. "Where will you go in order to . . ." I waved my hand in the general direction of the air.

"Miles and I set up a safe space." He glanced at the small

stone building we'd just passed. "Once I'm unconscious, I'll connect to a nearby raven and use their eyes to watch you. I'll only be moments away from you if you need me."

"What if there are no ravens?" I asked.

"There are always ravens near me."

"But—"

"If I have to come into the tower as a bloody pigeon, I will," he promised.

I smiled at that image as I turned to continue walking. "I'd better go. I don't want to be late. Olive said that's a big no-no."

Jasper sighed and put his hand on my lower back. We turned and began to cross the herringbone-patterned brickwork that made up the pedestrian path across the recently remodeled High Bridge.

Originally built in 1848 as part of the Croton Aqueduct, which brought water to the city from the Croton River in Westchester County, the bridge connected Manhattan and the Bronx over the Harlem River. The area now had the added bonus of the land surrounding the bridge, acquired over time by the city, being used to create north, middle, and south parks for the community.

Yes, the librarian in me had done her research before setting out. Coven meeting aside, I was interested in the history of the place and would have preferred a daylight meeting so I could really check it out as there were 102 acres of natural forest to explore in the park nestled between Harlem River Drive and Amsterdam Avenue in Upper Manhattan.

I knew Diego would love it as he was running around us

in great big loops. A hellhound with the zoomies, go figure. I couldn't determine whether he was just happy to be out in his proper form or if this was his way of maintaining a perimeter.

Abruptly, the bricks changed from the herringbone pattern to the more traditional staggered style. Jasper stepped forward with me only to be knocked back on his heels while I passed through unimpeded with Diego at my side. We were standing over the Harlem River now.

"Are you all right?" I spun around to face him.

"Yes." He brushed off his coat as if the shield had left lint on his person. "Annoyed, but otherwise fine." He glared at the water tower ahead. "This is as far as I can go, love."

I'd been expecting it, but I still hated to hear him say it. I nodded. I put my hand on Diego's shoulder, seeking courage. His muscles rippled beneath my fingers and I felt a surge of confidence. "Will you be able to fly in as a raven? What if the shield won't allow it?"

He cocked his head to the side as if listening to something only he could hear. He pointed to the tower. "Not to worry. My ride is already there. A shield can't keep me out."

"Good." I didn't bother trying to mask the relief in my voice. "Okay then. Be careful."

"You, too." His pale blue eyes glowed in the overhead light of the old-fashioned lampposts that ran along the iron railing and the taller fencing of the bridge.

I sent him a small wave and turned back toward the tower and started to walk. Without Diego at my side, I doubted I would have made it to the next section of herringbone brick, past another short squat brick building, and onto the path that wound through leafless trees that felt ominous in the dead of night. The park was deserted, and it creeped me out all the way down to the marrow of my bones.

"I hope I'm not dragging you into something bad, Diego." I absently rubbed his velvet soft ears as we picked our way along the leaf-strewn path. "If things go sideways, I want you to get out of there and go find Jasper. Do not worry about me."

Diego turned his head, and I could have sworn he rolled his red eyes at me with all the disdain of a teenager at peak attitude.

"I mean it."

I glanced at the tower set on the hillside above. It loomed over us and I searched the top of it, hoping to get a glimpse of the raven that Jasper would be inhabiting while he monitored us. I glanced at my wristwatch, wondering how much time we had left. Less than a minute!

"Oh, shit!" I grabbed fistfuls of my long skirt and cloak and started to run for the tower. Diego galloped beside me. We turned with the path, arriving at a set of wooden stairs.

A tiny woman, delicate in face and form, was standing at the top. She had a wild mane of red curls and was wearing a deep brown cloak over a pale yellow gown. I was relieved Agatha had been so spot-on with the dress code. The little witch was wringing her hands, looking nervous until her eyes lit upon me.

"Oh, thank goodness!" she cried. "You made it. Everyone is waiting. We have to hurry."

She clapped her hands together three times. One moment Diego and I were at the bottom of the steps, and the next we were standing in front of the stone tower. Much like walking through the magicked doors of the BODO, it felt as if my entire body was compressed and then released. I didn't enjoy it.

The witch led us inside through the arched doorway. Two large pipes ran up through the center of the tower and a metal spiral staircase lined the interior of the red brick wall, reminding me of the one that led down to the BODO at the Museum of Literature. The petite witch began to run up the steps, her feet barely touching the metal. I hurried to keep up while Diego brought up the rear.

"Hurry!" She dashed up the stairs. Over her shoulder, the witch called back, "My name is Tansy. I'm in charge of the membership of the High Bridge Coven."

"Nice to meet you." I was full-on mouth breathing now and thinking I wouldn't mind if she did that clapping thing again that got us where we needed to be without so much exertion. "Is it a large coven?"

She didn't answer and I thought she hadn't heard me. I was about to repeat myself, when she said, "It used to be."

"Did something happen?"

Tansy stopped running so I did, too, thank goodness. I leaned on the rail, trying to catch my breath while Diego paused beside me.

"Leadership recently made some changes," Tansy said. "Our high priestess removed the witches who were her second and third in command—the Hand of the Coven and the Spell Warden—replacing them with witches of her choosing." She paused and then added, "Some coven witches did not approve of the changes and left."

I got the impression Tansy was carefully selecting each word, scrutinizing them before setting them down between us.

This level of caution seemed excessive but then again, considering Odessa Van Doren was the high priestess in question, perhaps not.

"And how do you feel about change?" I asked.

She blinked and I knew I'd asked a loaded question.

"I'm just an initiate. I'm happy with whatever the high priestess decides." She reached out and took my hand. She pressed a flattened, oval-shaped penny into my palm, one of those embossed coins from machines commonly found at tourist attractions. She closed my fingers over it and put her finger to her lips. Her eyes were wide and I could tell she was terrified.

"Hurry!" Tansy began to run again. Damn it. I shoved the penny into my pocket to examine later.

"Where are we going exactly?" I asked. I had visions of Odessa luring me to the top of the tower only to throw me off.

"There are six levels in the tower," Tansy said. "We meet on the third."

That seemed less dangerous and I might actually make it halfway up this two-hundred-foot tower, I hoped.

Up and up we went, passing narrow wooden landings as we continued. Finally, we arrived at the third, which had several witches waiting. Not one of them even blinked at the hellhound beside me. Instead, they all bowed their heads, as did Tansy, when I stepped onto the platform. In greeting? I had no idea. Olive hadn't mentioned this.

Like me, they were dressed in long gowns and cloaks, and I felt as if I was wearing a witch uniform. Knowing that Agatha had woven protection spells into mine gave me a bit of ease. I scanned the faces of the witches in attendance for Odessa, but there was no sign of her. This didn't sit well with me, as

Olive had told me that the high priestess ran the coven meeting and greeted guests when they arrived. Where was Odessa?

I put my hand on Diego's back to steady myself. He leaned against me, which I appreciated.

It occurred to me that Odessa might have set me up. Instead of inviting me to join the coven, perhaps Odessa's plan was to capture me and take me and my grimoire to McWrath. I'd known all along that this was a possibility but now that it seemed probable, I wasn't feeling nearly as brave as I had when it was just a theory.

I took a quick count. There were five witches on the landing. If they decided to attack us, I was done for. Diego couldn't take them all, and my skill set was simply not up to this. I felt a surge of comfort come from my pocket as my grimoire tried to bolster my spirits.

A circle was drawn on the wooden floor in black charcoal just as Olive had said it would be, and a hum started to fill the landing. It was coming from the witches and sounded like the reverberation of a big gong. The witches took their places around the circle and began to sway, raising their arms. The hair stood up on my forearms. Diego emitted a low growl in his throat as an agitated ridge of fur appeared between his shoulders. The grimoire was oddly silent, as if it was trying not to be noticed. That couldn't be good.

A flutter of wings sounded behind me, and I turned to see a raven soar up through the center of the tower and perch on the sill of an arch-shaped window above. The bird turned its head and studied me with one pale blue eye. Jasper. I exhaled with relief.

My attention returned to the witches as the humming grew

louder and the swaying more exuberant as limbs were now involved. The witches began to move around the circle. It occurred to me that they were summoning someone or something? McWrath? I glanced at the women. There was still no sign of Odessa or Thorne, for that matter. Were they being called? What would I do if they appeared?

I pressed my back against the brick wall in a defensive stance that allowed me to watch the entire landing.

The low hum began to echo against the tower interior, and the witches started twirling around the circle with a sort of mad abandon that I found creepy and potentially dangerous, as they could topple over the railing or down the stairs with one misstep. And then, as quickly as they'd started, they stopped. It took me a second to realize it wasn't of their own volition. I watched as they levitated into the air to dangle about a foot above the floor. They were all suspended in place, a dazed expression on their faces. Terrifying!

This was not a coven meeting, at least not like any coven meeting Olive had prepped me for. I desperately wanted to turn around and run, but I forced myself to stand my ground with gritted teeth and clenched fists. I would not be scared off.

I took a steadying breath. The air felt like ice in my lungs. I stroked Diego's back just to prove that I could move. Diego turned his head toward me, indicating he was fine. I glanced up at the raven and watched him ruffle his wings, so he was clear as well. We were all free from the spell that had trapped the witches. Was it because we hadn't performed whatever ritual they'd just done? I didn't know. My lack of knowledge really bothered me, but there was nothing I could do about it at the moment.

A shimmer of brilliant light formed in the center of the circle, getting larger and brighter until it hurt to look at. I glanced away, shielding my eyes. When the light receded, I turned back to see the circle of witches were now hanging upside down as if they'd been turned over. Trails of different colored light, each witch's signature magical color, poured from the center of their bodies toward the middle of the circle where Odessa Van Doren stood in all her ice-blue and silver glory.

18

Odessa turned her head and stared directly at me. I'd wondered if she'd remember me from the gala. Well, there was no need to wonder anymore. She stared at me with a malevolence that felt violent.

"You actually accepted my invitation, baby witch." Her voice was low and rough and sounded as if it had been crafted of broken glass. Had she sounded like that at the gala? Was it because she was clearly evil? Hey, wait!

"Baby witch?!" I cried. *The audacity!*

"What would you call a witch who can't even master her own grimoire?" Odessa paced counterclockwise inside the charcoal ring. Her entire body was illuminated by the magic pouring into the circle from the witches.

"You're wrong." I felt compelled to argue even though she wasn't, not completely. I tried to sense the grimoire's feelings about this but it was like having a brick in my pocket. I wondered if it was trying to remain unnoticed to protect me, itself, or both of us.

"Am I?" She sounded amused. "Tell me, what spells have you mastered from the Donadieu grimoire?"

"Why would I tell you anything?" I asked.

"You came to the coven meeting," she said. "Was it because the handsome Rowan Thorne caught your eye?"

I heard the raven squawk on the window ledge, but I didn't look at Jasper as I didn't want Odessa to notice him. I doubted she knew of Jasper's ability, but I couldn't risk her going after him.

"That guy?" I scoffed. "All flash no substance."

She smirked. "Then I must assume you're here to use me to find out where McWrath has taken the *Book of Shadows.*"

Direct hit. Polite of her not to waste my time, I supposed. Still, she seemed so incredibly sure of herself. It annoyed me.

"Or maybe I'm just here to take over your coven." I crossed my arms over my chest and tipped my head to the side. "I hear membership is down."

Odessa's eyes narrowed. She flicked her fingers and an ice shard flew at me. Diego opened his mouth and flames shot out, reducing the would-be weapon to a puddle.

"Temper, temper." I began to walk clockwise around the outside of the circle. If she was going to posture, then so was I. Diego placed himself between me and the witches and kept pace, his red eyes never leaving Odessa. "I think it's obvious that you invited me here because you want something or you're acting on someone else's orders. I'm curious to know which it is."

Odessa tossed her hair and turned her face away. "Presumptuous of you to think *I* want anything from you."

I noted that she didn't deny acting on someone else's behalf, but I said nothing as I continued strolling around the circle. The witches remained suspended, their hair dangling just above the landing, their magic still swirling into the circle to Odessa. Would they fall when they were released? Were they even aware of what was happening to them?

I remembered what Tansy had said about the coven becoming smaller in number when Odessa changed her second and third in command. I glanced at the suspended witches and understood the motive of the ones who'd left, if this was the sort of change that had been implemented. I wouldn't be okay with this lack of personal bodily autonomy either.

Tansy in her pretty yellow gown was frozen with her arms out and her expression vacant. Her skin was even paler than it had been when she'd met me outside. It was almost as if she were being drained. Wait. My heart started to beat hard in a slow thud, a drumbeat of dread.

I glanced past the witches at Odessa. Was she more vibrant than when she arrived? She seemed to almost glow with her shining eyes and glass skin. I glanced back at the witches, studying their faces, and again at Odessa. Was my speculation wildly off base? Or was she using some sort of spell to drain these witches of their power to enhance her own?

I stopped beside Tansy. I reached out and touched her arm. Her skin was icy cold and I shivered.

"You want my power. You want to drain me like you're draining these witches," I said. It wasn't an accusation. It was a realization.

"You don't have any power," Odessa scoffed. I noted that she didn't acknowledge the rest of my statement.

"Don't I?" I asked. "I mean, I must, otherwise, why would

you invite me here? Unless it was McWrath who told you to invite me. He did, didn't he?" Odessa didn't meet my eyes. She was hiding something. "Is that your plan? To drain me of power and then turn me over to him? Is he here?"

"No, he isn't," she snapped. "This is between you and me."

"Brave of you," I said with more swagger than I felt. "I tied you up once. I don't see why I can't do it again."

Her face flushed a deep red and her nostrils flared. For an ice queen, she certainly had a hot temper.

"You can try." She raised her hands. Her fingers were curled as if she'd claw my eyes out if she could reach me, but she couldn't. I realized then that she was trapped inside her own circle, siphoning off the power of the other witches. If she stepped outside of it, I suspected she'd lose whatever power she'd taken. Was Odessa Van Doren a fraud? Interesting.

It had been my experience that the thing fraudsters loathed the most was being outed. I decided to go for it and see what happened.

"I think your power is stolen," I said. "Which means you're weak. Your cute little icicles can't touch me, not with my hell-hound beside me."

"Weak? Cute little icicles?" Odessa seethed. She was so angry, she was shaking. "You'll pay for that!"

She raised her arms, arched her back, and lifted her chin toward the ceiling. There was a horrendous *boom* and the interior of the tower was encased in a thick coating of ice. The temperature immediately dropped below freezing, and the suspended witches were covered in frost and icicles. Snow and sleet pelted us as a bitter wind whipped around the inside of the tower. Oh, shit. I may have overplayed my hand.

I stepped closer to Diego only to slip on the ice-coated floor. My feet shot out from under me and I instinctively grabbed the hound by the scruff, catching myself before I slid down the nearby stairs.

"Hang on to me!" The voice was low and deep as if it was coming from the bowels of hell. There was only one creature from hell that I was presently acquainted with.

"Ah!" I clutched Diego more tightly. "Did you just . . . *speak*?"

Diego glanced at me over his shoulder. *"A muzzle isn't really equipped to do more than bark or growl."*

My eyes went wide and I gasped. "Are you in my mind?"

"Excellent. Most humans take much longer to get there." Diego tipped his head to the side. *"I knew you were smart the second you got us out of that field at the market."*

"And you're sharing this ability with me *now*?" I glanced at Odessa, who was calling forth more snow, making it nearly impossible to see.

"If not now, when?" Diego retorted.

I opened my mouth to speak, but Odessa interrupted.

"How?" She glared at me. "How are you not frozen?"

I was not about to admit that my boyfriend had hooked me up with this sweet cloak that kept me warm and my bonus mom had dressed me in bewitched boots to keep my toes toasty. Instead, I went on the offensive and said, "Baby witch, my ass."

Odessa's nostrils flared. She lifted her arms as if she would blast more ice into the tower. I glanced at the witches. They would die of hypothermia if we didn't stop her.

"Can you do something?" I asked Diego.

"Are you suggesting I light the building on fire?" he asked.

"Could you do that?" I asked.

"If I wanted to." He sounded salty, as if I were doubting his abilities. I wondered if he was the hellhound equivalent of a teenager when in his natural state. A question for another time.

"I'm entering the circle," I muttered to Diego.

"Are you mad?"

"Just start heating up the room," I retorted. "These women will die if they're encased in ice for much longer."

Instantly the hellhound's body became a ball of flame. I felt the heat blast the side of my face and I quickly stepped away. Diego began to trot around the circle, and Odessa, distracted, spun in place to watch him, clearly trying to decide how much of a threat he posed. When her back was turned to me, I jumped between two of the suspended witches, into the circle. I could hear the cry of the raven above, but I didn't dare look at him. I didn't want to know what Jasper thought of my plan.

Instead, I pulled the hood of my cloak over my eyes and held my hands out in front of me, and using the lessons Olive had taught me to control the weather, I called forth the sun. While Diego heated the outside of the circle, I focused on the inside. The ball of bright red-orange light appeared between my hands and Odessa whipped around to find me in her circle.

"How dare you step into my circle uninvited?" She raised her arms to shield herself from the glare of the eye-searing orb.

I paid no attention to her as I focused on raising the sun up above the circle and using its heat to melt the ice that encased the entire two-hundred-foot interior of the tower as well as the snow and sleet that continued to blast the inside of the building. Between my small sun and Diego, the ice rapidly began to melt. There was rather more of it than I had counted on, and in moments, the floor of the landing was several inches deep in icy water. Well, hell.

There was a splashing sound and I glanced out from under the edge of my hood to see Odessa striding toward me while water pulled at her gown and churned around her feet. Her face was contorted with fury, her eyes wild and her lips pulled back from her teeth in a snarl to rival any hellhound's. She looked possessed.

She raised her arms, planning another icicle strike, no doubt, but Diego bounded into the circle and opened his mouth to blast flames at her like a mini dragon. It was really quite impressive.

Odessa shrieked and leapt back out of range, stepping one foot out of her protective circle. In the blink of an eye, she went from powerful and vibrant to a dried-out husk. By stepping out of the circle, she ended her magical connection to the witches. Her skin no longer glowed and her body appeared frail. The snow and sleet abruptly stopped, but the thick coating of ice she had manifested remained.

With a bellow of fury, Odessa bolted for the stairs. I watched in shock as she leapt into the air. She was suspended for a moment, just long enough to meet my gaze and cackle. A flare of pale blue light exploded from her chest and she vanished, leaving a lone snowflake behind. What the hell? The tiny bit of snow that was Odessa fluttered down the stairs. Diego barked and raced after it.

I was about to follow him when the witch beside me fell. I caught her upper body before her head crashed into the floor, but as I staggered under her weight, I noticed another witch about to fall. I lowered the first witch none too gently and caught the next one and set her down. I was racing to grab the third when Jasper appeared in the doorway.

"Help!" I cried.

He was beside me in an instant, assisting with catching the witches that were dropping like overripe fruit. Tansy was the last one to fall and we caught her together.

"The bottom of the tower is flooded," Jasper said. "And the stairs are still covered in ice."

"Diego!" I cried.

"He'll be all right," he said. "He's a hellhound, he can blast hellfire at anything in his way."

I nodded. Diego was singularly capable of dealing with ice and snow.

"If we can't go down, how are we going to get the witches out of here?" I asked.

"Your sun has melted the ice above us. We'll have to levitate the coven up to the room at the top," Jasper said. "It's our only way out until the ice is completely melted and the water gone."

"Then what?" I could hear the water churning below us and I didn't love the idea of being stuck in the top of the tower if Odessa doubled back.

"We'll figure it out when we get there." He led the way to the stairs, using his power to pull the witches along with us. I wished I could help him, but this was beyond my abilities at present. I focused on keeping the unconscious witches upright with their heads out of the freezing water on the landing as he began to float them up the spiral stairs toward the top of the tower.

When we had all five witches drifting up the spiral steps, I glanced out the windows that we passed at the grounds below, looking for Diego or Odessa. I didn't see either of them and my anxiety spiked. Where had Diego gone? What exactly did he think he was going to do? When we caught up to him, I was giving him a piece of my mind, after I hugged him.

We reached the sixth level, and I could see that Jasper was straining while using so much magic to carry all five bodies. He was breathing hard and his hair was soaked with sweat. Tansy was the last witch, and just before her body crossed onto the landing, she started to slip. I caught her under the arms and hauled her across the wooden floor.

"We have to stop!" I yelled at Jasper over the sound of the ice cracking under the heat of my little sun, which was hovering in the center of the tower. "You're going to harm yourself if you keep going."

He shook his head. "I just need to rest for a second. We can't leave anyone behind."

"We won't, but we should try to wake them," I said. "Isn't there something in the emergency pouch Olive provided that we can use?"

"Not for this many witches." He leaned against the wall, his chest heaving.

"We need Tariq and one of his potions." I started to pace the landing, watching the ice melt and keeping an eye out for Diego.

"You called?" Tariq appeared on the steps above us and I yelped in surprise.

"What took you so long, mate?" Jasper slumped down to the floor as if he didn't have the strength to stand for one more second.

"You just sent for us ten minutes ago," Tariq protested.

"Us?" I asked. "Are Miles and Olive with you?"

"Olive is down below, siphoning the water in the tower back into the Harlem River without trying to cause a flood, and Miles is on the grounds, helping Diego track Odessa."

"Track her?" I asked. "She escaped then?"

"I'm afraid so." Tariq looked grim. He shrugged out of his backpack and unzipped it, pulling out a small brown glass vial. He held it out to Jasper. "It's nettle. It'll restore your strength."

Jasper didn't hesitate but unstoppered the bottle and swallowed its contents. Next Tariq pulled out a different vial and handed it to me. "Put a drop on the witches' temples and the insides of their wrists. It's a rosemary infusion and should wake them up in a few minutes."

I nodded. I started with Tansy, gently dabbing the strong-smelling oil as instructed. Her nose wrinkled and she shook her head. It was working. I made my way through the women until I finished the last one.

Tariq was examining Jasper and I was worried that the nettle elixir hadn't been enough to restore his strength. He still looked extremely pale.

"We lost her." Miles arrived on the landing with Diego beside him. The hellhound looked weary and I didn't have the heart to berate him for scaring me. Instead, I hurried across the floor and gently put my hand on his shoulder.

"Are you all right?"

"Once outside, that annoying little snowflake vanished right in front of me."

"But you're unharmed?"

"My dignity is wounded, but that's it."

I laughed and threw my arms around his thick neck. *"Oh, Diego, I was so worried. Don't do that to me again, okay?"*

Diego let out an annoyed grunt. *"They're all staring."*

"I don't care," I said. *"Promise me you'll be more careful."*

"Fine," he agreed and then shook me off like a bad case of fleas.

I turned to find Jasper, Miles, and Tariq staring at us just as Diego had said.

"What?" I asked.

"Were you two communicating nonverbally?" Miles asked.

"Oh, well, yes, Diego can speak in my mind," I said. "If that makes sense."

"And you can speak in his, too," Jasper said. "Just now you were clearly conversing without words."

I thought about it and realized I had just done that. I glanced at Diego, but he was busy grooming his chest with his tongue.

"I suppose so." I shrugged. "We just discovered it in the thick of fighting Odessa."

"You discovered it," Diego corrected me. *"I knew all along."*

"And we'll be discussing your sense of timing in the near future. Does this mean you can read my mind?" I asked. Because that would never do.

"No," Diego said. *"Unless you direct your thoughts to me, I am completely shut out of whatever you're thinking. Much like your grimoire, I can feel your emotions, however."*

"You're doing it again, love." Jasper glanced from me to Diego.

"Sorry." I grimaced. "I haven't really had time to process it and I have questions."

"I'm sure you do." Miles started to laugh, but it was more of a wheeze than a guffaw. He shook his head and glanced at me and said, "Only witches and their familiars can communicate like that. You officially have a hellhound as a familiar. You really are a most uncommon witch, Zoe Ziakas."

19

"This is the last time I take the bottom of the tower when we have an assignment like this." Olive strode onto the landing with her dark hair looking wild, and mud spots on her long black trench coat.

"The water is out. Well done, Olive." Miles leaned over the landing to look all the way to the bottom floor.

Olive waved him off. She was not one for praise. Instead, she glanced around the landing. The witches had woken up and were huddled around Diego, whose entire body was aflame, making the area toasty warm.

"The High Bridge Coven?" Olive asked me.

"What's left of it. Apparently, Odessa booted her second and third in command." I pointed to the witches. "From what I observed, it seemed that Odessa was siphoning off their power to feed her own."

Olive went very still, as did Miles and Tariq. Jasper already knew what Odessa had done because he'd seen it, too.

"Zoe's right," he said. "Odessa used a summoning circle

to hold them and then she kept them in suspended animation while she drained them."

Tariq sucked in a breath. "That is an unforgivable crime in the magical world."

"Is it?" I asked. "I mean, it seems like it should be. What will happen to Odessa when it's discovered she's been doing that?"

"She'll be stripped of her power and banished by the Global Council of Magisters," Miles said.

I stared at him. We'd tangled with a banished dark witch before. "Because that works so well."

He gave me a sympathetic look. "The council has learned from its previous mistakes."

I decided to let it go for now. The witches were rousing, but they all looked punch-drunk. While my colleagues discussed informing the council about Odessa, I crouched down beside Tansy and asked, "Are you okay?"

Her smile was loopy and she said, "Never better." Then she cupped my face with both of her hands. An electric shock blasted through me and I felt as if I'd been hit by lightning. *"This isn't over, baby witch, I'm coming for you."*

Tansy slumped back against the wall, and I stumbled back. That had not been Tansy. It had been Odessa talking through Tansy, I'd stake my life on it.

I glanced at the others. "Does Odessa still have a link with them?"

"Potentially, until her spell wears off," Miles said. "Why?"

I didn't want to talk about it right now. I wanted out of the tower and away from here as soon as possible. I gestured to the huddled witches. "Do you think they'll remember anything that happened?"

"No." Olive's voice was annoyed. "They're of no use to us. Let's go."

"We're not just leaving them here," Miles said.

"Why not?" Olive asked. "There's five of them. They'll be okay."

Miles stared at her.

"Fine, what do you suggest we do with five magically blissed-out witches?" Olive asked.

"We're going to deliver them to their homes," Miles said. "Zoe, Jasper, you two go on ahead back to the museum. We'll meet you there and debrief then."

"Sounds good," I said. I took two steps toward the stairs, thrilled to be anywhere but in this tower, when my legs gave out and the next thing I knew, the floor was rising to meet me.

I heard a shout and then a pair of arms scooped me up, yanking me back up into the air just before everything went black.

"Zoe, are you all right?" Jasper asked.

I was more tired than I'd ever been in my entire life. I was lying on the floor but still cradled against Jasper's chest, so I assumed I'd blinked out for just a moment. I forced my eyes open and found four people and a hellhound staring down at me. I covered my face with my arm.

"I'm fine," I said. "I just got a little lightheaded."

Tariq pushed forward and gently moved my arm to shine a light in my eyes. "Her pupils are blown out like the other witches. I think when Zoe stepped into the circle to confront Odessa, Odessa took the opportunity to drain some of her power."

Reflexively, I patted my pocket where I kept my grimoire. It was still there. I felt worry coming from the volume and I patted the book again, letting it know I was okay. The book's relief flooded through me at the same time Diego licked my face. His breath smelled like barbecue from all the fire he'd been blasting, but I knew he meant well. I stroked his head, avoiding the flames that still rippled off his coat.

I moved out of Jasper's arms and tried to stand. He set me on my feet and kept a hand on my back in case I went down again, no doubt.

"I believe you're partially right, Tariq, but there's more." I gestured at Tansy, who was twirling her hair around her fingers and staring into space. "Odessa reached me through her."

"How?" Miles asked in surprise.

I explained the electric shock I'd felt when I touched Tansy and the voice that came out of the initiate that clearly wasn't Tansy's. I apologized for not telling them when it happened, thinking I could save it for the debriefing. "I really just want to get out of here."

Olive and Miles exchanged a meaningful look and Miles turned to me and said, "I believe you're right, Zoe. I think Odessa likely did steal some of your magic when you were in the circle, and I think she used it to track you through Tansy so she could threaten you. You're going to have to be extremely careful until we know where she is and what her motive is."

I nodded. Thankfully, I was just too exhausted to be afraid.

Miles turned to Jasper and said, "Take Zoe back to the museum. I don't want to risk that happening again."

"On it," Jasper said. He moved as if he planned to carry

me, but I sidestepped out of his grasp. I was not about to let go of my dignity.

"I can walk."

He leaned close, his eyes studying my face as if to see for himself that I was all right. I wasn't used to people fussing over me. For most of my adult life, it had just been Agatha. It was oddly comforting and yet a bit stifling.

"If you start to feel faint, tell me," Jasper said.

"I promise."

We headed for the stairs. Miles called after us, "There are several cars waiting. Have one of them take you to the BODO." He glanced at Diego. "You'll need to go back to your puppy form for the ride."

Diego shook himself from snout to tail as if he'd just come in from the rain. The flames on his fur vanished, as did the smell of charcoal. Or was it the scent of brimstone? Never having had an occasion in my life to come across brimstone, I had no idea. Once again, Diego was a cute little bundle of puppy energy and he raced for the stairs with an enthusiasm I couldn't muster.

Mabel's room was waiting for me when we arrived. I knew I was going to spend another night sleeping in my office, so I sent Agatha a text so she wouldn't worry if she went looking for me at my house. I didn't go into the details, but I let her know we were all fine.

Knowing that the rest of the staff would be arriving soon, I didn't linger in the tub and chose to put on the clothes I'd worn before dressing for the coven meeting instead of the comfy pajamas and robe the room had waiting for me. Pity.

When I stepped into the main room, Miles, Olive, and Tariq were entering the library through the heavy iron door. Jasper and Diego must have heard them arrive, as they exited Jasper's office at the same time.

Miles glanced at me and nodded in approval. "You look much improved, Zoe."

"I feel it." Diego took his usual spot by my side and I rested my hand on his shoulder.

My assurance that I was fine did not stop Tariq from approaching with his tiny light to check my pupils. "Back to normal," he declared.

"If you're using a loose definition of normal," Olive said.

I glanced at her in surprise. "Did you just tease me?"

She shrugged. "You held your own against Odessa. You're not completely useless."

"That's high praise from Olive," Tariq whispered, and I smiled. I'd take the win.

"Shall we debrief in my office?" Miles asked, although it wasn't a question.

We followed him into his comfortably cluttered space. A fire was crackling in the fireplace and a small feast was spread out on the coffee table, with roast chicken, beef stew, mashed potatoes, fresh hot rolls, and a salad. I'd had a cup of tea and some cakes in Mabel's restorative room, but now I found I was starving.

The others must have felt the same because for the next fifteen minutes no one spoke and the only noise was the sound of utensils on plates and the occasional smacking of lips as the meal was savored. I'd felt mended before, but now I was fully healed and ready to nap.

When everyone was finished, Miles brought out a decanter and poured us each a small glass of a vibrant green liquid. I reached for mine, but Jasper stayed my hand.

"Sip it," he advised.

I gave him a side-eye. "That strong?"

"It's not alcohol, it's one of Tariq's elixirs," Jasper said.

I turned to Tariq. "What does it do?"

He held his small glass up to the light, examining the color. "It's called essence of aetherleaf and it's a regenerative, much like the nettle juice I gave Jasper in the tower, but this one is extra. It restores magical energy, focus, and inner balance after grueling spell work or a battle. The silvery leaf from the aether tree is the main ingredient, although it has no scent or flavor."

Both Olive and Miles sipped theirs and they seemed fine. I held the glass up to my nose and sniffed. I glanced at Tariq. "I smell basil and rosemary?"

He nodded. "Holy basil, to be exact. It acts as a mental restorer and the rosemary clears away magical static."

"I didn't know there was such a thing," I said. "For the green color, I'm assuming spirulina."

"Correct." Tariq sipped his.

I sniffed the glass again. "Lemon balm and ginseng?"

"Soothes the nerves and ginseng increases stamina." Tariq lifted his glass, indicating I should taste mine. "Of course, there's also nettle for endurance and honey, which is a natural sweetener."

I took a tentative sip. It tingled on my tongue. It tasted like I was eating the weeds in my backyard. I tried not to make a *bleck* grimace and failed.

Tariq burst out laughing. "Your face."

"What? It's . . . healthy." I couldn't force the word *good* out of my mouth.

This time Miles laughed. "You say that like healthy is a bad thing."

"I think Ziakas would prefer it tasted like a pizza," Olive observed.

"You're not wrong," I said. I glanced at Tariq. "Sorry."

"No need." He waved his hand dismissively. "Taste is subjective, but you still have to drink it. You need it after what you went through tonight."

I glanced at the glass and sighed. "Okay to chug it?"

"Absolutely, just don't spit it back up or you'll have to drink it again." He glanced at Jasper. "Which has happened to others."

Jasper turned to me. "And why I recommended sipping it."

I nodded. "I'm more of a *jump into the deep end* sort of gal." I threw back the essence of aetherleaf and it hit the back of my throat with a punch, but I refused to have to drink it twice. I swallowed convulsively a couple of times until I knew it would stay down. I set my glass decisively on the coffee table.

"Is this why you were buying aetherleaf at the Midnight Market?" I asked. "To make this elixir?"

"It's one of the reasons," he said. "I use aetherleaf in several potions. There really is nothing that restores a witch or mage to full power as well as this elixir."

"Which is the only reason we all agree to drink it," Olive

said. "Now, about tonight, did you discover anything about McWrath?"

"No." I shook my head. "Odessa knew or suspected I was there to find out about him and the *Book of Shadows*. She essentially laughed in my face. Everything happened so fast. It was like being ambushed, honestly."

"Even from my perch above, it felt as if everything unraveled quickly," Jasper said.

"Did any of the coven members say anything of interest to you?" Miles asked.

"The only one I spoke with was Tansy when she met me outside to escort me in." I thought back to that meeting and then straightened up. The penny! I'd taken it from my cloak and put it in my pocket when I got dressed.

I pulled out the elongated and embossed penny and studied it. It was tarnished and dingy, and there was a fancy building pressed on one side of it with the name Lyric Hall beneath it. Why would Tansy give me a penny for an old building? Was she trying to tell me where I'd find Odessa? McWrath? The *Book of Shadows*? All of the above?

"Tansy handed me this penny before we entered the tower, and when she did, she put her finger over her lips to indicate I shouldn't say anything. Weird, right?"

"May I?" Miles held out his hand and I put the penny in his palm.

His eyebrows drew together as his brow furrowed. I glanced at Jasper to see what he made of Miles's reaction.

"What is it?" Jasper asked.

Miles handed the penny to Olive. She remained impassive, as always, but her eyebrow with the scar through it ticked up just a notch. She handed the penny to Jasper, who became immediately solemn. He handed it to Tariq, whose eyes went wide, and he exclaimed, "Kai!"

I'd only heard him use this Nigerian expression a few times and it was always when he was shocked, like when we had a councillor from the Global Council of Magisters arrive unexpectedly at the museum. As far as I could tell, it was not an expression of happy surprise.

Tariq glanced up from the coin. "Do you think the witch who gave you this was telling you that McWrath could be found at Lyric Hall?"

I glanced at the coin resting on his palm. "Maybe? She said she was happy with whatever the coven decided, but I sensed she was afraid." I paused to glance at Diego, who was sacked out in front of the fireplace, snoring. "The coin appears to be old. Is Lyric Hall a real place? Does it still exist?"

"Oh, yes, it exists," Miles said. "Lyric Hall is an old opera house on the Hudson River. Its heyday was the Gilded Age of robber barons, but it was too costly to keep up and has been deserted since the Great Depression. A few people have tried to bring it back over the years, but it's heavily warded, haunted, and inhabited by all manner of evil entities. No one has lasted longer than two weeks before they abandon it."

"And they never fully recover from the experience," Olive said.

A ghostly shiver that felt like icy cold fingers skittered down my spine.

"All right?" Jasper asked.

I propped my elbows on my chair arms and rested my chin in my hands. "Not really. We're going to have to go to this Lyric Hall, aren't we?" Even to my own ears, I sounded petulant. In my defense it had been a hell of a night.

Miles gave me a sympathetic smile. "I'm afraid so, but don't worry. I have every confidence we can handle this."

I noticed that Olive, Tariq, and Jasper did not jump right in and agree with Miles's assessment of the situation. I tried not to be too concerned, but I could feel the grimoire in my pocket and it wasn't emitting confident vibes. Rather, it felt anxious, like if it had fingernails it would be biting them.

I glanced at where Diego slept, envying him his ignorance of the situation.

"I'm not asleep." Diego's voice popped into my head.

"So, you heard?" I asked.

He shifted in front of the fire, rolling onto his other side, which I took as a yes.

"What do you think?" I asked.

"We're doomed."

Somehow it was so much worse hearing the truth from a hellhound.

20

For the next week, the BODO was abuzz with preparations for our visit to Lyric Hall. Miles had several very intense meetings with the Global Council of Magisters. They were decidedly unhappy with the *Liber Umbrarum* being missing and positively alarmed that it was believed to be in McWrath's possession. Miles convinced them that we were the best option for getting the volume back, and I suspected they were only too relieved to let us put our lives on the line and spare them the trouble.

Blueprints of the building were studied, and our emergency kit bags were loaded with whatever Olive thought we might find useful. Of course, she kept changing her mind and taking the kits back, so I stopped learning how to use what was inside, deciding to wait until she was officially finished. Instead, I spent my time going over the grimoire page that Freya had disappeared into on the off chance that it could lead me to my mom.

It was during one of these study sessions that Jasper found me in my office staring into the fire, which had a nice blaze going. His dark hair fell over his brow and he was wearing a pale blue Aran sweater that matched his eyes. His lips turned up when he spotted me seated by the hearth with Diego stretched out at my feet.

"Any luck?" He sat on the floor facing me.

I shook my head. "I can't decipher the code. There's been no sign of Freya in the BODO, so I don't think she's managed to come back and now I'm wondering if I'm supposed to go get her." I paused, hoping my grimoire would throw some sort of emotion at me in answer, but it was annoyingly nonresponsive. I sighed.

"Sorry, love." Jasper held out a hand to me. "Would a hug make it better?"

"Maybe." I let him pull me to my feet and wrap his arms around me. For a person who wasn't a hugger by nature, I sure didn't mind being held by him. In fact, it was the most at peace I'd felt in days. I rested my head against his shoulder and listened to the steady beat of his heart.

"This is very boyfriend-like behavior," I observed.

"Is it?" One of his hands slid up and down my back in a soothing stroke while the other held me close. "Didn't you tell me that you don't do emotional entanglements?"

"I did." My nerves flickered. We were overdue to finish the conversation about us that we'd started on the roof before we'd been attacked by the shadow. Finding out that Jasper was half-demon had given me more to consider, but as I pulled back to study him, I knew it didn't matter.

I was officially emotionally entangled with this demon mage and there was simply no denying it. Still, the librarian in me needed more information before making a decision. I stepped out of his arms and retrieved my grimoire, placing it on its shelf behind my desk. "But, of course, I have questions."

"Naturally." He gestured for me to continue before he crossed his arms over his chest as a small smile played on his lips.

"Given that you're fifty, I'd like to know if you've been married before. I mean, when I thought you were thirty-six, I knew it might be possible, but now that I know you're fifty, it seems probable and I'm just wondering how that worked out for you?" My words were rushed because even though I wanted to know if he'd been married, I also didn't want to know. The thought of Jasper deeply involved with someone else bothered me. It felt like jealousy, and having never felt that emotion before, I decided I didn't like it and refused to suffer it. I shrugged my shoulders, shaking it off, and then fixed my gaze on him.

"Married? Me?" He looked horrified.

"Yes, you," I said. "You could have been married multiple times for all I know."

"Oh, no, not me." He dropped his arms and planted his hands on his hips. "I've never been married. I don't even like going to weddings."

"Really?" I blinked in surprise and then confessed, "I don't enjoy weddings either."

"Is it the food, the music, or the cockeyed optimism of it all that gets to you?" he asked.

"All of the above," I said. "Although, I did go to one wedding between two booklovers when they held it in the library. They served tea and cake and after they were declared married, everyone was told to curl up with a good book and read for their two-hour 'reception.' It was glorious."

"It sounds perfect." Jasper laughed. "Zoe, love, you really are the perfect woman."

I felt my face grow warm and I glanced down at the top of my desk. "Just to be fully transparent, I've never been married either."

He said nothing, so I peeked at him as he ran his finger along the edge of my desk. He glanced at me from beneath his thick dark eyelashes. He looked ridiculously and heartbreakingly shy when he asked, "Any particular reason you haven't married, other than loathing weddings, of course?"

Diego lifted his head from where he was sprawled, and glanced between us. With a deep doggy sigh, he rolled over, facing away from us. *"Let me know when you two are done with all this goopy emotional stuff."*

"Mind your business," I responded.

I circled my desk to stand directly in front of Jasper. I tipped my head back so I could stare up at him and said, "I never met the right person."

An expression of relief passed over his face, and he slipped his arm around my waist and pulled me close. "Is that so?"

"It is."

He leaned down as if he would kiss me, but I put my finger over his lips and said, "And you?"

A slow smile curved the warm lips beneath my fingertip, and I felt a zing of awareness spark between us. I pulled my hand away and tried to pretend that my touching him or him touching me had no impact on my fevered brain, nope, none at all.

"I never met the right person either . . . until now." This time he leaned down and kissed me.

I would like to think I had the willpower to resist him, but I didn't. I wrapped my arms around his neck and pulled him in tight. All the worry I'd suffered while he'd been gone came bubbling up to the surface, and I just wanted to lose myself in him, in us, reaffirming that he was here in one piece and he was okay.

My hands ran over him as he kissed me in soft sips and deeper, more satisfying kisses that left me gasping for breath. With one hand I twined my fingers in his soft hair and with the other, I dug my nails into the roughness of his wool sweater, as I breathed in the scent that was solely his. Jasper. My Jasper.

When we parted, he cupped my face with his hands, holding my gaze with his. "Does this mean we're officially a couple?"

"Yes." The answer came out emphatically and Jasper grinned before he kissed me again, which was met with a deep doggy snore from Diego.

"Why do we have to approach by boat?" I asked. "Isn't there a portal or something we can slide through? If the place is haunted, there really should be a portal."

Jasper, Diego, and I were seated in the bow of the boat while Olive, Tariq, and Miles sat in the stern. Captain Merrin, who piloted the small craft, was an old fishing buddy of Miles's who also happened to be a river sprite.

Captain Merrin had been a ferryman on the Hudson for years. When he fell off his boat during a storm, he couldn't find the shore and began to drown. He brokered a deal with the river, offering his soul to it in exchange for his life. The river accepted and Merrin was bound to the river until it ran dry. I did not think the Hudson would be doing that anytime soon.

Merrin was short and stout, but his skin had an iridescent quality that reminded me of the translucence of water, and his eyes were a vibrant green. He was friendly and full of riddles. He wore his captain's hat with pride, and he was quick with a joke or a song. Truthfully, it was hard not to like him.

The bitterly cold winter wind made my eyes water even though the boat was moving so slowly it made almost no wake. Despite liking Merrin, I really wasn't a fan of deep, dark, freezing water and had it been left to me, I would have chosen to walk right up to the front door and confront head-on whatever McWrath threw at me. In other words, I would have been dead in about fifteen minutes, which was why I wasn't in charge.

"The wards around the house are primarily on the land. It's harder to ward over water, especially a body of water with a strong current," Jasper explained.

"Well, that is unfortunate." I burrowed more deeply into my cloak. Diego, in his hellhound form, leaned against one side of me, offering his warmth, while Jasper sat on my other side doing the same. I should have been toasty warm, but the cold I felt was deep in my bones and I knew it for what it was. Fear.

I was terrified. Going up against a demon as powerful as McWrath was unfathomable to me. The man . . . er . . . demon had managed to break into the vault of the BODO and steal the *Liber Umbrarum*. As far as I knew, no one had ever broken into the library before.

I believed Jasper's father was right that McWrath had used his shadow form to enter the museum, captured Miles and his aura to gain access to the BODO and its vault, and stolen the book. Having seen the entire museum become encased in a shadow, and given that the snippet of shadow we'd found belonged to McWrath, it passed the smell test.

"What are you thinking about?" Jasper asked me.

"The logistics of McWrath stealing the *Book of Shadows,*" I said. "I think your father's theory is right, but I'd love to hear McWrath admit it."

"You're not alone there," Jasper said. "Miles and I have gone over it ad nauseam. Given that Miles can't remember anything from the gala, we have no provable hypothesis. It's maddening."

The boat slowed and I glanced at the dark woods and the unlit opera house in the distance. There were no lights anywhere on the property. It was abandoned, so there shouldn't be lights, but the creep factor was ridiculously high on this rendezvous and I wondered yet again why we couldn't do this during daylight.

"We're almost there," Miles said. "Remember the plan. Expect everything and everyone you cross paths with to try and kill you."

The boat bumped against a rickety old dock, and Tariq and Jasper hopped out to hold the boat steady for the rest of us.

Diego waited for no one and jumped out onto the dock and started sniffing the old planks as if to ascertain whether there was any danger present. I followed Diego, grasping Jasper's extended hand to steady myself, leaving Miles and Olive to follow.

"Send the signal when you need me to pick you up," Captain Mirren said. He glanced at the group of us as if he never expected to see any of us again. Not encouraging. "A captain's lantern in the night, I guide you home with steady light. I sit where tides and shorelines meet. Tall, alone, I watch the fleet. What am I?"

"A lighthouse," our team said together, and Mirren nodded.

"Just so." He raised his hand in farewell and Jasper pushed his boat away from the dock. We watched him depart with only the rippling sound of the water breaking the silence.

We had planned our invasion of Lyric Hall using all the information we could gather. The difficulty was that most of the stories about the abandoned opera house were hearsay. We had no way of knowing what we were walking into and it put me on a razor's edge of anxiety.

The wind moved the bare tree limbs over us and I tensed, expecting the trees to snatch us. A plank creaked underfoot and I jumped, anticipating a hand grabbing my ankle from beneath the boards and pulling me into the cold, dark water. Jasper put his hand on my back to guide me, and I let out a yelp.

"Are you all right, Zoe?" Tariq asked.

"Sorry! Yes, I'm fine, just a bit keyed up," I said.

Tariq immediately dove into the large duffel he'd brought that was presently strapped to Diego's back. Unlike Olive's emergency kit bags, Tariq had brought everything and anything he thought might be useful from his lab. Diego had been outfitted with a harness to carry the bag for him as it would slow Tariq down too much to carry it himself.

"Here." Tariq handed me what looked like the sort of gummy people used to get high.

"No, thanks," I said. "I don't think a gummy would be advisable right now."

"It's not a hallucinogen." Tariq shook his head. "It's called a moon melt. It will sharpen your focus and relax you at the same time." I stared at him until he rolled his eyes. "It's lavender and mint based, I swear."

"I'll take one of those," Miles said. He held out his hand and I watched as he popped it into his mouth. To my surprise, Olive held out her hand for one as well.

She saw my expression and said, "It can't hurt."

Jasper took one, too, so I popped it into my mouth. It was refreshing and soothing at the same time. I felt my senses sharpen even as my heart rate slowed.

I reached out and put my hand on Tariq's sleeve. "I never should have doubted you. Thank you."

He smiled a slash of white teeth in the darkness. "Well, I can't blame you for refusing initially, you made a natural assumption."

"That's enough chatter. We don't want any of McWrath's spies alerting him to our presence," Olive said. "Let's go."

She stepped off the dock and onto the snowy riverbank. With her dark hair and dressed in her usual all black, Olive faded from sight in a matter of seconds as she strode into the trees, their branches folding in behind her as if to say they had her back. Interesting.

"After you." Jasper gestured for me to lead.

My steps were not nearly as confident as Olive's. The tree branches did not move out of my way, and I was forced to shield my face as I pushed into the thick woods behind her.

"Olive!" I hissed. "Where are you? Olive!"

"Shh." Olive hushed me from a small clearing. "You're loud enough to wake the dead."

"I get it. Because I'm a necromancer. Really funny." I was not amused.

"I thought so." Her pale face was the only thing I could see in the dark, and I realized that out here in the woods, she practically glowed. I'd learned she was a Fae witch, but we'd never discussed it. Obviously now was not the time, but I was decidedly curious as I watched her affinity with the natural world surrounding us.

"Are we all clear on the objective?" Miles asked as he, Jasper, and Tariq joined us.

"We are to split up and approach the opera house from different directions," Tariq said.

"The four compass points," Olive clarified.

"Exactly," Miles said. "Whoever manages to get into the opera house first will signal to the rest of us that they've found the entrance. Do you have your runes?"

I checked my pocket. Sure enough, the flat oval moonstone engraved with the witches' sigil for connection was there. We each had one. Whoever found a way into the opera house first would activate their moonstone and draw the other moonstones to it. Sort of like using walkie-talkies but with rocks.

Everyone mumbled affirmatively that they had their stone. Miles then reminded us of the compass point we'd been assigned to. Jasper and I had been paired to approach the house from the east, while Tariq and Diego took the west. Olive would head in from the south, leaving Miles the front door at the north.

I didn't like having the group split up even though I knew it made sense to cover more ground and be less conspicuous. As the least experienced witch, it was ridiculous for me to be concerned about these far-superior witches and mages, and yet, I was worried. I'd become very fond of them all over the past few months and I would be devastated if anything happened to any of them, including Olive.

"Be careful, everyone. Keep your guard up," Miles said and then he vanished. Olive was the next to disappear and then Tariq and Diego, who paused beside me to shove his head under my hand for a couple of scritches before he trotted off.

Jasper held out his hand to me, and I grasped his fingers with mine. As we stepped into the shadows together, I couldn't shake the feeling that something very bad was going to happen. We slipped between the trees as quietly as possible. I was impressed with our lack of noise and realized that Jasper must have muted us because there was no way I was tromping through the woods with the grace of a big cat when I usually thrashed around like a wild turkey.

"How do you know which way is east?" I asked.

Jasper pointed to the sky, which meant nothing to me, but I assumed he could navigate the stars like some old-timey sailor. It would have been impressive if it didn't remind me that he was a decade and a half older than me. Not that an age gap was such a big deal, but when the man in question was hot and likely to stay that way while I aged faster than him, well, the doubts started to creep in much like the fog that enveloped us at the edge of the forest.

We had been studying blueprints and old photos of Lyric Hall all week while we formulated our plan. I knew that the eastern lawn of the old opera house had once been a beautiful garden with statuary of Greek gods and perfectly manicured rosebushes in every conceivable color.

As soon as Jasper and I stepped into the garden, a thick suffocating fog began to swirl around our feet. Jasper's fingers tightened around mine. "Whatever you do, do not let go of me."

"This isn't a normal fog, is it?" I asked.

"No." Jasper's expression was grim. "We likely won't be able to see anything in a matter of seconds. I don't want to alarm you, but be prepared should anything or anyone appear."

I didn't like the sound of that at all. Who was going to appear? Bad guys? Minions? McWrath himself?

"Let's hurry." Jasper pulled me into the extensive garden. We raced along the gravel paths. There was snow-covered statuary everywhere and when we passed one particularly nubile woman carrying a strategically placed basket of fruit, I thought how tiring it would be to carry that basket for all eternity.

The fog was at our waists when we reached the edge of the garden bed closest to the building. I wondered if the others were already in place or if they, too, were racing the fog. I hoped they were ahead of it. The sooner we got into the opera house the better.

When I stepped one foot out of the garden, the fog thickened into a deep dense cloud that made it impossible to see anything. My equilibrium went bonkers and I wasn't even sure which way was up anymore.

"Zoe?" Jasper's voice seemed so far away. I squeezed his fingers to reassure myself he was right there. He immediately squeezed back.

"I can't see you," I said. Panic made my voice wobbly.

"It's all right, love," he whispered. "Listen, so long as you hang on to your connection rune, the vintage opera ticket that Miles found, and the bag of tricks Olive gave you, you should be safe even if we get separated. But let's not get separated, okay?"

"Okay."

I liked Jasper's confidence, but his charming British accent coming out of the fog like a disembodied voice didn't soothe the growing fear that Tariq's calming gummy was no longer able to banish. I couldn't shake the feeling that something very bad was coming for us and would be there in mere seconds.

We crept forward. Was it forward? I had no idea. I wasn't claustrophobic by nature, but not being able to see anything, including the person I was clinging to, made this feel like an out-of-body experience. The ground beneath my feet was the only thing I could be certain of—that, and the hand that held mine.

I should have known better than to tempt fate by even thinking such a thing. I stepped forward and kicked something big and hard with my right foot. I yelped as a spike of pain shot from my toes to my teeth.

I dropped Jasper's hand and hopped on one foot while I hissed a stream of expletives that would have sent my Mamie running for the soap. I limped in a little circle, trying to walk the pain off.

"Zoe, are you all right?" Jasper's voice came out of the thick fog as he reached for me in the darkness. Taking my gloved hand in his with a firm grip, he said, "You have to be more careful and don't let go of me. Not for one second."

"Sorry. I'm clinically clumsy." I flexed my toes to make certain none were broken. I was suddenly grateful to have chosen my steel-toed hiking boots for this expedition. Jasper said nothing more, so I felt compelled to nudge him. "Well?"

"Well, what?" he asked. He sounded impatient, which was not a tone I'd ever heard from him before. I wondered if he was feeling stressed and my chatter wasn't helping. Too late, I had to finish the bit now.

"Welllllll, when I say I'm clumsy, you're supposed to tell me I'm not, that I'm as graceful as a ballerina. If you want to maintain boyfriend status, you can't miss your cue." I was teasing him, but there was no responding chuckle or huff of laughter.

Abruptly, Jasper stopped walking and I slammed into his back. The fog made it impossible to see his face, and the back of his coat felt wrong. Jasper had been wearing his usual long black wool coat, and this was . . . velvet? I reached out a hand and patted his back where I knew his shoulder blade would be. My hand touched soft velvet and it was the top of his shoulder, making this body shorter by several inches. This person . . . being . . . whatever . . . was definitely not Jasper.

21

I tried to yank my hand out of his, but his grip tightened, painfully squeezing my fingers until I thought my bones would crunch.

"Stop struggling, Zoe, it won't do you any good." That voice. I recognized that voice. Fury heated me up from the inside out, and I opened my free hand and a ball of red-hot light sat in my palm, evaporating the fog that surrounded it. I raised it up to see. Sure enough, Rowan Thorne stared down at me.

He was dressed in a velvet cloak of midnight blue over a silver shirt and black pants and boots. His dark brown, almost black gaze met and held mine. His wavy shoulder-length white hair was styled in a half ponytail with only the top half of his hair pulled back. A lone wavy strand of hair framed his face, accentuating his feminine beauty.

"Let me go!" I snapped. I was seconds from throwing my ball of light at him.

"I'm trying to help you," Rowan hissed.

"Oh, sure, that's why you invited me to that coven meeting

where Odessa planned to drain me and then drown me." I wrenched my hand out of his. "Do you work for her? Are you one of her coven minions?"

In the glowing red light, I could see his jaw set. I'd pissed him off. Good. He had a long way to go before he matched my level of rage. I stomped forward, crowding him, pushing against his chest with my free hand and forcing him backward. "Where is Jasper?"

A look passed over Rowan's face that caused my heart to stutter in my chest. Was it fear? Sadness? Uncertainty?

Something inside of me went into a panic spiral. I'd just gotten Jasper back. I was not ready to lose him again. A polite way to describe what happened would be to say I lost my shit. Fury exploded out of me and I launched myself at Thorne, knocking him to the ground. I followed him down and kneeled on his chest. My orb of red exploded into streams of light that I used to stake him to the ground as if I were sacrificing him to the gods.

"Where is Jasper?" My voice was like nothing I had ever heard before, deep, growly, and rather terrifying.

Thorne wasn't impressed. He stayed passive under my magic, not even straining against the bonds that held him. His eyes narrowed and a slow smile curved his lips. "You care for him."

To my utmost mortification, I felt an embarrassed flush heat my face. I had never been comfortable expressing my feelings, and calling out my concern about Jasper's well-being because I cared for him as more than a colleague made me feel vulnerable and extremely uncomfortable.

"I care about all of my colleagues," I said. "Now where is he?"

Thorne wasn't buying it. In fact, he looked amused by my flustered state. I felt my grimoire in my pocket seethe on my behalf. I took heart in its support and decided to see what I could do with these magical tethers. I closed my fingers into two tight fists and moved them apart as if I was stretching something. My magical bonds began to stretch, pulling each of Thorne's limbs in a different direction. A look of surprise passed over Thorne's face and I felt a decided satisfaction.

"Where is Jasper?" I repeated the question while holding my fists steady.

Thorne glowered. I moved my fists apart, and the cords stretched his limbs until his back arched up from the snowy ground. Despite the icy cold weather, a bead of sweat slid down the side of my face. It was taking everything I had to hold him and I didn't know how much longer I could continue.

"I don't know!" Thorne yelled. His head was tipped back and his neck was straining. "Truly, I don't know!"

"Bullshit." I forced my hands farther apart until I was panting from the effort.

"All right, I'll tell you, just stop!" Thorne pleaded.

Good thing he caved, because my arms were shaking and I didn't think I could pull another inch. Still, I didn't lessen the hold. "Tell me where he is first."

"He's inside. McWrath has him," Thorne said. "And just so we're clear, I do not work for Odessa. I work for McWrath."

"Is that supposed to be better?" I asked. "McWrath stole the *Liber Umbrarum* from the BODO."

"You have to admit that's impressive. Has anyone ever stolen anything from the BODO before?" Thorne asked and I was pleased to see a sheen of sweat on his forehead as well.

"It's not impressive, it's criminal," I corrected him, refusing to answer his question. "Show me where Jasper is."

"Ask nicely," he said.

I glared at him. "Show me where Jasper is or I'll turn you into one of the statues in this garden, naked and with your private bits shrinkled from the cold. Not a great look for eternity, if you ask me."

It was a threat designed to scare Thorne into compliance, but instead he laughed. It was a great big bellowing sound that might have provoked a return smile from me if we had not been on opposite sides of things. His dark eyes glinted in amusement.

"I can see why Jasper is so taken with you, Zoe Ziakas," he said.

I rolled my eyes as I lifted my knees off his chest and stood. I was not discussing my relationship with Thorne. I kept the cords tight around his wrists and ankles, giving them enough slack to allow him to rise. "Take me to Jasper. Now."

Thorne rolled up to his knees. When he lifted his hand to brush the hair out of his eyes, I yanked the cord tight, keeping him from it. It wouldn't do to let him think he had free range of motion. He lifted one white eyebrow and I shrugged. He pushed to his feet and walked toward the large wooden door tucked into an elaborate stonework arch that was covered in overgrown vines.

Of course, the door creaked ominously when he pushed it open. I would have been disappointed if it hadn't. I held the lines of magic encircling Thorne's wrists and ankles with one hand while taking the connection rune out of my pocket with the other. I ran my thumb around the sigil of four arrows with their points meeting in the center three times in a clockwise direction until it started to glow. It would lead the others to this entrance if they hadn't found a way in on their own.

Thorne stepped inside and I followed. Miles had us study the floor plan of the old opera house so that we would know where we were when we entered. I knew that the east entrance door opened into a wing of offices and dressing rooms.

I was prepared for the long hallway with many rooms. Given the hall's decades of abandonment, I'd expected peeling wallpaper and moldy carpet and the dank smell of neglect. Logically, the interior should have been as creepy as the exterior. It wasn't.

Instead, bright wall sconces with fancy frosted glass lit the way, illuminating the rich Aubusson carpeting underfoot, the decorative plasterwork trimmed with gold, and several large malachite vases on golden pedestals set against the wall at precise intervals. I blinked as I took in a lavish and lush interior that looked as new as if it were in its prime.

"Gorgeous, isn't it?" Thorne sighed and leaned forward to smell the burgundy roses that filled the first vase. "The Gilded Age was truly magnificent, wasn't it?"

"If you like robber barons and the exploitation of the working class and the poor, sure." I gestured to the opulence, forgetting that my mannerisms were tied to him, and his right arm jerked forward and he cuffed himself on the chin.

He turned his head slowly in my direction and I wrinkled my nose and said, "Sorry . . . mostly. How is all this possible? Where did the fresh flowers come from?"

"McWrath is a very powerful demon." He shrugged. "Are

you positive you want to take him on for Jasper? Wouldn't it be better to meet with McWrath and negotiate your way out of this?"

"Negotiate?" I repeated. "No! I want the *Book of Shadows* back and I want my boyfr—colleague returned unharmed. There will be no negotiation. Now, lead me to Jasper."

"I really wish you wouldn't take that tone with me," Thorne said. "It's quite rude."

"And setting me up with Odessa Van Doren in the water tower, where she tried to kill me, wasn't?" I asked.

"That was unfortunate," Thorne said. "Odessa can be territorial."

"Territorial? What did she think I was going to do? Take over her coven?" I asked.

"She believes McWrath is more interested in you than she's comfortable with, and between you and me, she's right. You have great potential and could easily take her place if you aligned yourself with McWrath." He rubbed one of the rose petals between his thumb and forefinger, and its scent perfumed the air.

"How could McWrath be interested in me when we've never met? If he is, it's because he wants my grimoire," I said. I felt my book go cold in my pocket as if it didn't approve of me mentioning it. I resisted the urge to comfort it by placing my hand over my pocket. It wouldn't do to let Thorne know that I had it on me.

"I don't think that's the only reason." He shook his head and his white hair swayed just below his shoulders. "You're also young and beautiful—"

"Not that young, not that beautiful," I argued.

"And—" he continued undeterred, but I interrupted him.

"And in possession of one of the most powerful grimoires in existence," I said. "I know my grimoire is my value in the magical realm, you don't need to gas me up."

His white eyebrows lifted in surprise. "You don't see yourself as a valuable commodity with your looks, intelligence, and innate magical ability."

"Oh, I think I'm very valuable," I said. "Especially to myself. I don't particularly care if other people find value in me or not, and I certainly could not care less what a demon thinks of me."

He crossed his arms over his chest and leaned with his back against the wall. "Fascinating."

I didn't like his scrutiny. It made my skin feel itchy, and I couldn't stop myself from noting all the exits in the hallway. Where were the others? They should be here by now.

Thorne suddenly pushed off the wall. "Time to go. Someone's coming. I wonder if it's McWrath or maybe it's Odessa." His grin was wicked. "Wish I could stay to find out. Sorry, my dear, it's been . . . interesting. Please remember that I did try to help you."

"Go? You're not going anywhere—" I hadn't finished my sentence when he was gone. *Poof!* The magical cords I'd used to hold him lay discarded on the ground. What the hell? Had he been able to leave at any time and was just humoring me? I wanted to punch something.

Instead, and quite maturely I thought, I concentrated on my core, tapping into my magic. When I held out my hands, the discarded cords of red light were siphoned back inside of me, which was what I'd hoped would happen, although I really had nothing but instinct to go on. Cool.

Thorne had said someone was coming. Hopefully it was one of my colleagues. But if it wasn't, I needed to get out of the hallway. Back outside? No. The plan had been to get inside the building, and I wanted to find Jasper, whom I suspected was in here. I decided to try to find Tariq. Diego was with him and maybe he could sniff out Jasper's whereabouts.

I hurried down the hallway, checking the offices and dressing rooms as I went, hoping Jasper might be in one of them. He wasn't. The rooms were empty, but like the hallway, they were resplendent in their Gilded Age décor. Truly, I had never seen so much gilt and mother-of-pearl inlay in my life.

I exited the hallway through a green-velvet-curtained doorway and found myself in the corridor that led to the seats in the main theater. If I crossed the auditorium, I might be able to find Tariq and Diego or at least be on the west side of the building when they entered. Assuming they were still outside stuck in the fog, I could let them in.

Decision made, I stepped into one of the curtained alcoves that led to the seats. A man with heavily pomaded silver hair and a very stylish mustache stepped in front of me.

I jumped with a small cry. "Oh, hi, can you help me? I'm looking for a tall, dark-haired man, speaks with a British accent."

"Ticket, please." He bowed his head slightly. He was wearing a burgundy uniform of a matching jacket and pants with pale blue piping along the collar and cuffs. It was an old-fashioned style that I'd expect on a bellhop or an elevator operator from the previous century. An outline of the opera house along with the name Lyric Hall was embroidered onto the upper left lapel of the jacket. This man worked here or . . . he had at one time.

It took me a moment to realize he wasn't fully corporeal and I could see through him if I squinted. Great, a ghost usher.

His face was impassive as he repeated, "Ticket, please."

I stared beyond him at the huge theater and noted it was brightly lit as if expecting hundreds of operagoers to arrive, and yet it was completely empty.

"I don't have—" I started to say and then remembered that I did have a ticket. Miles had said that sometimes theater workers who loved the theater more than life occasionally refused to leave. Which was why he'd found old tickets from the Lyric Hall's heyday and reproduced them magically just in case we ran into any old staff that lingered. "Oh, wait, just a second, I do have my ticket."

I reached into my pocket and pulled out the duplicated ticket. "Here you go."

"Very good, miss." The man took my ticket and turned to escort me to my seat.

I followed him down the steps into the theater, through the rows and up to the front, where he directed me to a seat in the fifth-row center. The seats were narrow and embroidered in an opulent tapestry of green, red, blue, and gold. The usher waited for me to sit, so I sat. I had no idea what a ghost usher would do if a guest refused to sit, and I didn't particularly want to find out. I figured once he left, I'd sneak out and find the others and hopefully Jasper.

The need to scream my colleagues' names until they appeared was roiling inside me, but after talking to Thorne, I didn't want to bring any more attention to myself than I already had. If Odessa and McWrath were here, they could show up at any time. The feeling of being utterly alone swamped me. I wasn't one to wallow or feel sorry for myself, but in that moment, I was feeling so out of my depth, it was hard to breathe. I forced myself to hold it together.

The usher turned and walked away and I went to get up, but I couldn't. There was nothing tying me to the seat, but I couldn't budge. It was as if I'd been glued in place. I pushed against the armrests and wriggled and wiggled, but I couldn't get any leverage to rise.

The light dimmed and eerie music started to play from the orchestra pit. A feeling of deep foreboding came from my grimoire and I was right there with it. This was some *Phantom of the Opera*–level shit that I was truly not prepared to deal with.

The music swelled. I scanned the dark theater looking for the usher. He was nowhere to be seen. It was just me in the theater and it made me feel vulnerable, as if I were the lone target at a shooting range.

Was McWrath here? What about Odessa? Why had Thorne gone along with being tied up only to ditch me? Did he know about the show? Was there a show? Panic caused the blood to pound in my ears, and I could barely hear the creepy music over the thumping bass beat of my heart.

The music reached a crescendo and the curtain started to open. I could almost hear the hushed delight of decades of operagoers, eager to watch the show. The usher appeared in front of me and began to clap, but his ghostly hands made no sound. He glared at me until I raised my hands and began to applaud. It sounded weird, a slow clap that echoed in the immense hall. Satisfied, the usher faded away, disappearing from sight.

A single spotlight snapped on, lighting the center of the stage, and there, standing with his head and arms limp, was Jasper. I stopped clapping and cried out. I tried to get out of my seat, but I couldn't budge.

Tears of frustration sprang to my eyes and I started to yell, "Let him go!"

The usher appeared in front of the stage and whooshed at me, flying over the tops of the seats. He stopped inches away from me, put his finger over his lips, and gave me a hard stare. I closed my mouth and he disappeared.

The music began again with a boom of the timpani drum. My gaze shot to the stage to see Jasper yanked upright like a marionette. I gasped. It wasn't *like* a marionette, Jasper was actually dangling from several magical cords, ice-blue in color—Odessa!—and he was awkwardly forced to step lively across the stage. When it looked as if he'd trip, he was yanked sharply into the air and then plopped back down.

It was too much. I fought against the hold in my seat, trying to break free. I realized I was panicking and made myself be still. Watching Jasper forced to high kick to the music was going to break me. Where were the others? Why was no one here to help me?

The music changed and a backdrop was lowered behind Jasper. It was a poorly painted and very two-dimensional scene of a street of generic shop fronts. Despite myself, I watched, terrified to see what happened next. When Olive appeared as a marionette just like Jasper, I thought I might have a heart attack.

Olive's dark gaze went straight to me in the audience, and it felt as if she were trying to pull me toward her by sheer force of will. The chair was not giving me up, however, and I ended up feeling like a human taffy pull.

"Stop it!" I cried. An evil *bwa ha ha* responding laugh from backstage was the only answer, and I'd have bet my way out of this hellscape that it belonged to Odessa.

Before I could protest any more, Tariq and Miles were trotted out. The music became so loud there was no way to shout over it. I watched helplessly as my colleagues and friends were subjected to the torture of not having control of their bodies. They were forced to skip and dance and jump ridiculously high. I was terrified Miles was going to throw his back out, and still the music and dancing went on and on.

When the music changed and my four colleagues were left hanging, suspended in the air with their feet hanging a foot off the ground, very reminiscent of the witches at the coven meeting, I knew something even worse was about to happen, but I couldn't fathom what.

As the music became a farcical discordant noise, Diego came out from behind one of the poorly painted shop fronts. Like the others, he was being controlled like a life-sized puppet, but he was dressed in a polka-dot clown suit with a pointy hat on his head. He was in his full hellhound form, and the mocking cruelty of the costume and the woebegone expression on his face made a fury boil up inside of me that felt volcanic.

I should have known it would have been too lucky for Diego to have escaped; besides, he was too loyal for that. Also, I should have been emotionally prepared that whatever Odessa had in store for me would be something designed to break me. It was fair to say the witch, and I meant that in the mean sense, not the magical one, had succeeded.

"If you would be so kind as to put me out of my misery, I'd be eternally grateful." Diego's voice sounded in my head.

"That's not going to be necessary," I answered.

I put my hand over the grimoire in my pocket and muttered, "Don't freak out."

The grimoire responded by flooding me with feelings of reproach, as if it was all in on my fury and how dare I doubt it. Okay then.

I filled my lungs with air and then used the trick that Miles had taught me when the Books of Dubious Origin collection occasionally got out of hand, much like it had the night of the gala. I tapped into my core magic to make my voice as loud and as long as a slow-moving rumble of thunder.

"Enough!" I bellowed. I might have overshot because my chair immediately released me and I fell, banging my knees on the hard floor. Also, the magic that held my friends vanished and they were instantly dropped, sprawling onto the stage in a tangle of limbs.

I pulled myself to my feet and ran toward them. The ghost usher tried to stop me, but I blasted right through him, which he did not enjoy, judging by the expletives he yelled.

I vaulted onto the stage and raced straight for Diego. His magical bonds had vanished, too, and I ripped the clown suit off him and threw it on the floor in front of him.

"Burn it," I said.

"With pleasure." Diego opened his mouth and flames shot out, melting the horrible costume and scorching the historic hardwood floor. I didn't care. In that moment, I would have been happy to burn the entire building down.

Instead, I ran backstage. I was hunting Odessa and I would not rest until I found her. I ran between old pieces of scenery and props stacked here and there, jumped over coiled ropes, and found the metal ladder to the upper level. I was four rungs up when an arm wrapped around my middle and I was plucked off.

Instinct took over, but instead of using magic, which was not entirely intuitive yet, I balled up my hand and tried to punch whoever had grabbed me. My fist was caught by a large hand at the same time I was set on my feet. I spun around to find Jasper standing there, his hand around mine.

"It's okay, Zoe." He used my fist to pull me into his arms. "You did great. It's okay."

"She's up there," I protested, pulling back and pointing to the scaffolding. "I heard Odessa. I'm not done with her."

"Oh, I'd say you are." Miles joined us, brushing his clothes off from where he'd fallen. "That was quite the banshee screech you let loose."

"Excuse me?" I asked.

"Banshee. You." Tariq had a finger in his ear and was wiggling it as if trying to clear it.

"That's not possible . . . is it?" I asked. Diego trotted to my side and sat leaning against me as if in solidarity.

"Lyra Luna would have been proud," Jasper said. "You managed to break the spell that held us."

"It had to be Odessa," I said.

"Probably." Olive was fastening her hair at the nape of

her neck with a hair band. "We can't know for certain because you blasted her into next week with that yell of yours."

"For real?" I asked.

Miles waved his hand in a more-or-less gesture. "Not exactly into next week, but you definitely fried her for a bit, making this an opportune time to search the building for the *Liber Umbrarum.* If we split up, we can search the place before Odessa regains her powers. And be mindful, we have no idea where McWrath is or who else is on the premises."

"Oh, right." In all the chaos, I'd forgotten that our purpose was to retrieve the *Book of Shadows.* "About that." I turned to Jasper and said, "Rowan Thorne is here."

22

Jasper went very still. "You saw him?"

"More than that," I said. "I tripped in the garden and suddenly I was holding *his* hand and you were gone. Where did you go?"

"No idea," Jasper said. "I remember you tripped, then I stumbled in the fog, lost consciousness, and woke up in that macabre marionette nightmare."

The others all nodded so I assumed their experiences were similar.

"What did Thorne say?" Jasper asked. "What's he doing here?"

I shrugged. "He said he works for McWrath and he seemed very impressed by McWrath's break-in at the BODO. I thought I was successfully using my magic to hold him, but then Thorne said 'someone is coming' and he poofed right out of the bonds I'd used."

"Wait." Olive held up her hands. "You managed to tie up Rowan Thorne?"

"At the time, I thought so, but he got out of it so easily, I realized he'd been playing me," I said.

"Did he mention in what capacity he works for McWrath?" Miles asked.

"No." I shook my head. "He seemed to think my time here would be better spent negotiating a position for myself in McWrath's regime rather than looking for the *Book of Shadows*."

"Bloody hell." Jasper ran a hand through his hair in frustration.

"All right, keep an eye out for Thorne as well," Olive said. "This place is huge and we have a lot of ground to cover if we're going to find the *Liber Umbrarum*."

"Quite right," Miles said. "So far we've been assaulted by blackout fog and held captive by a witch. Who knows what else this opera house has in store for us. Doubt everything you see, feel, smell, hear, and touch. Trust no one, even if they present like one of us. Use our secret code to identify yourselves to each other, and keep your magic at hand. Clear?"

"Yes," we answered as one.

Miles sent us in four different directions. Diego refused to leave me this time, and so it was that I found myself wedged between Jasper and Diego as we set off to examine the south side of the opera house. Miles had tried to send us back to the east side, but I knew that if there was any energy left in the egomaniacal witch from hell—Odessa—she would be aching to brag about forcing a witch, three mages, and a hellhound to prance around the stage at her command. I was banking on finding her backstage, reveling in the humiliation she had caused. And if I had managed to put her magic on the fritz for even a moment, well, I wanted to enjoy that, too.

Jasper took my hand as we entered the largest dressing room, clearly built to house the star of the show. I took comfort in having him with me and tightened my fingers around his.

Then I remembered thinking I was holding his hand only to discover it was Thorne. I dropped his hand and leaned back, putting some distance between us while studying his familiar light blue gaze, his arching black brows, high cheekbones, square jaw, and full lips. It was him, I knew it was, but still . . .

"Ink fades." I said our secret code.

"Knowledge doesn't," he responded perfectly.

"I'm sorry. I knew it was you. I did." I stepped forward and hugged him tight.

"It's all right. After your experience with Thorne, I don't blame you for checking." He returned the embrace, with an arm around my back and one pressing my head against his shoulder. He kissed my hair and said, "Quite smart of you, actually." He put some space between us and cupped my face. "When we retrieve the book, we'll take up where we left off."

"Promise?" I asked. My voice was lower than I'd ever heard it, and his pupils flared just the tiniest bit.

"Hang on." He tugged me close with one hand on my lower back and the other buried in the hair at the nape of my neck. His lips were just a breath from mine when he said, "Put your arms around me."

I did as I was told, locking my body tightly against his and cursing every single stitch of clothing that was between us.

"Excellent." His voice was as rough as the rub of his wool coat against my cheek. "We'll take up right here." His eyes twinkled when he added, "I now have this position committed to memory." Then he kissed me quick and released me to go back to examining the room, starting with the contents of the vanity.

I blew out a steadying breath. Was it possible to internally combust from sexual frustration?

"No." Diego sniffed his way around the room. *"Also, ew, gross."*

"You weren't supposed to hear that."

"Then you should keep your thoughts to—" Diego froze in place.

"Diego, what is it?" I hurried to his side, terrified that something bad had happened to him.

In three strides, Jasper was beside me. "Diego, what scent have you found?"

I glanced at Jasper. How did he know it was a scent?

"A demon was here and he carried something with the scent of centuries." Diego turned his head to me and I saw flames light his eyes.

"The *Book of Shadows*?" I asked out loud so Jasper would know what we were talking about.

"Yes."

"He says the book was here and so was a demon," I said.

"Can you track it?" Jasper asked.

Diego didn't bother answering. He kept his nose to the ground and followed the scent along the baseboard until he reached a door that blended almost seamlessly into the wall. Jasper and I followed and the three of us pondered the door for a beat.

"All right then." Jasper began to tap around the wainscotting until there was a click and the door popped out from the wall, allowing Jasper to pull it wide open. Darkness greeted us.

"Is this normal in a backstage dressing room?" I gestured to the gaping maw of nothing in front of us as a shiver of dread wriggled through me.

"No idea." Jasper moved me behind him and said, "I'll go first. You two wait until I say it's okay."

"I don't have a good feeling about this," I said. "Diego, can you scent the book in there?"

Diego sniffed the air. *"Yes."*

Damn it. We had to go. We had no choice.

Jasper held out his hand and an orb of light appeared. His signature magical color was black and so was the light he crafted. The ball pulsed a shade of blue violet, glowing brighter when it lit upon anything emitting fluorescence.

"Be careful." The words came out before I could check them. Of course he was going to be careful. He didn't need to hear me say it. Putting the words out there was my own way of trying to control the outcome. If only I could.

Jasper reached out and squeezed my hand. Not making any promises but offering reassurance all the same.

I held my breath as he stepped into the closet. He took two steps and both he and his orb of light disappeared, swallowed by the darkness without a sound.

No, no, no! Not again. I was not prepared to lose him twice in the space of an hour or two or however long we'd been in this godforsaken opera house.

"Jasper!" I shouted. Diego pressed up against my side, the hair of his scruff raised as he growled through his teeth.

There was no answer. There was nothing.

"We have to follow him." I grabbed Diego's scruff with one hand and made my own orb of bright red light with my other. "On three. One, two, three."

Together we stepped into the closet only to find nothing beneath our feet, and my light was snuffed immediately as we dropped through the emptiness. I screamed but no sound came out of my mouth. Panic thundered through me. Were we going to fall to our deaths? Had Jasper? Was he already dead?

"This is an illusion. I can smell the magic. Do not let go of me!" Diego ordered.

"I won't," I promised.

As if Diego's observation dimmed the power of the illusion, our descent began to slow. I maintained my grip on him while I tried to find my magic. The darkness was complete, and I needed light to get my bearings and find Jasper. I was concentrating so much on pulling up my magic that I started when we landed with a thump in what appeared to be the stern of a boat. Great, another boat.

I sat up, still clutching Diego by the scruff. The boat was a large wooden vessel that had a wheelhouse in the front. It was still nighttime, but when I glanced up, there were stars in the sky overhead instead of the unrelieved darkness we had fallen through. A cool breeze tugged at my hair and I could hear water breaking against the hull that rocked ever so gently.

"We're on a boat," I said, stating the obvious.

"Are we?" Diego asked. He didn't seem convinced.

"What do you mean? Is this an illusion, too?"

"The magic here is strong," Diego said. *"Don't trust anything you see."*

I hadn't thought I would ever miss the creepy opera house,

but now I was wishing I was anywhere, including Lyric Hall, but here. Were we on the Hudson River? We'd have to be. Did Lyric Hall have its own ghost ship? Was that what we'd landed on? Who was piloting the craft? Where was Jasper? Was he somewhere on the boat?

I rose to my feet, still maintaining my grip on Diego. I think we both preferred not to lose contact. "We need to check things out."

Diego didn't respond. He simply pressed himself against my side, moving with me when I glanced over the side at the frigid black water below. Was it real? I felt as if I were going mad trying to parse out if I was in another illusion or not.

The door to the wheelhouse opened, and I glanced inside the well-lit space to see Jasper in a passionate embrace with Odessa Van Doren.

23

Disbelief kept me rooted to the spot. Jasper? With Odessa? She was pressed up against him, her fingers tangled in his hair, kissing him as if she were giving him the breath of life. Just like my grimoire had turned green over my affection for the bookwyrms, I was certain I was turning a sickly shade of the same. I tried shaking the toxic feeling off, as I had before, but it didn't work.

Jealousy, an ugly emotion if ever there was one, twisted through me like poison. I couldn't stop it, and the fury it ignited in me was fierce. I wanted to storm into the wheelhouse and rip them apart. Then I wanted to punch Jasper right in the mouth. We had just declared our coupledom and now he was tossing me aside for Odessa—of all witches!—well, hell hath no fury and all that.

"Are you done?" Diego asked, breaking into my seething fantasy of pitching Jasper overboard.

"I haven't even taken a swing at him yet," I argued. *"So that would be no."*

"That's not Jasper," Diego said.

I stared at the couple. I'd spent enough time daydreaming about the man to know him when I saw him. I was about to say as much when Diego continued, *"I know what Jasper smells like. That's not him."*

It took a beat for his words to penetrate and when they did, a sweet surge of relief bubbled up inside of me. Not Jasper. Of course it wasn't him. The logical part of my brain kicked in, overriding my silly heart. How could I have believed it for even a second? I was disgusted with myself and supremely annoyed at the show I now realized was for my benefit.

"Then who is it?" I asked.

"I don't know, but they want you to think it's Jasper, and I think you'd be wise to play along until we can find the real Jasper," Diego said.

"Can you try and sniff him out?" I asked.

"If you can cause a scene." Diego lowered his head to the deck and began to snuffle along the boards.

"Oh, with pleasure," I assured him.

Odessa wanted to play? Well, all right then. I tossed my hair back and focused on my initial fury, bringing it back to the surface. I strode forward, slamming my hand against the open door and banging it into the wall.

"You son of a bitch!" I cried.

The couple broke apart. Odessa put her hand to her throat and batted her eyelashes. "Oh, dear, how did you get here?" She was a terrible actress, which inexplicably annoyed me even more. Her face was plump and glowy, and her eyes sparkled. I realized that she hadn't just been playing with my colleagues when she'd strung them up like puppets. She most likely had been draining them of their magic at the same time, which had protected her from the blast of my fury. So much for my banshee cry.

"I followed him!" I snapped. I pointed at the man who looked so much like Jasper it made me pause. What if Diego was wrong? What if it was Ja—no. I knew better than that. I would not let them torture me with their mind games.

The man spread his hands wide in a *whoa, whoa, whoa* type of gesture, reserved for men who screwed up but thought they could gaslight their way out of it. Jasper would never.

"Now, love, you've got the wrong idea," Not Jasper said. And damn, he was good. He sounded just like him. Again, a worm of doubt wriggled in my brain, but I flicked it away. I trusted Diego to find the real Jasper. Also, there was something off about this Jasper. I couldn't say exactly what it was, but I didn't get the fluttery feeling in my chest when this man looked at me that I got whenever Jasper was nearby.

"Wrong idea?" I cried. Both Odessa and Not Jasper assumed defensive stances.

I could see Diego out of the corner of my eye. He was headed around the wheelhouse to the bow. Had he gotten a lead? I had to buy him time. The bigger the scene, the bigger the distraction. I pulled up my magic, but instead of using it on the two of them as they no doubt expected, I used it on the boat.

I sent my magic all over the vessel until it was aglow with my signature color, red. If we were on the Hudson, I could only imagine what people would think if they saw us floating down the river. Next, with a circular motion of my right hand, I sent the boat spinning clockwise in the deep dark water.

Odessa and Not Jasper looked wide-eyed as if they hadn't expected me to punch back so hard. Little did they know, I was just getting started. They both grabbed on to the control panel at the front of the wheelhouse as I made the motion again but faster and the boat's spinning intensified.

"What are you doing, you crazy witch?" Odessa cried.

I held up my hand in a *stop* gesture and the boat halted, sending Odessa to the floor. She braced herself with her hands, blowing a hank of blond hair out of her face, and I used my left hand in a counterclockwise motion to reverse the boat's spin in the opposite direction, knocking her to the floor again. What a shame.

Not Jasper did not fall but rather stood braced for anything as he stared at me with a narrowed gaze. I realized I had to maintain the part of furious girlfriend so I spat, "You chose the wrong witch, asshole." At the very least it felt good to call this imposter names.

"Oh, come now, love, this meant nothing." A slow smile curved his lips and he lowered his head and glanced at me through his lashes. His attempt to charm me pissed me off so much that I reversed the boat's direction again, catching Odessa off guard. She rolled across the floor and this time decided to remain down, but not him. He still stood. How annoying.

The real Jasper had spent weeks teaching me how to manipulate energy before he went on his mission to retrieve the *Liber Umbrarum*. I'd practiced intensively while he was gone, hoping to show him how I'd improved when he came back. I'd even decorated Agatha's Christmas tree without ever touching an ornament. Since Jasper had returned, we hadn't had any time for me to show him how I'd improved, but now I was relieved that I'd practiced so much.

"Is Jasper on the boat?" I asked Diego.

"Yes, he's below deck and as far as I can tell unconscious," Diego answered. *"Might not be the best play to sink the boat."*

"Can you get to him?" I asked. *"Also, it would be safer for you to be below."*

"I'm your guardian," Diego argued. *"I don't leave you."*

"I don't need you right now, but Jasper does."

"Fine. But I can hear everything that's happening and will be there in a nanosecond if you need me."

"Thank you. Now go."

"You have skills," Not Jasper said.

"You sound surprised." I decided to call his bluff. "Don't you remember all of those hot, sweaty, passion-filled nights we spent together with you teaching me everything you know?"

There hadn't been any sweaty nights between us . . . yet, but the imposter's answer would tell me how much he knew about us.

"Oh, gross. I'm going to be sick," Diego said. I ignored him, focusing on Not Jasper.

"How could you have forgotten what it was like between us?" I feigned a sob and turned my head, watching him out of the corner of my eye.

The pale blue of Not Jasper's eyes flickered to a brown so dark it was almost black. Thorne! I should have known. He'd said he was working for McWrath, but clearly he had something going on with Odessa, too. That did it.

Very dramatically, I raised my hands and took all of my magic pulsing around the boat and used it to lift the vessel into the air. I was done playing games. I wanted the *Book of Shadows* and Jasper, and I wanted to go home. I was so over this macabre nonsense. These two minions to the demon McWrath could explain to him how a baby witch brought them down.

"You are magnificent," Thorne said. He looked enthralled.

"Are you mad? She's going to kill us!" Odessa screeched from the floor.

"What did you expect when you betrayed me?" I scanned the water's edge and realized we were just offshore from Lyric Hall. Excellent. I guided the boat toward the opera house, feeling the wind rip through the open door of the wheelhouse and whip at my hair and cloak. I was pushing the limits of my abilities and fighting not to look like it.

I lifted the ship higher to clear the trees and then lowered it onto the snow-covered lawn. My nose was frozen and my fingers felt as if they were made of ice. I could barely hang on to the boat and ended up setting it down none too gently.

There was an ominous crack of wood, and I wondered if I'd damaged the hull. Oops.

"Diego, are you and Jasper all right?"

He didn't answer. I tried not to panic. I needed help. Where were Miles, Olive, and Tariq? Had they been captured like Jasper? Were they locked away in the opera hall? How was I supposed to deal with Thorne and Odessa and McWrath, wherever he was, all by myself?

Thorne started to walk toward me. I sent him a disgusted look, which I didn't have to fake. I turned and strode out of the wheelhouse. Thorne followed. He started to slow clap, and I couldn't decide if it was in a mocking way or if he was sincerely impressed that I had just flown a boat—a freaking boat!—back to the opera house.

Once outside, I spun around and lifted my chin. I crossed my arms over my chest to hide how much they were shaking after the amount of magic I had just expended. Still, I had to keep up my jealous pretense until the others arrived. "Don't try to flatter me. You're dead to me, Jasper."

"Aw, love, I hope you don't mean that." Jasper strolled around the corner of the wheelhouse with Diego at his side.

I pointed at Not Jasper. "It's Thorne. He tried to convince me he was you."

"But you didn't believe it."

"No." No need to tell him right now that Diego had figured it out first. I was confident I would have once my jealousy passed.

Jasper's gaze met mine and his lips tipped up in one corner. He looked as handsome as ever and I felt almost weak with relief when I registered the same fluttery feeling I always felt when he was near. I had no idea how to play this and then realized I simply didn't care. I broke into a run and threw myself into his arms. Jasper caught me, lifting me up and holding me tight.

"You're all right," I cried, tears of relief welling in my eyes.

"Thanks to you." He kissed me quickly and then moved me behind him to stand with Diego. I felt his mood shift immediately into one of cold fury. "Really, Thorne? Still working for McWrath? Is that how low you've sunk?"

Not Jasper flickered almost as if he had a glitch. Thorne appeared, then Jasper, then Thorne, but it wasn't Thorne who remained in the end. It was something else. Diego pressed closer to me as if to protect me, indicating that the bad vibes I was getting were spot-on.

Horns, the first thing I noticed when Thorne's white hair changed to black was that he had horns poking out of his dark hair. He also had deep crimson skin, yellow eyes with elongated pupils, and muscles. The demon was a wall of pure muscle. He reminded me of Lord Griffin, who was the only other demon I'd ever seen in his true form, as this demon was bare chested, wearing only silk pants with a geometric pattern on them and a pair of fuzzy slippers, which seemed incongruous with the rest of him.

"Did you really think you were dealing with that halfling Rowan Thorne?" The demon's voice was so deep it echoed on the night air. This had to be McWrath. I felt my stomach drop to my feet. I'd taken on McWrath? I felt a bit woozy at the realization and put my hand on Diego's scruff to steady myself.

My grimoire in my pocket felt like a block of ice. I suspected, knowing that the demon wanted it, the poor thing was panicking. I put my hand over my pocket in reassurance, but it remained closed off.

"McWrath." Jasper didn't sound surprised. "Hiding behind Thorne's image doesn't seem like you at all. And here I thought Thorne was working for you when he showed up at Crooked Alfie's, but it was you disguised as Thorne all along."

"I wasn't hiding." McWrath scoffed. "Most witches respond poorly to demons even with their true form hidden. Since you did me the favor of taking Thorne out of commission by turning him in to the Global Council of Magisters, I knew it was unlikely he and I would be moving in the same circles. I merely used Thorne's likeness to infiltrate the enemy camp." He glared at Jasper, looking him over with his lip curled back in a sneer, making it clear who he thought the enemy was.

"Enemy?" Jasper gasped as if in surprise. "You consider me your enemy? I think I'm hurt."

How he could banter with the demon was beyond me. I wanted to run, flee into the night, and here they were trading insults like we were in a comic book. Men!

"You stole the *Liber Umbrarum* out from under me," McWrath growled. He sounded pissed.

"Alfie chose to sell it to me," Jasper argued. "I can't help it if he likes me more."

"He's going to get us killed," Diego said.

"I'm sure he knows what he's doing," I said.

"Perhaps you should prepare your grimoire just in case," Diego said. *"Because Jasper has the* Liber Umbrarum *on him and if McWrath figures it out, he will kill us all."*

"How did Jasper get the book?"

"It was on the boat."

"Are you sure?" I asked.

"Yes, I can scent it on him."

"Alfie is a weak-willed human with more money than brains who deserves every misfortune that befalls him," McWrath raged.

"Alfie is a sad old man living the last of his days in hiding no thanks to you," Jasper snapped.

"He won't be hidden for long," McWrath vowed. "When I find him, he'll learn the error of his ways."

"If you find him, which you won't." Jasper glanced back at Diego and me and said, "We're done here. Let's go."

"You're not going anywhere, Griffin."

Jasper stared him down and said, "Try and stop me."

McWrath's head tipped to the side. His eyes narrowed and his crimson skin began to darken. Uh-oh.

"The witch and her grimoire stay with me," McWrath said.

"The hell she does," Jasper countered.

"I should have killed you when I had the chance," McWrath snapped. "It was my respect for your father—"

"You mean your fear of my father," Jasper corrected him.

"Fear? Pah!" McWrath raged.

"We really need to go now," Diego said.

"I know," I hissed. Hiding behind Jasper, I pulled my grimoire from my pocket. I was running on fumes magically and desperately needed help. With shaking fingers, I withdrew a needle from the magical kit Olive had given me and pricked my finger. As Jasper and McWrath continued exchanging insults, I squeezed my finger until a drop of blood beaded up and then dropped onto the lock. I really needed a quicker way to access this book.

"We need to get out of here right now," I whispered to the grimoire. "Preferably to a place McWrath can't go. Can you help me?"

The grimoire popped open and started flipping pages, back and forth until it stopped on the page I'd been studying for weeks. It took me a second to place it. It was the same page Freya had disappeared into.

I put my hand over the page, and the symbols began to rearrange themselves. The words reformed and moved as I tried to read them.

"That's it. We're done talking," McWrath announced. "If you and that mangy mutt want to live, you will leave the witch and her grimoire with me."

"None of that is happening," Jasper said at the same time I thought it.

"You don't understand," McWrath said. "This isn't negotiable."

"I'm afraid it's you who doesn't grasp the situation. There is no deal to be made here," Jasper countered. "And you're absolutely mental if you think I would ever let you near her."

"You act as if you think you have a choice!" McWrath's voice boomed across the boat.

I glanced at my book. We had to get out of here now. I looped my arm through Jasper's while keeping my grimoire clutched in my hand. I grabbed Diego by the scruff of his neck and muttered the letters that had reconfigured on the page. "Per vias temporis, transitus aperiatur."

I repeated the phrase, which I knew was roughly translated to "through the pathways of time, let passage be opened," three times, when a bright red-hot light split through the night with a boom so loud it sounded as if I'd cracked the sky in half. Jasper whirled around and put his arms about me as if to keep me safe from the very thing I was manifesting.

I heard McWrath cry out in fury as the light circled us with a tornado-like wind. I clutched my grimoire and Diego so hard, I was afraid I was hurting them, but I didn't dare lessen my grip. The swirling wind squeezed us so tightly, it felt as if I was compressed to the point of my bones breaking. I didn't even have the lung capacity to scream from the pain.

As quickly as it appeared, the constriction vanished and

we dropped to the floor, too weak to stand. When I opened my eyes, I noted we were no longer on the boat but rather the three of us were crouched on a parquet floor that looked exactly like the one in the Museum of Literature.

Had the grimoire brought us home? Jasper was protectively curled up around Diego and me, and I peered over his shoulder to get my bearings. I was relieved to be safely away from McWrath but realized instantly that instead of the Museum of Literature I knew and loved, this place looked more like someone's home and we were right in the middle of their private library.

"Zoe, are you all right?" Jasper removed his arms from around me and studied my face.

There were two women standing beside a desk at the end of the room. One was elderly and the other middle-aged. Despite their Gilded Age attire, I knew the younger one immediately, and it appeared she recognized me, too.

"Zoe?" she asked. Her voice was exactly as I remembered it and so was the worried look in her eyes. I felt my throat get tight and I swallowed hard, trying to pull it together enough to speak.

"Hi, Mom," I said.

24

Juliet Donadieu, my mother, gasped and covered her mouth with her hands. Her face became very pale and she swayed a bit on her feet, but the diminutive, silver-haired woman beside her clutched her arm, steadying her.

"Breathe, Juliet dear," the woman said. "Freya told us she would come."

I glanced at the woman's face and recognized her from the portrait upstairs in the Museum of Literature. Mabel Stewart. Jasper must have recognized her at the same time, as he jumped to his feet and helped me to mine. Diego, for his part, stayed curled in a ball until his transition back to a puppy was complete. Then he popped up and began wagging as if he was just delighted to be here.

I stood there, out of breath with tears stinging my eyes, unable to move. I was terrified that I was hallucinating. I turned to Jasper and whispered, "Pinch me."

He looked at me with a tenderness that almost broke me. "You're not dreaming."

"But if you pinch me, I'll know for sure," I countered.

"Or you could go hug your mum and let that be the proof." His voice was gently encouraging as he closed the grimoire I still held.

I stepped forward on shaky legs, but that was as far as I got when my mom dashed across the space between us and grabbed me in her arms. She was sobbing so hard I couldn't understand her, but I heard the words "worried," "waited," and "it's been so long." She stepped back and cupped my face, her gaze darting across my features as if trying to take in every change the years had wrought.

"Oh, Zoe, my dearest girl." She pulled me into a hug so tight I thought I was moving through time again. I clutched her close, hanging on to her as if she might disappear.

I could hear voices and knew it was Jasper talking with Mrs. Stewart. A door opened and closed, and when my mother released me, I discovered we were alone in the small private library except for a slender gray volume perched on the corner of the elaborate writing desk. The front cover of the book was the face of a cat, and a tail dropped from the spine and swished across the desk. Freya. Miles's beloved book-cat who had leapt into my book as if she knew exactly what she was doing.

"Hi, Freya. You scared me to death when you vanished into the grimoire." I wiped at the tears that were coursing down my cheeks and glanced at my mom. "She doesn't look repentant."

"Cat." Mom shrugged. She cupped my face and wiped away my tears with her thumbs. "You know how cats disappear and then suddenly reappear?"

I nodded.

"Freya does it all the time," Mom said.

"So, she can use the grimoire?" I asked. "Even though she's not a Donadieu?"

"She can use anything she wants," Mom said. "She is crafted from ancient magic and not bound by our rules."

I gave Freya a side-eye. I had more questions but my mom hugged me tight and I focused on her, not wanting to miss a moment of this precious time together.

"I knew you would come. I knew one day when the grimoire was yours, you'd come to see me. Oh, Zoe." Her words ended with another sob and she hugged me again.

We held each other and wept for all the years we'd missed and for all the moments that had been taken from us, but also for the joy of finding each other again. When the tears began to dry, Mom led me to a sitting area in front of a fireplace.

"Are you hungry? Tired? Cold? Can I get you anything?" she asked as we sat on a tufted burgundy love seat with an elaborately carved wooden frame.

I glanced around the room, which was peak Gilded Age, and then at her, taking in her clothing, a lace-trimmed ecru shirtwaist with puffy sleeves and lots of fussy buttons over a navy-blue A-line skirt that reached the floor and boasted three rows of ruffles along the hem.

"I'm fine, thanks. No, that's not accurate." I turned to her and asked, "What year is it? Was that Mabel Stewart? Are we in the Museum of Literature? How long have you been here?"

"Let's see, it's the ninth of April, 1897. Yes, that was Mabel, and you are in her home, which will become the Museum of Literature. I've been here for a year as I'm currently employed as Mabel's personal librarian," Mom said.

"You are?" I asked in surprise.

Mom nodded. "I always wanted to tell Agatha that I became a librarian, too, but I couldn't risk giving either of you any information that could put you in harm's way. Since you made it here, I assume you've figured out how the grimoire works." Mom tapped the book I still held clutched in my hand.

"Ha! I wish." I set the book on the marble and mahogany coffee table. "I've spent months trying to translate it, but I can't." I hated admitting that I was a failure to my mom when I hadn't seen her in forever, but there was no avoiding it.

"Oh, Zoe, you can't translate it," she said. "No one can."

"What?" I asked. "Why didn't Mamie tell me that when I saw her?"

"You saw Mamie?" My mother's eyes were round. "How?"

I sighed and leaned back against the love seat. "I have so much to tell you. Wait. How much can I tell you? Will it impact your life if I do?"

My mother tapped her lips with her index finger as she considered my question. "Well, given that you're in possession of the grimoire, I realize I have passed on in your timeline."

My throat got tight and I grabbed her hand and laced our fingers together. "It was six months ago—"

"No." Mom interrupted me. "Don't tell me anything about that. Whatever happened was what was supposed to happen—"

"But—"

"No buts." She shook her head. "Death comes how it comes. We don't get to choose." A shadow crossed over her face, and I knew she was thinking about my father.

"I can tell you this," I said. "For a long time, I didn't understand why we were always moving or why you dropped me off at boarding school and left me in Agatha's care, but now I do and I'm grateful for the sacrifices you made for me."

My mother's face crumpled and she pulled a lace-trimmed handkerchief from her sleeve and pressed it to her face. "It was the hardest thing I ever had to do, but I'd have done anything to protect you."

"I know." I squeezed her fingers in reassurance. "I'm sure Agatha would want me to tell you that she loves you and misses you, too."

Mom smiled and said, "Is she well?"

"She is. I can't wait to tell her that I saw you," I said. "She'll be thrilled."

"Please tell her that she was right and I'm sorry," Mom said.

"For what?" I asked.

"She told me not to make you vow not to do magic," Mom said. "I was wrong. I was so blinded by my grief over losing your father and my desire to keep you safe that I asked you to deny the very essence of who you are. I made your life more difficult than it had to be and I'm so sorry."

"Mamie said that you'd had a change of heart," I said.

My mother closed her eyes for a second and took a deep breath. "So, Mamie and I made up, too?"

"Yes." I nodded. "She loves you very much."

A little sob slipped out and my mother cleared her throat. "Okay. Enough of that. I don't know how long you'll be here, so there are some things I need to explain."

"I'm listening." I released her hand after one more squeeze and picked up the grimoire. "You can start with what you meant when you said no one can translate it."

"During the witch trials, one of our ancestors spelled the grimoire to hide itself in an indecipherable encryption to keep the book from being used as a proof of witchcraft," Mom said. "In fact, to the witch hunters of the time, it fashioned itself into a pious little tome that only the most virtuous would possess."

"Clever." I glanced at the book and noted the feeling of pride that pulsed from it.

"Also, the grimoire was spelled to remain coded and only respond to the witch who possessed it when the grimoire deemed it necessary," Mom said.

"Seriously?" I looked back at the book. "I'm not sure the book should have that much discretion." I felt a flare of what I could only describe as indignation coming from the book, which made me smile.

"But you have unlocked it and it does show you the spells you need," Mom observed.

"Yes, but *only* the spells I need," I protested. "Which is really annoying."

"It's intentional," Mom said. "As I said, our ancestor spelled the grimoire's contents into an unbreakable code to prevent anyone from deciphering it just as she sealed it with a blood oath so that only a Donadieu can open it."

"But how can I access all of the spells in it?" I asked. "There are hundreds."

"There are." Mom nodded. "Between you and me, I think some of them are rather useless."

My jaw dropped in surprise.

"Not all of our ancestors were as good at the magical arts as they'd like to think," Mom said. "Which is why the grimoire vets the spells you need when you need them. The grimoire is—"

"A sentient being?" I asked when she paused for a beat.

"You've discovered that, too." She smiled. "You always were very quick."

She looked so proud that I felt the same spike of happiness I felt when I was a kid and she gushed over my report card or clapped when I did a cartwheel.

"You've formed a connection to the grimoire, haven't you?" Mom asked.

"If by that you mean can I read its emotions? Yes." I nodded.

"That's good," Mom said. "The closer you bond, the more easily the book will work with you. And once you learn the spells, you won't need the book to show them to you. You can use them at your discretion."

"So, if I learned a summoning spell for someone who's crossed over, I could use it without the book?" I asked. "Because I managed it once but haven't been able to again."

"Yes, you could, but it takes very strong magic to bring a person back over the veil," Mom said. "Also, you need to be in a place with a lot of magic, like a ley line."

"Or a magical battle?" I asked.

My mother put her hand over her heart as if even thinking about such an event caused her anxiety.

"The entire staff of the BODO was with me," I assured her. "I was perfectly safe." I saw Freya roll her cat eyes at my big fat fib from where she sat on the desk behind my mother. I ignored her.

"That sort of setting would give you enough magic to call someone," Mom said. Her eyes had a faraway look, and I wondered if she'd ever managed to call my father back across the veil. It seemed too personal a question, so I focused on the situation at hand.

"So, practically speaking, I can use the same incantation that got us here to bring us back?" I asked.

"Yes, so long as you let the grimoire know where you want to go." She patted my hand as if she just needed to connect to me. "What did you ask when you used it to bring you here?"

"I asked the grimoire to help us get to a place where a demon couldn't reach us," I said.

"A demon?" Mom went very still, except her hand on mine tightened to the point of pain. I winced and she immediately loosened her hold. "Sorry, I find demons troubling."

"No kidding." I fretted my lower lip between my teeth while thinking of my BODO colleagues. "When we go back, will it be to the moment we departed, or will the time that passes here be the same as there?"

"If you spend a day here, when you go back, it will be a day later," Mom said. "You age the same here as you would there. There are certain things even hopping through time can't erase."

I thought about our abrupt departure from the opera hall. I had no idea where Miles, Olive, or Tariq were or what McWrath would do to them if he found them. It was concerning.

"Now I have some questions for you. What brought you here? Who is the man you're with?" Mom asked. "And when did Lilith deliver the hellhound I sent?"

"You can tell Diego is a hellhound?" I asked.

"Of course." Mom looked slightly insulted.

"Wait! Lilith is the name of the Ash Mother?" I asked. "And you know her? You had her deliver Diego to me?"

"Yes, I know her. Much like I'm working for Mabel now, I worked for Lilith for a time," Mom explained. "She seems harsh but she's really . . . well . . . socially awkward. It was one of my more fun jobs while on the run. You know how much I like dogs."

"How did you know Diego would be my familiar?" I asked.

"I didn't," Mom said. "I just wanted you to have a hell-hound for protection, so I told Lilith that if and when you stepped into your power with the grimoire, she should give you the pick of her latest litter, and because she liked me, she agreed."

I sat there with my mouth hanging open until my mom reached over and gently closed it.

"Can you tell me what brought you here?" Mom asked.

"Do you want the long version or short?" I shook my head, trying to focus.

She smiled. "Short for now."

"Jasper, Diego, and I were escaping from that demon I mentioned," I said.

Her eyebrows lifted.

"His name is McWrath and he stole the *Liber Umbrarum* from the vault in the Books of Dubious Origin collection," I said.

"The *Book of Shadows*?" Her eyes grew wide.

"That's the one. We were in the middle of an altercation when I turned to the grimoire for help." I stroked its cover as

I spoke, and I felt a feeling of contentment come from it. "It opened and I placed my hand on the page, recognizing it as the same page Freya had disappeared into. It deciphered the spell into words I could read, and the next thing I knew we were here."

"You've managed to call a soul across the veil and time hop in the few months you've had the grimoire." My mother cupped my cheek and gazed at me in wonder. "You are remarkable."

This. This was what I'd missed all those years that my mom had popped sporadically in and out of my life.

"I've missed you, Mom," I said.

"I've missed you, too." She tucked a loose strand of my hair behind my ear. We were the last two in a long line of witches, and in my own world, I was it. The end of the Donadieus. The desperate need to learn as much as I could as fast as I could filled me.

"Which one of our relatives thought coding the book like that was a good idea?" I asked. If ever I could pull that witch forward, she was going to have some explaining to do.

"I believe it was Josephine Donadieu," Mom said. "She saw too many of her coven die for their witchcraft and she believed hiding the book's contents in an indecipherable code would keep the possessor of the grimoire safe."

"Oh." I tried to imagine living in a time where there were witch trials and executions. The mere thought of watching Jasper, Agatha, or any of the BODO members be burned at a stake made me pause. I couldn't fault Josephine for trying to save her people. I knew, without a doubt, I would have done the same thing.

There was a knock on the door just before it opened, and Mabel Stewart entered the room with Jasper and Diego. She smiled at the two of us on the love seat and asked, "Do you need more time to catch up? I don't want to rush you, but—"

"A demon is after the *Book of Shadows*," Mom said. "We need to help them."

Mabel nodded. "But first, tea, I think."

She gestured to a cart in the corner and it rolled forward. While I watched, the silver teapot poured out several cups of hot tea.

"Here you are, dear." She handed me the first one.

"Thank you, Mrs. Stewart," I said, reveling in the warmth of the bone china cup in my hands.

"Call me Mabel," she said. "Your mother has told me so much about you, I feel as if we're well acquainted."

"All right." I nodded in agreement and sipped from my cup, letting the warmth of the tea seep into my body.

I felt a sharp pang of hunger hit my middle when Mabel took the three-tiered plate off the cart and set it on the table. I recognized it as one that Miles had shown me before.

"This plate is from Louis XIV," Mabel said. "Simply tap one of the plates three times and your desired food will appear."

Jasper and I shared a smile, and I knew he was remembering Miles and Tariq teaching me how to use this plate. While Mabel passed out linen napkins and small serving plates, Jasper told me about his tour of the Stewart home. Mabel had been kind enough to take them to the kitchen, where Diego had been given a turkey leg. This explained why he was now sacked out in front of the cold fireplace, snoring.

Mabel gestured for us to help ourselves and I went right for the sweet plate, tapping it three times and happily munching on my petit fours while Jasper chose the lower plate that conjured meat pasties. I'd had no idea how starving I was until I, too, added a couple of pasties to my plate. No one spoke while we ate, but I got the feeling that both Mabel and my mom were thinking about what they'd learned from us.

When Jasper and I set our plates down, Mabel leaned forward in her seat and asked, "Do you have the *Book of Shadows* with you?"

Jasper glanced at me as if to ask whether I thought he should trust Mabel or not. I understood his caution as we'd been fooled by false appearances before. Still, my mother was here and she worked for Mabel. I nodded.

Jasper dipped his head once in acknowledgment and reached into his coat pocket and pulled out the familiar burgundy leather book with the brass studs. He set it on the table next to my grimoire, and both Mabel and my mother leaned close but didn't touch the volume.

"It's smaller than I expected," Mabel said.

"For something that can alter reality, you'd think it would feel more ominous," Mom agreed.

"That's two of the set," Mabel mused as she reached forward and picked up the burgundy book in her thin age-spotted hands.

"Two of the set?" Jasper asked. "I'm sorry, but that sounds as if you think these two books are connected."

Mabel nodded. "They are."

Jasper and I exchanged a quick look of confusion.

"How?" I addressed the question to my mother.

"The Donadieu grimoire is also called the *Book of Echoes*," she said. "Because the most powerful spell it contains can bring back the dead rather like an echo bounces sound back."

I felt an uneasy shiver pass through me and it took me a moment to realize that it wasn't me. Rather it was my grimoire responding to the name.

"Explain, please." I glanced between my mother and Mabel, not caring who told the story so long as someone did, and quickly.

Jasper's big warm hand landed gently between my shoulder blades in a calming gesture and I closed my eyes for a beat, willing myself to be chill.

"During the height of the Enlightenment, about one hundred and fifty years ago—" Mabel paused and her brow crinkled in thought. "Wait. That would be almost three hundred years for you." I nodded, encouraging her to keep going.

"Yes, well," Mabel began again. "During that time where the scientific mind ruled, five of the most powerful magical texts were brought together by those in possession of them and they were magically bonded as a set."

"Why?" Jasper asked.

"Protection," Mabel said. "Having the books magically bonded meant that whoever possessed one of the books could access all the books through the bond. The idea was if any witch or mage or what have you was imprisoned or sentenced to death for being in possession of one of the books, then the knowledge wouldn't die with them because any of the other four keepers of the books could access the tome that was left behind."

I frowned as I tried to grasp what Mabel had just said.

"So, I'm not the last person to be able to use the grimoire so long as another of the four book keepers steps in and takes my place if I die?" I asked.

"Precisely." Mabel sipped her tea.

"And it also means I could wield the *Book of Shadows*?" I asked, feeling distinctly uncomfortable.

"Yes," Mabel said. "You or any demon. Unlike the *Book of Echoes*, which is a grimoire crafted by witches and spelled to the succession of the Donadieu witches, the *Book of Shadows* was written by demons one thousand years ago and can only be possessed by a demon unless, of course, another being uses it through the bond of the five books."

I glanced at Jasper and noted his features were tight as if he was struggling to keep some inner conflict inside. He cleared his throat and asked, "How about a half demon? Can a half demon access the *Liber Umbrarum*?"

Mabel tipped her head to the side and studied him. Her brows lifted in surprise and she said, "There is only one way to be sure. Why don't you try it and see?"

"Wait." Mom sat up straight. "Who's a half demon?" She pointed to Jasper and asked, "You?"

It was clear from her tone that she did not approve.

"It's okay, Mom," I said.

"It most certainly is not," Mom said. "Demons are not to be trust—"

Whatever she was about to say was cut off by Mabel as she put her hand on my mother's forearm in a calming gesture. "From what Jasper has told me about his family, I believe he is honorable."

"He is," I insisted. My tone was defensive and when my

mother glanced at me, her eyes narrowed. I was certain my feelings for Jasper were written all over my face.

"Zoe—" Mom began, but I shook my head.

"Later. We need to know more about all of this before we go back," I said. "And we have to go back. We left our colleagues behind. We must make certain that they're safe."

"Quite right," Mabel agreed. "Jasper, would you care to try a spell out of the book to see if it will respond to you?"

Jasper looked ill at ease, and I couldn't tell if it was the censure from my mother or his own discomfort at being half-demon. I leaned against him and said, "Try it. We need to know."

With great reluctance he picked up the burgundy book. When he opened it, I felt a tingle of excitement, and it took me a moment to realize that it was coming from my grimoire. It was . . . *happy*?

Jasper studied the first page with pursed lips. I glanced over his shoulder to see if his book was written in the same cipher that my grimoire was. Instead, I saw what I recognized as Medieval Latin, indicating that the book was one thousand years old, as described.

Jasper flipped through the pages, studying each spell until he found one that caused his eyebrows to tick up. "This one should do it." He glanced at me. "Don't fret."

I frowned at him but he rose and moved across the room, reading from the book as he went. As I watched him, his form started to glitch much like Thorne's—or rather McWrath's—had on the boat. I felt my heart drop when I saw the wavy dark hair on the back of his head turn white and form unruly tufts.

When Jasper turned around, I found myself staring at Miles right down to the glasses that slid down his nose.

My mother and I gasped in unison while Mabel didn't seem that surprised. "It appears a half demon can utilize the *Book of Shadows*."

Jasper glanced down at his clothes, which had transformed to Miles's usual corduroy pants and elbow-patched cardigan sweater over a plaid flannel shirt.

"Mirror?" I asked Mabel. At her blank stare, I said, "Looking glass?"

Mabel gestured to a small one hanging on the wall behind the door. I stood and pulled Jasper over to it so he could see his transformation himself. When he caught sight of his reflection, he let out a shocked exhale and then turned to me. "Am I shorter? I think I am."

I glanced at him and noted that I didn't have to tip my head back to look at him. "Yes, the spell got everything just right."

Jasper turned back to the mirror and touched his face. "Amazing."

"More like terrifying," Mom said. "Imagine giving a demon that sort of power."

"Much as I'd like to dive into your issue with demons more deeply," I said, "at the moment, I want to test the theory that if a witch has one of the books, they can use any of them."

I held out my hand, and Jasper gave me the book. Like him, I turned and walked across the room, muttering the same spell he had while firmly keeping in mind the person I wanted to replicate. I felt the warmth of the magic in my core give way to the sensation of roots sprouting from inside of me and spreading out to my skin and hair and toenails. It was distinctly uncomfortable, but I ignored it and kept focusing. When the sensation stopped, I turned around. Mom and Jasper both let out shocked cries while Mabel appeared mostly intrigued.

"You look just like Olive," Jasper said. He tugged me in front of the mirror, and I immediately touched the eyebrow with the scar. I couldn't feel the scar beneath my fingertips, so it wasn't an actual transformation so much as a glamour. Weird.

I tried to keep the facade, but I could feel my magic fading. It felt like the snapping of a rubber band all over my body when the glamour disappeared and my own features returned. I glanced at Jasper and noted he still looked like Miles. He closed his eyes and his image glitched and then he was Jasper again.

"Let's never tell them that we did that," I said.

"Agreed." Jasper grabbed my hand and squeezed my fingers as if to reassure himself that I was actually me again.

I led him back to our seats and faced Mabel. "We need to know about the other three books and where they might be. McWrath clearly knows about the connection between the *Book of Shadows* and the *Book of Echoes*, which is why he came after me. If those other books are out there, there's no question he'll pursue them as well, especially now that we have two out of the five."

"Yes, of course." Mabel nodded. "This is one of the reasons I started collecting books of dubious origin. To keep questionable witches, demons, and others from using these powerful books for evil intentions."

"We'll make certain that McWrath can't get his hands on either of these books," Jasper promised. "But Zoe's right. If the other bonded books are out there, we have to find them, too. If having one of the books gives the possessor permission to access the powers of the other four bonded books, assuming they have them in hand, then having all five together would make their power limitless and they'd become unstoppable."

"Exactly. They'd be able to rule the world both non-magical and magical," Mom said. She glanced up and her eyes were wide with fear. "Stay here, Zoe. Stay here with me and Mabel and your grimoire."

"Mom, I can't . . ."

"You have to," Mom interrupted. Her expression was fierce. "I won't lose you again."

25

It was clear that she was terrified, and I wanted to acknowledge her fear while also staying steadfast in my purpose.

"I'm sorry, Mom, but I can't stay," I said. "You more than anyone must understand the obligation I feel to keep my colleagues safe."

Mom stood up. Her long skirt twitched around her feet as she began to pace the room. "So, I'm supposed to just let you go back with this half demon?"

Mabel sighed. "I understand your hesitation, Juliet, I do. But Jasper is also half-mage, the son of a Swedish witch, from whom he has the rare gift of aviankinesis, and Lord Eliath Griffin, a demon who is also British aristocracy."

"Let me see," Mom said to Jasper.

Without hesitation, he pushed up his sleeves, revealing the raven tattoos on his forearms. Hugin and Munin, ravens who hear and see all.

My mother pursed her lips as if this proof of his mage ability changed things and she didn't like it.

"Wait a second." I turned to Jasper. "Is your father alive in this timeline?"

Jasper looked uncomfortable and then admitted, "He's very young, but, yes, he was born in 1890."

I put my head in my hands for a moment and took a long slow breath. My boyfriend's father was 136 years old. Cool, cool, cool.

"See?" My mother pounced. "It's not natural for a witch and a demon to become involved."

I held up my hand in a *stop* gesture. "Conversation for another day." I raised my head and turned to Mabel. "Tell us what you know about the other books, please. It's important."

Mabel rose to her feet. "Why don't you two come with me? I want to show you something. The house staff will be arriving soon. We can talk more securely elsewhere. Bring your books and your hellhound with you."

Jasper and I rose and picked up our spellbooks. I crouched beside Diego where he was still sprawled in front of the fireplace.

"Come on, buddy, we need to get going." I patted his head and he started with a snort and rolled onto his belly. He pushed to his feet, shaking himself from head to toe. I followed Jasper, and Diego followed me. My mother fell in behind us as if that were the best place for her to keep an eye on Jasper.

I swallowed the sigh that wanted to slip out. I had expected Jasper's half-demon parentage to be a challenge for me, mostly because his father scared the bejesus out of me, but I had not anticipated ever having to share this information with my mother or her having such a negative response.

We walked through the mansion and I marveled at the same parquet floor and decorative oak paneling on the walls. The room that was now a museum was in its former glory as a grand ballroom and Mabel led us to the end of it where the door that led down to the Books of Dubious Origin collection of the future would have been.

There was no familiar iron door. Instead, Mabel used magic to move one of the wall panels, revealing the same spiral staircase that I knew so well. We trudged in single file down the three flights of stairs, following Mabel and the golden orb of light she manifested. There were no lasers or doors to be magicked through. Instead, we walked along the tunnel, illuminated by Mabel's light until we came to a large oak door. Mabel again used her magic to open it and we stepped into the BODO.

So much was the same. The large main room, the three stories of open shelving accessible by two spiral staircases, the wrought iron railings containing the collection, and the beautiful ceiling overhead that reflected the sky so that the inhabitants didn't feel suffocated by being underground.

"It looks the same," Jasper marveled. "Although in our timeline, the shelves are packed."

Mabel smiled at him. "That is gratifying to hear. I brought you here because it will be less conspicuous if you leave from here."

Mom started to protest but Mabel shook her head. "You know she has to go, Juliet."

Given the searing red light and tornado wind our departure was going to kick up, I knew Mabel was wise to keep our departure hidden from view.

"Now, before you go, let me quickly tell you about the other books," Mabel said. "Although, truthfully, I don't know much. The legend of the bonded books has been whispered about for years, but with no hard evidence of such books, it's been believed to be just that—a myth, a tall tale, a legend."

"What are the other books?" Jasper asked.

Mabel bit the tip of her thumb as she paced back and forth, as if being in motion would help her gather her thoughts. She dropped her hand and said, "According to the rumors, the five bonded books were the *Book of Shadows*, the *Book of Echoes*, the *Book of Whispers*, the *Book of Secrets*, and the *Book of Destiny*."

A shiver coursed through my book as she listed the titles. "Why are they called by those names?"

Mabel dropped her hand and turned to face me. "Like your grimoire, they're each named for the strongest spell within their pages."

"Our grimoire can call forth the dead," Mom said. "But we're not really bringing people back, merely an echo of who they once were."

I thought about Mamie when I'd called her to me. She'd been tangible. I'd hugged her. But, much like an echo, she'd faded when my magic wasn't strong enough to hold her. I nodded. The name made sense.

"And the *Book of Shadows* is demon-bound," Jasper said. "Demons weaponize their shadows, and the book's ability to alter reality is definitely shadow magic, the sort of thing done in the shadows and not something of which the Global Council of Magisters would approve."

"Definitely not," Mabel agreed. "The other books are named

as aptly as these two, I suspect, but given that no one has seen them in decades, I can't say what spells they possess that warrant their names or if they still exist."

"You've given us plenty of information to start a search," I said. I could feel the librarian inside of me crackle to life with the desire to track down every bit of information I could on these five bonded books. There was no doubt in my mind that McWrath's endgame was to acquire all the books, because as my mom had pointed out, it would allow him to easily rule the world.

I turned to Diego, who was busy licking his chest. "Time to transform, my guy."

He stopped grooming his fur and as he straightened up, he became the fearsome, red-eyed guardian beast that looked as if he ate bats for breakfast.

"That's disgusting. Bats are entirely too bony," Diego protested.

"Whatever," I said. *"Did you have a nice nap?"*

"Delightful," he responded. *"Now say a proper goodbye to your mother. She's very sad."*

I glanced at my mother and saw the shimmer of tears in her eyes. It hurt my heart and I wished I could stay, but we'd been gone for hours and I had no idea what we'd find when we went back. I just hoped I could direct the spell to take us to our friends, wherever they might be.

"Mom, I promise I'll come back as soon as I can," I said as I approached her. "Now that I know I can manage this, I hope to come and visit often."

My mother's lips trembled and she fidgeted with the handkerchief in her hands. "I'd like that."

"Me, too." I hugged her hard, taking in her scent, which was exactly as I remembered. It made my heart hurt and with one more quick squeeze, I let her go. I turned to say goodbye to Mabel, who was speaking in low tones with Jasper but turned to smile at me when I approached.

"Thank you for taking care of my mom," I said.

Mabel waved off my thanks. "Juliet takes better care of me than I do of her. I'm lucky to have her, especially since my beloved Thomas has passed away." A look of deep sadness crossed over her face and I knew the bone-deep grief she was feeling. I reached out and squeezed her hand.

"Come back to us whenever you can," Mabel said.

"I will."

Jasper finished speaking with my mother. Whatever he'd said seemed to ease the suspicion in her eyes a bit when she looked at him. He and Diego took positions on each side of me, and I clutched my grimoire close as I grabbed Diego by the scruff while Jasper stood behind me with his arms around my waist.

"Bye, Mom," I said. "Bye, Mabel."

The two women linked arms, and I found it comforting that my mother had established a good life for herself with people who cared about her. I closed my eyes and thought about our colleagues as I muttered the same words, "Per vias temporis, transitus aperiatur," that had yanked us away from our own timeline to here.

The light and wind assaulted us just as fiercely as they had the first time. I genuinely thought I might be sick when it felt as if my bones were being ground to bits. And then it was over.

We collapsed onto the floor, and as soon as my hand smacked the decorative parquet flooring that I knew so well after months of walking on it, I was certain I had failed and we were still in Mabel Stewart's home.

"Oh, no, we're supposed to be with Miles, Olive, and Tariq at the opera hall." I pushed up to a seated position within the protective circle of Jasper's arms.

Jasper let me go and straightened up. "What exactly was in your mind when we time hopped?"

"I concentrated on our colleagues at the opera house, but it brought us here instead." I patted Diego's back, assuring myself that he was okay. He nuzzled my hand in answer.

Miles strolled out of his office and stared at us on the floor. He was wearing a pair of flannel plaid pajamas with a blue robe and leather fleece-lined slippers. Given that we were three floors belowground, I had no idea what time it was or why he was dressed as if he was either going to sleep or just waking up.

"Miles, you're here!" I cried with relief. I hadn't messed up, and the spell had brought us back to our colleagues in the BODO.

"I am, but where have you three been? We haven't seen you in days," Miles said.

"Days?" Jasper and I asked together.

"But we were just at Lyric Hall with you a few hours ago," I said.

"Lyric Hall?" Miles cupped his chin with one hand in his thinking pose. "I think if I'd seen you there, I'd remember it. We went there hoping to find the *Book of Shadows* but it didn't pan out."

"But we have—" I began, but Jasper grabbed my arm and when I glanced at him in question, he shook his head.

"Miles, where are Tariq and Olive?" Jasper asked.

"In their offices," Miles said. "We just got back from the opera house a bit ago and we're all feeling a little out of sorts."

"Why did you go to the opera house to search for the book?" Jasper asked.

Miles frowned. "Someone told us to go there. Huh, I can't remember who it was now."

Diego let out a low growl, which confirmed it. Something was off with Miles.

"But you didn't find anything there?" I clarified.

"Nothing. The place was a rotted-out shell and not safe to enter," Miles said. "We walked the perimeter but couldn't risk going inside."

I exchanged another puzzled glance with Jasper. It was almost as if Miles's memory of the actual events had been erased and replaced. Could the spell from the *Book of Shadows* that altered reality do that?

It was then that I noticed Miles's eyes. They held a vacant quality that I had only seen one other time, and that was when the dancers had been possessed the night of the gala. Miles had clearly been bewitched.

"McWrath must have spelled him before we found the *Book of Shadows* on the boat and escaped Lyric Hall with it. I don't think a banshee can help us this time," I said to Jasper, dropping my voice so Miles couldn't hear.

"No, she can't." He turned toward the other office doors and called out, "Oy! Olive, Tariq, we need you!"

I moved in close to his side and hissed, "How do we break the spell?"

Jasper met my eyes with his light blue gaze and whispered, "We can both utilize the *Book of Shadows*. There has to be a counterspell in the book that we can use."

"Of course!" I felt like slapping my forehead, but as Olive and Tariq stepped out of their offices to join us, I refrained.

"Keep them distracted and I'll see if I can find the spell," Jasper said.

"Nice of you to join us," Olive said. She was dressed all in black, but this time it was a long fluffy black robe over a pair of black pajamas and a very trendy pair of black kitten-heeled mules. While Olive was always stylish in her basic black, the kitten heels seemed . . . odd.

Meanwhile Tariq was in blue-and-white-striped flannel pajamas and had a dark blue eye mask pushed back on his forehead as if he'd been asleep.

"What's going on?" he asked through a yawn. When he saw us, he yelped. "Zoe! Jasper! Where have you been?"

"What time is it?" I asked. "Why are you all dressed in pajamas? Are you sleeping here?"

"If you'd been with us, you would know that we left the opera house at two in the morning after being nearly frozen to death," Olive said.

"We created our own heat bubbles," Tariq said to me. "It wasn't that bad."

"When we finally got back here, Mabel's room divided into three, one for each of us," Miles explained. "We were so tired, we decided to sleep in our offices."

"We were that pathetic when we arrived, not that you two care," Olive said. "Where have you been, anyway?"

Maybe it was Olive's tone, but I felt Diego's hair rise on the back of his neck. He'd already growled at Miles.

"Why don't you go sleep in my office," I suggested to Diego, not wanting him to cause a ruckus. *"Jasper and I can handle this."*

He tipped his head to the side as if he'd argue when a yawn snuck out of him, opening his massive jaw and causing his tongue to curl. *"Fine. Yell if you need me."*

I watched him disappear into my office before I glanced behind me at Jasper, who had his back to the group as he thumbed through the demon-bound book looking for the appropriate spell. I faced the others and studied each of their expressions. Tariq and Olive both had a vacant stare, much like Miles.

I didn't know how the altered-reality spell worked. If I challenged their memories, would they become combative? There was only one way to know.

"Jasper and I were with you at the opera house," I said. All three of them flinched as if hit with an electric shock. Was that how an altered reality worked? The truth became jarring.

"Sorry, Zoe, but I think we'd remember," Tariq's voice was gentle but firm.

"Not if someone used a reality-altering spell on you, you wouldn't," I said.

"I would know if I'd been bewitched," Olive snapped.

"Would you?" I countered. I thought back to the Midnight Market and how she hadn't been affected by the reality-altering spell at all. Why now then?

"Easy," Jasper muttered from behind me. "I said to distract not enrage."

"Right. Sorry." I tipped my chin up. "I have very different memories of the opera hall."

"I'm sure you do, since you weren't there," Olive chided me.

Miles held up his hand. "Let's hear her out." He turned back to me. "Zoe, tell us your version of tonight's events."

"All right." I glanced at Olive and said, "But no turning me into a doorknob if you don't like what I have to say."

"I would never." Olive sniffed. "You'd be a dishrag first."

"Great." I took a deep breath and told them everything, minus the part about Jasper having the *Book of Shadows* because until they were back to normal, I didn't want to risk having them do anything that might have been programmed into them by McWrath, such as murdering Jasper for the book.

By the time I finished the story of our adventures at the opera house, giving an abbreviated ending of Jasper and me escaping McWrath, all three of them were looking at me in sheer disbelief.

"I was *not* a puppet!" Olive snapped.

"You were all puppets," I said. "And Odessa Van Doren was in command of you."

"I can't imagine why Zoe would make any of this up," Miles said. "And it would explain a few things."

"Such as?" Olive asked.

"The missing hours," Tariq said. "None of us can remember leaving the BODO or arriving at the opera house or what we did at the opera house for a few hours before we remember wandering around the building and through the woods." Olive sent him a dark look but Tariq shrugged. "It's true."

"Zoe's version does fill in those gaps," Miles agreed. "And if our memories were altered, it would explain why we believe they weren't with us and why we think we haven't seen them for days. Jasper, what do you think?"

Jasper stepped out from behind me, holding his book behind his back as he recited a spell that sounded like medieval Latin, "Veritas revela, umbrae cadant."

My librarian mind immediately translated it to "as the truth is revealed, let the shadows fall." Which made sense since it was a spell from the *Book of Shadows*, after all.

Unlike the drama of the time hop, this was a gentler spell. It felt as if a ripple of energy shot out from Jasper to the far reaches of the room.

Miles staggered on his feet. Olive clutched the back of a chair, and Tariq sank onto the floor right where he stood, landing in a seated position with a thump. Tariq glanced up at Olive and said, "Zoe was telling the truth."

"I gathered," Olive said. "I remember it now, all of it." Miles pulled out a chair at the large round table where we held meetings, and Olive gratefully sank into it. She rested her head on the table and said, "I *was* a puppet. Mad respect to Odessa Van Doren then."

I tipped my head, studying her long dark hair splayed across the table. The Olive I knew would be vowing revenge and planning exactly how she was going to make Odessa Van Doren pay.

Miles took a seat as if standing required too much energy and glanced at Jasper. "Is that . . . did you just use the *Book of Shadows*?"

"I did," Jasper said. "Turns out it's a spellbook by and for demons."

"Kai!" Tariq exclaimed as he rose from the floor and joined the others at the table.

Jasper and I took the remaining seats. I rested my chin on my hand. I was exhausted and I hadn't even emotionally unboxed the reunion with my mom yet.

Miles turned to me with his dark eyes as sharp as ever and asked, "You said that you used your grimoire to escape McWrath but you didn't say how. What happened, Zoe?"

"I used a spell in my grimoire to travel here," I said. I saw them nod as if it made sense that we would escape to the BODO. After a beat, I added, "Except when we arrived, 'here' was in 1897 and Mabel Stewart was in residence."

26

Tariq's jaw dropped, Olive's eyebrows shot up, and Miles smiled. It was a slow smile that caused his entire face to crinkle in the purest expression of joy.

"You did it." He beamed at me. "You used the grimoire to travel through time."

"Yeah." I felt an embarrassed heat flood my face and I glanced down at my hands. I realized I was still in my coat and took my grimoire out of my pocket and set it on the table.

"She was spectacular," Jasper said. "Saved our lives, no question."

"Well done, Zoe," Olive said.

Praise from Olive? And she'd even called me by my first name. I felt my face grow even warmer.

"I'd say it was nothing, but that would be a lie," I said. "Time hopping is not pleasant, but it was worth it."

Jasper reached over and squeezed my shoulder. He knew that seeing my mother again had been huge for me. I turned my head and saw the empathy on his face, and it gave me a shot of strength I hadn't known I needed.

"It was a quick trip, but we discovered something about the *Book of Shadows* and my grimoire, which apparently is also known as the *Book of Echoes*."

Tariq, Olive, and Miles glanced at my family grimoire, and judging by their startled expressions, they'd heard the name before.

"The Donadieu family grimoire is the *Book of Echoes*," Miles repeated as if he had to hear the words aloud again to make sense of them.

"Of course," Olive said. "Because necromancers bring back echoes of the past."

"Exactly." Jasper nodded.

"I can't believe you got to meet Mabel Stewart," Tariq sighed. "That's so cool."

"There's more," I said. "Apparently, the reason McWrath was so hot to get my book is because the two books are bonded."

Jasper set his book on the table beside mine. I felt that same tingle of happiness coming from my grimoire and wondered at it. I glanced up to see if anyone else felt the connection between the two volumes or if it was just me. It was then that I saw it. A glitch. A rip in the fabric of the glamour.

"And they're not the only—" Jasper began, but I interrupted.

"Olive, can you do me a favor and make one of your light orbs?" I asked. "It's so dark in here and I'm just too tired to craft one myself."

Olive's scarred eyebrow ticked up and she looked away from my direct gaze. "I'd love to, Zoe, but I'm afraid that enchantment we were under really wore me out."

"I can do it," Tariq volunteered.

"No." It came out harsh and Tariq blinked in surprise.

"Sorry, it's just that I'm really curious as to how Olive was bewitched by the reality-altering spell at the opera house when I'd thought she was immune. Wasn't that what you said at the Midnight Market, Olive? That those spells don't work on you?"

"Obviously, McWrath has been practicing." Olive flicked a bit of lint off her robe's sleeve.

"It's also interesting how you've called me Zoe twice when Olive has never called me by my first name before," I said. "And kitten heels? Really? You should have done your homework more carefully . . . McWrath."

Olive's eyes narrowed, and the irises that were normally so dark they looked black flared yellow and all hell broke loose.

Diego came out of my office as if he'd been launched. The glamour on Olive melted away and McWrath stood in the middle of the BODO in all of his crimson-skinned, curly-horned demon glory. Jasper grabbed his book and mine and yanked me down to the floor under the cover of the table.

White-hot light lit the room, and I knew Miles was using his magic to contain McWrath.

I peeked over the edge of the table and saw McWrath throw back his head and laugh.

"You think you can hold me, old man?" McWrath roared. "I wore your body like a cheap suit and used your aura to break into the vault and steal the *Book of Shadows* and you had no idea."

I sucked in a breath. Jasper's father had been right. McWrath had used Miles! I saw Miles's white light waver with uncertainty and then he hunkered into his magic and snarled, "Thanks for the lesson. You can be certain that will never happen again."

A blast of bright white light lit the entire BODO and I ducked back down behind the table.

"Take the books and go, love." Jasper shoved the books into my hands. Diego skidded to a stop beside me. "Get her out of here, Diego."

"But I can help," I protested.

"Getting these books away from McWrath is the greatest good you can do." Jasper kissed me quick. "Go!"

Damn it. I knew he was right. Diego put himself between me and the fight, which now included Jasper's black light and Tariq's silver. I loved them all dearly, but I didn't think McWrath was the sort to be held by three mages' magic no matter how powerful they were.

Clutching the books to my chest with one arm, I tried to figure out where to go. It had to be a place where McWrath wasn't. A chair exploded next to us and Diego moved his body between it and me. I peeked over the edge of the table to see how it was going and noted that volumes from the shelves were dive-bombing McWrath, who stood in the center of three ropes of magical bonds. Jasper, Miles, and Tariq, the three musketeers, were holding on so tight that their muscles were straining, their jaws were clenched, and sweat was beading up on their foreheads.

I had to leave to give McWrath a reason to depart as well. Without the books, there was no purpose for him here. There was really only one place to go. One of our people was missing and I needed to find her.

"Hang on, Diego," I said. I grabbed him by the scruff as I closed my eyes, focused on Olive, and muttered the spell that would deliver me where I suspected I was needed most.

We landed back in the opera hall theater with a hard thump. I hated this place so much my fight-or-flight response kicked in on an adrenaline surge that almost had me sprinting out the door.

"Why can't we ever land on a nice fluffy couch somewhere?" Diego grumbled.

"You really are a complainy adolescent, aren't you?" I asked. *"Be grateful we're away from McWrath and help me find Olive."*

Diego started sniffing the ground. I rose to my feet and followed him, tucking each of the volumes into my cloak pockets. The theater had the same feeling of expectation about it. Was it real or something else set up to keep me off-kilter?

I was following Diego so closely, looking for clues on the ground, that I didn't notice another presence until I saw a pair of shiny black shoes. I jerked upright and there stood my buddy the ghost usher.

"Ticket?" he asked.

"Don't have one." I tried to walk around him but he stepped in front of me. Diego growled, but our man of the snappy outfit and pomaded hair did not care. Truly, what could a hellhound possibly do to him?

"Ticket?" he repeated.

"Oh, for fuck's sake." I slid my hand into my pocket and my fingers closed around a slip of paper. Could it be? I pulled it out and sure enough it was the same ticket I'd given him before. Had Miles spelled it to be returned to me? Wouldn't put it past him.

"This way, please." The usher began to bounce down the rows to the same seat I'd sat in before.

"I can't," I said. "I'm looking for someone."

He came back at me in a rush, stopping mere inches from my face, but I held my ground. I wasn't afraid of no ghost.

"Sit down!" he ordered.

Okay then. I sat where I was told. With one last irritated look at me, the usher departed.

"We're not actually doing this again, are we?" Diego asked.

"Oh, hell no," I said. *"As soon as that curtain opens, get ready to charge the stage. Odessa is behind this, I'm sure of it."*

The phantom pit orchestra began to play an eerie tune and I steeled myself to see Olive trotted around the stage as a giant puppet. I felt queasy at the thought but shook it off. We would grab Olive and get her out of here and be back at the museum as fast as we could.

The curtain began to open and I was about to push up out of my seat when I fell back in shock. There was a giant puppet on the stage, but it wasn't Olive. It was Odessa!

As we watched, Odessa performed an awkward ballet. When her gaze met mine, her eyes shot blue fire. She was livid. She opened her mouth to speak but no sound came out. I didn't have to think too hard to determine who the puppet master was for this show. I rose from my seat, more than a little surprised that I was able to do so. I saw the ghost usher out of the corner of my eye and held up my hand, and said, "No."

Diego and I strode to the stage, climbing up the stairs along the side and stepping behind the curtain into the wings. I stared into the darkness until I could see the ghostly pallor that was Olive. I stood on one side of her and Diego sat beside me as we watched her control Odessa's arms and legs, forcing her to twirl and jump and prance just as Odessa had done to Olive and the others.

"I like this woman, I really do," Diego said. I ignored him.

"Are you almost done, Olive?" I asked.

"Maybe in another year or two, Ziakas. Now go away." Olive bounced her hands, making Odessa hop like a bunny.

"McWrath is in the BODO," I said.

Olive dropped her hands and Odessa went limp. "What?"

"McWrath glamoured himself to look like you and has been in the museum with Tariq and Miles for the past few hours," I said. "I assume he left you here because he knew that his reality-altering spell wouldn't work on you, plus, he wanted to steal your identity."

"What did he do to them?" Olive demanded. I glanced at where Odessa was hanging like a rag doll. Clearly Olive's revenge was completely forgotten when her colleagues were in peril.

"He altered their memories of tonight, disguised himself as you, and now Miles, Tariq, and Jasper are trying to contain him," I said. "He's after the *Book of Shadows*, which Jasper stole back, and my grimoire, which is apparently also known as the *Book of Echoes*."

"Your grimoire is the *Book of Echoes*?" Olive repeated. "Of course, I should have guessed. He must know that they're connected."

"He does," I said. "Wait, you know that?"

"Of course, Ziakas," she snapped. It was so nice to have cranky Olive back. "How did you get here? We have to go back immediately."

"What about her?" I gestured to Odessa.

"She has drained her last witch," Olive said. She turned away from me and shouted, "You can take her now!"

I watched as a black-robed figure stepped onto the stage. The being pushed his hood back and a head of white hair in a half ponytail was revealed. Rowan Thorne!

"Olive, no!" I cried. "You can't trust him. He works for McWrath."

"Excuse me?" Thorne asked. "Do I know you?"

Another robed figure stepped out of the shadows and pushed back his hood. He was short and robust with round eyeglasses and a curled mustache. Recognition hit me instantly. Marvello from the market, keeper of bookwyrms and odd objects.

"Marvello?" I asked just to be certain.

"Nice to see you again, Zoe," Marv said. "I see you know my fellow sentry."

"Sentry?" I asked.

"They work for the Global Council of Magisters," Olive said. "They transport those who use their gifts for nefarious purposes to the council for judgment."

"But you"—I pointed to Rowan Thorne—"were here all night."

"Sorry, ma'am, I have no idea what you're talking about. Marv and I have been hustling all evening. It's been a banger night for bad behavior," Thorne said.

"But Jasper said you were no—" I cut myself off, thinking that insulting Thorne might not be my best play.

Thorne's white eyebrows lifted. Now I had his attention. "Are you talking about Jasper Griffin?" The intensity of his dark stare gave me pause.

"Yes." It came out hesitant even to my own ears.

"He's a friend of yours?" Thorne asked. I didn't feel the need to explain we were actually a couple, so I just nodded.

"Jasper used to be my friend, too. He turned me over to the council last year, and my sentence was to work for them or lose my magical ability. I've been working for them ever since." He looked rueful. "Tell Jasper I said . . . thanks." It looked as if the words cost him, but it was clear Thorne had chosen to turn his life around, however reluctantly.

I decided to take him at his word. "Just so you know, a demon named McWrath has been impersonating you."

"Well, shit," Rowan cursed. "I did a job for him about five years ago. Damn it, you do one deal with a guy and he takes your likeness. That's just rude."

"Demons." Olive shrugged.

I turned to Marv. "I thought you kept a booth at the Midnight Market."

"That's just a side hustle." Marv waved his hand dismissively. "The wife says I have too much stuff, so I sell it there to keep her happy."

A glass ball on Thorne's belt lit up. "We have another call. We need to go."

"Take her." Olive snapped her fingers and Odessa was released from Olive's magical bonds. The mages caught Odessa in a web of orange light before she hit the floor. Marv wrapped the web around her and then, with her floating in between them, they took three steps forward and vanished.

"What was that?" I cried.

"As Marv said, they're sentries for the Global Council of Magisters," Olive said. "I've done a lot for the council, so they agreed to let me have a moment with Odessa before they took her away."

"What will happen to Odessa?" I asked.

"Nothing that she doesn't deserve," Olive said. "Now how did you get here?"

"I used the spell in my grimoire to time hop," I said.

"Finally making yourself useful, Ziakas?" Olive asked. "Let's see it then."

I swallowed hard and grabbed Diego by the scruff and looped my arm through Olive's. I focused on our colleagues, repeated the spell three times, and hoped that we weren't too late.

This time I was certain my bones actually were ground to a fine powder. When we landed on the roof of the museum, I was so relieved to have made it, I sucked in a deep breath and pushed all thoughts of the pain out of my head.

"Excellent." Olive stood up and strode toward the door that led inside. "We can sneak in and see what's happening."

"I wouldn't rush in there if I were you." A deep voice spoke from the shadows, and I felt Diego's fur rise under my hand as he bared his teeth and a low growl sounded in his throat.

Olive immediately formed an orb of blue light and sent it up into the air, illuminating the rooftop. Out of the darkness strode Jasper's father, Lord Eliath Griffin, and beside him was his doorman, Corey, from Griffin's antiquities shop.

27

"Eliath." Olive said his name as if it bored her.

"Olive." Lord Griffin sounded equally unimpressed.

"Corey." I greeted him with all the friendliness I could muster given that he still looked like he could rip a person's head off their body.

"Zoe." Corey grinned, and a gold tooth winked at me in the glow of Olive's light.

"If that's all the niceties," Olive said. "We have a situation."

She started for the door, and Diego and I fell in behind her.

"You can't beat McWrath," Lord Griffin said.

"Oh no? Watch me," Olive retorted.

"He wants the *Book of Shadows* back and he won't stop until he gets it," Lord Griffin said.

I felt a flutter of fear come from the pocket that held my grimoire. I wanted to comfort it, but not at the risk of Lord Griffin noticing. With my nerves as frayed as they'd ever been, I was annoyed by the chitchat, and I sounded an awful lot like Olive when I snapped, "Your son is in there. Do you plan on helping us help him, or are you just going to stand in the way?"

Corey's eyes went wide while Olive looked at me with a glint of what I thought might be pride. Much to my relief, Lord Griffin just rolled his eyes and said, "Of course I'm here to help, which is why I am advising against running in through the only entrance where he's sure to grab you." Lord Griffin paused to glare at me. "Especially while you're carrying the very books he seeks."

"He's not wrong," Diego said.

"Hush."

"Then what do you suggest?" Olive asked.

"I have an idea, but you're going to have to trust me," Lord Griffin said.

"Why would we do that?" Olive countered.

"Because if you don't, the BODO will be destroyed," Lord Griffin said.

Olive crossed her arms over her chest and stared out at the cityscape. The brightening sky to the east indicated that sunrise was coming, which felt ominous. I had no reason to believe that we were running out of time except the feeling in my soul.

"I think we have no choice," I said.

Olive glanced at me and nodded once. "Fine." She turned to Lord Griffin. "What's the plan?"

"This is so weird," I said. I held my hand up in front of my face and noted that I could see through my fingers, my hand, my sleeve.

"You get used to it." Corey shrugged. I glanced at the portly man who was now, like me, a shadow of his former self.

"We're going to slip under the door and down the staircase to the library," Lord Griffin said. "Once inside, we'll assess the situation."

"I'll assess the situation," Olive corrected him. I stared at the two-dimensional dark gray shadow that was now Olive. So strange.

Lord Griffin had used his demon ability to make the four of us into shadows, and to my surprise the transformation hadn't hurt. Quite the opposite, I felt lighter. It was as if he'd taken away the burden of being in a body and I felt oddly buoyant.

"Stop bouncing," Lord Griffin said to me, and I immediately tempered my enthusiasm for my new form. "While McWrath is distracted, we'll sneak inside. Keep to the shadows and he might not notice that we're there. Now follow me and stay close."

Diego had not been transformed and would wait on the roof and act as a lookout in case McWrath brought in help.

"*I'll stay in touch.*" I tried to pat Diego's head but my hand went right through him.

"*Oh, ew.*" He shook his head as if I'd slimed him. I tried not to be offended.

Lord Griffin dropped to the ground and slid beneath the door; Olive went next, then me, and Corey brought up the rear. It was so much easier than I'd expected. As we slid down the stairs, I marveled at how different moving through the world as a shadow was.

When we reached the doorway at the bottom of the stairs,

Lord Griffin paused before he left and said, "If I tell you not to follow, go back to the roof immediately."

We all nodded in agreement. My nerves ratcheted up as I had no idea what we were walking . . . er . . . slithering into.

Lord Griffin disappeared and then we heard him whisper, "Come on then."

Again, we slipped through the crack between the door and the floor until we were huddled in an alcove at the top of the library. We could hear the chaos below and I slid to the railing to get a glimpse of what was happening.

The tables and chairs resembled kindling and the books had stopped dive-bombing McWrath, obviously realizing that they couldn't fight against so much power.

Olive slid up beside me and took in the scene below. "This is bad."

"Yup," I agreed.

McWrath was no longer being held in magical bonds. Instead, he was the one with the upper hand, or rather hands, as he had sprouted several more arms and was brandishing a sword, a mace, a shield, and an axe with all of them.

Miles, Tariq, and Jasper were throwing everything they had at him. Tariq's pajamas were torn and his eye mask gone. Raising a large wooden bowl, he tossed the contents at McWrath, coating him with a glowing green slime that I could smell all the way up here with my two-dimensional nose. I gagged. McWrath's body became red hot and he burned the slime off, making the stench even worse.

Miles's glasses were perched so far on the end of his nose, I was certain they'd fall off. Still, he threw up a shield to contain McWrath. The demon tried using his weapons on it, but the shield wouldn't give. He stomped around in a circle, bellowing in fury. I felt a surge of satisfaction until McWrath hit it in the same spot with all his weapons at once, causing the shield to splinter right down the middle. Damn it.

Jasper had a cut on his head and blood was running down the side of his face. Still, he held his arms out and I watched him cast a spell that called forth the authors of the books surrounding us. Under his command, a squad of ancient mages and witches attacked the demon with spells that immobilized him, shields that prevented him from fighting back, and curses that tripped him and covered his eyes with a magical blindfold. I heard Lord Griffin grunt with what sounded like approval.

"That's how you do it," Lord Griffin said. "To beat a demon, you don't use brute strength. You destroy their essence. McWrath wants to be the most powerful magical being, but he is being attacked by those he can never match."

McWrath was going down under the onslaught until he grabbed the wizard Merlin by the throat and in a blink, he shape-shifted into him. McWrath spun them around in dizzying circles until it was impossible to tell which of them was the book-borrowed Merlin and which was McWrath.

The fighting immediately ceased as the squad didn't want to harm the magical legend. Jasper, Miles, and Tariq were now at a standoff with two Merlins and a crew of famous witches and mages who had no idea what to do. Jasper gestured the others away and they vanished, but the two Merlins remained.

"Well, that's a problem," Corey said.

"Or it's buying us some time," I countered. "I have an idea. Cover me."

"Is she serious? Does she think I'm going to let my son's survival rest on her?" Lord Griffin asked Olive.

Olive shrugged. "Then might I suggest we get down there and help him?"

"Perfect," I said. "I just need a minute. Can you switch me back to my old form as soon as I'm in my office?"

"Of course." Lord Griffin looked insulted by the question.

"Excellent." I didn't wait for his response but slid down the steps toward my office as swiftly as I could.

I was betting that there was only one way McWrath was going to gain control of the situation and that was to use his most powerful weapon. It was the one that allowed him to break into the BODO's vault, the one he used to attack us on the roof, and it was what Lord Griffin would call his essence. Now that I had assumed a like form, I understood the power that McWrath, a shadow demon, wielded and I knew how to defeat it.

Once inside my office, my shadow started to expand. I felt as if I were a balloon being blown up. Gone was my two-dimensional semitransparent state. I was fully corporeal again. In moments, I heard Olive, Lord Griffin, and Corey join the fray.

"Diego, I need you," I said.

"Of course you do."

I shook my head at his arrogance and hurried over to the cabinet. I stored the two bonded books and retrieved the bottle containing the lightning storm I'd made and set it on my desk. When I had fought off McWrath on the roof, I'd used the power of night, but this time I needed more. I needed a source that was blindingly bright that I could weaponize, and lightning was just the ticket.

"I'm right outside your door." Diego's voice spoke in my head.

I opened the door and blinked at the chaos that met my gaze. With the added forces of Olive, Lord Griffin, and Corey, McWrath was outmatched and he knew it. I watched as one Merlin flung the other away from him and McWrath assumed his full demon form. Lord Griffin did the same, and I glanced across the library to see a look of alarm pass over Jasper's face. He and his father might be at odds, but Jasper was clearly worried about him.

I knew that, being outmatched, McWrath would fall back on his essence, so to speak. While other demons could become shadows, he had the ability to use his shadow as an assassin, a thief, or a route for escape.

"When he turns into a shadow, pounce," I said to Diego. The hellhound assumed a pointer position.

We watched as our friends and allies hit McWrath with everything they had. He fought them off, even trading blows with Lord Griffin. When he staggered back and glanced from side to side with his yellow slitted eyes, I knew he was looking for an escape.

"Get ready," I said to Diego.

Sure enough, one second McWrath was there and the next he was gone. I heard our friends cry out, but my eyes were locked on Diego. With a roar, the hellhound pounced, landing squarely on a shadow that was creeping its way toward the nearby spiral staircase.

"Zoe!" Jasper cried out, but I waved him off.

Feeling as if I were using the last little bit of magic inside of me, I called up the warmth from my core as I opened the bottle, letting my storm out.

The wind and rain were fierce, but I didn't care. I focused solely on the lightning. I needed to grab on to it. I caught a bolt in one fist, and the heat seared my palm, but I didn't let go. I grabbed another with my other hand and pulled their fire into me, recharging my magic and giving my magical bonds the power of white-hot lightning. I pulled in more and more strikes as they came until I felt as if my insides were on fire. Only the freezing rain falling from the dark cloud above me kept my temperature down.

"Hurry! I can't hold him much longer!" Diego cried.

"Jump!" I ordered.

Diego leapt off the shadow on command and I held out my hands and sent many-fingered bolts of lightning around the shadow, lifting it from the floor and caging it in a ball of flashing lightning that it couldn't escape.

An ear-piercing shriek came from the ball and I squinted against the lightning strikes to see McWrath in his demon form, trapped inside a prison that wouldn't allow him to be a shadow ever again.

"I'll be damned," Olive said. "She did it."

That was all I heard before I collapsed into a strong pair of arms that caught me right before I hit the floor.

We sat around the table Miles had restored. We were all battered and bruised, and beyond exhaustion. Tariq had used one of his magical diffusers to rouse me, and was busily tending all our injuries, including his own. I sat in the protective circle of Jasper's arms with salve on my palms for the lightning burns when Thorne and Marv along with two other sentries came and collected McWrath, as he was considered high-risk.

Jasper left me for a moment and I saw him talk to Thorne. I supposed Jasper was apologizing for believing the worst of him. To Thorne's credit, he seemed to accept the apology.

"Feel free to stop catching magical transgressors," Marv said. "We have two more hours left of our shift and would like to have some peace and quiet."

Tariq laughed. "We aren't leaving this room. I promise."

As soon as the sentries took their three steps forward and disappeared, I felt a surge of relief come from the entire collection surrounding us. Jasper's squad of mages and witches from the books had been returned to their tomes, and Miles had sent the books back to their original shelves. The ones that had sustained damage that required magical mending, like Merlin and his grimoire, had been sent to Tariq's lab, where he would tend them as soon as he finished with us.

"Zoe, how did you get the idea to use your lightning?" Miles asked.

"Lord Griffin said to vanquish a demon, you have to go after their essence," I said. "The darkness of night had absorbed him on the roof, eradicating his power but also allowing him to escape. I figured that an opposite force, lightning with its erratic blasts of light, would render his shadow useless and also contain him."

"Well done," Miles said.

"Yes, quite impressive," Lord Griffin agreed. I would have

been pleased with the praise, but he glanced down at his suit with a look of disgust. "If you'll excuse us, Corey and I will be off. I don't think I can stand to be this filthy for another second."

"Of course," Miles said.

Lord Griffin and Corey stood up.

"Hey . . . Dad," Jasper said. Lord Griffin turned around with a curious look. "Thanks for your help."

An expression of deep emotion passed over Lord Griffin's face. If I had to put a name to it, I'd have said he was feeling moved. He swallowed and nodded and cleared his throat.

"I'm always here for you, son." Then he and Corey became shadows and disappeared.

The room was silent for a beat and then Tariq spoke. "If no one else is going to say it, I will. We have to make a decision about these books."

I'd retrieved the *Book of Shadows* and the *Book of Echoes* and placed them in the center of the table, not feeling comfortable with them out of sight.

"I'll keep my grimoire just as I always have," I said. "And Jasper can take charge of the *Book of Shadows*."

Jasper looked at me with his eyebrows raised.

"You're part demon," I explained. "As such, you can use it. I can, too, because of its bond with my grimoire. I don't think keeping it in the vault is a good idea. Better to keep it hidden in plain sight."

Miles nodded. "I agree. Are you willing, Jasper?"

"Of course," he said.

"That's sorted then," Olive said. "Anything else?"

"Yes," Tariq cried. "Do you really think McWrath is the

only one who'll come after these books? From what Mabel Stewart told Jasper and Zoe, it's clear the bond the two books share has been known for centuries. That sort of potential power is a temptation many witches and mages and others won't be able to resist."

I glanced at Jasper. "We have to tell them."

"Agreed," he said.

"What?" Olive glanced between us with her scarred eyebrow raised as if she couldn't believe there could be more bad news after the night we'd just had.

"There are three other books that are also bonded to these two," I said.

"Are you saying what I think you're saying?" Miles asked. "I mean, I've heard rumors, but I thought they were just that."

"Not rumors." I shook my head.

Tariq slumped back in his chair. "Five bonded books?"

"According to Mabel Stewart." Jasper nodded.

Olive crossed her arms over her chest and frowned. "What are they?"

"The *Book of Shadows*, the *Book of Echoes*, the *Book of Whispers*, the *Book of Secrets*, and the *Book of Destiny*," I said. "And whoever possesses all five could easily rule the world, both magical and non-magical."

"Miles, is this true?" Tariq asked.

Miles cupped his chin in thought. His eyes glinted with excitement. "The story of these bonded books has existed for centuries, but because none of the books were ever seen, it became the stuff of legend, but now that we have two of them, I have to say yes. I believe there are three more, and I believe as the Books of Dubious Origin department, it is our duty to find them."

Tariq slowly lowered his head to the table. "I knew he was going to say that. I knew it."

"Cheer up, Silver," Olive said. "Think of the quest to find these missing books as job security."

"Ha." Tariq let out a laugh that sounded like a sob.

A big blocky head plopped into my lap and I scratched Diego's ears.

"What do you think, love?" Jasper asked me.

"I think . . ." I paused as I noticed everyone's attention was on me. "I think we're going on a quest."

Jasper grinned, Miles chuckled, Tariq moaned, and Olive looked bored. But I knew that no matter how we each felt about the quest, we were going and we were going together because that's what families do.

ACKNOWLEDGMENTS

Writing the Books of Dubious Origin has been an exercise in letting my imagination run wild. Truly, some of the scenes, specifically the magical ones, have surprised even me as I was writing them. I kept asking myself, "Where did that come from?" No idea.

I do know it has been an absolute joyride from the first word until the last. All that to say, I am very grateful to my editors, Kate Seaver and Amanda Maurer, for joining me on this adventure. You always make my work that much better. And thanks to my agents, Christina Hogrebe and Jessica Errera, for having my back when I come up with the latest thing I want to try. I couldn't do any of this without your support and encouragement.

Thank you to the publicity and marketing teams, in particular Kaila Mundell-Hill and Kim Salina-I. Your tireless work on behalf of the book is much appreciated.

I have always had amazing covers, but Brandon Dorman has made the covers of this series absolutely magical and I am so grateful for his brilliant artistry. And special thanks to

Kristin del Rosario for her brilliant book design. It is next-level.

Special thanks to my tireless assistant, Jenel Looney, whose creativity in promoting my work knows no bounds. Also, you're truly the most organized person I know. Shout-out to the Xuni team for my fabulous website.

Lastly, many thanks to my family, Chris Orf, Beckett Orf, and Wyatt Orf, and my dear friends—you know who you are—who are endlessly patient with my deadlines, work-aholism, and inability to talk about anything but whatever book I'm currently working on. I love you all more than words can ever say.

Keep reading for an excerpt from
Jenn McKinlay's novel

The Summer Share

Hannah

"Good morning, travelers," I said to the camera on my phone, which was perched in its holder on the dashboard of my vintage Volkswagen van.

Bang! The right-front tire lurched into a pothole on the sorely neglected road.

"Ah!" I took my foot off the gas and swerved out of the danger zone. The van didn't shimmy or pull, so we hadn't popped a tire. *Hallelujah.* I'd had enough flats in my career as an online camper van enthusiast to know when Buttercup—yes, my baby had a name—was in trouble.

Dude, my Great Dane rescue, lurched to his feet and shoved his big blocky head in between the front seats—to offer assistance, no doubt, as he was always helpful like that. I reached up and rubbed his soft, floppy ears.

"It's okay, buddy. We're almost there." I tapped the camera off on my phone. Given the poor condition of the road, I figured it was better to record my content for next week after we arrived.

I turned my attention back to the narrow lane. There was enough room for only one car so I really hoped no one approached me from the opposite direction. Because with vibrantly green grassy marshland squeezing the road on both sides like a too-tight corset, there was no place for me to go except into the brackish muddy water.

I scanned the area, looking for the cottage where my Pops had spent every summer for as long as I could remember. The Outer Banks had been his special place in his later years. No one in the family had ever been invited into his fishing sanctuary. It was just him and his solitary weeks spent on the water. I think we accepted the banishment only because he kept us supplied with enough grouper, red drum, and little tunny for the entire winter.

Now that I was here, my chest felt tight with a fresh wave of loss for the man who had been my number one fan, my champion, and my best friend. Inhaling through my nose, I slowly exhaled out my mouth, trying to control the grief that had been ever present since the moment Pops had passed four weeks ago.

The van lurched into another pothole. "Damn it."

When I was a kid, Pops and Nana brought me to the Carolina shore for weeklong summer vacations. My memories were full of sand between my toes and ice cream cones, marathon Monopoly games when it rained, and generally just basking in the adoration of two of my favorite people.

When they divorced, in a split my dad called the most amicable parting of ways in the history of marriage, the vacations stopped. Nana started dating while Pops continued his trips to the Carolina shore but he went by himself, making this place his own.

Another large divot appeared and I refocused on the road, weaving around the treacherous-looking pit. The marshland fell away as Buttercup rumbled onto firmer ground and the road widened just enough for two vehicles to fit with a fine hair between them.

Dude and I followed the curved lane, passing by several houses tucked back amid a copse of enormous live oaks. The way the modest cottages were nestled under the massive trees with their thick trunks, wide canopies, and arching limbs, it felt as if I'd stumbled into a sort of magical forest. I glanced at the numbers on the homes and knew I was getting closer.

Excitement zipped through me. I was overcome with curiosity to see the place where Pops had spent so much of his life by himself. Separated from the other residences by a stand of smaller sand oaks was a lone white clapboard house with dark green trim and matching shutters, all of which were closed over the windows. I felt my lips curve up. This was exactly the sort of place where I could picture Pops spending his days, fishing and boating, enjoying the quiet after so many years as the local news anchor in Providence, Rhode Island.

The van chugged to a stop and I turned the key in the ignition off. I double-checked the metal numbers tacked onto the side of the house. Eighty-one. This was it. Dude let out a small whimper and wiggled as if he, too, knew that we'd finally arrived. I turned and patted his shoulder. "Let's check it out."

I opened my door and Dude clambered over the seat—all

150 pounds of him—almost knocking me down in his haste to follow me, as if afraid I might leave him behind. He trotted forward two steps and immediately lifted his leg on the trunk of a crape myrtle, identifiable by its peeling brown bark and thick clusters of bright pink flowers. I couldn't blame him; a dog has his priorities, after all.

I took a beat to take in the house in front of me. A sense of déjà vu hit me right in the chest. I had been here before. I was certain of it. I remembered thinking in my little-kid brain that this house was a sentient being, that the dormer windows on the second floor were eyes, the front door a nose, and the porch a wide smile. I supposed it might just resemble the house I'd stayed in with Pops and Nana, but I felt certain it was the actual house.

I remembered Pops had let me ride my bike on the wraparound porch and we pretended I was a race car driver doing laps until Nana declared I was making her dizzy. When had Pops bought the house that we'd rented for our vacations, and why hadn't he ever told me?

I marveled at the place that held a decade of summer memories. When Nana returned from her vacation, I'd call her and ask if she knew this was our old rental. I put my hand on the stair railing and studied the place. Upon closer inspection, the house was less charming and more woebegone in appearance. The roof had missing shingles, the gutters were stuffed with leaves, and several of the shutters were missing slats and in a few cases hanging drunkenly from their hinges.

The paint was peeling and green moss was growing thick in the shadows and crevices. Knee-high weeds filled the front yard, covering the crawl space below and curving up onto the porch railing as if intent upon swallowing the house whole. Several tree limbs had fallen in the yard, probably from recent storms.

Given the state of the outside, I hated to imagine what the inside looked like. A month had gone by since Pops had passed and his estate settled. I knew it had been several months since he'd come down here to fish. I had no idea if he had anyone checking on the house or not. I was assuming not. During those months of vacancy, I feared a wild critter or two might have taken up residence and would now claim squatter's rights.

"Do not bite anything in the house, especially if it moves," I said to Dude. He tipped his head to the side as if he found this order confounding. "I'm serious. You don't know their medical history, if they have fleas, ticks, or rabies. No biting." He opened his massive muzzle and yawned. "Oh, I'm sorry. Am I boring you?"

I pulled the key to the cottage out of the side pocket of my beige cargo shorts. The house was much smaller than I remembered, but given that I'd been living in my van for the past five years, it felt like a castle to me. Not for the first time I wondered why—out of all the members in my family—Pops had left his summer place to me. Was it because I presently lived in a van? Unlike the rest of my family, my grandfather had never tried to dissuade me from my current life choices.

Pops had followed me on the socials and actively engaged in my posts. I'd always thought he was proud of me for going my own way when my career in journalism came to an unexpected and tragic end at the same time that my husband announced he no longer loved me and ended our marriage. But maybe Pops had given me the house so I had a safe place to land when I was tired of my nomadic lifestyle. If so, he'd been right. After several years of nonstop traveling—some might say running away—lately I'd been getting the urge to plant myself somewhere and put down some roots, or at the very least take a sabbatical from the daily quest for content.

I climbed up the steps, fully prepared for the boards beneath my feet to give way. They did not. They even supported Dude. The front porch was empty except for two large white flowerpots on each side of the front door that contained the dried husks of what had once been some sort of large plants. Geraniums? Roses? I couldn't tell.

It seemed an unexpectedly cheerful aesthetic for a man's fishing retreat. I tried to remember if Pops had been a plant guy. He'd never remarried after his divorce from Nana, and I couldn't remember any plants in the bachelor residence Pops had maintained down the street from my parents' house in Little Compton, Rhode Island. He and Nana both lived in that neighborhood. When Nana married George, my bonus grandpa, Pops had been the one to give her away.

Another wave of grief hit me. How could a man who had loved his family and friends as fiercely as Pops had be gone? There'd been no warning. No time to say good-bye. The lump in my throat was hard and I tried to swallow it down. Pops hadn't seemed himself the last three months of his life. His contagious laugh, a deep throaty chuckle, was seldom heard and the sparkle in his eyes was dim. Whenever I asked him what was wrong, he pushed away my concerns, blaming it on aging, but it never sat right with me. I should have persisted. Now I would never know what had been on his mind during those last few months.

Guilt and regret honed my grief to a sharp edge. I glanced at the door in front of me. Ever since my dad had handed me the key to the house, I'd pinned a lot of hope on finding solace in this place that Pops had loved so well.

I slid the key into the dead bolt and twisted it until it clicked. I turned the knob and pushed the door open. Well, I tried to push it open. The humidity had swollen the door shut and I had to put my shoulder into it. Dude watched me encouragingly as I used the force of my entire body to ram the door. When it gave way with a groan of protest, I stumbled inside.

With the exterior shutters closed over the windows, the light was weak. I reached for the switch by the door and flipped it on. Nothing happened. No electricity. Great.

I squinted into the gloom and as my eyes adjusted I noticed dust sheets covered the furniture, and the place smelled musty. It hit me then that the last time Pops had been here, he must have closed it up knowing he wasn't coming back. Otherwise, why would he have used dust sheets when he'd popped down here once a month and every summer?

I crossed the front room to the closest window, turned the latch to free the interior sash, and pushed it open and then the screen as well. The clasp to the shutters was on the inside, so I quickly popped it and pushed the shutters wide. I swear I felt the house sigh in relief as I lowered the screen. I did the same with three more windows until there was enough light to see and air moving through the house to push out the musty scent of neglect.

Dude prowled through the living room, the dining area, and the kitchen—his favorite room, of course. His nose was pressed to the ground and he snuffled his way through, looking for any snacks that might have been left behind.

I followed him, taking in the vintage cooking space. White appliances and rounded oak cupboards. Hello, 1994. I recognized the same interior aesthetic from my baby pictures in my parents' old photo albums.

I opened the large window over the sink and unlatched the shutters, pushing them wide. The view from the back of the house boasted a monstrous live oak to one side, a sloping woefully overgrown lawn, and a narrow dock that ran fifty yards through the tall grass to the wide waterway that ran through the center of the marsh. Wooden stairs led up to a small shack on a large platform raised on stilts. That had to be where Pops cleaned his fish and stored his boat during inclement weather.

Below the shack was a lower platform that sat on the edge of the wide channel. I noticed a boat was tied up to it. It was not Pops's boat, as his was moored at the marina in Little Compton. He might have left the house to me but the boat was his pride and joy and had been bequeathed to my dad, his only child. And yet there beneath Pops's fishing shack was a boat . . . and a fisherman.

I'd been worried about critters squatting at the house. It hadn't occurred to me that a person might have done so. Fantastic. The lawyer for Pops's estate was due here at any minute. This was so not what I needed right now.

From this distance it was hard to get a sense of the man. The sun glinted off his thick, wavy, dark brown curls, his broad shoulders were snug beneath his T-shirt, and as he cast his line, his muscled calves flexed beneath his knee-length shorts as he strode along the rocking planks with purpose. He was pale as if he didn't get enough time outside and yet he looked entirely too comfortable on Pops's . . . er . . . *my* dock. I decided I was going to have to go say something. I patted my pocket for my phone, realizing then that I'd left it in the van.

"Come on, Dude. I don't want to confront anyone without the ability to call for backup if things get weird or nasty."

Being a woman, traveling on my own, I had become very savvy about always having my phone fully charged and on hand. If I got a weird vibe, I called someone and started talking about where I was and what I was doing immediately.

I turned, expecting my ginormous shadow to follow. He did not. Instead, Dude nudged open the back door with his nose. Not hard, since it had apparently been left OPEN! Clearly, the trespasser on the dock with the boat had been in Pops's house. The audacity!

"Dude, don't go out there!" I ordered. He went out there. Damn it!

I slipped through the door, hoping the man on the dock didn't notice us, and hissed through gritted teeth, "Stop, Dude, get over here right now." He didn't.

Instead, he let out a deep *woof* of greeting and started to gallop across the yard and down the dock toward the poor bastard standing on the edge of the platform, holding a fishing pole and having no idea what was about to hit him.

Author photo by Hailey Gilman

Jenn McKinlay is the award-winning *New York Times*, *USA Today*, and *Publishers Weekly* bestselling author of several mystery and romance series. Her work has been translated into multiple languages in countries all over the world. She lives in sunny Arizona in a house that is overrun with books, pets, and her husband's guitars.

VISIT JENN MCKINLAY ONLINE

JennMcKinlay.com
JennMcKinlayAuthor
McKinlayJenn